FAR FROM CAMELOT

RYLEE HALE

FAR FROM CAMELOT
Copyright © 2024 Rylee Hale

Written by Rylee Hale
Cover image by Fer Gregory/Shutterstock.com

ISBN 979-8-9867508-9-7 (paperback)
ISBN 979-8-9867508-8-0 (ebook)

PUBLISHED BY VICIOUS CITY PRESS

NOTE FROM THE AUTHOR

When I wrote *Far From Neverland*, I didn't plan on writing more retellings. However, I had so much fun with it and was blown away by the love that book received, so I decided to turn it into a series.

The books in the Far From series will all be contemporary fantasy retellings that take place mostly **far from** the locations of the original tales.

As always, please stay safe and check the trigger warnings if needed.

For specific content warnings, playlists, and to sign up for my newsletter, please visit my website: www.ryleehale.com

To those who believe that magic exists in the real world and that bad boys in all black have a heart worthy of love.

Hatred kept me paralyzed; love moved me.
Hatred kept me in the dark; love illuminated me.
Hatred kept me existing until your love brought me back to life.

—DETHRONE THE QUEEN

1

MERLIN

Over a thousand years ago.

As the Battle of Camlann rages on, eddies of gray smoke rise into the warm night air, thick and acrid and swirling. The clashing of swords and cries of men ring across the field, and the scent of blood and sweat is carried on the wind, permeating every inch under the obscured sky.

The Knights of Camelot have fought a hard battle, and I've done everything in my power to help and protect them. Even with the aid of my magic, many have fallen, but many more have been victorious and proven their worth. Gawain and Percival remain in competition for most enemies struck down, while Bedivere and Tristram have had too many close calls.

And Arthur?

King Arthur is unstoppable while he's wielding Excalibur.

My eyes find him through the sea of warring knights. His blond hair is plastered to his forehead with sweat, and his face and armor are sprayed with the blood of other men. His ocean blue eyes shine beneath the silvery light of the moon, and the smile he gives me is one of a king on the verge of victory.

However, all it takes is a split second distraction, my attention stolen just long enough to divert an arrow off its course with a flick of my wrist, the projectile missing Galahad by mere inches. When I turn my gaze back to Arthur, the angel of death from my premonition is approaching.

Mordred.

"Arthur!"

My warning comes too late.

The King turns to face his adversary—his own *son*—swords already driving forward, each hitting their mark. Excalibur strikes Mordred at the same time Mordred's sword pierces Arthur's chainmail, right in the vulnerable spot between the steel plates of armor.

Time stops.

Everything from the clanging of metal to the stench of blood fades into the distance.

"Arthur!"

The cry rips from my throat as I stumble forward, tripping over fallen bodies and dropped weapons as I struggle to reach him, the effort of moving like trying to wade against a rapidly rushing current. My ears ring with my own cry as I watch Arthur fall to his knees, Excalibur slipping from his hand onto the bloodstained ground.

I saw this.

I saw this and thought I actually had the power to stop it.

But I never did.

Despite blood blooming through the chainmail over his lower abdomen, there's a deranged look in Mordred's eyes—eyes the same ocean blue as his father's—that I will never forget.

They shine with victory.

I reach Arthur just as he's falling backward, and I drop to my knees to catch him before he can fall to the ground. In my periphery, Mordred stumbles back and collapses. But, right now, my sole focus is on Arthur.

My king.

My *friend*.

"Stay with me," I plead desperately as I stare down into his eyes that are glossing over.

"I'm sorry I failed you, Merlin." He chokes on his words along with the blood that fills his mouth, spilling over his lips. "Failed Camelot."

"It is I who failed you, Arthur."

The men around us haven't stopped fighting, but I can sense eyes on us. I can't feel much else past the anguish and grief and defeat. It feels like a living, breathing entity inside me, something I can physically feel burning through my veins just like the magic that lives there too. The weight of it is even heavier, crushing me from the inside out.

I've known Arthur Pendragon since he was a boy, watched him grow into the king that Camelot deserved, the one the kingdom had waited for since his reign was foretold.

The king who's just died in my arms.

A vicious cry of agony rips from my chest, my very soul, shredding me apart.

The sound is amplified, traveling leagues across the lands, cracking the hard ground beneath me, fissures in the earth snaking out like a spider's web. It's only then the noise of battle fades.

Arthur's dead weight is heavier with the armor, and I have to use a burst of what magical strength I have remaining to lift him and rise to my feet.

"It's over, Merlin."

The mirth in Mordred's voice makes me feel nothing. I'm numb to everything that's not this devastating sorrow. Not even when I allow my gaze to briefly fall to him do I feel satisfaction at his fatal wound. His inky black hair that sweeps his shoulders is drenched with sweat, his youthful complexion pale compared to the triumph still shining in his eyes. He's so young compared to my two hundred years, and, yet, I feel no sympathy for his imminent end.

I feel nothing for him at all.

Even if magic was capable of healing mortal wounds, nothing in this world would make me wish to save him.

I don't know how I manage to find my voice after practically tearing open my throat, but when I do, it's raw and deep and sounds foreign to my ears.

"I hope you die a slow and painful death, Mordred."

I turn my back on him, the son of the king, the once Knight of Camelot, the man who only ever wanted Arthur's throne.

Before I can walk away, Sir Gawain is there, picking up Excalibur off the ground, the magical blade stained with blood. If only it had been magical enough to save Arthur.

If only *I* had saved Arthur.

Gawain places the sword on top of the king's body in my arms and gives me a solemn nod. I can't find it in me to return the gesture.

Heading across the battlefield that's littered with the bodies of fallen knights, I set my gaze ahead. Out of the corner of my eyes, the king's knights kneel, bowing their heads over their swords. I can't look at them because if I do, I'll only be reminded of how badly I failed them *all*. I'm already drowning in the guilt of failing Arthur.

It's only when I reach the edge of the field, pushing through the line of trees until I'm obscured from the battle, do I allow the weight of Arthur to bring me to my knees. I can't carry on.

I bow my head, saying a silent prayer for my fallen king and friend. When I lift my gaze once more, we're at the edge of the Lake of Avalon. I can feel the last of my magic fading, leaving me, from the effort of transporting us so far. Mist swirls in the distance. The surface of the water sparkles from the reflection of the winking stars, the sky here not cloaked by smoke.

Resting Arthur gently on the rocky ground, I take Excalibur in my hand and rise to my feet. Approaching the bank of the lake, I stand there and stare out over the water, unsure of how much time passes before I realize there are tears streaming down my face.

I failed.

Part of me wishes I had stayed behind to watch Mordred die.

With a gut-wrenching roar, I raise the sword in the air and hurl it into the lake.

It doesn't even get the chance to hit the water before a delicate hand is breaking through the surface and catching it by the hilt. Then the hand is lowering back into the water, taking Excalibur with it.

Removing my purple cloak from my shoulders, I toss it onto the rocks behind me before stepping forward until my feet are wading into the water.

"Nimue!"

The Lady of the Lake appears a moment later, rising above the surface without so much as a splash, clothed in a white dress, blonde hair long and flowing around her face as though she's still under the water. She hovers above the lake and glows like an angel.

It's easy to see why I once loved her.

"I'm sorry, Merlin," she says, her lilting voice like melodious bells. "You have to let me take him now."

A small wooden boat appears from the mist in the distance, sailing toward shore. It scrapes against the rocks, and I move back to Arthur's body, lifting him one last time into my arms. I'm so numb that I don't even question what it is I have to do. I place the king into the boat, folding his arms across his chest.

Leaning over him, I place a kiss against his forehead. "Goodbye, my king. I'm so sorry I failed you."

As the boat begins to float back across the water toward the mist, I drop to the rocks on my knees.

"Please, Nimue," I say, voice cracking and fresh tears in my eyes. "You have to take me too."

"You do not belong in Avalon, Merlin."

"Then take me somewhere else. Anywhere else. Somewhere far away."

She appears to consider it, then says, "Camelot still needs you. Arthur needs you."

Arthur is dead.

None of her words register. The only thing that *does* register is the breaking of my heart. *I'm* broken, and I don't know if I'll ever be whole again.

"Please, Nimue," I say again. "I can't stay."

"Come to me, Merlin."

I stand, my legs shaking beneath me as I step into the water. Nimue begins to retreat, and I follow her like she's the beacon of my salvation, the only thing in this universe that can take me from this pain.

The water swirls around my waist, rising higher as I journey deeper, following the light of the Lady of the Lake as she takes me somewhere far away.

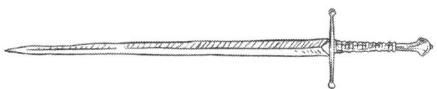

Present day.

The alarm clock blares, and I nearly knock it off my nightstand as I swat at it to shut it up. I groan and roll over, bringing my pillow with me to bury my head beneath it.

All I ever have now are nightmares, memories of a past I wish I could forget. I almost miss the premonitions. I haven't had one in centuries, mostly out of touch with my magic after all this time. When I first arrived in this world, magic had its place. Then it was a sin punishable by death. Now, no one believes in it. For a long time, it's simply been safer to keep most of my magic bottled inside, using the bare minimum when I need it.

A weight settles on my back, claws kneading into my bare flesh.

"Ouch. Fuck," I grumble, tossing the pillow away.

The cat leaps off my back, landing gracefully beside my head. When I turn to look at the orange tabby, he meows in my face.

"Good morning to you too, Percy."

He meows again, then pounces away. I roll my eyes at the impatient feline as he bounds toward his food bowl.

I've only had a handful of pets in my very long life, just as afraid of forming attachments to them as I am to humans.

The cat's name is Percival, another pet that I've named after one of the Knights of Camelot.

I guess there's a part of me that *doesn't* want to forget.

After forcing myself out of bed, I decide to take care of myself first, using the restroom, then brushing my teeth as I stare at my reflection in the mirror. Some mornings, like today, my own reflection surprises me. I've allowed myself to grow old many times—white hair, wrinkles, all of it, which allows me to stay in any one place for a longer period—and then I'll reverse what aging has done to me. It's one of the rare occasions I use that much magic.

I've seen my face reflected back to me at so many different ages so many times that, occasionally, I forget how old I'm claiming to be. Right now, I can pass for late-thirties.

Hearing Percy meowing loudly in the other room, I hurry out of the restroom and into the small kitchen.

The New York City apartment is a modest studio over the small bookshop I own and has dark wood floors and exposed red and black brick walls lined with overflowing bookshelves. It's filled with mismatched furniture—a small, yellow couch, blue sheets on the bed, and stools in different shades of green at the bar that separates the kitchen from the rest of the space.

In the last thousand years—I may have lost count—I've lived on every continent, in many different countries and states. Money is never an issue because that's one of the other times I allow myself to use magic.

But for the last century or so, owning a little bookshop in New York City has been…I guess you could call it a dream of mine. Not that I have many of those anymore. It's in one of the quieter parts of the city, which suits me perfectly.

Percy circles my leg as I open a can of food, purring and rubbing his head against my calf.

"Greedy little shit," I mutter affectionately as I spoon the food into his bowl, and he immediately begins to gobble it down.

After showering and shaving—doing so without magic like a normal human because that's what I'm supposed to be now—I get dressed in jeans and a soft, navy blue sweater, then finish up my morning routine by checking on my plants that are scattered around the only window in the place. I'm not sure if it's my magic or my soul that still requires a connection to nature, but I have to find little ways of maintaining it, especially in the city.

I water each one that needs it, whistling an old tune as I do—who knows how old some of the things in my mind are. Afterward, I pay a little attention to a sad-looking pothos vine hanging from the ceiling. My fingers graze one of its wilted leaves, and it slowly begins to come back to life, turning from brown to a vibrant green, its vine growing an extra inch.

My plants get a little of what's left of my magic too, but that's the end of it.

On my way out of the apartment, I give Percy an affectionate stroke down his back before walking out the door and locking it behind me.

Since the bookshop is only downstairs, I don't have to travel far to get to work. Not that I consider it *work*. It's more something to keep me busy, to fill the time of my eternal existence. That sounds sad, but it's not. I'll admit I've suffered a few dark times with the threat of eternity hanging over my head, but I've learned how to make this time feel the most fulfilled, as fulfilled as I possibly can.

Even after living in this world for over a thousand years, there's never been a shortage of books to read.

I open the store early most days and sit behind the counter reading while customers filter in and out. It never gets busy, which is more than fine with me. The few people who do walk through the door are usually those who still appreciate the smaller shops, the older books, the distinct musty scent with hints of mahogany, leather, and vanilla.

The walls of the shop are similar to those of my apartment upstairs—exposed red and black brick—though they're mostly covered from the hardwood floors to the ceiling by bookshelves, more shelves creating almost cramped aisles throughout the space. Two windows at the front let in a little natural light that pour over the plush red armchairs that sit in front of them.

I worked here for a couple of years before I bought the place from the old man who owned it before. It's clear this place has always been cherished.

The front door opens in the early afternoon, the tinkling of bells ringing through the small store. I look up, already knowing who to expect.

Sure enough, Willow is traipsing up the middle aisle with two cups of coffee in her hands, one hot and one iced. She drops the hot one in front of me before leaning her hip against the counter and taking a large gulp of her iced coffee as condensation drips past her fingers.

"Good morning, Merlin," she says through a yawn.

"It's the middle of the afternoon."

"Well, it's morning for me." She gives me a toothy grin as I take a sip of my bitter, black drink.

Willow works at the bar directly across the street, the Stone Crow, which complements my store, Writ in Stone, as well as anything, I suppose. The spirited girl in her late-twenties came in one day a couple of years ago, rips in her jeans and purple streaks in her blonde hair, searching for a first edition copy of *The Secret Garden* for her girlfriend at the time. I managed to track one down for her, and she's refused to leave me alone since. I'm sure it's simply because she feels sorry for the old, lonely man who runs the small bookshop that doesn't get much business.

I prefer ancient man living in blissful solitude who is exactly where he wanted to be when he moved to New York.

Someone else may consider the two of us friends, but I don't have those anymore.

At least, I try not to.

"You gonna come by for a drink after you close up this evening?" she asks, looking at me with those round doe eyes of hers, the streaks in her hair pink these days.

"I wasn't planning on it," I tell her honestly, waving the book in my hand.

The ice in her cup clinks as she throws her hand out to the side. "Oh, come on! You owe me a good tip after all the coffees I've been bringing you this week."

Except I know it's the tips I leave that she uses to buy our coffees because she doesn't like to accept money from me. She nearly threw a fit the first time I left her a twenty, and she's been bringing me coffee ever since.

"And here I thought you were doing that out of the kindness of your heart."

"Well, that...*and* the tips." Her following smile takes up half her face, and we both break out in laughter, hers a lot louder than mine. "Plus, we have some new bands playing tonight."

She reaches into her back pocket and pulls out a bright orange flier that's been folded several times. Straightening it out, she slaps it on the counter in front of me. I peer down at it, not recognizing any of the band names, but, admittedly, she's piqued my interest.

I appreciate music as much as I do books. Both adequately help to quiet my mind. It may have taken my ancient ears some time to appreciate some of the newer genres like hard rock and metal—of which the majority of the bands that perform at the Stone Crow play—but I like them nearly as much as jazz now. Willow may have made me promise to never drag her to another jazz bar after the first and last time.

When Willow clears her throat, I look up and follow her gaze to my hand that's on the counter beside my coffee, my fingers drumming a random beat on the pale wood. Her brow arches knowingly, and I quickly cease my tapping to fist and flex my hand.

The restless drumming became a habit many...*many* years ago, and Willow has often called me out on it, mostly in a soft, concerned, maternal kind of way. She guessed quickly that it was a nervous tic, though she chalked it up to anxiety. She wasn't completely wrong, but she didn't know it was also because my hands often felt on edge without magic to keep them busy. I may use a little here and there, but it's nothing compared to how often I used to rely on it.

It's also usually her excuse to convince me to come have a drink with her because I *clearly need one*.

I never said she was the best influence, but I know she means well.

Sighing, I give in and say, "I'll come by for a little bit, all right?"

The corners of her mouth pull up even higher. "That's more like it. Later, Merlin!"

Willow spins around with the grace of a dancer and exits the shop, the chime of bells left behind in her wake.

For a moment after she's gone, I stare down at my hand. My fingertips tingle with repressed magic, this innate need I've had all my life that I've had to water down to nearly nothing compared to what it was and who it made me in Camelot.

I don't miss it. Or, rather, I don't *let* myself miss it. I like this life and who I am now. I've liked most of the lives I've crafted for myself over the centuries. However, when I think too hard about it, I know *something* is missing.

After taking another sip of coffee, I pick up my book and get back to reading.

There's no point in missing a life long gone, one I'll never get back.

2

MORDRED

The tour bus rocks gently beneath me as it travels over the highway in…Pennsylvania? I think? We've been on the road for a few weeks now, and I can hardly be bothered to remember where the fuck we are at any given time. I know we're on our way to New York where we have a few gigs lined up over the next couple of weeks in the city, but don't ask me where we're going after that. That's all Ava.

My fingers pluck over the strings of my electric guitar, the music coming through my amp headphones as I sit in my usual spot—the corner of the smallest bench with my heavy boots propped up on the small table. My tongue plays with the ring in my lip absentmindedly while I concentrate on the new song I've been working on.

My bandmates are around here somewhere. Hell, they could be right in front of me, and I probably wouldn't know with how engrossed I am in the new song I've been working on—and with the way my messy, black hair falls like a curtain over my eyes.

I've been in this world for…seven hundred years? Eight hundred? Fuck, I lose track of a lot of things. It happens when time no longer has any meaning to me. Most days, I exist in some kind of time-space vacuum. It takes a great deal of brain power to remember the names of the people I surround myself with, hopping from one found family to the next, even though the mere idea of *family* makes me sick. It's better than being alone though. I tried that for nearly a century, and that…well, it was dangerous to myself and anyone around me.

After that dicey time in my life, it was music that helped heal me. Not that I'll ever consider myself *healed* from my sins, but it was as close as I'll ever get. Since then, my life has revolved around music and magic, one my sanctuary, one my vice.

My mother's a sorceress. I could never give up magic even if I wanted to. Which I don't.

When someone smacks my feet, I sigh internally before looking up, shaking my hair out of my face to see Wesley… Fuck, no. That was a different one. This one's Will. He stands there, staring at me expectantly.

Heaving an audible sigh this time, I remove my head-phones and let them fall around my neck before snapping, "What?"

Behind him, Ava giggles. "Uh oh. He's in one of his moods."

"Am not," I huff, my tone way too pouty to back up my denial and only causing Ava to laugh louder.

Will is our other guitarist. Ava's our drummer, and she's also responsible for booking most of our gigs, along with keeping the peace between us. Her twin brother, Anthony, is our bassist and our current bus driver. I met the twins a few years back in England, and when we decided to move to the states together and settled down in LA, that's where we met Will.

They're all pretty familiar with my *moods* by now, as Ava likes to call them. She says I brood a lot, but, really, I think my *moods* are just when I'm trying not to give in to all the impulsive and intrusive thoughts that get worse and worse from the boredom that comes with an eternal existence.

And all the bitterness.

The first thing I think about when I wake up and the last thing I think about before falling asleep is King Arthur. My father. Not because I miss him. Fuck no. It's because of how his fate altered the course of my life forever. I felt *so* much relief after I killed him, when I finally felt my blade drive clean through his body, taking something from him as important as the thing he had denied me.

Unfortunately, that relief was short-lived.

"When are you going to share that new song of yours with the class?" Will asks, breaking through my thoughts as he crashes down on the bench on the other side of the table.

"Eventually. Or never if you keep bugging me about it."

Will looks over at Ava where she lounges on a larger couch and nods. "Definitely in one of his moods."

As they share a laugh at my expense, I roll my eyes and reach over my guitar to pick up the freshly rolled joint off the table. I dig into the pocket of my jacket and fish out my lighter, sticking the joint between my lips before lighting the end. I let the smoke swirl around the steel bar pierced through my tongue before inhaling deeply.

"Could you at least open a window when you do that, Mordred?" Ava chastises from behind the alternative music magazine she's back to flipping through.

I have to stop and check myself before I throw the window beside me open with nothing more than a flick of my wrist. It takes a lot of self-control to keep from using magic around people when I'm so used to using it when alone. I've been with Ava and Anthony for so many years that I've considered sharing that part of myself with them, but considering the catastrophe that was the last time I was open about my magic…well, it's a bad idea.

I manage to open the window all by myself like a good little mortal, then sit back and take a few more hits of the joint. After I've had my fill—never taking more than I need to calm the fuck down—I pass it over to Will, who takes it and greedily sucks it down, coughing in between deep drags.

I suppose I have more than one vice after all.

But who was I to not fall victim to the whole "sex, drugs, and rock 'n roll" scene? It's been my entire personality for the last several decades. It may as well have been in my blood.

Right after cunt sorceress of a mother and self-righteous king of a father.

Everyone goes through their rebellious phases. Mine has just lasted several centuries.

"Attention, children," Anthony calls from the front of the bus. "ETA to the hotel is about an hour."

Without a word to the others, I return my headphones to my ears and let the drugs and music do their thing. Now if only I had the sex…

I probably could. Will has flirted with me enough and is cute as fuck. But I learned a long time ago not to shit where I eat. It's exhausting enough as it is finding people I can vibe with, who can put up with my unending shit, and who I don't constantly feel the urge to put their heads on a spike. Throw in something that usually makes mortals turn uncomfortable or clingy or hostile, things tend to get messy.

However, all my bandmates could tempt me if I let them. Will is a deceptively straight-laced, tattooed momma's boy who can pass surprisingly well for a hedonistic bad boy. He sometimes reminds me a lot of a young Ernest Hemingway.

Good 'ol Ernie.

Don't ask.

I think I have a thing for the refined gentleman type. Even better if they're closeted freaks with internalized homophobia that makes them hate themselves.

I love it when they hate themselves.

But, then again, I'm not too picky.

The twins are two sides of the same gorgeous coin. Artemis and Apollo—if the god and goddess had flawless, dark brown skin and alluring onyx eyes, along with quirky personalities and eccentric styles. Anthony never plays a show without wearing *something* with a horrendous paisley print, and Ava has about a million brightly colored leggings she wears beneath short skirts. I might be the frontman, but they sure do draw attention when we're all on stage.

Maybe I'll be able to find a hook-up after our gig tonight. I haven't gotten laid since we've been on the road. Not because it's difficult. I've had plenty of offers.

I tend to go through these phases. Blurs of faces and bodies, so much sex I think my dick might fall off. Then long periods of nothing, barely even getting myself off. It's been a while this time, and I think I'm ready to break the dry spell.

I don't get much more of my newest song finished before Anthony is parking the bus and we're all grabbing our shit and clambering out. Before we head inside, we unhook the van we've been hauling around with us so that it's one less thing we have to do when it's time to head to our first gig in the city later tonight.

The hotel we're staying at is nice. And expensive. Tall ceilings, dark wood, marble floors, massive and ornate chandeliers. There's a lot of modern art hanging on the walls and a bar off to the side of the lobby. I think there's even a rooftop pool.

Understandably, the four of us get a number of curious and suspicious looks as we check in and head to our rooms.

The rest of the band believes that I inherited an ungodly amount of money from some distant, deceased relatives, and that's how I've been able to afford things like equipment, vehicles, and lodging wherever we go, not to mention the fancy condo I share with Ava and Anthony back in Los Angeles.

Of course, I can't tell them the truth about the source of all the money.

Hint...*it's magic.*

We all head to our separate suites. On the thirteenth floor. Because I'm a dick.

"I fucking hate you, Mordred," Ava mutters as she swipes her key at the door beside mine.

"You love me, and you know it." I blow her an obnoxious kiss in response to her glaring daggers before entering my room.

Ava's a bit superstitious, and I can't help but get a kick out of it.

After dumping my bag by the door, I walk into the main space and take in the view of the city through the floor-to-ceiling windows. The sun is peeking between buildings on its descent toward the horizon, but I wave my hand, closing the curtains against the fading daylight anyway.

Shedding my jacket and black Henley on the nearest chair, I make my way through the suite. It's all gray walls, modern furniture, recessed lighting, and pristine white sheets on the bed.

Another vice of mine is luxury.

In the restroom, I splash some water on my face, deciding to get an hour nap before we need to leave. My reflection catches my gaze in the mirror, my black jeans slung low on my hips and offering a clear view of the prominent scar along my left hip, visible even beneath all the artwork tattooed on my body. I never got it fully covered, even though I should have. It's the one Arthur gave me the night I killed him. The one from Excalibur, the one that nearly ended my own life.

The only reason I still pay it any attention is because of how much I hate it, the near constant reminder. It's an ugly mark that doesn't reflect the truth, the truth of how beautiful that moment really was.

It's a physical scar that has no mental equivalent whatsoever.

There are plenty of things magic can't do. Magic can't get rid of this scar outside of an illusion. Magic couldn't heal me from that wound. I had to recover on my own.

After Merlin left me for dead.

The source of the scar doesn't haunt me like the scar itself does, marring my perfect body while my mind has only experienced relief and triumph from what happened that night. If anything, it's a reminder of how weak I was to let the promise of victory distract me enough for Arthur to take a piece of me too.

I'll never regret my choices.

Never.

No matter what came after.

Exiting the restroom, I move over to the bed and crash onto the cloud of a mattress, face buried in the down pillows. With absolutely nothing weighing my mind down, I'm out like a light and sleep like a baby.

3

MERLIN

Business was slow today—nothing new there—which gave me time to finish reading my book, along with an adequate excuse to head over to the bar for just one drink.

It's nearly eight o'clock when I get started on shutting down for the evening. I sweep the entire store, straighten up a few of the shelves, and close out the old register that I never bothered replacing after I bought the place. I have a separate tablet for card transactions, but the antique register completes the vintage feel of the shop, the main reason I chose to keep it.

After shutting off all the lights, I head back to the counter with only the glare of the street lamps outside filtering in through the front windows to guide me. I left the flier that Willow dropped off earlier today out for a bit of advertising for the bar. Not that I expect the kind of customers I get to be interested in the kind of music that's going to be playing there tonight.

But the chances of anything happening are never zero.

I go to grab the flier, but the moment my fingers touch the bright orange paper, the world around me is swept away.

Everything is black.

Save for a beam of bright light in the distance, like I'm in a tunnel.

There's something silhouetted against the glow. A chair? It's large with a high, pointed back, blocking most of the light that shines behind it like a halo.

A throne.

Something whooshes right past my head, the flapping of wings. The black bird flies toward the light, weaving in and out of the darkness before landing on the highest point of the throne.

I take a cautious step forward, my feet heavy like I'm moving through mud.

The bird cocks its head at me.

A raven?

A crow.

It releases a caw.

Then turns to stone.

Closer to the throne now, I can make out a figure sitting there. It's a woman, her long, black hair cascading over her shoulders in waves. I can't make out her face clearly, shrouded in shadows.

I take another step, and her mouth curves in a spine-chilling smirk.

Slowly, the parts of her I can see begin to crack, fissures spreading up and down and across her delicate body, like she's a fragile rock. Before my very eyes, she turns to stone, just like the bird still perched above her. Even her crown transforms.

A moment later, the queen *crumbles.*

As though she was nothing more than a protective layer for another, the debris falls away and a different figure takes her place.

I take one more step forward.

I can see the man's face more clearly, a face that's hauntingly familiar. Black hair that once swept his shoulders, now shorter. Blue eyes that glimmer through the darkness like mystical waters. A twisted, black crown rests on top of his head.

He smiles.

I'm pulled from the vision as quickly as I entered it, gasping for air as though I hadn't breathed the entire time. I lean over the counter, hands gripping the edge with white knuckles as I catch my breath.

No, no, no.

Fuck no.

I haven't had a premonition in a century at least. Why now?

Throne.

Crow.

Stone.

Queen.

Plucking up the flier, I grasp it tightly, the paper nearly ripping in my shaking hands as I turn it toward the light from the street lamps. My gaze roams down the names of the bands until it lands on one, and my blood turns to ice.

Dethrone the Queen.

It's not possible.

Mordred is dead.

Then again, I've never had a premonition lie. I've never had a premonition not come true, despite the many times I've tried to thwart them. Sometimes my premonitions are more symbolic, sometimes realistic. Sometimes they're a blend of both. This one was more symbolic, but the meaning was clear.

I stand in the middle of my shop, staring down at the paper in my hand, my heart racing a fierce, rapid tempo in my chest, pounding violently against my ribs.

Mordred is fucking dead.

But…*what if*…?

It's not possible…is it?

I think back to that battle over a thousand years ago, when Excalibur pierced Mordred's armor. A millennium may have passed, but I remember it clearly as though it were only yesterday. With the amount of blood seeping through the chainmail and slipping through his fingers as he held his hand to his wound, bleeding on the ground as I carried Arthur away, there's no doubt that he was severely injured. Magic wouldn't have been enough to heal him, not mine nor his. But…I suppose…with a skilled enough physician…

Fuck.

Mordred's alive.

And he's going to be at the Stone Crow. He could be there right now. Right across the street…

This premonition has rotten timing. When I would get them regularly, they would usually be days in advance, sometimes months. Not fucking *minutes*. I must really be losing touch with my magic. Either that, or it's determined to taunt me, having no mercy when it comes to showing me that my nightmares are returning in the flesh.

If I had this premonition days ago, maybe I could've gotten out of the city like a goddamn coward.

But am I really a coward if it's because I don't want to murder a man in cold blood? Because *that's* the thought currently swirling around my addled mind.

I've never killed in cold blood before.

Even as a sorcerer back in Camelot, I killed men, sure, but it was always in defense of myself or others.

But Mordred?

I have no doubts I'll feel the urge to strike him down the moment I see him. Despite being born of magic and demons, I was always known as Merlin the wise, the *good*. If I was to see Mordred after all this time, I fear I would let my demons win, that I would give in to that part of me that had to fight so hard to resist the dark side of magic.

And, yet…there's another part of me, a morbid curiosity to see if it's true. And to know why *now*. Does he know I'm here? Has he tracked me down?

Is this a trap?

My curiosity ends up winning.

Crumpling the paper in my hand, I toss it into the small bin behind the counter, then head out of the shop, locking up behind me. The moment I turn to look across the street, I find myself frozen again. The sign for the bar hangs above its door, a stone crow perched on top of it, identical to the one from my vision after it was petrified.

There's still that part of me that wants to run, but I shut it down.

I have to know.

The street I'm on isn't a busy one, but I still head down to the nearest crosswalk. Being overly cautious is better than being reckless. Then again, I am willingly walking into a place where a certain mortal enemy of mine is undoubtedly inside, and that's pretty damn reckless.

The Stone Crow is a decently sized bar considering its location. It's not usually that busy, but tonight it is. The crowd immediately has me more on edge than when I first stepped inside.

Wooden stools in front of a long bar counter line the left wall that's full of shelves of liquor. The front of the building holds tables and booths packed with patrons, servers weaving their way around with trays of drinks held high. Under the dim lighting, there are a lot of low, murmuring voices, laughter, and the clinking of glass. It smells of beer, bar food, and stale cigarette smoke.

At the back of the bar, there's a small platform stage where it looks like the first band is packing up their equipment. None of the members are Mordred. I know that less because I can't *see* him and more because I can't *sense* him.

If he was in the same room as me, I'd know it.

Trying my best to ignore the spike of my heart rate and the dread pooling in my gut, I head over to the bar, beelining for the one empty stool and taking a seat.

Willow's easy to spot a few feet down the bar, mixing a customer's drink, smiling easily and chatting animatedly with him like she doesn't have a care in the world. *Lucky her*. She pours his drink from the shaker, and then her eyes find me.

"Merlin!" She waves at the man, then bounds gracefully over to me, motioning to another bartender to switch spots with her. "Want your usual?"

"Make it something a little stronger?"

My voice comes out shakier than I expected, nearly giving out, but she's kind enough to ignore it as she turns to grab a bottle from one of the shelves behind her. She retrieves a glass and pours a hefty amount of amber liquid into it. Her hand barely lets go of the glass before I'm picking it up and swallowing a large gulp.

"Everything okay?" she asks, brows knitted.

I don't drink much, and Willow knows it. Whenever I come to the bar—which is only once or twice a week, if that—it's usually for just one drink, two at most. Just enough to give me the time for a little human interaction outside of the shop.

"I'm good," I lie, completely unconvincingly.

Willow's hand comes across the bar, stopping an inch above my own where my fingers are drumming on the counter. We both grind to a halt, and she pulls her hand away.

"Sorry," she murmurs.

She got the impression a long time ago that I don't care for being touched, and I suppose...maybe she was right. So I never said anything to the contrary.

"Not a problem." I flex my hand and take a sip of my drink, appreciating the burn more this time. "Just a long day."

"You know..." she starts, smiling and moving past her faux pas as she leans over to rest her elbows on the sticky bar. "Bartenders double as therapists. So, if you need to talk..."

"That might be awkward considering you're also kind of my friend."

"*Kind of?*" She straightens with a look of mock offense. "Well, we'll see if this *kind of* friend brings you coffee anymore."

That manages to coax a small smile to my lips. "You *are* my friend," I correct.

"That's more like it."

I guess I do have *one*.

Any illusion of peace I may have felt from talking to Willow is immediately sucked away when there's a prickle at the base of my spine. Something changes in the air inside the bar. There's no doubt in my mind as to the source.

Magic.

It's been some time—I can't even remember how long—since I've felt the presence of magic. It was something that was common, something I was used to, back in Camelot and in the early days of my time here. It's been more prevalent in certain parts of this world, even up until somewhat recently. I expected to feel it at some point during my time in the city with how congested it is, but I haven't. I had begun to suspect magic had completely died out.

Maybe it has with the exception of me and Mordred.

Knowing that's who's in the room with me, I fix my gaze down on my drink as my knuckles turn white around the glass. I don't know exactly where in the room he is, but I can't bring myself to seek him out.

Not yet.

"Merlin." Willow's voice barely reaches my ears. It's like I'm underwater, everything sounding far away. "You're turning white. Did you see a ghost or something?"

The painful cliche is a little too on the nose.

"Not yet," I answer in a whisper.

"What?"

"Nothing."

"Okay, well…you're being weird. I'm going to get back to work."

Willow's nothing if not blunt.

After she moves along the bar to help other customers, I nurse my drink, still unable to look toward the stage. The band starts testing their equipment, random drum beats and distorted guitar notes pealing through the din of the bar.

"Hey, they haven't started yet!"

My eyes are drawn to the front door by the voice, and I see a group piling in, wearing mostly black, some with splashes of color. The leader is a girl with thick eyeliner and short hair that's half black and half bright blue. My gaze tracks them through the building until I realize how many people in the bar have migrated to the back, a crowd filling the floor in front of the stage. I suppose even bands that play in small dives like this can have fans.

I quickly look back down at my drink before I can see anything—or *anyone*—else.

The noises of the band stop, and a hush falls over the bar. Then a voice comes over the PA speakers.

"I'm Mordred le Fay, and we're Dethrone the Queen."

My spine stiffens, and all the air is sucked out of my immediate vicinity. If there was any doubt in my mind before, there's certainly none now. It may have been over a thousand years since I've heard that voice, but it hasn't changed.

After that short, dismissive introduction like he can't be bothered to say more to his audience, the band jumps right into their first song, a hard rhythm of distorted guitar and reverberating bass and heavy drums.

The fans start screaming, and I still haven't looked at the stage. I don't know if I *can*, if I'm physically capable of it at this point.

But I'm *not* a coward.

So I look.

Mordred is at the front of the stage, fingers moving deftly at both ends of his guitar. He looks the exact same as I remember him, and, yet...different.

He wears all black—ripped, black jeans; black combat boots; black military style jacket over a black T-shirt. His black hair is shorter than it used to be. Where it once swept past his shoulders, now it's cut just below his ears in a messy style. He has the same ocean blue eyes, framed by a thin border of eyeliner, and his jaw is still sharper than any other I've ever seen.

My gaze moves down to the guitar he plays—a pure white Gibson Les Paul that's juxtaposed against all the black. Even his nails are painted black, and the backs of his hands are tattooed, the artwork continuing up and disappearing beneath the sleeves of his jacket.

While he plays, his eyes are closed and his body sways on stage, as though he's completely consumed by the music, like he's giving himself over to it.

He takes a step toward the microphone stand in front of him.

The moment he opens his eyes, they're already on me, like he knew I was there the entire time. Somehow, he can see me past the purple-tinted spotlights.

Oh, right. He has magic too.

Even as time seems to stop, he never ceases his playing, never misses a beat or a note. His eyes sear straight through me, holding me captive.

I can't look away.

Is he doing that purposefully, creating some kind of link that I'm incapable of breaking? It feels like it. Like he won't *let* me look away. It's possible too, considering how strongly I can sense his magic, how fiercely it suffocates my own while both of our power saturates the air inside the bar. It shouldn't surprise me how his overshadows my own, not with how little I use it these days.

Then again, maybe the only reason I can't look away is because of the overwhelming force of my anger. I thought maybe I would experience fear in the face of Mordred returning from the dead, maybe a fresh wave of mourning, but I feel none of that.

My initial expectation was true.

All I feel is *fury*.

And *hatred*.

Our intense staring begins to feel like a challenge the longer it goes on.

Then he fucking *smirks*.

His mouth finds the mic, and he starts to sing. His lips move, but I hear none of the words that slip past them, neither one of us having looked away. It's as though he's singing directly to me, despite my extreme loathing louder than anything coming through the speakers.

It's not until their first song is over that whatever spell held our eyes locked breaks. I look away, back down at my drink, then I down the rest of it.

"I love you, Mordred!"

The shout comes from one of the girls in the crowd, and I roll my eyes before I can stop myself. They probably wouldn't feel the same if they knew the man murdered his own father. Or maybe they would. What do I know?

Mordred doesn't respond. I can feel his eyes still on me, and his silence is unsettling. When my gaze drifts back to the stage, it's like he was waiting for me to look again.

With another smirk, he says into the mic, "This next song is called 'Sins of the Father.'"

The head turns of his bandmates pull my attention to them as they all share a look, like Mordred has gone off script. But they're quick to recover as their frontman starts the song with a guitar solo.

Has his gaze left me for a second?

Refusing to give him any kind of satisfaction, I return once more to my glass, only to be disappointed when I remember it's empty.

Willow's there to save the day, holding up the bottle of liquor in front of me in offering, the music too loud as drums and bass join the guitar to hear anything else. I nod and slide my empty glass across the bar.

"*Bow down...bow down...*"

Maybe it's the raging river of wrath and enmity boiling hot in my veins that's keeping me from wanting to listen to the lyrics of Mordred's song. Or maybe it's because I'm certain he only means to taunt me with it.

"*I was sinful at birth.*"

I shouldn't be surprised that he can sing. A thousand years is enough to perfect any skill. Still, it's caught me off guard now that I'm not hypnotized by only his eyes. His voice is low, deep, growly.

"...*this wicked legacy of mine...disease in my veins...*"

The burn of the liquor is the only thing keeping those murderous waves at bay, keeping me from releasing them in a literal storm clear across this bar.

"...*cycle of sin and sorrow...chain that can be broken...*"

I want to fucking kill him.

"...*this curse of mine...*"

By the time the song ends, my glass is once more empty. Willow fills it again wordlessly, her concern radiating around me but not touching me, not with the bubble of everything hot and awful surrounding me, made from the fumes bleeding from my very pores.

I won't kill him.

I tell myself this despite the overwhelming, near-debilitating desire to do so. As the band moves smoothly into their next song, I'm still trying to convince myself not to become a cold-blooded killer. It's a battle between the human and the demon in me, as though an actual angel and devil perch on my shoulders.

With how hard I'm fighting against thoughts of avenging Arthur's death, visions bathed in blood, of all the ways I could do it, I'm surprised the death grip on my glass doesn't shatter the damn thing.

I'm not this person.

By the time the band's set is over, I've finished four glasses of whatever it is Willow's been serving me. At this point, I don't know if the alcohol is calming me or heating me up more.

Willow's voice sounds far away as I leave my stool, ignoring both her calling my name and the movement happening on stage as the band breaks down their equipment.

The gushing of fans begging for autographs fades into the background with the rest of it.

This isn't me.

I head to the other side of the bar, through the hallway that leads to the bathrooms and the back door. Pushing the door open, I step out into the dark alley, the crisp, night air hitting me in the face and doing nothing to soothe these scary thoughts.

I won't kill him.

Even though I really fucking want to.

4

MORDRED

I sensed Merlin the moment I stepped on stage. Or, rather, I sensed his magic. It was weak, much weaker than mine, but it was familiar. It's been a long time since I felt Merlin's brand of sorcery, but I'd recognize it anywhere, even as feeble as it was.

Watching him squirm was the most fun I've had in a while. I could barely keep my eyes off him the entire time I was performing. Or as we finished our set and started packing up our equipment. Or as I stepped to the edge of the stage to sign autographs on T-shirts and tits—*just another night for me*—my gaze following him all the way to the back door.

There's a magnetic force that I have to fight against that's trying to pull me in his direction, to taunt him and haunt him further. But even though I can be a dick, I'm not about to make my bandmates haul our equipment out by themselves.

I can only hope Merlin's waiting for me. I bet he is. Something tells me he can't resist this pull either.

The next band starts bringing their instruments on stage as we finish packing up our own and lugging them out the back door where our van waits in the alley. The others chat idly with each other, knowing I'm not much of a talker after shows. I chug a bottle of tepid water and prefer to rest my vocal cords.

Fine. I just don't like to talk at all, riding the high of performing in silence.

And, this time, the high of giving Merlin hell.

"Hey, man," Anthony says after stowing his bass in the cab, the white T-shirt beneath his black and pink paisley shirt completely soaked through with sweat. "What was up with changing the setlist in the middle of the show?"

Of course, I knew I wouldn't get away with my brooding silence this time.

"Felt like the right move at the time," I answer, my voice always a little deeper after a show. I lean against the side of the van as Ava and Will wrestle the last of the drums inside. "I knew you guys could handle it."

"Yeah, you're lucky we're a bunch of badasses." Ava hops down out of the van and straightens her short, black skirt that she's wearing over lime green leggings tonight. "A little heads up would've been nice though."

"Last minute call," I say with a shrug.

Ava eyes me with suspicion, no doubt wanting to ask me the reason but deciding not to press it.

After slamming the van doors shut, Will stands beside me and flings an arm over my shoulders. "How about a few drinks before we head back to the hotel?"

We all smell like sweat and cigarette smoke, but not one of us cares. Will always cares the least of us all. He's a toucher.

Ava rolls her eyes. "Not if you guys are going to make me DD again."

"I'll volunteer this time," Anthony offers.

I can still feel Merlin's magic nearby, so I know he's stuck around. My gaze drifts down the alley where the shadows are thick. I consider using a little magic to see through them, but it was risky enough doing that on stage so I could lay eyes on him past the spotlights. I don't need to see him though.

I know he's there.

Waiting.

"You guys go ahead," I tell them, ducking out from under Will's arm. "I think I'm going to go meet up with an old friend."

"You have friends?" Ava asks teasingly.

I give her a one-finger salute, and she laughs.

"Want us to wait for you before we head back?" Will asks.

"Nah. I'll find my own way. You guys have fun." I start walking backwards away from them, toward the shadows instead of the street. "Don't do anything I wouldn't do."

"So nothing's off the table then?" Anthony calls back as he opens the back door to the bar for the rest of them, music from the other band filling the alley.

I laugh just long enough for them to hear me. As soon as the door closes, all sounds of music and laughter die.

Turning around, I make my way into the shadows. Even the noises of traffic become muffled the deeper I go and the darker it gets. I don't use magic to improve my sight even though I could. Maybe I should be afraid, concerned that the only reason Merlin is still here is to kill me. I may not know who he is now after over a thousand years, but I know that's not who he once was. I'm not afraid of him.

Then again, I'm not sure of the last time I actually *felt* fear.

Stepping into the darkest part of the shadows, I tilt my head, straining my ears. I haven't seen or heard him yet, but I *know* he's here.

"It's been a long time, Merlin," I call blindly into the shadows.

"Not long enough."

He slowly steps out from behind a tall stack of wooden pallets, and I can't keep a smirk from spreading across my entire face even if I wanted to. His tension is palpable, and the desire to push all his buttons is too damn great.

"How long has it been? A thousand years?" I take a step forward. "Give or take a few decades?"

His jaw ticks, and he holds a hand out. "Stay away from me, Mordred."

I don't listen. I take another step. "Aw, you're gonna hurt my feelings."

"What feelings?" he scoffs.

I bark out a stiff laugh. "Fair."

When I step forward again, this time, he takes a step back. I tilt my head, my eyes naturally adjusting to the lack of light so I can see him better. He looks practically identical to the last time I saw him—short brown hair that's a bit wind-swept, russet eyes that are a rich, deep reddish brown, and just a hint of stubble. Even his jaw is set just as hard, like he wants to reiterate those exact same words he left me with all that time ago.

I hope you die a slow and painful death, Mordred.

"I said stay back!" he snarls like he's a trapped animal.

"Am I supposed to fear you, Merlin?" It's as though there's a hook in the corner of my mouth, my smirk only growing. "Because I'm only afraid you'll be disappointed. Again."

"Don't you dare."

He doesn't have to elaborate. I know he doesn't want me to bring up the last time I *disappointed* him.

"Don't I dare what?" I ask with faux innocence.

"You think I won't hurt you?"

I click my tongue before licking it over the ring in my bottom lip. "I think you *want* to hurt me. If you *can* is another matter."

"You remember who I am."

It's not a question because of course I remember. He would never let me forget. He was the greatest sorcerer in Camelot, and he knew it. It's not that he was arrogant about it; in fact, despite being the most powerful wizard, he was rather humble about that fact. It was one of the reasons my mother loathed him so much. And one of the reasons I admired him.

Eh...

Maybe *respected* is a more appropriate term.

"I think I can confidently say who you are isn't who you *were*. Your magic is weak, Merlin. Did you think I wouldn't be able to sense it? When was the last time you used it? Do you even remember how?"

His eyes narrow. "You think you're more powerful than me?"

"Yes," I answer simply with another tilt of my head. "Shall we have a demonstration?"

The fire escape above him creaks and groans. The two steel side rails of the ladder grow unnaturally downward, extending so fast that Merlin has no time to react before they're wrapping around his wrists like vicious snakes and pulling him back against the wall. The ends lengthen further to bind around his ankles. He struggles, but we both know only magic can fight against magic.

I step forward, turning until I'm standing in front of him, grinning up at him, his feet a few feet above the ground. "Come on, Merlin," I taunt. "If your magic's still more powerful than mine, why not fight back?"

He stops struggling, panting from the effort. My eyes linger on the way his chest rapidly rises and falls. His lips form a thin line, and he simply glares at me.

"What's the matter? Can't remember how?"

I'm pressing for a real answer because something in me needs to know the truth. Merlin without magic feels...*wrong*. He must be able to sense it because he changes the subject.

"What are you doing here, Mordred? Have you really waited a thousand years to find me and kill me?"

I take a step forward, having to crane my neck a bit to look up at him, satisfied when his entire body stiffens. "You were never this vain before. Not everything's about you. I didn't even know you were here."

That seems to catch him off guard. "You expect me to believe that?"

"I'm just living my life, Merlin." I shrug, extending my arms wide. "We were bound to run into each other eventually. It's a small world and all that."

His eyes narrow further, and I wonder if he can sense the untold truth behind my words. After a moment, his expression almost softens. "Why did you leave Camelot?"

Fuck that.

I refuse to talk about that.

It's my turn to scowl. "You're the one strung up, not me."

"Clearly, killing Arthur didn't have the desired effect. Do you regret it?"

My jaw clenches until it aches. I wasn't planning on actually hurting Merlin, but I'm dangerously close to doing just that.

Moving closer, I glare up at him. "You remember who I was too. What the fuck do you think?"

I had quite the reputation among Arthur's other knights. I was the despised, illegitimate son of the king, the one who often went down into the city and murdered and raped without any regard. Of course, many of those accounts were often exaggerated or completely fabricated. But none of them cared. I clung to that reputation because it gave me the conviction to do what needed to be done.

"If you're looking for any sign of shame or possibility of salvation, save your strength. Not only do I feel no guilt over it, I *liked* it."

His face falls, and he shakes his head like he doesn't want to believe it.

Good 'ol, Merlin.

"You always foolishly believed the best in people, and that's why you failed."

His body jerks forward, and he's fighting against his restraints again, no doubt with the desire to attack me.

I laugh, easing some of my own tension that Merlin created as I goad him. "*Magic*, Merlin. Come on. You can do it."

He falls still once more.

He looks good all tied up. Fighting. Panting.

My cock twitches.

Woah. What the fuck?

I did *not* intend for my thoughts to fly so far into left field.

My dick really needs to check itself. Merlin may be attractive, but I never looked at him like that. I may like them a little older—at least physically because no mortal is older than I am—but...come on. He's *two hundred years* older than me. Fucking ancient. I wouldn't fuck the Lady of the Lake just because she's older.

Fuck. This is *Merlin*, for fuck's sake.

I really do need to get laid. That's all it is.

Pushing those thoughts way, way, *way* back, I close most of the short distance that's left between us. That proves to maybe not be the best idea. I have to force my gaze to stay on his face instead of his crotch that's right in front of me.

"You look like you want to murder me," I say, amused.

"I'm not you."

"Oh, ouch." I frown with mock offense. "You're right though. You couldn't hurt a bug, could you?"

"I've squashed plenty. I'll squash you too, Mordred."

I click the bar in my tongue against my lip ring in an attempt to control the amusement on my face. Reaching out, I casually walk my fingers up his thigh. "More like I'll crawl beneath your skin, darling."

He thrashes against his steel binds. "Don't fucking touch me!"

For the first time, I see a hint of fear in his eyes. It's faint, mostly eclipsed by his anger and animosity, but it's there nonetheless. The only other time I remember ever seeing him afraid was the night I killed Arthur. Merlin has never been a coward.

I chuckle to myself as I take one small step back.

Just like Merlin without magic, Merlin afraid feels just as wrong. However, that last part doesn't bother me as much, instead sending a sick thrill through me. I want to be the one to coax it all out of him. All his magic and his fear.

"Have it your way, Merlin." I stare up at him, making sure to give him one last smirk. "I have a feeling I'm not done with you though."

"I'd be perfectly content not seeing you again for all eternity," he snarls, no trace of fear left.

"Well, I'll be in the city for a couple of weeks. If we don't run into each other again, I guess I'll see you in another thousand years."

As I turn my back on him, I wave my hand in the air. The metal binding Merlin creaks behind me, and I hear him drop to the ground with a grunt. I bid my farewell with another casual wave of my hand, moving out of the shadows and back down the alley.

For some reason, I don't feel like finding a warm body to fuck anymore. Maybe I'll explore the streets of New York some before heading back to the hotel.

Crawling under Merlin's skin was better than any hook-up I could've had instead.

5

MERLIN

The water raining down from the shower isn't nearly hot enough to boil away Mordred—the memories of his face or his words or his touch. Despite the fact he only touched me over my jeans, I still can't stop scrubbing that spot on my thigh. The skin has turned red to the point of pain, yet I continue with the abuse until I can no longer feel him there. At least as much as I could before.

By the time I finally exit the shower, I've lost count of how many times I've washed my entire body. After drying off, I slip into a pair of boxers and crash onto the bed on my back. Percy leaps up and curls up at the foot of the bed, softly purring.

I'm almost mad at myself for not using magic to fight back tonight, but Mordred wasn't entirely wrong. I'm not confident in my abilities like I once was considering I barely use those powers anymore. Not only that, but it's better if

Mordred believes I *can't*. If I had tried and magic came as naturally to me as it once had, there was also the chance I wouldn't be able to stop until he was dead. And I promised myself I wouldn't kill him.

But there's still that small part of me that regrets not going through with it anyway.

Not only can I not stop thinking about how strongly I hate him, I can't help but wonder *why* he's here. I wish he had answered the question about why he left Camelot because now those thoughts are going to poison my mind as much as my contempt for him.

There have been times, sure, when I've pondered the fate of the kingdom after Arthur died and I fled. However, for the most part, I've left the past in the past. It doesn't matter what became of Camelot because I've left that life behind me.

But what if I doomed Camelot by leaving? What if I let Arthur down?

Fuck.

I *know* I did.

I hate myself almost as much as I hate Mordred.

Staring up at the ceiling, I have a hard time shutting my mind off. I roll over onto my side, then my stomach, then my other side, eventually ending up on my back again. For probably about an hour, I toss and turn with these thoughts so loud that they drown out the sounds of the city.

It's not until I finally make a decision that I'm able to relax. I'll keep to my apartment and my shop for the next couple of weeks. I won't risk running into Mordred again.

By the time morning comes, I'll forget this entire night.

"Get on your knees."

There's a face in front of me, blurry, everything a little hazy. Stinging pains like pin pricks twinge in spots around my face and ears and neck.

Slowly, the face in front of me comes into focus. First, it's the eyes—as blue as a clear ocean. Then, metal glints from his lips and his ears, his inky black hair falling over his forehead. For some reason, my subconscious mind doesn't recognize him until he smirks, showing off his teeth. Just like he did on stage and in that alley…

"I said get on your knees, Merlin."

For some other inexplicable reason…I do.

I can't understand or explain what's going on in my head. There's something like unease, bordering on panic, but it's getting buried deeper and deeper under something else—a kind of calm, a quiet repose.

The sound of a zipper echoes in my ears, reverberating off of what, I don't know. Everything but Mordred is still a blur.

He's the only thing that's clear. So is his cock as it bobs in front of my face, already hard.

*And…*pierced.

Just like the jewelry in his face, the metal appears to glimmer from several places. Mordred's deep voice drifts from above me, but I can't make out the words, too transfixed.

I hate him, but I want to taste him.

Again…I do.

Just as the first salty drop of precum hits my tongue…

I bolt upright in bed, gasping for breath. Sweat clings to my entire body.

And I'm…*hard.*

That is the furthest thing from okay.

What the fuck *was* that?

Completely ignoring my aching erection, I quickly get out of bed, fleeing like it was the scene of a crime. It's still dark outside the window, but a glance at the clock says it's early morning, about an hour earlier than I normally get up. Which is fine. I'll just get an earlier start to the day because there's no way I'll be able to go back to sleep.

As hard as I try to forget what I saw in my sleep, I can't.

I refuse to believe that was a premonition. Of course, that would mean my subconscious was dreaming about Mordred's dick, and...that's not ideal either.

I hate him.

I hate him more than I've ever hated anyone or anything. And that's saying something considering I've been alive for over a millennium, with plenty of time to find other things to loathe more than Mordred le Fay.

By the time I'm entering the shower, my erection has faded. My conscious mind is clearly more sane than my subconscious one.

Still, it can't stop replaying that vision. Dream. Whatever it was.

I wish I could claim it was neither.

There's no way in hell I would ever kneel for that evil bastard.

Despite the steam filling the small shower, a chill sweeps down my spine when a disconcerting thought hits me. What if it *was* a premonition? What if he did something to me? Manipulated me, fucked with my mind? I wouldn't put it past him, even if the only purpose was to humiliate me.

Maybe I should try to shake some of the rust off my magic...

I wish it was possible to scrub my brain like I did my body last night, to cleanse my mind, wipe that vision completely from my memory.

Since waking, I've actively avoided thinking about the fact that I've never once been able to stop a premonition from coming true. Denial is keeping me from freaking out more than I probably should be.

Making this a shorter shower than last night's, I get out, dry myself off, and wrap the towel around my waist while I brush my teeth and shave. After throwing on some clothes, I strip the bed and carry the sheets to the laundry, like I can erase nonexistent evidence of what I had seen while tangled up in those sheets.

I feed Percy, take care of the plants, then lock up and head downstairs. I'm tempted to lock myself away in my apartment all day, but I need the distraction of work. And books. I've read everything I have in my apartment, so I need to pick out something new.

I'd rather be lost in literature than in my own head.

It's still a little early, so I spend nearly twenty minutes browsing, being a little too picky, until I find something interesting enough that I haven't read before—*After Dark* by Haruki Murakami. I take the book to the counter, open up the shop, then sit down to read.

The book is short, so I finish it a little after noon. It's also a mindfuck. Just like my life currently is.

But it succeeds in its purpose to distract me because, also like everything else, I'm left without any concrete answers, abandoned with only my own guesses and assumptions. However, it's a lot more preferable to speculate the possible truth behind every surreal event that happened in the story than it is to speculate the truth behind my hopefully-not premonition.

It's late afternoon, and I've buried myself in another book—*The Alchemist* by Paulo Coelho—when Willow steps inside the shop. She doesn't walk further in than that, just a step, leaning her back against the door once it closes, holding the usual two coffees in her hands.

Looking up at her, I arch a brow at her odd behavior. "What?"

She peers at me, narrowing her eyes. "Are you… approachable right now?"

I sigh and place my book down on the counter. "Was I that bad?"

"You had twice the amount to drink than you normally do," she says, finally moving forward. "Which still isn't that much, but it was…concerning."

She's right. After four drinks, I was feeling the kind of buzz I hadn't felt in a long time, but it was a necessary one. Of course, it was gone the moment I confronted Mordred in the alley. It wasn't enough to last or to leave me with a hangover this morning, but I should probably avoid being so reckless.

Especially around *him*.

I just couldn't help it when I saw him. All my inhibitions went flying out the proverbial window.

Which probably doesn't bode well for…

Nope.

"I apologize," I say, quickly redirecting my thoughts before they can completely derail into a fiery train wreck. "I wasn't quite feeling like myself last night."

Not a lie.

Willow sets my hot black coffee on the counter and gives me a small smile. "How are you feeling today?"

"Better."

A half truth.

"Good. And my offer still stands if you need to talk about it."

"Thanks." I pick up the coffee and take a sip. "Aren't you off today?"

"I am." She bites her lip while swirling her drink, ice clinking. "But I was wondering…"

I grin and lean back in my seat. "Oh, here we go."

"Hey, it's nothing as bad as that jazz club you dragged me to!"

"That was not *bad*. You just don't have taste," I tease in jest.

She scrunches her nose. "Not *bad* taste."

I laugh and shake my head. "What is it?"

"One of those bands that played last night, Dethrone the Queen, is having their next show over at Twister's tonight. I was wondering if you wanted to go with me."

The moment the name of Mordred's band leaves her lips, my body instinctively freezes up, my muscles taut and full of dread and anxiety. I *was* doing a decent job at not freaking out, but the thought of seeing him again has that repressed panic bubbling to the surface. I was so intent on avoiding him at all costs, but I know myself. It's damn difficult to tell Willow no.

"There it is again!" She points to my face and furrows her brow.

"What?" I ask, my voice coming out too thick.

"That look. Like death warmed up. What's up with you?"

I lower my gaze and sigh again. I don't like the thought of lying to Willow, but, more than that, I need to get this off my chest, loosen this tight feeling just beneath my ribs. Maybe if she knows the truth—well, *part* of it—she'll let me say no to going.

"You know their frontman? Mordred?"

She nods.

"I…" I clear my throat. "I kind of know him. From a long time ago."

The way her eyes widen is almost comical. "*You* know *him?*"

Something about the way she says that gives me pause. "What is that supposed to mean?"

"Well, he's...you know. And you're...you know."

Crossing my arms over my chest, I try not to grin at how flustered she is. "Spell it out for me, Willow."

"He's...cool. And young. And hot. You're...old and boring."

She doesn't even have the decency to sound guilty, but I still have to suppress a chuckle. Willow has that effect. She's a rare ray of light even when things are the darkest. Not to mention that being viewed as the antithesis of Mordred is the highlight of my week.

"If I'm so old and boring, why invite me to the show? Surely you have cooler and younger and hotter friends than me."

Taking a sip from her straw, she shrugs. "I thought you'd make a good wingman."

"Wingman?"

Willow leans over, plops an elbow on the counter and her chin in her hand, and stares off into space. "Ava," she whispers wistfully.

"And Ava is?"

"You know Mordred, but you don't know the others in his band?"

I hesitate, then answer, "It's been a long time since I've seen him."

She stands up straight again and takes another sip from her coffee. "Well, Ava's their drummer. I'm pretty sure I made a fool of myself last night when they all came to the bar. Though, she did invite me to their show tonight, so I guess that doesn't mean I completely struck out. Thinking about it...Mordred was the only one not there last night. Was he with you?"

The question is innocent enough, but it still makes my jaw tick. "We...caught up."

"Damn. He must have done something really fucked if you hate him that badly."

That's an understatement.

"Yeah, well...I'd rather not talk about it."

"Okay," she says, nodding respectively. "I won't make you go tonight, but I still think you'd make a much better wingman than any of my other friends. I swear I'll stick up for you if anything comes up."

She bats her eyelashes at me, kind of contradicting the claim she wouldn't make me go. She knows how charming and convincing she can be.

But the more I think about it, the more the temptation pulls at me. For one reason only. If there's *any* part of me that would ever be willing to do anything like I did in my vision, I have to know. I have to know if my perception of Mordred has changed. It's certainly not my *feelings*. My hatred for him will forever be a poison in my veins, but maybe there's a kind of gravitational force that I haven't acknowledged. Even the thought makes me sick.

But I have to know.

I have to know if I need to be prepared to fight him.

Or if I'll have to fight myself.

I'm positive I'll live to regret this for the next thousand years, but I eventually nod and say, "All right. I'll go."

6

MORDRED

I haven't been able to stop thinking about Merlin all day. It's kind of annoying if I'm being honest. I haven't been this fixated on something other than music in a long time. But I can't help it every time I remember how thrilling it was to rattle his cage, to watch him squirm. If getting under his skin was that much fun, I imagine burrowing *inside* it would be even better.

Fuck.

Every now and then, those thoughts sneak up on me without my permission. I shouldn't have restrained him because...*damn*. He looked good like that.

But...again. This is *Merlin*.

I desperately need to reorient my thoughts before I do something stupid like attempt to act on it. Then again, if I'm determined to provoke him to the point of using magic, that's one way of going about it.

But I don't have a fucking death wish.

Merlin without magic is entertaining. Merlin *with* magic is dangerous.

Considering my head has been elsewhere all day, I haven't made shit for progress on the new song I've been working on. The others went to do a little sightseeing while I stayed behind at the hotel. I realized last night that the city hasn't changed all that much since the last time I was here, so I chose to hang back. They're used to leaving me to my own devices, especially when Ava decides I'm in one of my frequent brooding moods like she did this morning before they left.

This time, I think she mistook distracted for brooding.

About an hour before our gig is supposed to start, I meet the others downstairs at the van, and Anthony drives us over to a place called Twister's. I make an effort on the way over to ask them how their sightseeing went, and they all eagerly share. The place we show up at is a similar dive as the Stone Crow, about the same size and just as busy as the night crowd arrives.

"You're not going to change the setlist on us in the middle of the show again, are you?" Ava asks as we all hop out of the van and start unloading the equipment.

"Nah, I think I got it all out of my system last night," I answer vaguely, knowing they won't understand quite what I mean.

And it's a goddamn lie.

I don't think fucking with Merlin will ever be out of my system.

While Anthony goes to check in with the manager, I lean against the side of the van, resisting the urge to light up and take a quick toke. I had a few hits back in my hotel room—it's easy to deal with the smell when you have magic. But I've been restless all day, and it hardly helped.

Will leans against the van beside me, bumping his shoulder against mine, the goddamn toucher he is. "You okay, man? You've been acting a little strange since last night."

"Stranger than usual?" I ask with a grin.

"I guess not." He returns my grin and shrugs. "I guess it's more like a feeling."

"That attuned to me, huh?"

A blush rises in his cheeks. "I wouldn't say that. But we are bandmates, after all."

Anthony comes out the side door of the bar and tells us we've got the go-ahead to start setting up.

I give Will a pat on the shoulder. "I'm all good, man. Let's do this."

The moment I step inside the bar and onto the stage, I feel him. Well, I feel his weak ass magic. I don't seek him out; I have no doubt he knows I'm aware of his presence. Instead, I ignore him because the idea that he could possibly crave my attention is too deliciously sweet. There's a reason he's here, and I'm certain it's not a coincidence.

It's not until all the equipment is set up and I step up to the mic with my guitar that I let my eyes land on him, immediately like I knew where he was all along. The way he tenses has me smirking behind the microphone.

After giving my usual short introduction to the crowd, we jump right into the first song. Just like last night, I can't take my eyes off Merlin.

He's standing with a young woman with blonde and pink hair who I'm pretty sure I recognize as one of the bartenders from the Stone Crow. It's difficult to know for sure because I had been so completely focused on the man on the opposite side of the bar last night. She's bobbing her head and swaying to the music while Merlin stands rigid beside her looking stiff and out of place.

And, of course, it wouldn't be Merlin without that twitch in his jaw and the pure fucking death glare he's giving me.

Maybe he's come to kill me after all.

The thought causes me to smirk wider as I sing into the mic, my gaze permanently fixed on Merlin, like I'm singing to only him and no one else in the bar.

It's not until halfway through the second song that I let my eyes move away from him to roam around the crowd, giving them all a fraction of my attention before it returns right back to where it really wants to be.

If my bandmates could see how little interest I'm paying the rest of our audience, they'd probably chastise me, especially Ava. We have a decent little cult following, and I'm sure they wouldn't appreciate it if I alienated what fans we have. For example, the girl with the black and blue hair in the crowd whose tit I recall signing last night with a permanent marker. She's the kind of fan I wouldn't be surprised to see at every show we have in the city over the next couple of weeks.

But fuck it. It's not like this band can ever be bigger than we are.

Before I can let myself think too much about that, I take my step back during the third song, letting Will take the front of the stage for his solo. As we switch spots, he briefly grabs my ass, and the crowd makes more noise.

Will's a talented guitarist. They're all talented musicians. Too talented for the way I hold them back.

When Ava starts off our last song with her drum solo, I return my whole focus to Merlin once more. Somehow, he looks far more uncomfortable than he did even a moment ago. He's not so much glaring anymore, his brow furrowed deeply as though he's in physical pain. More likely, it's a mental kind of torment.

Either way, I want to know the exact cause.

It'd be amusing if it was simply my face.

Before our last song ends, I watch Merlin lean over into his bartender friend's space and speak into her ear, having to talk loudly over the music. Despite the risk of using magic so publicly, I do so I can catch what he says. Mortals are always so oblivious to it anyway.

"I'm sorry, Willow. I have to go."

I use magic again, a spell to track his movements as he weaves his way through the crowd and out the front door, a dim prismatic haze only I can see lingering in his wake.

We finish our set, sign a few autographs, and start packing up our equipment and hauling it back out to the van. Once it's all loaded in the cab, I pull out my phone and check it, glancing at the screen as though I'm reading a text.

"Hey, guys. Sorry to do this to you again," I tell the others as I stuff my phone back in the pocket of my jacket. "That friend from last night wants to meet up."

"Are we ever going to get any of your precious time while we're in the city?" Will asks with a playful grin but with a hint of genuineness to his question.

Anthony pats him on the back like he can sense his despondence.

I may be quiet a lot of the time and often keep to myself, but I usually make a point of setting aside more time than this for my band, hanging out with them at least a little during each of our stops.

"I'll make it up to you guys tomorrow. Promise."

"That's fine." Ava shrugs with a smile like she can't be bothered. "I have a date waiting for me inside anyway"

"You work fast," I tease.

She scoffs. "You're one to talk."

Ava and Anthony were around during my last...whore phase, for lack of a better term.

"Hey, I've been on my best behavior lately."

Even in the dim alleyway lights, I can make out the blush on Will's cheeks. Ava just laughs like I told a funny joke and starts heading back toward the door.

"You guys have a good night," I say as I start walking away, this time toward the actual street. "We'll do something tomorrow."

When I reach the street, I look left and right, searching for a sign of the spell I placed on Merlin. I find it easily, like a shimmering ribbon winding its way down the sidewalk from the front door of the bar, fading the further Merlin travels. I follow it, its black and purple hues glistening like an oil slick.

The spell mostly follows a path along the sidewalk, weaving around street lights and corners and occasionally directing me to cross a somewhat busy street. The bar we just played at is only a few blocks from the Stone Crow where we played last night, and that seems to be the direction in which Merlin is heading.

Sure enough, that's where the spell leads.

Well, it leads directly across the street, the mystical ribbon disappearing through the door of a small bookshop called Writ in Stone. I can't help but grin at the possible significance.

An idea comes to me, and, instead of walking across the street and simply letting myself in through the front door, I close my eyes. Take a breath. A brief moment of concentration. When I open my eyes again, the street and the night sky are gone, replaced with the inside of the shop.

And Merlin.

He's standing in the same aisle I just materialized in, in front of a tall shelf with a stack of books in his hand. For barely a second, he remains oblivious to my presence before his body goes rigid when he senses my magic.

Then, slowly, his head twists to the side, and his jaw clenches. "How are you here?"

I smirk even though the look in his eyes is a little harder to translate than usual. "Magic. You know, that thing you used to excel quite well at."

He turns back to the shelf and places a book between two others. "Good. Then use it to leave. You're not welcome here."

"I'd say you're hurting my feelings again, but, well, we've already established I don't have those."

Leaning my shoulder against the nearest bookshelf, I cross my arms over my chest and observe him as he proceeds to place a couple more books on the shelves. He's as stiff as ever, but I can tell he's making an effort to remain calm.

"Did you not hear me?" he snaps when I haven't made a move to leave.

He's still not looking at me, and I'm not sure why that pisses me off. Ignoring his question, I ask one of my own. "Why did you come to the show tonight?"

I didn't think it was possible for him to tense up even more, but he does. There's something off about him. He's even more on edge than he was last night, which is surprising considering it was our first encounter in a thousand years. The fact that I can't figure him out is pissing me off too.

"Willow asked me to go. I did it as a kindness to a friend."

"Bullshit." I push off the wall and take a step forward.

His body immediately spins to face me, defensive.

"You want to know what I think?"

"Not particularly."

"I think you're obsessed with me."

He laughs without any true amusement and turns back to the shelf to stock more books. "Of course you do. Because you're an arrogant prick."

"People are often obsessed with the things they hate," I rationalize.

"I may hate you, but I'm far from obsessed."

After placing the last one of the books he's holding on the shelf, he turns once more and takes a step like he's going to move past me, aiming for a wide berth. I move in front of him instead, and he stops. He steps back, and there's a subtle flicker of fear in his eyes, similar to what I saw there last night.

"Why did someone like you decide to settle down in NYC?" I ask, genuinely curious.

"What does that mean?"

None of his animosity has faded since being in such close proximity to me, and I want to soak it all up.

"For starters, you're nervous in crowds. You also don't like being touched."

"Sounds like you're the one obsessed with me if you've noticed all that."

I smirk wide, showing my teeth. I could probably deny it, but it might be a lie. I'm obsessed with inching my way beneath his skin, seeing just how far I can burrow in.

Some of that fear in Merlin's eyes is still lingering, and suddenly he's fidgety, shifting on his feet, rubbing the tips of his fingers against his palms. His gaze has left me, causing my amusement to fade. Taking your eyes off a possible predator isn't a good idea if you're afraid of them.

"Did something happen?" I ask before I can stop myself, hating the way I sound almost…*concerned*.

If Merlin is going to be afraid of anyone, it's going to be *me*.

He falls still, his eyes snapping back to mine. His jaw clenches again. "No."

Lie.

Tilting my head, I study him a little closer. "Did you have a premonition?"

Merlin was always famous for his visions, one reason his counsel was highly sought after in Camelot. It wouldn't surprise me if he did have one, even if his magic is as weak and out of practice as it is.

"No."

Another lie.

I narrow my eyes as though that will help me see straight through him to whatever he's keeping locked up.

What are you hiding, Merlin?

If I wanted to, I could force him to show me, use magic to burrow into his mind. Not only would I have to catch him off guard, but if he decided that was the moment he was going to fight back, I'd be leaving myself vulnerable. Though it might be worth it if it provoked some of his own magic that's been lying dormant for who the fuck knows how long.

Changing the subject—or maybe biding his time until he figures out how to deal with me—he asks, "Why did someone like you decide to start a band?"

I grin at his counter question to my own previous one and reply similarly. "What does that mean?"

"For starters," he says, playing the same game, "you're immortal. Surely you know what would happen if your band makes it big and someone recognizes you decades later when you haven't aged a day."

"Hey, if Lestat can do it, why can't I?"

He stares, unamused.

"Fine. Why do you think we haven't made it big?" I almost laugh at the way his brows draw together in bemused surprise. "I may be reckless, but I can be careful when I need to be. I have no interest in ending up as a science experiment. But, come on, you have to admit an eternal existence can get boring. We have to do *something* to keep ourselves entertained so we don't go insane."

Merlin actually takes a step toward me, not close enough to touch, but close enough I can nearly feel the fury radiating off him. "I won't be your next source of entertainment, Mordred. Get the fuck out of my shop."

"You know, I'm actually trying to be civil here."

"You thinking you have any right to be here is the furthest thing from civil."

Fuck, I love how much he hates me.

It makes me want to push every single one of his buttons, let him fight me and watch him squirm until he can't anymore, until that fight completely bleeds out of him.

"I think I've been pretty nice," I tell him, cocking a brow. "Tell me. Have I hurt you?"

"Don't do that." He takes another step forward, a small one, careful not to get too close, like he's a cautious rabbit approaching a sleeping lion. He lowers his voice to a deep rumble. "Don't pretend you're something you're not, Mordred. A thousand years can't erase the darkness that's inside you. You think I can't still see it? All that evil swimming around in your soul? That despicable, vile wickedness has eaten away at every corner that might have long ago held any semblance of good. From the moment you decided to kill your father, you've been nothing but a monster."

It's not until he finishes speaking that I register the ache in my jaw, the pain in my chest. It's my turn to take a step. Despite being close enough to touch now, he doesn't back away.

Lowering my voice even deeper than his, I snarl, "For someone once known as the wisest wizard in Camelot, you sure don't know shit."

I don't know what compelled me to say that, to bare that smallest hint of my soul that he hates so much, hardly a sliver that sleeps within the darkness he sees so easily. It slipped out along with the anger he aroused in me, but I quickly lock it all away again, forcing every muscle in my body to loosen.

"Tell me again how you liked it," he says, practically growling now.

Now even my signature smirk is back in its place. "I *loved* it."

This time, he doesn't look hurt or shocked. "Then how about you tell me why you're really here if it's not only to torment me?"

"Oh, it's definitely to torment you. But there's more to it. I really am itching to rouse that slumbering magic of yours."

"Why? What reason could you possibly have? You're not the type to have suicidal tendencies."

I can't help but laugh at that. "At least you know you have no chance of putting me down unless you have the full strength of your powers back. Even so, I'm not worried about that."

"Then why?"

I play with the bar in my tongue a bit while I scrutinize him closely, wondering just how much he knows, how much I should tell him. Clicking the bar against my lip ring, I sigh. "Do you really not know you're meant to return to Camelot?"

A deep line appears between his brows. "What?"

Poor Merlin. I relish in his stunned expression and the next blow I'm about to deliver. Just to make sure it's an effective bombshell, I take another step until there's two feet between us and lower my voice to a deep whisper.

"You're meant to return to Camelot, Merlin. To bring Arthur back."

7

MERLIN

I'm meant to *what?*

Surely this is Mordred fucking with me even more.

Arthur's dead. He died. I know he did because I witnessed Mordred kill him. I carried his lifeless corpse to the Lake. Even if it was possible to bring Arthur back, why would Mordred tell me that? Why would he want to *help* me do that?

"You're so full of shit."

At the same time that I realize I instinctively lowered the volume of my voice to match his, I also register how close he's standing, having been too distracted by what he was saying. The awareness comes with an extra shock to my senses when I catch his scent in the air. Beneath the sweat and stale cigarette smoke he probably picked up from his show, there's something else.

It sparks a memory, a more recent one—a Renaissance faire I went to several decades ago, more out of curiosity than anything else. The costumes weren't terrible. Many of the demonstrations like woodcraft and leatherwork were surprisingly accurate. The jousting inspired quite a few memories of the tournaments among knights back in Camelot. Of course, the promiscuity and the hacked Elizabethan English being belted out left and right made me cringe.

More than anything, that faire was a conflated blend of more than just the Renaissance. It was an experience, but I'd never claim historical accuracy.

But...the smell.

It was the scent carried in the air—beneath the food and beer and body odor, originating mostly from candle making demonstrations and wax and oils and perfumes in shops. Smells have the power to conjure memory, and it was that particular one that evoked the most visions of Camelot, of home.

Staring into Mordred's gaze, I suddenly loathe him even more as that scent fills my nostrils. Like incense, a mix of cedarwood and patchouli.

His eyes remind me of Arthur.

His scent reminds me of home.

Fuck, I hate him.

I finally take a step back.

"I guess I can't blame you for not believing me," he says with a shrug. "I'm more surprised you didn't know. You know, with your habit of seeing the future and knowing all about destiny and shit."

My head is fucking spinning. Half an hour ago, the biggest question mark taking up the most space in my mind was the possible premonition I woke from this morning. But I've already solved that one.

I felt shitty leaving Willow at the bar like I did, but I had seen what I went there to see, what I needed to see. Which was *nothing*. No answers, no possible explanation or reason as to why I would willingly do what I did in that vision.

Admittedly, Mordred is...attractive. Objectively. *I guess.* After living as long as I have, you learn to appreciate the candid beauty of a person. And Mordred *is* beautiful. But he's also *evil*. The fact that he's physically appealing isn't enough to erase the ugliness inside him, to make me blind to it. Neither is the amount of time it's been since I was intimate with someone—it's difficult to count the number of years since something when there's been so many of them. After a thousand years, that carnal urge isn't always as strong as it once was.

And it certainly wouldn't be with Mordred.

That's why I ran out of there. Because no answer *was* my answer. I was convinced that premonition couldn't possibly come true. I probably should've gone straight up to my apartment, but I wasn't quite ready to face my subconscious, a deep, dark part of my mind that feared rattling my shaky conviction.

But now *this*?

"Why should I believe you?" I cross my arms over my chest, the act feeling a bit too defensive after the direction my thoughts just took.

I have no reason to be defensive.

For once, Mordred's mask falls, not to reveal whatever rage simmers beneath the surface, but a more solemn seriousness. "I killed my father, and I would do it again. I hated him. He turned his back on me."

When he moves forward again, I hold my ground. And my breath.

"That's the truth. You know it is. It was my destiny to kill Arthur, but...it was always his destiny to come back. The once and *future* king."

The words are familiar. I think I've heard them before.
But…

"You're lying."

A crease forms between his brows like he's just realized
something. He tilts his head in that way he does that's discon-
certingly both leering and alluring. "Have you always lived
your life in denial, Merlin?"

Briefly, I fear he's aware of those…*other* thoughts still
swimming around in my mind. But, no, he can't be. Not that
I'm in denial about that either.

"I'm not in denial."

"That's what people in denial say."

Fuck him.

"I'm cautious." My words come out between clenched
teeth because I feel that familiar urge to kill him again.
"Especially when it comes to snakes like you. And it makes
absolutely no sense that you would kill Arthur and then try to
convince me that I'm meant to bring him back."

Mordred moves back so he can lean his side against a
bookshelf, like he's settling in.

I'd much rather him fucking leave.

"Did you know Morgan promised me the crown if I killed
Arthur?" he asks, casually like he's discussing the weather.

"I figured as much."

"She betrayed me."

"Am I supposed to be surprised? Or sympathetic?"

He shrugs, looking away. "Neither, I suppose."

"So what? Mommy Dearest convinced you to kill Daddy
and then turned her back on you too so you decided to flee
Camelot?"

His jaw ticks, but I can tell he's trying to keep some
composure. I'd give him credit for that if I didn't hate him as
badly as I do.

"Something like that." His eyes find mine again, and I feel the weight of their severity. I'd almost rather be subjected to the mocking grins. "She convinced the kingdom that she was Arthur's half sister, meaning not only was I the king's illegitimate son, but I was also the product of incest."

I frown. "Morgan wasn't Arthur's half sister."

"No, she wasn't. But she was convincing enough. As far as all of Camelot was concerned, I was forbidden from ever taking the throne."

"So you threw a tantrum because you couldn't be crowned king and ran away?"

His eyes darken, and the memory of that vision flashes through my mind. I'm pretty damn certain that I'm not strong enough to fight against his magic—not yet—so I probably shouldn't keep testing him.

"I stayed for a while," he says, looking away again. "Over a hundred years. I didn't want to believe that killing Arthur was all for nothing. So I stayed, continued doing that witch's bidding. Turns out...she destroyed Camelot far worse than I would have."

"You're claiming you're the lesser of two evils?"

"Not lesser." Slowly, his smirk begins to return, and for some troubling reason, it eases the tension in my body. However, when his gaze moves back to me and sweeps over me from bottom to top until it meets mine, that tension returns and doubles. "Just a different brand."

"Then what's your plan? Arthur and I overtake Morgan because you couldn't do it on your own so that you can kill Arthur all over again?"

Mordred moves away from the bookshelf he's been leaning against to stand in front of me once more. "I don't care about Camelot anymore. Arthur can have it. But I wouldn't mind my witch of a mother getting what she deserves."

"If that's what you wanted, why didn't you track me down sooner?"

It's not that I'm quick to believe him; I'm just trying to understand why he *wants* me to believe him. It's not like he couldn't have found me sooner. Magic would've made that easy.

Something flashes in his eyes, there and gone so fast I barely catch it, let alone identify it.

"Even I believe in destiny," he says, brushing it off. "I honestly thought you'd find your way back on your own, and, if you didn't, we'd cross paths when we were meant to."

I haven't given much thought to destiny in all this time, not since leaving all that behind in Camelot, not even when I'd still have the occasional premonition. Two premonitions in two days might be enough for me to consider it. Not that that last one has anything close to do with destiny…

"Seeing you again sure as hell doesn't feel like fate."

He moves closer, closer than before, *too* close, while some force I don't understand keeps me from retreating.

"Maybe you'll change your mind when I coax all the magic out of you," he says, voice low and deep. Eyes locked on mine, he licks his bottom lip, his tongue brushing over the ring there. "Maybe I'll coax out even more than that."

Now I realize what it was, that force. Stronger now, it's the urge to wrap my hand around his throat and slam him back into the wall of books. Steal all his air. Watch the light fade from his eyes.

"You're a fucking poison," I snarl.

Because I don't like these thoughts, his darkness infecting me to the point of a murderous rage I don't recognize in myself.

"Monster. Snake. Poison. I've been called far worse things."

"Get the hell out, Mordred."

For a moment, he doesn't move, content on invading my space, that light in his eyes sparking as though he's contemplating riling me up even more.

Finally, he shrugs and steps back. "You know how to find me if you want magic lessons, darling."

And then he's gone, a light breeze caressing my face from the disturbance in the air.

Darling.

Fucking *darling*.

I've never hated a word so much.

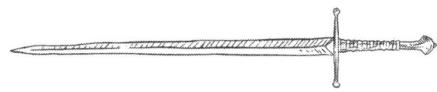

"Camelot still needs you. Arthur needs you."

Nimue's words have haunted me all night and day.

And Mordred's...

"Have you always lived your life in denial, Merlin?"

I will never admit that Mordred was right, but...maybe he wasn't entirely wrong either.

Even after the Lady of the Lake told me that Arthur needed me, I chose to ignore her. Or not believe her. Instead, I made the decision to run away.

Did some part of me know that Arthur was meant to return one day? Maybe. If I did, why did I abandon him? Was I that scared of failing again? Of facing Arthur after failing him so miserably?

What else have I been living in denial about?

I'd rather not examine that question too closely.

At least I haven't been plagued by any more possible premonitions in the past thirty-six hours. Once again, I've spent the day buried in books, and it's nearly closing time already. Willow didn't come in today, but she had the day off again. I might have checked Dethrone the Queen's schedule online to see they weren't playing a gig tonight, so I assume Willow may have spent the day with Ava.

I've never minded solitude. Unfortunately, today was a bad day for that. I haven't been able to get out of my own head. I remember nothing of the book I spent the day reading.

On the plus side, by the time I trudge upstairs, feed Percy, and crash in bed, my mind is too tired to fight against sleep.

When I wake the next morning, it apparently got all the rest it needed because it goes right back to work, asking the question I had been barely avoiding all day yesterday.

Am I going to return to Camelot?

I don't fucking know.

One thing I do know for certain is that I don't need Mordred's help reigniting my magic. Sure, I might have lost sight of my true powers over the years, but I can find my own way back to them without him.

However, the idea of practicing on him sure does have its appeal…

The day passes in another blur of too many heavy thoughts, and in the afternoon, Willow's right on time walking through the front door of the shop. However, this time, she has a slight scowl on her face and only one coffee in her hand.

"I didn't bring you one," she says matter-of-factly as she stops in front of my counter, taking a sip from the straw of her iced latte.

I suppress a grin because that would probably just get me into even more trouble. Instead, I nod with understanding. "I deserve that. I'm sorry for leaving you the other night."

Her gaze slowly softens, and she sighs. "You really can't stand to be around him, can you?"

I shake my head because I can't tell her more than I already have.

"I'm sorry I kind of forced you to go. But you're still an ass for ditching me."

I let myself grin at that. "I know. I really am sorry."

"You know, he doesn't seem all that bad."

That sounds suspicious.

"I mean, of course, I'm on your side no matter what, but—"

"Willow?"

"Yes?" She gives me a wide, innocent smile and bats her eyelashes.

When I tilt my head, I'm reminded too much of the way Mordred does that and quickly straighten it. "What makes you say he doesn't seem that bad?"

She grimaces and averts her gaze, staring down at her coffee as she swirls it around in the cup. "I might have…hung out with Ava and the band yesterday."

And, just like that, all that heavy weight I've been feeling for the past two days is suffocating me all over again. It's not that I'm worried Willow would have shared anything with him that I'd rather her not have—the only secret I'm keeping from Mordred is that absolutely-not-a-premonition. It's the fact that the son of a literal witch is intent on infiltrating every aspect of my life.

When I haven't said anything for several seconds, she looks back up, still grimacing. "Are you mad at me?"

I wish I could be, but I can't.

"Of course not."

"But you're not happy about it."

It's not a question.

"Of course not," I answer again, but this time with a faint smile.

"I swear no one talked about you. I mostly spent time with Ava."

"It's fine, Willow. Really."

It's not, but, again, I can't take it out on her.

"So," she starts, clearly itching to change the subject. "Coming to the Crow tonight?"

I don't have to think about it long. I know Mordred has another show at a different venue tonight, but I have no intention of going. I should probably hole myself away in my apartment, but...

"Yeah. I could use a drink."

Or two.

8

MORDRED

I kept my promise and spent nearly the entire day with the band yesterday—with the addition of Ava's new girlfriend Willow. Lesbians work fast.

All I really did though was tag along while they all did even more sightseeing, trying my best to be conversational but often too consumed with thoughts of Merlin to offer anything more than vaguely interested mumbles and halfhearted suggestions of where to go. Willow had plenty of destinations to take us to anyway. It also took great effort not to talk about Merlin or ask Willow invasive questions about him.

I hadn't planned on revealing as much as I did to Merlin the other night. He needed to know about Arthur, but he didn't need to know how Morgan betrayed me. Or how I felt about it. Because I'm pretty sure that was written all over my face.

I hadn't spoken about it in almost a thousand years. My mask was weak.

Most of today, I've spent back in my hotel room, attempting to focus less on thoughts of Merlin and more on this damn song that doesn't seem to want to be written at all.

When the band and I get to our gig that night, I half expect—maybe more than half—to see Merlin there, but he's not. I wish I could deny the disappointment I feel at not getting to watch him squirm from my spot on stage. The result is a less satisfying show than the previous two.

However, afterward, Ava suggests we all go get drinks at the Stone Crow—so she can see her girlfriend, no doubt—and I jump at the opportunity.

The moment we walk through the front door, I zone in on Merlin sitting on a stool at the bar and relish the way his back almost immediately stiffens.

There's that satisfaction.

Not wanting to seem too eager to everyone else, I let Ava lead us to the bar where Willow is already making moon eyes at her as she approaches. Ava leans over the bar and gives the bartender a lingering kiss.

"You look cute tonight," Ava says as she takes a seat.

"You look cute every night," Willow counters. "I like your leggings today."

They're paint splatter print with neon pinks and oranges.

Ava leans forward with a playful grin. "I like your *legs*."

Willow blushes.

Anthony groans. "Get a room, you two."

"Later?" Ava asks.

Willow nods enthusiastically. "Definitely."

Now that the others have claimed two stools to the left of Ava, I head to her right where there are two open seats between her and Merlin. I step up to the one closest to him, loving the way his knuckles are turning white around the glass in his hand and the fact he hasn't looked up at any of us.

"Well, if it isn't my bestie Merlin!"

The moment I extend my arm to drape it over his shoulders, his head snaps up, glaring with a raging fire in his eyes.

I want it to burn me.

Instead, I hold up my hands in mock surrender and take a step back, unable to stop the invisible hook that's tugging up the corners of my mouth. I slink one stool over and slowly lower myself onto it, leaving one between us.

"I'll just sit here then?"

"Hey!" Willow snaps, demanding my attention. "You might be Ava's bandmate, but if you fuck with Merlin, you fuck with me too."

I give her my best innocent smile, which, let's be honest, isn't at all convincing. "Noted."

Willow turns back to the others and asks "Drinks?" like she's not even asking me.

"You know what I like," Ava says.

The other guys, however, are staring between me and Merlin.

"Wait. What's going on?" Will seems the most interested, leaning forward farther than necessary to see around Ava. "Who's Merlin?"

"He's an old friend."

"Reluctant acquaintance," Merlin corrects me, having gone back to staring down into his glass.

Well, that could've been worse.

Willow slides a glass with something colorful in it across the bar to Ava. "They're like mortal enemies or some shit."

That's better.

"What has good 'ol Merlin told you about me?" I ask her, propping my elbow up on the bartop and resting my chin in my hand.

"Other than you're a dick and he hates you, nothing."

I belt out a laugh because even that's nicer than I would've expected.

Willow looks over at Merlin. "I can always have Gabriel haul his ass out of here and rough him up a bit if you'd like."

"Don't worry about it." Merlin throws back the rest of the dark liquid in his glass, sets it back on the bar along with a few bills, and stands. He gives Willow a tight smile. "Have a good night. Thanks for the drinks."

Peering over my shoulder, I watch as he heads toward the door, wondering just how many drinks he had. But he doesn't seem to be swaying like that first night I saw him crossing the bar, even if it had only been slightly. He must not have had as much tonight.

At some point while watching him walk away, my gaze inadvertently falls to his ass.

Dammit.

Just as the door closes behind him, Ava slaps me in the back of the head.

"Ow," I mutter, turning back to them and rubbing my head because, fuck, that actually kind of hurt. "What was that for?"

"Why do you have to be such an ass?" Ava hisses.

"It's part of my charm." I look at Willow and grin. "She's still upset that our rooms are on the thirteenth floor of the hotel."

"Jokes on you, buttercup. Thirteen's my lucky number now after last night."

Willow's cheeks turn as pink as the strands in her hair.

Anthony groans again. "Hello. Hi. Your brother's right here."

"Hey, bro." Ava waves her hand flippantly in the air, but her gaze is still firmly set on her girl, shamelessly eyefucking her from across the bar.

Will and I both laugh.

I stay for a while longer, letting everyone else do most of the talking since all I can think about is following after Merlin. The others have all had a drink, and by the time Willow finally breaks her visual fucking session with my drummer to ask if they'd all like another, I still haven't been offered one.

Taking the hint, I sigh and stand from the stool. "I think that's my cue."

Willow's heart eyes that had been all over Ava moments ago immediately turn into daggers when she looks at me. "What did you do to him? I've never seen Merlin hate anyone before."

Shrugging, I start walking backwards toward the door. "I'm just that special I guess."

I leave it at that, and Willow doesn't pry further. Turning around, I exit the bar and walk a few steps down the sidewalk. I stop directly across the street from Merlin's shop, leaning against a light pole and staring at the building.

The lights downstairs are all off, no movement on the other side of the dark windows. My gaze drifts upward to where I'm almost positive there's an apartment where Merlin lives. There's a single window, a dim light on somewhere behind it.

Once the dastardly idea comes to me, there's no talking myself out of it.

It's not like he doesn't already want to kill me…

I close my eyes.

When I open them again, I'm inside his small studio apartment, standing between the bed and the couch. I turn in a circle, taking the place in with its random colors and mismatched furniture. It's not where I would've pictured Merlin living, but, then again, he's probably had a dozen different homes that steadily became less and less *him*.

Something touches my leg, and I nearly startle. I look down to see an orange tabby rubbing his head against my calf. He peers up at me and meows.

"Give me a minute, Percy!"

Merlin's voice comes from where I assume the bathroom is, and I realize the shower has been running only when the water is turned off.

Bad timing to pop into his apartment unannounced. My dick takes way too much interest in the images now running rampant through my mind. I'm surprised he hasn't sensed me in his home yet.

It's warm in the apartment, so I decide to take off my jacket and make myself at home. Looking between the bed and the yellow couch, I figure the latter is safest, so I settle there.

At least I didn't appear directly in his bed. The thought had occurred to me.

As soon as I sit down, Percy the cat leaps into my lap, kneading on my leg a bit before curling into a ball and purring. I wish Merlin had a revolving chair in here so I could spin around as soon as he enters the room, cat perched on my lap while I cackle like some cheesy movie villain. I suppose I could always conjure one. But Percy is already too comfortable, and I'm not about to break that universal rule.

I'm evil, but I'm not that brand of evil.

Maybe next time.

I'm stroking the cat along his back when Merlin comes out of the bathroom. In nothing but a pair of boxers.

Holy fuck.

He notices me immediately. "What the fuck, Mordred?!"

Did Merlin always look this good? Because…

Holy fucking fuck.

Give me a break. My brain is barely working.

"Are you kidding me with this shit?" he snarls as he quickly snatches a pair of gray sweatpants off the back of a chair and steps into them.

Nooo. Don't put on more clothes.

He continues bitching about my presence while I haven't said a goddamn word, barely paying any attention to what he's saying. I'm too preoccupied by the way his slightly tanned skin highlights his taut muscles that ripple with anger and tension. I have muscles too, but where I'm more lean, Merlin's body is all hard and firm and sculpted perfection.

Stray droplets of water drip from his brown hair, landing on his shoulders before cascading down over his chest and through the valleys of his abs.

I want to lick them off.

"Get the fuck out of here!"

Percy has long since jumped off my lap since Merlin started shouting, and I'm forced to lean over to conceal my raging hard-on.

Goddamnit, Mordred. He really would fucking kill you.

"What had you so distracted that you didn't sense me, Merlin?" I ask, finally finding my voice and plastering that smirk I know he loathes so much right back on my face. "What were you thinking about in the shower?"

"Breaking and entering my shop is one thing," he says, ignoring me, seething, voice still raised. "But you can't just break into my home!"

"Technically, there was no breaking in involved."

I really need my dick to soften, but it has no plans of doing so with the way Merlin is glowering at me. All that delicious heat and rage. Water still rolling down his bare chest...

"Mordred!"

Oops.

"What'd you say?"

"Tell me what you want so you can get the hell out."

I lean back, at the same time bringing my right ankle up to rest on my left knee because, yeah, this stiffy isn't going anywhere. I might love riling Merlin up, but he doesn't need to know I'm hard for him.

"I was only curious if you made a decision about returning to Camelot."

"I haven't. And you hanging around like a parasite isn't going to help."

"Parasite?" I arch a brow and purse my lips. "That one's not bad. I think I prefer monster though."

He stands there, chest almost dry and heaving and turning red with all his anger and hatred. "I'll call you whatever you want if you'll just get the fuck out."

Both my brows rise now. "Whatever I want, hmm?"

"Mordred, *please*."

Well, my cock loves that.

He pleads with his eyes, dejected and exasperated, like all that fight is finally starting to bleed out.

"Beg harder," I say before I can stop myself.

Merlin blanches, his face falling further. "What?"

"Or you could prove to me that you have the chops to go back to Camelot," I say, changing the subject so I can hopefully get off this damn couch soon. "I can't in good conscience send you off without at least knowing you can take care of yourself."

"You don't have a conscience."

"Fair."

"And I'm perfectly capable."

Except he turns his back on me, proving the opposite.

He takes a step toward the door, like he's planning on opening it and attempting to throw me out.

I raise my hand and, with practiced precision, effortlessly conjure a bolt of lightning and hurl it in his direction as though it's coming straight out of my palm. It's not bright and white. It's black with flashes of violet, like that oil slick ribbon I followed to find Merlin the other night.

The lightning strikes him square in the right ass cheek.

I barely contain my squeal of delight as the bolt singes through both layers of clothes, leaving behind a small hole, a little smoke, and a view of his reddened flesh. Merlin barely makes a sound, a faint grunt, his shoulder bunching, the muscles in his back flexing.

As the lightning dissipates, fading into nothing but a thin, lingering smog, Merlin turns slowly to face me, his eyes darker and more dangerous than ever. Maybe even more so than when he told me he hopes I die a slow and painful death.

"Why are you so intent on testing me?" he snarls.

"If you can't fight me, you certainly won't be able to fight Queen Morgan." I've finally gotten my dick to go down to something closer to a semi, so I feel confident enough to stand. It's not like he'll look down there anyway. "Come on, Merlin. Show me a little magic, and I'll go."

"I don't have anything to prove to you."

"If you want me to leave, you do." When I take a few steps toward him, I can tell he resists the instinct to retreat, even as I match his daunting glare with a taunting smirk. "I could always give you a reason to fight me."

"Stop," he says, but the word is weak. "Stay away from me, Mordred. I mean it."

I stop a few paces away from him, tilting my head as I observe that same shifty kind of fear I saw in him the other night in his shop. The kind that's hiding something beneath it, that makes me want to dig my way to all his secrets like they're buried treasure.

"You're hiding something, Merlin. If it's more than just your magic, then I'm going to find out. Fight me if you can."

If he can, this is going to hurt me a lot more than it's going to hurt him.

Giving him no other warning, I pounce, closing the distance between us. He's fast, but I'm faster, taking his head between my hands, gripping hard. His own hands come up, wrapping his fingers around my wrists in an attempt to pry them away, but I'm already burrowing my way in, delving into his mind.

"Get on your knees."

I see my own face.

Merlin drops to his knees.

I'm jolted out of Merlin's premonition by a magical shock, but when I'm back in my own mind, I still have his head between my palms.

Yeah, that fucking hurt.

But I can't seem to let him go. His hands are still around my wrists, his nails digging painfully into my skin, undoubtedly drawing blood. His russet eyes are locked with mine, still swimming with that terror, heightened now. But there's more.

Maybe a dash of lust?

Certainly fury.

Curiosity gets the best of me, and when I grind my hips slightly against his, my aching erection meets his own hard cock.

I let out an astonished breath. "Oh."

9

MERLIN

Reliving that damn premonition was like a nightmare all over again. Except it made me hard. Again.

My nails dig into Mordred's tattooed flesh even deeper until I feel the warmth of blood beneath my fingertips. It doesn't change the way he's looking at me—with a craving, a hunger. If anything, his ocean eyes appear to flood with it all.

And even though there's a part of me I hate that feels it too, I feel enraged more than anything.

"How fucking dare you," I growl a split second before I release one of his wrists to wrap my hand around his throat instead.

His hands fall from the sides of my head as I turn him and slam him against the wall. He doesn't fight me, even as my grip tightens. His eyes spark, and his smirk stretches across half his face.

"You break into my shop. My home. Now my mind. Give me one good reason why I shouldn't kill you right here."

"Because you're still hard." He thrusts his hips forward, once more grinding our cocks together to prove his point.

I should back away. Release him and force him to leave. But...damn that part of me that doesn't *want* to. I haven't been this close to another person in so long, and I hate that the heat of his body feels *good*. That his pulse beating beneath my palm sends a different kind of thrill through me. That he looks as good as he does—black hair sexily disheveled, tattoos covering both his forearms. Even that cursed smirk is doing something to me.

"If you wanted to be in control, all you had to do was say so," Mordred says, breathless. "But you looked pretty submissive in that premonition of yours."

"That will *not* be coming true."

"You really do live in denial, don't you, Merlin? Have you ever had a premonition that didn't come true?"

"I'm not gay."

I'm grasping at straws now, scrounging for any excuse, anything to say to hide that *damn fucking part* that actually wants him, to push it back into whatever dark depths it came from.

"More denial," he says like he wants to laugh. "We've been alive for over a thousand years. You expect me to believe you've never been with another man in all that time?"

"I didn't say that."

He groans, and it sounds...appreciative?

It's true. Living as long as I have, I've had different experiences with different partners, even if the number is probably low for someone of my twelve-hundred years. Still, I didn't exactly lie when I said I wasn't gay. I've never considered myself gay, bisexual, or anything else. I've never felt the need to. *That* isn't denial. It's not confusion. It's simply a choice to not define my sexuality.

"It's okay. You don't have to put a label on it," Mordred says as though he's infiltrated my mind again. "But the fact is…"

He grinds his hips against mine again.

I moan.

Fuck.

"You want it."

Taking advantage of my weakened state, he grasps tightly onto my wrist that's connected to his throat by my hand, twists it savagely until my grip falters, and spins me around. I grunt as my back hits the wall, taking his place. His hands come down on the wall on either side of me, caging my head in. He leans forward, his warm breath ghosting along the shell of my ear.

"Tell me how badly you want it, darling," he whispers.

And then he *bites*.

It's not a cute little nibble. He takes the soft flesh of my ear between his teeth, bites hard, and tugs. I let out an embarrassing noise that's somewhere between a whimper and a moan. My cock jerks; my boxers feel too tight.

I've officially lost my mind.

A twelve-hundred year existence hasn't been enough to drive me to the brink of insanity, but apparently my dick wanting Mordred is what's finally done it.

His mouth travels down to the side of my neck and bites me there too, sucking on the tender skin, making me moan louder.

That dreadful thought I had before creeps back in.

"What are you doing to me?" I ask, sounding pained.

Mordred pulls back just enough to meet my gaze with lust-drunk eyes. "You think I'm using magic to manipulate you?"

Isn't he?

That would make it so much easier to explain what's happening to me.

"You want to hear something fascinating?" His hand touches the side of my face, his thumb hooking under my chin to tilt my head back. "I'm not."

He leans forward again, and his mouth latches onto my throat that he's given himself access to, biting and sucking until I feel like he's everywhere, giving me all those stinging pains I felt in my premonition.

"But I hate you," I manage. It comes out less matter-of-fact and more like a plea to understand.

"I know, Merlin." His lips skim to the other side of my throat, nipping at my skin. "It turns me the fuck on."

"No." I try to shake my head, but it barely moves. "I can't."

After sucking on one spot at the side of my neck for so long I'll be surprised if he hasn't left a mark, he pulls back again, panting now. "Want to know what I think?"

Not particularly.

But with how fucking confused I am right now, I'm willing to hear it.

"I think you held the weight of Camelot on your shoulders for centuries and you never truly let go of it. This is that part of you that needs to let go."

When his hand moves to the back of my head, fingers threading through my hair, I realize how much he's touching me. How much I'm *letting* him touch me. He tugs on my hair, yanking my head back further, provoking another moan as my chest heaves with every harsh breath.

"You want this because you need it. You need to let go, to submit, even if it's to me."

"I hate you," I say again, as though hoping it can snap me out of this.

"Keep saying that. You're only making me hotter."

He's touching me too much.

I want this too badly when I shouldn't.

My breaths turn heavy, erratic, so harsh it hurts, my head hazy with the struggle to keep air in my lungs.

I try to shake my head again, clear the panic, but something stops me, a familiar sensation—the other one I also felt in that vision. A calm, a kind of floating, a gentle wave crashing over me, carrying me away from the impending attack.

It's not natural; it's magical.

Mordred may not have been using magic a moment ago, but I think he is now.

He rolls his hips against mine, and the friction against my aching cock shatters whatever remaining resolve I have. Forgetting all about magic, I practically melt against the wall.

"That's it, Merlin. I don't want to hurt you. I just want it to feel good. If it helps, you can be in control next time."

Next time?

I should be fighting against those words, but they barely reach me through the barrier of this euphoric haze I'm swimming in. I should be fighting against *him*. Because this is *Mordred*. But my dick certainly doesn't care about that right now. Maybe it's whatever he's doing to me, or maybe the hate is turning me on just as much.

"Let go and let's make that premonition come true." He grabs my chin in his other hand to bring my face back to his. "Get on your knees."

I stare into the pools of his eyes, and I'm no longer swimming.

I'm fucking drowning.

"I said get on your knees, Merlin."

There's no way I'll be able to find my way back to the surface now, so I let the tide pull me in, let the water pull me under.

I drop to my knees.

His hands move to the zipper of his jeans, and I watch with rapt attention, bewitched by his darkness that shouldn't be calling to me the way it is. The black aura that surrounds him harmonizes with the tattoos on the backs of his hands and the black polish on his nails. It's bad and wrong, and I want it.

When he frees his hard cock, taking the base of it in his hand, the truth of my premonition is confirmed.

He's indeed pierced down there too. Five in total. Three barbells make up a Jacob's Ladder down the underside of his shaft. The curved bar of a Prince Albert sticks out from the tip, and another called an apadravya is pierced vertically straight through his crown.

I may have done a little research on dick piercings after that premonition…

What I failed to realize in that vision is just how big he is. He's uncut, like me, but he's so hard, his foreskin retracted to show off every glimmering piece of jewelry.

It's kind of beautiful.

Yeah, I've definitely lost my mind.

Above me, Mordred groans. "Fuck, you look good down there." He gives his cock a rough stroke, a pearly bead of precum glistening at the tip.

I hate him, but I want to taste him.

So I do.

I lean forward and swipe my tongue over the head of his dick, collecting the salty drop, the taste mingling with that of skin and metal.

"Don't tease me, darling." His hand brushes through my hair on the side of my head, the touch gentle. *Too* gentle.

I don't want or need his gentleness.

My attempt to glare up at him feels weak even to me. "Stop calling me that."

He seems to sense what it is I really need and grasps my hair tightly in his fist. "I'll call you whatever the fuck I want while you're on your knees for me. Now suck, *darling*."

Any chance I have to respond is lost when he hauls me forward, the tip of his cock pressing against my mouth. My lips part, and he thrusts between them, skin and metal gliding along my tongue until I feel him in the back of my throat.

I gag.

Fuck, it's been ages since I've done this.

But when he pulls back to let me breathe, I chase after him because I haven't had nearly enough. I lick across his Jacob's Ladder before taking him as far as I can without gagging this time.

"Fuuuck, Merlin."

I look up in time to see his head rolling back on his shoulders before his gaze lowers to me again. It darkens, and his grip in my hair tightens. When I moan around him, he groans, his hips rocking with more fervor as my cheeks hollow and I suck with just as much eagerness.

"You're so fucking good at that," he growls as his free hand smacks against the wall above me like he has to hold himself up.

I can't help but grin around his cock.

"Fuck. You're not as much of a prude as you seem, are you?"

Pulling back and letting his dick slip from my mouth, I peer up at him. Drool and precum drip down my chin, and my voice comes out raw and gravelly. "A thousand years in *this* world? What did you expect?"

He growls again. "Don't fucking stop."

My mouth opens as he forces me back onto his cock, metal gliding across my tongue. I lick and slurp and suck until his legs are shaking, as though his knees are about to give out from the pleasure I'm giving him. My hands go to the sides of his thighs—whether to hold him up or myself, I'm not sure. My dick is so hard and aching, and if I looked down, I'm certain there'd be a wet spot on my sweats.

"Fuck, I'm gonna come. Can you take it?"

My nails dig into his thighs as I take him deeper, swallowing around his thick length, demanding he give it to me. And he does. His cock throbs in my mouth, his hips stutter, and the warmth of his release pours down my throat.

I swallow it down, every drop.

The sounds of our combined panting fill the small apartment after I let his softening cock slip from my mouth. He continues leaning forward, his weight held up by the wall, catching his breath.

It's not long before he's hauling me to my feet, and, before I can start swaying, he's pressing me back into the wall. The sea I'm still swimming in is rocky, dense clouds obscuring all rational thought.

He tilts forward.

His mouth is an inch from mine.

The spell finally breaks.

I turn my head to the side before his lips can touch mine.

Grabbing my chin hard, he forces me to face him and growls, "Let me taste myself on you."

When his mouth comes at mine again, I violently yank my head away. "I'm not letting you kiss me."

"So you'll suck my cock, but you won't kiss me?" Anger laces his words. When I don't answer, his hands go to my sweats, fingers hooking into the waistband. "I knew I should've tied you up. At least let me return the favor."

Grasping his wrists, I shove him, and he stumbles back several steps. "I don't want you to touch me."

"Are you fucking kidding me?!"

He's pissed. I can hear it in his voice and see it swirling in those blue depths of his eyes.

I'm not sure what he expected. That trading blow jobs would make me forget everything? Make me forget how much I hate him?

That I wouldn't catch his manipulation?

"You lied to me, Mordred," I snarl, my rage matching his. "You did do something to me. Don't fucking deny it."

"I didn't lie when you asked. I didn't make you want me." He takes a step forward but keeps distance between us. "You were already well past that point, Merlin. You were damn near on the verge of a panic attack because you couldn't turn your fucking head off! You needed to let go, and I helped you."

"*Helped* me?!" My lips curl in disgust. My erection has long since faded, and now all those other urges when it comes to him are returning in full force. "Get the fuck out, Mordred. Leave, or I will hurt you. And you know I can."

I know he felt that little burst of power I used to force him from my mind. It may not be enough to match his, but I suspect it wouldn't take much to push me to that point.

His magic may not have been what made me want him, may not have been the catalyst that ultimately brought me to my knees—because I would've eventually gotten there on my own anyway—but it was a manipulation nonetheless.

This is *Mordred le Fay*, and I shouldn't be the least bit surprised.

"Fine. You want to hate yourself for enjoying something for the first time in gods know how long, that's your choice." He gives me his back, walks over to the couch, and snatches up his jacket before heading to the door and yanking it open. He stops long enough to scowl at me over his shoulder. "Enjoy wallowing in your self-hatred."

The moment the door slams behind him, I lean back against the wall, my head landing with a soft thud. I screw my eyes shut and inhale a deep lungful of air and immediately start panting for breath again, starving for oxygen as though I haven't breathed since Mordred tried to kiss me.

I hate admitting when he's right.

But he is.

I fucking hate myself.

10

MORDRED

I usually love it when men hate themselves for wanting something they feel like they shouldn't, but this time, for some inexplicable reason, it pissed me the fuck off. I was so furious I couldn't even magic my way out of there. I didn't trust myself not to materialize right into a wall and had to use the damn door instead like some pathetic mortal.

And then I locked myself in my hotel room for the next two days. We didn't have a gig either of those nights, and Ava had texted me to let me know they were all going out again yesterday. I skipped, like the brooding buzzkill I am.

I spent the last two days between ordering room service, smoking, lying around in the bed on wrinkled sheets, and working on that godforsaken song.

Who am I kidding? That disaster will never be finished.

I accused Merlin of hating himself, but if that goddamn pity party I spent all day having yesterday is any indication, I might be guilty of the same thing.

It's the next morning, and now I'm restless. We have another show tonight, but the entire day stretches ahead, just me and this room. I doubt the others are going to invite me out again when I keep turning down offers.

I consider making an appearance at Merlin's shop, but I don't feel like either of us have had enough time to cool off. We were both so furious that night that I'm almost surprised we didn't end up killing each other. Am I a piece of shit for using magic on him the way I did? Probably. But, fuck, I wanted to touch him. Taste him.

He and I together is a bad idea, a powder keg ready to explode.

Wrong.

But...fuck, it felt so right.

I don't remember the last time I felt such intense pleasure.

Merlin may have been birthed by a human and bred by demons, but his mouth is a gift from the gods.

I won't deny that I want him.

There's a knock on the door, and I groan as I roll out of the disheveled bed, nearly pulling the covers clear off the mattress on my way. I pad across the hotel room in nothing but a pair of boxers. I have a Do Not Disturb sign on the door, so I swear if it's housekeeping...

I open the door to see my three bandmates standing on the other side, Ava front and center. They're all wearing pajamas, Ava's unsurprisingly bright and colorful, and holding an assortment of snacks and drinks that appear to be from a vending machine—bags of chips, pastries, candy, and sodas.

"What are you doing here?" I grumble sleepily.

I'm not exactly a morning immortal.

"Movie day!" Ava exclaims before pushing her way past me. "Care to put some clothes on?"

She's far too chipper for...after ten in the morning according to the digital clock on the small desk. Whatever. It's still too fucking early for this shit.

The others follow, and I move out of the way before closing the door behind them. When I turn to them, Ava's already dumping the snacks on the coffee table in the living area of the suite. Will stands there awkwardly, glancing at the scar that stretches across my hip and quickly averting his gaze.

I do what Ava suggested and step into a pair of sweats and pull a plain black T-shirt on over my head. They've all seen the scar, but they know I don't talk about it.

"We would've come for a slumber party last night," Ava says as she plops onto the middle of the couch. "But we were all a little hung over. You know, having fun *without* you like usual."

"And clearly you can't take a hint," I mumble.

Okay, I'm being an asshole, but...what's new?

They all glare at me, but it's Anthony who speaks up.

"We can all take the hint that something's going on with you."

"Nothing's going on," I lie.

"I told you I had a feeling," Will says as he moves over to the couch and sits beside Ava. "We know you pretty well, Mordred. We're used to your..." He peers at our drummer, and she nods her head encouragingly, as though she's his mentor in meddling. "Your moods. But there's more to it this time."

I cross my arms over my chest. "How about you all get the fuck out?"

Great. Now I sound like Merlin.

Will ignores me. "Ava says you've always been broody, but you've been acting more so lately. Does it...Does it have to do with that Merlin guy?"

My jaw clenches so hard it aches. "No."

"I knew it!" Ava bounces on the couch like she's just heard the most exciting gossip of the century. "You've been acting strange since our first night in the city. And all that tension, oh my god."

"Sure." I roll my eyes. "*Murderous* tension."

Anthony leaves my side to take a seat on the floor beside the coffee table, probably to be closer to all the snacks. "I bet the hate sex is hot."

"It would be if we were having it."

I'm not about to tell these fuckers about the best blow job of my life. That memory belongs only to me.

Will chuckles, but his cheeks flush pink.

"I don't suppose you want to tell us all about it?" Ava asks, wiggling her eyebrows, unable to fight her baser instincts of being a nosy brat. Then she scrunches up her face and adds, "Not the sex, obviously. But what the hell is up with you two?"

"Not even a little bit."

Even if I did want to talk about it, there's not exactly a story I could spin that would be even close to the truth.

She huffs and picks up the remote for the television. "Fine. But if you do need to talk, we're here. In the meantime, stuff your face and watch bad TV with us. You need to loosen up."

Despite her curiosity and meddling, Ava always respects boundaries when they're put in place, and the others follow suit since she's basically taken over the role of mother hen. Most humans aren't like that; most humans push and push like they've lost their will of survival. It's one reason I've stuck with Ava and Anthony longer than I usually do anyone else.

Still, I know they won't leave without threatening bodily harm. And I suppose I could use the company instead of wallowing in self-hatred just like Merlin probably is.

Moving around the table, I take the spot on the couch on the other side of Ava, choose a cheese Danish from the pile of snacks, and settle in to watch whatever cheesy action movie she just put on.

At least Ava doesn't accuse me of brooding for the rest of the day.

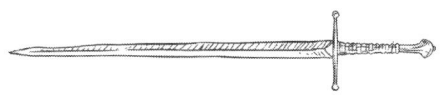

Later that evening, after they've left a mess in my hotel room and we've all gotten ready, we head to our gig. This one's a little deeper into the heart of the city, so I don't expect Merlin to show up.

Still, when we take the stage, I feel disappointed that he didn't.

It's fucking ridiculous.

I'm ridiculous.

It's like I'm thriving off his hatred, his attention, his obsession. When he's not giving all of that to me, it's as though a hole opens up inside me. It widens and deepens, becoming a hungry abyss that swallows everything in its path.

Even my talent apparently.

My performance tonight is sloppy at best. My bandmates don't sugarcoat it either.

"What the hell, Mordred?" Ava says as soon as we're back outside and starting to load up our equipment. "I thought we helped today?"

"You did," I tell her sincerely. "I was just having an off night." I clear my throat, swallowing my pride, and add, "I'm sorry."

She gives me a sympathetic look that makes my skin itch, but she drops the issue for now as we all fill up the van. They let me have my routine silence while we work, having a conversation among themselves I can't be bothered to pay attention to.

I can't explain why I've been thrown so off-balance, like the world is tilted on its axis. Playing with Merlin has been fun. I had the best blowjob of my life. But I've become addicted to his hate, and going three days without a fix is fucking me up.

"That settles it then," Ava says as soon as the doors to the cab are shut. She turns to me with her hands on her hips. "We're going to the Crow, and you're getting drunk tonight."

"Do I get a say in this?"

"Absolutely not," says Will with a grin.

"And if Merlin's there again?"

It's the only question that matters, but I probably should've kept it to myself. I'm not usually so open, even with my bandmates. It started when I shared more than I meant to with Merlin about Morgan, and now apparently there's a short circuit somewhere between my mouth and my brain.

Merlin really did break me.

Anthony shrugs. "Get drunk and bang it out."

"Come on," Ava says as Will turns his back to climb into the van. "You haven't been drunk since we got here. It's New York City. That's just wrong. I'll even DD."

I consider bailing, but...*dammit.*

Getting drunk and banging it out with Merlin sounds too fucking appealing.

Not that I expect that to happen, I tell myself as I hop in the van and Anthony drives us away from the venue. However, there's still that pesky desire to see him, to make sure he hasn't forgotten about me. To make sure I haven't lost what progress I've made digging under his skin.

Even if he loathes me more now than he did before, as long as I still have my place there, then all is right in the world.

We arrive at the Stone Crow, and when we walk inside, I spot Merlin in his usual seat at the bar. He's wearing a navy turtleneck sweater, and I imagine the sight of my marks all over his throat and have to repress a groan. He's talking to Willow, *smiling* at her. Even though he can undoubtedly sense my presence, nothing about his demeanor changes. His back doesn't straighten. His muscles don't stiffen. He doesn't fall silent.

Like he's not affected at all.

That pisses me the fuck off.

Either I've lost my touch, he's lost interest, or he's playing a game.

Any one of those would be enough to send me into a rage, but at least the latter has the least chance of casualties.

Fine, Merlin. Two can play.

I let my bandmates move ahead of me and take their seats before I plop my ass down on the stool on the far side of all of them, sitting directly beside Will. Will peers down the bar at Merlin, then back at me with an uncomfortable—but what might be meant as comforting—smile.

Willow slides two feet to the side, leans over the bar, and proceeds with her usual flirting with Ava. Anthony, Will, and I all wait patiently while rolling our eyes.

I purposefully avoid looking at Merlin, instead striking up a conversation with Will and ordering drinks since Willow is actually inclined to serve me tonight. It probably has something to do with how much less tension there is, or the fact that I'm not antagonizing her friend.

Little does she know...

There might be more tension between me and Merlin than there's ever been before, and that's saying something. We're just both ignoring it to piss the other off.

Or maybe Merlin's doing it because he really does want to pretend, because he wants to forget everything that happened between us the other night.

I won't fucking let him.

I consider that maybe there's some part in the deep recess of my soul that's littered with dust and cobwebs that feels rejected. He swallowed my cum but wouldn't let me touch him. If my soul worked right, I'd say that stung.

However, I'm me. I can easily get over that. But letting him *forget* it?

Hell no.

I'm two drinks in, and before I can figure out how to remind him, to make sure that memory is burned into him, he stands, telling Willow he'll be right back. My gaze follows him as I try to subtly peer over my shoulder, watching him stroll through the bar toward the hallway in the back. The only things back there are the restrooms and the back door.

The temptation to follow him is there, but I decide not to, still playing the game. I'm determined to beat him at it.

However, just as I move to face ahead again, I see a man stand and follow Merlin. He's big, bald, and wearing a leather vest. Before either of them can disappear around the corner, the stranger grabs Merlin by his elbow.

I'm seeing fucking red as I watch Leathervest lean over and say something in Merlin's ear before I can magic my sense of hearing in order to catch the words from across the room. Merlin gives him a stiff nod, and they walk toward the back door instead of the restrooms he was originally heading to.

Oh, fuck no.

This wave of possessiveness is new, but I'm a pretty go-with-the-flow kinda guy.

I say nothing to the others as I down the rest of my third drink, which is unfortunately not enough to feel the effects of the alcohol through my mounting, dangerous fury. Visions of violence flash through my mind's eye as I rise off my stool.

"Good luck, buddy," Anthony mumbles as I walk away, clearly assuming I'm on my way to finish the *banging it out* portion of the night.

I'm about to bang someone's head into the wall until their skull's caved in.

The rest of the bar blurs and darkens at the edges of my vision like I'm marching through a tunnel that's slowly closing in on me as I head toward the back door.

I'm not sure what I expected to find out in the alley, but I don't think it was the scene I walk out to.

They're both out here, standing about ten feet apart. Merlin's staring at Leathervest, looking...bored.

Even while the other man aims a gun at his head.

The stranger's eyes widen upon seeing me, but he doesn't lower his weapon. The door to the bar slams shut behind me, the sound reverberating off the dark walls of the alley. The dumb fucker moves his gun between me and Merlin, like he's not sure who the biggest threat is.

Hint: it's me.

I can already smell the blood.

Taste the violence.

This should be fun.

11

MERLIN

I had every intention of disarming this thug and scaring him off after he approached me in the bar and told me he had a gun and wouldn't hesitate shooting people if I didn't come outside with him. He's a special breed of dumb, and I wasn't afraid of him.

But now Mordred's here, and I'm experiencing a little consternation. There's mischief and murder in his eyes, and I'm unsure of how to de-escalate this situation before he gives into those instincts of his.

"Don't let me interrupt," Mordred says as he subtly waves a hand over the door. I hear the lock click before he leans casually against the wall. "Please, continue."

The poor bastard across from me furrows his brow as he peers between us, confused by the unexpected turn of events. "Well, since I have two bunnies in my trap now, you can give me all your money too," he says, voice gruff and a little less steady than it had been before Mordred's arrival.

He scoffs. "I'm a musician who plays in a bunch of shitty bars. You think I have money?"

The man alternates between targets again, and every time he aims his weapon at Mordred, my jaw clenches, and I think I can translate what's shining in Mordred's eyes. Because I feel it too—the power of the much stronger predator staring down a weaker predator who's encroaching on his prey he's already claimed.

Mordred is *my* prey.

No matter whoever is who in each of our minds, I won't condone killing, even if it is some lowlife crook.

"Fine." The guy points his gun at me, and some of my tension eases. "I know you own that little shop across the street. You have money. Hand it over."

Mordred laughs, and the sound echoes eerily through the alley. "You really are a fucking moron, aren't you?"

"What the fuck did you say, punk?"

"Hey." I get the guy's attention when his weapon moves to Mordred again, speaking calmly in the hopes of keeping this from turning into a bloodbath. "You might want to keep that thing pointed at me."

Mordred continues leaning against the wall and peers over at me. "Aw, my knight in shining armor."

"I don't care if he shoots you, Mordred," I say dismissively.

Except, I think…I might?

I'm the only one who gets to hurt him.

"I just don't want him to give you a reason to kill him."

"Oh, that's going to happen anyway," he says, eyes flashing with wicked promise.

"Man, fuck you both!" The scumbag once more moves his gun between us. "Just give me whatever you fuckers have!"

Mordred takes a step away from the wall.

"Mordred…" I caution.

"Don't ruin my fun, Merlin."

I don't mind Mordred scaring the prick, but I'm growing increasingly worried he won't stop there. Do I even want to stop him? I don't give a fuck that this guy threatened me, but I'm still seething every time that gun is trained on Mordred.

All those demons I worked hard learning to repress are rattling their cages.

"You can't make him scream," I tell him, hoping he'll have a little fun with the vermin before releasing him like a fish. "It'll attract too much attention."

"No screaming." Mordred snaps his fingers. "Check."

The man opens his mouth, but no sound comes out. He's playing his role of a fish well as he flounders, hand shaking around his weapon, fear creeping into his wide eyes.

"You might want to get out of here," I warn him. "He might not look like it, but you're dealing with a monster."

Mordred turns a smile on me. "Thanks, darling."

He *would* appreciate me using his preferred designation. I'd almost find it endearing if it wasn't true.

Instead of choosing the smart option and running away, the thug raises his gun higher, trembling as he moves it between me and Mordred, trying to decide who to shoot first. A disappointed sigh slips from my lips as I ready myself to stop a bullet. I expect Mordred to extract the gun from his hand, but it's more like he's waiting, taunting, *hoping* he'll shoot.

"Mordred," I urge him again.

The next time the weapon is aimed at me, the man's finger itches at the trigger.

Before he can pull it, his head snaps violently to the side. His large body drops and crumples to the ground in a pathetic heap.

Everything falls silent, and that silence stretches on and on. And on.

I stare at the corpse across the alley, struggling for some clarity in the midst of the storm of emotions warring within me. He shouldn't be dead. His death was unnecessary.

I've always been a protector at heart. I fought to protect my mother until her end, until her fragile human existence could stand no more. I fought to protect my friends, knights of Camelot. I would have given my life to save Arthur's.

I should *not* feel any amount of satisfaction that the man who threatened Mordred is dead.

"Well," Mordred starts, breaking the silence, "that was a bit anticlimactic."

I look over to see him staring at the man on the ground, face scrunched in a frown. Is he frowning because he hoped to have more fun than that? Or is it because he's feeling things he shouldn't be feeling too? It's times like these I wish I could read his mind.

"What the fuck did you do, Mordred?" I ask, my voice surprisingly steady and quiet.

"Were we..." His gaze flits between me and the dead guy, then he grins with faux innocence. "Were we not on the same page?"

"Obviously not," I snap, my volume rising.

Mordred turns his body toward me and tilts his head. "Do you expect me to apologize? He was nothing more than scum."

"Of course I don't expect you to apologize. You never apologize for anything."

"Please tell me this isn't about when I tried to help you the other night."

My lip curls. "Right now, this is about the fact that you just committed murder. Do you make a habit of that?"

"Of course not," he says nonchalantly. "Not that I have a problem with it. And not that I'm particularly concerned with getting caught, but I think it'd become an issue if I was sentenced to life in prison and never died."

It's clear he's trying to lighten the mood, but I'm so far from amused that all I can do is glare at him.

He sighs heavily, looks back to the fallen body, and waves his hand. The crook disappears with a thin wisp of black and purple smoke that quickly dissipates in the thick air. "There. All better."

I shake my head. "Like it never happened, huh?"

"Come on, Merlin. He was a waste of perfectly good oxygen."

"Is that why you did it?"

His jaw ticks. "No."

"Then why?"

He takes a step toward me, his eyes sparking with rage and something else I can't quite put my finger on. "Because he dared to touch you," he says, voice low and menacing. "Threaten you. Only *I* get to do that. You're mine."

For the second time in only a few minutes, everything goes quiet. There's a subtle change in his eyes, widening a fraction as though maybe he didn't mean to say that. But with the added depth to those oceans revealed, I see what it is I couldn't name before.

The same thing I think I felt when that gun was aimed at him.

Possessiveness.

I shake my head again. "I'm not yours, Mordred."

He moves closer, and when he's two feet in front of me, he reaches for the collar of my sweater, slowly as though he expects me to hit his hand away. I should. The instinct is there. But I don't.

Lowering the fabric to expose my neck, his eyes zero in on my throat. "My marks on you say otherwise."

It takes some self-control not to let my eyes flutter when his fingers brush my skin. "You manipulated me."

"That again?" He drops his hand, letting my turtleneck slip back into place. His eyes narrow, closing off my access to any vulnerability he might have been showing. "I told you I didn't make you want me. I didn't make you forget who I am or what I've done. As you damn well remember, I killed my own father. So if you think I feel bad for using a little magic on you—to save you from a fucking panic attack I might add—then you've forgotten who I am all on your own."

I haven't, but if I had, he'd be doing a damn good job at reminding me.

Because he's sure as hell reminding me of those desires to fucking kill him.

Giving into my hatred and anger, I wrap my hand around his throat and force him back several feet before slamming him into the nearest wall. Staring into his eyes, I'm met with a reflection of my own rage.

How have we not killed each other yet?

"I haven't forgotten who you are, Mordred." I lower my voice to a deep growl as I tighten my grip around his neck. "But you will never manipulate me with magic like that again, no matter my mental state. Is that fucking understood?"

His chest heaves, and I realize mine is too when it brushes against his. His heat, his scent, it all envelops me until our fury mingles with something else. Something more dangerous, more potent.

He says nothing, only offers that infuriating fucking smirk of his.

"I mean it, Mordred." My voice comes out more breathless than before. I refuse to believe the lust that's shining in his eyes is another reflection. "Your addiction to my hatred is going to be the death of you. The next time, if you pull that shit, I will end you."

The last of his rage seems to fade as his tongue darts out over the ring in his bottom lip before he bites it. "Next time?"

"I didn't mean it like that."

"I think you did."

He rolls his hips, and his erection rubs against my semi through our jeans. I didn't even realize I was getting hard.

Well, fuck.

"And what if I told you it's just the thought of killing you that's getting me hard?"

"I'd say you're in denial again."

My hand leaves his throat to tangle in his hair instead, gripping it hard by the roots. "I don't want you, Mordred." *Yeah, denial.* "You're a fucking monster."

He's completely breathless, panting, shamelessly grinding his cock against mine that's fully hard now. "I could be *your* monster."

"Is that what you want?"

I inch my face closer to his, and his eyes are on my lips as he leans forward. I tighten my grasp in his hair and yank him back. He moans with both arousal and disappointment.

"So fucking needy. Is that what you want, Mordred?" I ask again. "To be my little monster?"

"Fuck," he groans softly. "Yes."

"Then fucking prove it."

When I push on the top of his head, he falls easily and eagerly to his knees.

12

M🜏RDRED

When I felt the weight of Merlin's hand on top of me, I wanted nothing more than to sink to my knees for him. So that's what I did. And that's where I'm at, moving in a blur— already clawing at the button of his jeans, popping it open, lowering his zipper, fucking yanking his pants down.

Am I desperate?

Yes.

I'm dying to feel his cock in my mouth, craving the taste of him, longing for him to fill me with his cum.

I hope he's fucking brutal.

The moment I free his erection, practically salivating at the glistening drop at the tip, I dive forward, wrapping my lips around him with a wanton moan.

"Fuck," he grunts as he thrusts deeper into my mouth.

I go at his dick like I'm on death row and he's my last meal. It's not that I'm trying to compete with him or show him up because I'm pretty sure no one in this world or the next has the cocksucking skills he does. But maybe my enthusiasm will make up for our differences.

Because I am very, very enthusiastic about sucking his cock.

At the same time, however, I'm itching for his hate and whatever brutality he'll offer. His hand is still in my hair, but his hold isn't tight enough.

Pretending that my sole mission is to provoke him into showing me the full extent of his cruelty, I tug his jeans and boxers down even further, increasing my access. In truth, I just want to touch him every-fucking-where.

Continuing to suck him with more and more eagerness, I add a finger into my mouth alongside him, stretching my lips further. I suck and suck, slurping around his cock until both it and my finger are drenched with saliva.

When I slip my finger out of my mouth, I cup his balls, rolling them in my hand while my other hand grips his thigh, digging my nails into his skin.

He moans, and it turns into a grunt of frustration when I pop off his dick. I lick over his head, then down his shaft. My hand slips past his balls just as my mouth gets to them, and I nip at the tender flesh with my teeth at the same time I press a finger against his taint.

He bucks his hips and groans. "You fucker."

I chuckle, letting my mouth travel to the side and my finger journey further back. I lick my way up and over his hip before moving back down to his leg. My finger that's still wet with saliva finds his hole, and I tease his rim while he's panting and cursing above me.

The moment my teeth sink into the meaty flesh of his thigh, I thrust my finger inside him.

"*Fuuuck.*"

His grip tightens in my hair, and he attempts to yank me back, but I only bite him harder, sucking until he's hissing and groaning in pain.

Eventually, he pulls me off him and glares down at me with all the malice I'm fucking *hungry* for. "You like to bite, huh, little monster?"

"I like to *mark*." I thrust my finger deeper in his ass until his eyes flutter. "I like to mark *you*."

"Keep your finger where it's at," he demands in that breathy voice I love. "I'm going to fuck your head into this wall."

Fuck yes.

Staring up at him, holding his gaze, I open my mouth and stick out my tongue. He wraps his free hand around the base of his shaft and rocks his hips forward, gliding his dick across my tongue a few times—undoubtedly feeling the hard metal of my piercing—before ramming it into the back of my throat.

The force has my head tilting back, slamming against the wall behind me. The blow isn't as hard as I expected, but the stars dotting my vision are fucking beautiful.

He carries through with his threat, fucking my mouth, each thrust knocking my head into the wall. It's not enough to break my concentration of fucking him right back, driving my finger in and out of his ass. When I add a second, his assault becomes more intense.

Faster.

Harder.

I loved making Merlin submit to me, but I think I might love this side of him more.

Or maybe it's a tie.

My cock is painfully hard, straining against my jeans. Fuck, I'm close to coming in my pants like I'm fucking two-hundred years old again. With my hand that's not currently busy with Merlin's ass, I reach down and rub against my erection through my jeans, just needing a little friction.

When I moan around Merlin's cock, he yanks me off.

"Don't even fucking think about coming."

It's only when I try to peer up at him, his deep, commanding voice pulling at me, that I realize my vision is blurred.

"Fuck," he breathes as his thumb swipes across my cheek. "You're even more beautiful with tears in your eyes."

I'm beautiful?

Wait. Did he say...*tears?*

I'm not sure which part of that I want to unpack first. I don't remember the last time my eyes...leaked. Have I even witnessed my own tears since coming to this world? I'm pretty certain I haven't. I've never even cried when I've been fucked to within an inch of my life like Merlin's currently doing to me.

However, that fact pales in comparison to the fact that Merlin called me beautiful.

His thumb that wiped at my cheek presses against my lips, and I open my mouth to suck on it, tasting the saltiness of my own tear.

"You don't get to come, Mordred," he growls, like he's enjoying torturing me. "This is punishment for manipulating me. Do you understand?"

I nod, the motion slow and weak.

Truthfully, I never minded being edged or denied an orgasm. Sometimes I like it.

But I don't tell him that.

Merlin could do whatever he wants to me, use me however he pleases, and I think I'd enjoy every fucking second of it.

He pulls his thumb from my mouth and replaces it with his cock again, picking up the same wicked rhythm as before as though the intermission never happened.

My head strikes the wall again, over and over, even as I scissor my fingers in and out of Merlin's tight hole.

Fuck, I want my cock inside there.

I don't know who is matching whose rhythm and pace, but we're each plunging inside the other harder, faster, deeper with each thrust. I'm pretty sure I hit Merlin's prostate when he practically roars over me, the sound echoing in the alley. He drives his hips forward twice more before he's filling me up, cum shooting down my throat. I barely manage to catch and keep a little in my mouth because I want the taste of him to linger.

As soon as his orgasm passes, he's taking a step back, and my mouth and fingers immediately miss the warmth of him. He hauls up his boxers and jeans, tucks himself in, and then he's back on me, hauling me to my feet like I did to him the other night.

I lean back against the wall for support, my cock still hard and throbbing and aching for a release I know I won't get. My vision is still blurry, but my gaze somehow finds Merlin's lips.

He shakes his head. "No."

I stick out my tongue weakly, showing off the little bit of cum I hoarded like treasure in an effort to tempt him. He groans but makes no move for it. So I swallow it down greedily.

"All for me then," I say with a shrug, throat raw and deliciously sore.

He glares at me but asks, "How's your head?"

Reaching up, I rub the back of my head and wince. "Ow. Tender."

Merlin smirks, and the sight gives me pause. It's a smirk, not a smile, but I've never seen his lips turn up at the corners like that while looking at me. I'm sure it's just my state of vulnerability after being so thoroughly fucked in the mouth that makes me feel something about it.

"Good," he says. "How about your cock?"

I groan and thrust forward just enough to grind my erection against him. "Still hard and hating you right now."

"Good," he says again, and I don't miss the sadistic edge in his voice.

"And here I thought you learned to control your demons a long time ago, Merlin."

"I can control them just fine. I just let them come out and play when you're around."

Now it's my turn to smirk. "They're welcome to come out to play whenever they want."

His face falls only slightly as he takes a step back, though he still appears at least a little less tense than usual. "Be careful what you wish for, Mordred. I might be able to satisfy them a little by torturing you, but trust me when I say they'd much rather make you pay in blood."

Aaand…just like that, my erection deflates.

Not because Merlin still hates me—I still love that. But despite the immense pleasure I get at crawling under his skin, I didn't live this long just to die.

It's a dangerous line I've been flirting with since first laying eyes on him.

It's the sincere way he says it that has his words clutching my arousal in their claws and carrying it away.

Still, I keep my smirk, my only mask, fixed firmly in place. "Noted."

He looks away, runs his hand through his hair, and lets out a heavy breath. "What do you think the chances are that Willow and your friends are going to have something to say about us being gone so long?"

"Oh, a hundred and ten percent."

I couldn't give a fuck if the others know exactly what we've been doing, but I can tell Merlin would rather not deal with it.

"Let's not go back inside," I suggest.

"Yes, disappearing together is much less obvious."

"I want to take you somewhere."

His gaze flits back to me, and his eyes narrow suspiciously. "Where? A ditch?"

I let out a low chuckle. "You might want to kill me, Merlin, but I have no desire to kill you."

He still appears apprehensive as I take a step forward and offer out my hand. He stares down at it without taking it.

"It won't bite. Not like me."

His hard gaze meets mine, but I swear there's a flicker of amusement somewhere deep in the reddish hue of his russet eyes.

Winning.

"I won't ask you to trust me because I know you don't," I tell him with a sincerity that feels uncharacteristic. "Just... take a risk. Live a little. I dare you."

He contemplates for several seconds longer. I don't know if it's the dare that convinces him—he's not one to turn down a challenge—but he finally puts his hand in mine. Even though I saw it coming, his touch is warm and takes me by surprise.

I grip his hand, tight, as though I'm afraid of letting go. "Hold on."

And then we're gone.

13

MERLIN

The moment we arrive wherever it is Mordred's taken me, I release his hand. I'm getting far too comfortable with his touch, and I need to crush that ease of touching him before I start craving it.

Taking in our surroundings, I see we're standing in an open field under the cover of a star-filled night.

"Where are we?"

Mordred points behind me.

I turn, and I'm struck still by the sight.

Stonehenge stands in the distance beneath the expanse of the night sky that stretches above and all around us like a dome. It would be early morning here, the sun not yet having approached the horizon. Stars glitter against a velvety backdrop, the Milky Way visible, reaching into the heavens like a highway for the gods.

I haven't been here in centuries, and the memories of this place bombard me from all directions.

"Why are we here?"

"Come on," Mordred says without answering the question.

He transported us within the fenced perimeter, and when he starts heading in the direction of the monument, I apprehensively follow.

"Mordred," I caution. "You know this place is guarded?"

"Don't worry," he says, moonlight spilling over his pale features as he gives me a faint smile that shouldn't calm me as much as it does. "They can't see us. We're invisible."

We approach the ancient stones, and I can already feel the power within them as Mordred leads us into the center of the ring. I watch him as he comes to a stop and lifts his face upward, glittering stars reflected in the oceans of his eyes.

"How much of your magic do you think still exists in these stones?" he asks with his gaze still on the sky above.

Again, he surprises me.

"You knew?"

He looks at me, and when he smirks, it's different than all the other times. "That you built this place? Of course I did."

Stonehenge is technically much older than I am. However, before Arthur was born, the Lady of the Lake sent me to this world, several thousand years into the past, with instructions on how to build a magical site that would survive millennia. Much of my blood, sweat, and magic lives here to this day.

Could she have known that I would return? That I would *need* to return?

My magic has never truly left me. Faded, yes. I've always known there was a chance that if I needed the full extent of my powers again one day, that I may not be able to find my way back to it.

Is that why Mordred brought me here?

"Your magic is unique, Merlin," he says as he starts to circle me and his eyes move around the weathered stones. "I came here once, a long time ago, and I could sense it easily. I knew it was your magic that made this place. I was even more certain when—"

He cuts himself off, but he doesn't stop his slow circle, moving closer to the stones. The silvery glow of the moon shines over the side profile of his face as he reaches out to skim his fingertips over the rough surface of one of the monoliths. His jaw tenses, his face scrunched with the weight of whatever he was about to say.

"When what?" I press.

He shakes his head, refusing to look at me.

"Mordred, if me trusting you is something you're actually interested in, then you have to talk to me."

I only say that to get him to talk. I don't think I'll *ever* trust him.

Continuing his walk around the stones, forcing me to turn in a stationary circle to follow him with my gaze, different emotions flit across his face as he wrestles with whatever he's not telling me.

Nearly a minute later, he finally stops and faces me. "When I saw you shortly after."

Caught off guard for too many times tonight, I frown. "What? Here? When?"

"Over four hundred years ago. Not too far from here actually."

That sounds about right. I was probably somewhere around London back then.

"How did I not sense you?"

He shrugs, then continues on his circular path. "There was a lot more magic in this world back then. It was easy enough to conceal my own magic behind it all. But even with all that magic around, yours would always stand out, especially back then when it was a lot stronger."

"Why didn't you confront me back then?"

He falls silent again, this time for twice as long before he says, "It wasn't the right time."

There's more to it than that. It's obvious, but I'm hesitant to pry further. He's keeping things close to his chest, and it's not that I'm worried about setting him off—though he undoubtedly has anger issues I should be wary of. But like his touch that I'm becoming too accustomed to, I don't need to be acquainted with the rest of his demons lest mine become intimately familiar with them.

I've already witnessed him murder a man and was less affected than I should've been.

"The fact is," he says, stopping and facing me again, "you need your magic back, Merlin. All of it."

"I still don't understand. You're the one who killed Arthur. You hate your mother too, I get that. Why do you feel so strongly about this that you'd try this hard to return my magic to me?"

Even though I don't want to pry, I have to about *this*.

He stares at me for a tense moment. When his gaze drifts down to my hand dangling at my side, I realize my fingers are tapping against my palm. I don't know if it's the amount of sheer power in this place, but the rhythm feels more frantic, more desperate.

"I already told you. I hate both my parents, but Morgan is a plague that needs to be wiped out. You and Arthur are the only ones who can do that. If that means you fulfilling your destiny to bring back my sorry excuse for a father, then I'm going to push you toward that fate." As he speaks, his eyes darken and his voice lowers dangerously. "And I'm very good at *pushing*."

Again, I get the sense there's more to it, but before I can decide if I want to push *him*, I'm sent flying backward.

My back lands on the hard ground, and all the air is expelled forcefully from my lungs. I gasp and cough, and when my eyes flutter open, the stars above me appear closer, multiplying as my vision blurs. I blink until the slight dizzy spell fades.

"What the fuck, Mordred?" I choke out as I push myself to my feet.

It comes as no surprise to see the smug smirk on his face. When he holds out his hand, palm up, I prepare myself for another blow. Instead, a silver gauntlet materializes in his hand. He tosses the armored glove at my feet.

"Is that supposed to be funny?" I wave my hand, and the gauntlet disappears.

Like with the body in the alley back in New York, there's a wisp of smoke. Instead of black and purple, it's an ashy blue.

Mordred slowly claps his hands, the sound reverberating off the stones. "Look at that. He does have magic!"

"I never denied it. I don't know why you think I have to prove myself to you."

His jaw ticks. He has a reason, but he won't tell me what it is.

"You have to prove yourself to me because I'm trusting you to return to Camelot and deal with that witch. I won't let you go until I have faith you actually have what it takes."

"That's not the whole truth, is it?"

"Fuck you, Merlin! You think you know everything, but you don't. And you don't need to. All you have to do is get back in touch with your magic so you don't fucking fail again."

The sound of a cage rattling echoes in my head.

My demons want free.

I might just release them.

"What the fuck did you just say?"

"You heard me." He takes a step forward, tilting his head in a more menacing way than he has before. "You failed Camelot. You failed Arthur."

He's goading me.

I *know* he is.

And…fuck, I hate that it's working.

My hands ball into fists at my side.

He takes another step forward until we're two feet apart. His smirk is gone, and in its place is a look of disgust. "And then you fled Camelot like a fucking coward."

Have fun, demons.

I raise a fist, pull back, and let it go. The force of the hit to his face sends his head to the side. He stumbles and sways but remains on his feet. He blinks several times, then reaches up to swipe his thumb across his split lip. Blood glistens at the corner of his mouth as he looks back at me.

"I know your demons want more than that, darling."

They do, so I raise my fist again.

This time, he catches me by my wrist before I can land another punch, then twists my arm violently behind my back. A sharp pain shoots through my shoulder as he spins me around. He forces me a few steps forward until he shoves me face-first against the nearest monolith. His body presses against my back. He increases the pressure on my arm, causing me to grunt.

"*Magic*, Merlin," he whispers harshly in my ear. "Use fucking magic and stop hitting like a bitch."

"Fuck you. Get the fuck off me."

His warm breath against the shell of my ear and the side of my neck makes me shiver. I sense it coming before it happens. He bites the lobe of my ear, fucking *hard*, harder than he's bit me any other time before.

Just like I've become familiarized with his touch, my dick has developed a conditioned response to his teeth. I bite my tongue, but I can't stop the moan escaping from deep in my throat as my dick jerks in my jeans.

His voice lowers to a more deadly pitch, his lips ghosting along my ear, as he says, "Make me."

Somewhere beneath my skin where he's managed to burrow inside is that piece of me that doesn't want to make him, that doesn't want to lose his heat, his all-consuming presence. But I have to make myself try or he'll never release his claws.

I stop struggling against him physically, reaching out with my magic to the ancient stones.

It's there.

I can *feel* it.

But it's like it's rejecting me.

Maybe it's as ashamed of me as I am that I'm allowing Mordred to have this devastating, profound effect on me.

I try. I try. And I try again.

Nothing.

My shoulders fall, crumpling under the weight of defeat.

"Giving up so easily?" Mordred asks, his deep voice still filling my ear as though he's inside my head. "Again?"

Rage flares in my chest once more, but it's not enough.

"You're a failure, Merlin. A coward."

More.

"You ran away with your tail tucked between your legs."

A spark flares along my palm that's pressed against the cool, rough stone, the one that's not still being held behind my back.

Give me more.

"You forgot all about Camelot, didn't you? You abandoned its people, Arthur's knights, the entire kingdom. They needed you, and you let them all down."

Maybe he *is* in my head.

It doesn't feel like Mordred is the one saying these things to me. It's as if he's plucking out the thoughts from my own mind and throwing them back at me, like they're using him as their host, his voice their catalyst.

The power from the stone becomes stronger, vibrating beneath my hand, through my bones.

Just a little more.

"You let me murder Arthur right in front of you. You couldn't stop me. You still can't stop me. In fact, you love this, don't you? You love my hands on you that are covered in his blood. You'd let me have my way with you. How sick are you, darling? I'm the king's killer, and you can't fucking get enough of me."

It's my fury with us both, my hatred for us *both*, that ignites the flame.

That returns my magic to me.

The power in the stone helps, but the burst of it comes from within me, a flash of lightning, like static electricity, all bright and silvery blue. It wraps around my hand, travels up my arm, covering me like armor.

Mordred cries out behind me when the lightning hits him, his hold on me released.

I step back from the stone, watching as my beautiful magic envelops the monolith, bolts crackling and striking out toward the ones on either side of it. As I turn slowly, I watch as the lightning jumps between the stones, engulfing each— even the broken and fallen—in an electric cocoon until they meet on the other side and we're surrounded by a monument of rock and voltaic energy.

When my eyes land on Mordred, who's fallen to the ground in the center of the circle, I see the blazing white-blue lightning reflected in the deep oceans of his eyes. They're wide, staring up at me as though I'm a god.

"You did it," he says in awe.

I have my magic back, yes.

Unfortunately for him, so do my demons.

"I told you to be careful what you wish for, Mordred."

14

MORDRED

"I told you to be careful what you wish for, Mordred."

Well, fuck.

I knew what I was doing when I provoked him. Or...I *thought* I knew what I was doing.

However, it was the only way I knew how to dig deep enough to where he buried away his magic, to stir it in its deep hole he's kept it locked away in until it finally came spilling over.

But now?

I might've fucked up.

I hardly recognize his voice. It comes out harder and harsher, just like the gaze that's currently burning its way into my defective soul.

Fear is an almost foreign emotion to me, but as I stare up into Merlin's eyes that look a shade more red than they naturally should, blazing like an inferno, I'm slowly becoming reacquainted with it.

"I had to do it, Merlin." At least my voice is as steady as ever. "You know I did."

"Thank you for reminding me who we both are."

Lightning continues striking all around us, crackling in the air that's lit up electric blue. He takes a step forward, but I don't move. I remain on the ground, a sign of submission that damn near kills me.

"My magic is no match against yours," I say, like he needs the reminder, half hoping an unfair fight is beneath him, that he wouldn't murder anyone—even me—in cold blood.

I might be an arrogant prick, but even I can admit that Merlin has always and will always be the most powerful sorcerer to ever exist.

As much as it pains me to acknowledge it.

"Then maybe it'll bring you some comfort to know that this will be over quickly."

The detached tone of his voice sends a literal shiver down my spine, and I *hate* how an emotion I haven't felt in centuries can suddenly become so all-consuming in the face of Merlin's demons and my sins.

A bolt of lightning strikes the ground a foot from me, singeing the grass and leaving a black scorch mark in its wake.

"Fuck!"

I scurry backward in the grass, keeping my eyes on Merlin's. There's a look in his that has another spark of terror wrapping its tendrils around my throat and squeezing the life out of me. Or, more like, it's the *absence* of a look. Like there's nothing there.

Empty.

A void.

"Merlin, please." Now my voice is anything but steady. Fuck.

I don't feel fear. I don't beg.

But more than the threat of imminent death, there's something about the cold way he stares down at me that's constricting that damn beating thing in my chest, wrapping around it like a noose.

"How did you expect this was going to go, Mordred?" he asks in that same distant tone. He takes another step, and I scoot back another foot. "I've told you time and time again how much I've wanted to kill you. But you were right. I was out of touch with my magic for too long that I probably couldn't have. Thanks to you, I've found my way back."

Maybe I should've waited another four centuries after all.

"You won't kill me," I say with a conviction I don't feel.

He takes another step, but I'm left with nowhere else to go when my back hits the stone behind me.

"Why? Because we sucked each other off? Did you think that would mean anything to me? Make me choose to look past your sins? The way you ruined my life? Was that your plan all along? Bewitch me with dick?"

"Fuck you, Merlin. I helped you, whether you choose to see that or not."

"From what you've told me, you've only helped *your-self*." He crouches down in front of me, holding my gaze with his cold one. "Unless you have anything else to tell me?"

Unfortunately, he's right, and anything else I have to tell him would only prove that point further.

"I already told you everything you need to know."

"Yet you're still keeping secrets like the spineless snake you are."

My jaw clenches, and my nostrils flare. I try to grasp onto that anger to mask my fear, but when I speak, my voice trembles like a goddamn coward. "I can't stop you if you really want to kill me, so go ahead and get it the fuck over with."

Once upon a time, I didn't fear death.

But things change.

"I'll give you a chance, Mordred. One truth."

I purse my lips, sealing them in a tight line.

He stands, his eyes darkening at my refusal to give him what he wants. The lightning around us flickers and sparks and grows in intensity. I can feel it at my back, sweat trickling down my spine from the heat. Or the fear.

I wince.

Then I'm blurting out one truth, the only one I can give him.

"I was afraid!"

His brows dip, but his eyes remain cold.

"Four hundred years ago." My chest heaves with each erratic breath. "When I saw you, I was afraid. That's why I didn't show myself."

One corner of Merlin's mouth twitches upward, and the sight is downright creepy with the empty void that's swallowed his eyes. "Are you scared of me, little monster?"

"Yes. Fuck you for making me admit it. Are you happy now?"

He stares down at me so long that I stop breathing, the only sound in the air around us that of the buzzing and crackling lightning. Then he speaks one word that feels like damnation, like the sealing of my fate.

"No."

Lurching forward, he leans down and grasps the sides of my jacket in each hand and hauls me up easily, all the magic coursing through him giving him a burst of superhuman strength.

When he slams me against the stone, I hiss and grimace and groan at the electric shocks against my back, the current lighting up my veins.

"I'm the furthest thing from happy, Mordred," he snarls as agony crashes over me. "How could I be since you brought your darkness back into my life? Since you opened wounds that never fully healed? Fuck me? Fuck *you* for existing."

"Merlin…"

There's an apology somewhere on the tip of my tongue, but I bite it back. I'm not going to lie and apologize for something I'm not the least bit sorry for.

I won't lie even to save my life.

"But you're right about one thing, Mordred."

The jolting lashes all over my back begin to weaken and wane. The white hot lightning dancing around the stones like live wire starts to die down. When Merlin's eyes darken again, it's with something different than the void from before, something not quite wrath either.

"I can't fucking get enough of you."

Wait…

I've barely wrapped my mind around those words before his lips come crashing down on mine.

Bruising.

Punishing.

Like he's channeling all his hate into this one kiss.

I fucking love it.

Of course, the abrupt one-eighty from being scared for my life to being kissed within an inch of it is giving me whiplash. But I kind of love that too.

"Fuck, I hate you," he growls before taking my bottom lip, ring and and all, between his teeth and biting, no doubt taking his revenge for all the times I marked him.

My deep moan gets swallowed up when Merlin thrusts his tongue in my mouth and I taste a hint of my own blood. He presses his body against mine, trapping me between him and the rock. When he rolls his hips, I let out another moan as his erection grinds against mine. He devours me with his mouth, takes me apart with each thrust, every blessed bit of friction.

His fingers move from my jacket, skimming up my throat, then they're in my hair. He takes a fistful to yank my head back, like he has to pull me away because he can't pull himself away.

"Why did you have to make me want you?" He stares down at me with eyes that are so *full* now, completely opposite from the blank vacuum they were before.

Merlin is brimming with hostile lust, a venomous desire that's infected my veins, a toxin I hope there's no cure for.

I fist the front of his sweater with both hands, push him back a step, then spin us both around until it's his back against the stone. His hand slips from my hair, and his shoulders fall, the tension vanishing the moment I take back control.

He's wound so tightly with magic and hate that this is the only way he can let go. He might deny that I help him, but I'm going to do it anyway.

"You think I wanted to want you?" I whisper against his lips as I slide my hands down his chest toward the bottom hem of his sweater. I slip them beneath the fabric, then glide my hands back up, palms on fire as they coast up his bare abs. "Trust me, I didn't."

We're both panting heavily. The mystical lightning that surrounded us has receded, but the sky's grown a lighter shade of blue, promising the imminent arrival of the morning sun.

My hands find Merlin's nipples, and he moans as I pinch them between my fingers. I thrust my hips forward, grinding against him over and over. The next time a low, rumbling noise comes out of him, I capture the sound in my mouth as I kiss him just as hard as he kissed me. I even bite his bottom lip so his blood can join mine.

His lips part, inviting me in, and I lick my tongue against his. He takes me deeper, his tongue moving around the metal bar in mine. I press my lips to his harder, his soft ones yielding for me.

"Fuck, Merlin," I groan as my lips start to roam down to his jaw. I nip him there too. "Ever since I had you tied up and at my mercy, I've fucking wanted you. Speaking of…"

Removing my hands from beneath his sweater, I grasp both his wrists, hold them together, and stretch them up over his head. He doesn't stop me even though he could.

As I pin his wrists against the stone, the rock on either side shifts, wavering like an illusion, before it grows. It swells up and over his wrists until both sides connect like a bridge, effectively binding him in place.

"There. Now I can have my way with you." I punctuate my point with another thrust of my hips and another bite to his jaw. "You were going to kill me, Merlin." I lower the turtleneck of his sweater to bare his neck. "How should I punish you?" I ask before I latch onto his throat with my teeth.

He hisses even as he tilts his head back to give me more access. "I wasn't."

After sucking on his skin long enough to leave a mark, I pull back to meet his gaze. "What?"

"I wasn't going to kill you." He looks at me through hooded eyes, already so far gone. "Like you said, I know how to control my demons."

"So what? You just wanted to scare me?"

He nods weakly.

"Mission accomplished, asshole." I grip his jaw in my hand as my other one moves back to his chest, pinching his nipple through his sweater. "For the record, I don't do fear. Or begging. So I'm going to have to make you pay for that."

"Do whatever you want to me."

I groan and thrust against him again. "Careful, Merlin. You submit so beautifully, but I've learned one thing," I say, peppering kisses and nipping bites along his throat as I speak. "When I'm in control, you need the calm that comes with submitting. When you're the one with the power, I need your chaos. I don't know if I can exercise restraint not to show you mine and rip you the fuck apart."

"I can handle your chaos, Mordred," he whispers in a low, breathless voice.

"Fuck, Merlin."

I'm straight up dry humping him now as my bites turn more vicious. Bloodthirsty. Ruthless. He meets me thrust for thrust, whimpering and hissing as I alternate between kisses, licks, and gnawing and sucking on his flesh.

When I pull back, a wicked smirk tugs at the corners of my mouth, and I look up to see Merlin's eyes swimming with lust. "You're welcome for your necklace."

Fresh bruises and teeth marks decorate his neck from one side to the other, and the sight has my cock begging for release.

He groans, but the sound of displeasure can't fully disguise the hunger in his eyes. "You're lucky I have plenty of turtlenecks."

"Of course you do. Boring old Merlin. But you're anything but boring, aren't you? It's just an image." I lean forward, nip at his ear, then whisper against it, "The truth is you're fucking filthy and want to be stuffed full of my cock."

A shudder sends a tremor through his body.

"Are you going to beg for it, darling?"

He leans his head back enough just to catch my gaze and gives me a feeble attempt at a glare. "I don't do begging either."

"Not yet you don't." My hands finally move down, sliding down every inch of his body along the path to the button of his jeans. I pop it open, reach inside his boxers, and wrap my fingers around his dick. It hasn't been long since he fucked my face, but he's hard as the rock he's bound to. "Before I'm done with you, you'll be begging me to fuck you."

His eyes flutter, and he leans his head back against the stone as he thrusts into my hand, letting out a long, rumbling moan.

While I let him use one hand, I use my other to undo my own jeans and pull out my cock that's just as hard as his. Twin beads of precum glisten at both our tips as I line our dicks together and wrap my hands around them.

"*Fuuuck.*" Merlin opens his eyes so he can look down and enjoy the show as I run a palm over both our heads to collect the precum.

When I look down too, I add a generous amount of spit, using that and the precum to coat us both as I start to stroke us together. My gaze finds Merlin's face, and he stares down in a captivated lust haze as my tattooed hands and black painted fingernails move around our shafts. The metal bars of my Jacob's Ladder glide along the underside of his cock, no doubt adding even more sensation.

"You like that, darling?"

"Fuck yes. You feel so good. Especially those fucking piercings."

"They're all for you right now."

Both our voices are husky, our panting breaths fanning the flames of desire as I pick up the rhythm. When his breathing becomes even faster, his moans louder and more frequent, I know he's getting close.

"You want to come for me, Merlin?"

"Yes."

I smirk. "Beg me for it."

He shakes his head with barely any movement. "Never."

I have half a mind to stop, to get myself off and leave him hanging like he did to me earlier, but I'm already so fucking close. Stopping now when he feels so fucking good rubbing against me would torture me just as much.

"You will." I lean forward to take his bottom lip between my teeth and bite him again. "Next time you have a premonition, it's going to be me fucking you. You're going to know how good my cock inside your ass feels, how it feels to be filled with my come. You're going to want it. You're going to beg so sweetly for it."

"Fuck." His warm breath kisses my lips before his mouth comes down on mine in another brutal kiss. He moans and mumbles through the heat of our breaths, "Mordred…"

"Yes, darling?"

"I'm gonna come."

"Come all over us, Merlin."

Our cocks erupt seconds apart, his release triggering my own until our cum drenches our dicks and my hands. I slow my movements, stroking us through our orgasms as we breathe in each other's air.

Only seconds pass before I sense the tension returning to Merlin's body.

"Let me go," he says, voice stiff.

"Don't you dare fucking freak out on me again."

"I'm not. Just…let me go."

I don't believe him, but I do as he asks after I wipe my hands on the rock on either side of him and then tuck us both back into our clothes. The rock binding his wrists cracks and fractures and crumbles away. The moment his hands are free, he fists my jacket like he did before and turns us. He slams my back against the stone, and when the air rushes out of my lungs from the impact, he's there to swallow it with a fierce open-mouthed kiss.

If I thought I was addicted to Merlin's hate before, it's nothing compared to the pure malice he puts behind his savage kissing, bruising and bloodying my lips. Every rough touch lights me on fire, every lash of his tongue against mine sparking hotter and hotter.

It goes on and on until we finally come up for air.

"I think I'm starting to love hating you," he says, his body still pressed against mine, our chests heaving in sync.

"Welcome to the club."

His lips twitch, but they don't quite form a grin. After a moment, he takes a step back, putting distance between us that I instantly despise.

I think it's pretty clear I'm not finished with him. Not by a long shot.

Merlin shifts his gaze, looking out to where the sky is quickly softening to a pale blue, a thin band of gold breaking the horizon.

"I guess we should get out of here," he says as he runs a hand through his already disheveled hair.

"Right." I give him my signature smirk, but something feels off about it this time, more forced than how it always comes so easily. "You're welcome for the orgasm. Again. Even after nearly killing me."

Another flicker of faint amusement passes over his face. "Good night, little monster."

Merlin vanishes, leaving only a gentle disturbance in the air and deserting me clear on the other side of the world.

It's probably for the best.

I think I might be fucked.

15

MERLIN

Over a thousand years ago.

"You sent for me, Your Grace?"

"Yes, Merlin," Arthur says from his position on the throne. He hands a scroll off to one of two of his knights who stand before him.

They both turn and head across the throne room to leave.

"Please close the doors on your way out," Arthur calls after them.

Both knights bow their heads to the king before exiting and shutting the large double doors with a resounding thud that reverberates off the stone walls.

Arthur stands the moment they're gone and immediately begins to pace the length of the grand hall. His brow is pinched, a clear signal he's lost in pensive contemplation and I need to give him a moment to collect his thoughts. I stand there silently with my hands behind my back while he continues to pace back and forth.

After a couple of minutes, he removes his crown and places it on the arm of his throne as though it's nothing but a burden.

I know at times like this it is.

Rounding the throne, Arthur stops on the other side and peers at me over the high back. "Did I make a mistake in knighting Mordred?"

My spine straightens at the question even though I knew it was coming.

I've known Arthur since he was a boy, and I've always been there for him. He's come to seek me out whenever he needs advice, whether trivial or significant, whether it's about war, his people, or love. I've failed him more often than I care to admit, yet it would seem he'll always believe I'm more wise than I really am.

I don't know what I did to deserve Arthur's friendship, but I'll cherish it as long as I live and do everything in my power to protect it.

When it comes to his son, however, things become complicated.

Staring into Arthur's eyes, I see those blue oceans that are deep with all his complex feelings toward Mordred. Right now, they're full of sadness and disappointment that's masked with indignation. I've always been capable of seeing past his masks to what's really in his heart.

"I assume he gave you his reasons for what he did?"

Arthur releases a heavy breath as he moves away from the throne and resumes pacing. "He claimed the man was beating a child."

It happened early this morning while Mordred's patrol was down in the city. They came upon an older merchant who was beating a young boy of twelve. According to the other knights who witnessed it, Mordred asked no questions before killing the merchant with his sword.

"The child had stolen several loaves of bread because he and his younger sister were going hungry," I say, my eyes following Arthur. "Not that that's an excuse for the boy's actions. At the same time, that's not exactly an excuse for what that man did."

"It's not an excuse for what Mordred did either."

"No, it's not," I agree.

"That's not how we handle things. Mordred is constantly going against what it means to be a Knight of Camelot, and his actions will only inevitably make the people fear the knights rather than respect them."

"You're right again."

"Do you believe everything the other knights say about him?"

Rumors abound concerning Mordred's immoral tendencies. It's been said that he goes into the lower villages to kill and rape, but no one's ever been able to find evidence as to his crimes, nor has anyone come forward to accuse him. I followed him one night away from the main city, but I quickly lost his trail. I suspected he sensed me and used magic to cover his tracks.

"There's no proof," I offer. "Have you considered that the knights treat him the way they do because they're following the lead of their king?"

Arthur stops his pacing and turns to face me. "What does that mean?"

"You don't exactly hide your contempt for him."

The truth is, I don't believe rumors. Mordred may have been raised by his mother, but he chose to leave her, chose to come to Camelot and pledge his loyalty to Arthur and become a knight. That alone deserves the benefit of the doubt. Even if I do watch him like a hawk.

"Do you blame me for that, Merlin?"

"He's your *son*, Arthur."

"Only because his mother bewitched me in order to conceive him."

"He's not Morgan le Fay."

The king lets out another heavy sigh, returns to his throne, and sinks down into it. "I cannot accept him in that way, Merlin. I went against my better judgment and made him a knight, but I will never make him crown prince."

"And you know I respect your decision, Arthur."

"What do I do about this?" he asks, looking at me with pleading eyes.

"You can't show him any special treatment since you've chosen not to claim him as the heir to your throne. However, if you show him less respect than you would your other knights, then he'll continue to be ostracized by them, which, in turn, will only make him continue to act out."

"He respects me less than my other knights do."

"Respect works both ways, Your Grace."

His brows lower in a pained expression. I don't usually use honorifics with Arthur when we're alone, our friendship far past that. It's a reminder of his position, and he knows it judging by the war raging behind his eyes.

"You believe I treat him too harshly?"

"I believe you unfairly hold his mother's sins against him. You have no obligation to claim him as your son considering the deceit that brought him into existence, but since you did knight him, then he at least deserves the respect you show every other knight."

His face relaxes, and he eventually nods. "You're right, of course. As always, I appreciate your counsel, Merlin."

"You know I'd do anything for you, Arthur."

The corners of his mouth slowly tilt up. "As your king?"

I grin back. "And as my oldest friend."

That night, I have a premonition that proves Arthur had been right about Mordred all along.

A fortnight later, I fail him.

Present day.

Last night was one scene of a shit show after another. Yet, somehow, it was one of the best nights I've had in...well, a very long time.

My mind was racing when I popped back inside my apartment straight from Stonehenge where I left Mordred, but after I fed Percy and got a shower, I slept like a baby. I'm not sure if it was because I was exhausted from the powerful burst of magic returning to me or from two orgasms. Probably both.

It's early morning, and I'm back behind the counter in my shop with a book in my lap as usual. However, I haven't read a word all morning, staring at the same page as the ink all bleeds together.

I *should* be thinking about returning to Camelot, about when I should leave and what I need to do to prepare for abandoning my life here. I owe Arthur. Even after all this time, I *miss* him. The promise of his return should be all that's on my mind, of seeing my oldest friend again, of bringing him back and helping him reclaim his throne.

But instead of thinking about that, I'm thinking about Mordred. More specifically, trying to pick out *one* thing I regret from last night. Because I need to regret something. I need something to drive me away.

Do I regret the dead guy?

No.

As much as I should be condemning Mordred for killing the man, I know who Mordred is, and I can't hate him for it more than I already do. Besides, there was a part of me—a dark part—that wanted to see the motherfucker dead for daring to threaten Mordred.

Do I regret making Mordred believe I was going to kill him?

No.

I have never—not even a thousand years ago—seen Mordred afraid like that. For a brief time, it quenched my demons' thirst and made them shut up enough for me to enjoy what he did to me afterward.

Do I regret *that*?

Also no.

I may feel no remorse for anything that happened last night, but that doesn't mean it hasn't all left me completely stupefied. Too many times this morning I've found myself subconsciously slipping a finger beneath the turtleneck of my sweater—today, it's a deep, rich purple—just to feel the warmth of the bruises that really do look like a necklace. His marks. His sign of possession I really shouldn't love as much as I do.

Last night, I felt things for Mordred I never thought I would. Defensiveness. Possessiveness.

To be clear, I still hate him more than I've ever hated anyone. And that's why this is all sorts of complicated and fucked up.

It doesn't help that Mordred is obviously hiding things. Maybe it's nothing to concern myself with. Maybe it's not relevant enough to worry about. But I can't control that urge to peel back all his layers and discover whatever secrets he's keeping.

Of course, I'd never force my way into his mind like he did to me. That was dark magic, something I've always known he's exceptionally skilled at thanks to his mother, and I'm still pissed at him for it. There's a difference between murdering in defense of others—which, admittedly, is what he did last night and what I could have been pushed to doing myself had that man's gun been aimed at Mordred instead of me when he nearly pulled the trigger—and using dark magic to invade a person's mind, the one place they're meant to be safe.

He was trying to provoke me into using magic, but I won't defend him.

Fuck. Isn't that what I'm doing for everything else he's done?

I can't sit here anymore.

I'm feeling too anxious in my own goddamn skin.

Tossing my book onto the counter, I get up and attempt to preoccupy myself with cleaning. I'll probably have to sell the place, so the least I can do is make sure the shop is spotless. I could use magic, but I need the distraction.

I spend the rest of the morning and early afternoon dusting, sweeping, and organizing books on the shelves.

It doesn't help. I can't get Mordred out of my head.

He did exactly what he threatened to do. He crawled beneath my skin.

I already looked up Mordred's band's schedule and saw they don't have a show tonight. I don't know why I even looked though. Even if they were playing, I wouldn't go. I need to put distance between us before I do something stupid like actually start caring.

I'm on edge every time the front door opens, like I'm expecting someone else to come through it.

It's never Mordred.

I shouldn't *want* it to be.

The next time the door opens, it's Willow who enters the shop. I peek out from one of the back aisles, and she strolls over, practically shoving a hot, black coffee in my hands.

"Spill."

Shit. I guess I should've expected this.

"Are you talking about the coffee?" I ask with an innocent smile. "Because I'd much rather drink it."

She rolls her eyes.

Okay, that was a bad joke.

"You and Mordred both disappeared last night."

"Did we?"

After I finish straightening the books I just returned to the shelf I was working on, I head back through the shop to the counter, taking a sip of coffee on the way.

"Merlin, you're killing me!" Willow follows me and leans against the opposite side of the counter as I take a seat. "Anthony swears you two went to go bang it out. Will didn't seem to like that theory."

"Will?"

"Yeah. I've kind of gotten the impression he's got it bad for Mordred since I've been hanging out with them all. I thought about telling him to go for it, but not if you two are...you know. So are you?"

"Are we what?"

"Banging it out!"

I laugh and shake my head, trying and failing to ignore this fresh wave of possessiveness that's coming over me. It's ridiculous because if Will wants Mordred, I should let him have him. He probably doesn't hate Mordred like I do.

But…then again…does he *want* Mordred with the same intensity I do?

Fucking hell.

"Willow…"

"Fine, fine!" She holds her hands up in surrender. "I'm being nosy. But, just so you know," she adds with mischievousness gleaming in her eyes, "you're not fooling me with that turtleneck."

A heat flares up from beneath said turtleneck until I feel it rising into my cheeks. She can see it judging by the flash of cunning pride in her eyes.

"I knew it!"

"I still hate him," I say, like that's any kind of defense.

"Oh, I'm sure you hate him *real* good." She wiggles her brows, which only makes my face flame hotter. She takes a sip of her iced coffee, then taps the straw against her lips pensively. "He's got…chaotic bottom vibes."

I press my lips into a thin line, refusing to give anything away. However, the image of Mordred on his knees in that alley as he accepted all my rough chaos flashes in my mind— not only accepted it, but *loved* it. I'm suddenly thankful for the counter that hides the view of my cock twitching in my jeans.

She arches a brow. "No? Cinnadom?"

"Cinnadom?"

"Yeah. A cinnamon roll Dom."

"You're going to have to forgive this old, *boring* man. What the hell is a cinnamon roll in this context?"

She snickers. "You know. Sweet. Innocent. Adorable. Far too precious for this cruel world."

I can't stop a scoff from clawing its way up my throat. "Trust me, that doesn't describe Mordred at all."

"Okay, so *burnt* cinnamon roll. He is a rock star, after all. But you have to admit he can be sweet when he wants to be."

"Mordred? Sweet?"

"Because he dared to touch you. Threaten you. Only I get to do that. You're mine."

His words from last night come back to me, and...I *guess* in his own twisted, possessive way they were kind of sweet.

Willow shrugs. "Maybe not to you because, you know... you *hate* him so much," she says, voice dripping with sarcasm that I try to ignore. "He's been nice to me though, and he cares about his bandmates. Ava wouldn't put up with his shit if he didn't."

"All I hear is a lot of defending him and forgetting about the fact that I really do, honestly, legitimately *hate* him."

"Whatever you say, Merlin," she says in a singsong voice with the same sarcasm as before. She starts backing away from the counter, skipping backward. "See you later?"

"Not tonight."

"I get it. You're way less tense today, so you probably don't need anything to help loosen you up tonight. Like a drink. Or orgasms."

She giggles and rushes out the door before I have time to reply.

I'm definitely *not* less tense today. If anything, I'm more so. But I suppose I can understand why she'd think that. Two orgasms in the past twenty-four hours would undoubtedly give that illusion.

But the fact is I don't want to risk running into Mordred tonight. I can't see him until I know how to deal with these conflicting emotions. Until I can reconcile the part of me that still hates him and the part that, well...at least doesn't want to kill him anymore.

Until I can bring myself to say goodbye.

16

MORDRED

Over a thousand years ago.

This is Arthur's last chance. I shouldn't even be giving him more chances after he's rejected me time and time again, but I'm willing to go against all my mother's wishes and give him this last one. *One. Last. Chance.*

Kneeling on one knee in front of the throne, I peer up into Arthur's eyes that are a spitting image of my own. I loathe that I share something as meaningful as the eyes with this man.

"Stand, Sir Mordred."

I do, hating the way he spits out my name like he can't stand the taste of it.

"You requested an audience?"

"I did, Your Grace." I glance to the left of Arthur where Merlin stands. He's *always* there. "I requested it alone."

"Merlin stays. Tell me what you want."

I shouldn't blame Arthur for the harsh, curt way he's speaking to me—at least, not *this* time. He looks and sounds completely wretched, racked with grief at having lost his wife to another man. Just a couple of nights ago, Queen Guinevere ran off with Sir Lancelot, one of Arthur's trusted knights and friends.

Despite what some of the other knights say, even though Lancelot was one of the only knights who accepted me as one of them, I never encouraged him to seduce the queen. I never *dis*couraged it either, but that's besides the point.

I shouldn't feel this elated by Arthur's misery, but I do. However, this is also his opportunity for this last chance I'm giving him.

"In light of recent events, I was hoping you might reconsider your decision as to my position. You have no queen, no heir. None but me."

The slight raise of his brows is weak, tired. "You think I should crown you prince?"

I take a deep breath. "Yes, Sire. Whether you like it or not, I am your blood. And you need an heir."

Come on, Arthur. This is your only chance. Take it.

"How dare you," the king snarls as he stands.

Saw this coming.

"You are taking advantage of your king's broken heart and attempting to manipulate the situation to your advantage."

I *was* attempting to manipulate the situation, but to *his* advantage. Of course, I can't tell him that.

"You may be my blood," Arthur continues, sneering down his nose at me, "but that was not a decision I made myself. I do not claim you as my *son*; therefore, I will never claim you as my prince."

"Your Grace."

Arthur turns to look back at Merlin. They have some kind of silent conversation while I stand there seething, drowning in rage and enmity and bitter resentment until I can't breathe. My jaw aches, clenching so hard I swear my teeth will crack.

After nearly a minute, Arthur lets out a heavy sigh. He returns to his throne and sits down, appearing even more tired than before.

"Please keep in mind, Mordred, that I did not have to grant you knighthood." He speaks more calmly than before, but it's as if it pains him to do so. "But I respected you enough when you came to me to do so. I will not, however, consider crowning you prince, and I will entertain no further requests as to this matter. Is that understood?"

"Of course, Sire." I grind my teeth as I bow my head. "I will not bring it up again."

"You may go."

I have to repress the urge to scowl at the king, but I at least allow myself to glare briefly at Merlin before I turn to leave.

My mother was right all along.

And Arthur Pendragon just signed his death sentence.

That night, I slip out of the city and into the forest to meet my mother like I do a couple nights a week.

Merlin follows me.

Of course he does.

It's not the first time.

It's also not the first time I use magic to cover my tracks, taking a couple of different routes until I'm positive I lose him. After going over the plan for Arthur's demise with my mother—Lancelot's betrayal is the perfect catalyst for war, a battle, Arthur's last—I return to the castle undetected.

The next day, I'm on edge and still brimming with fury. When I witness a merchant beating a young boy, I can't contain my rage. I impale the man on my sword, imagining him as my father.

Soon.

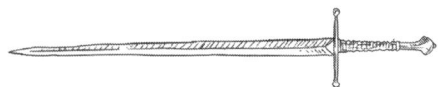

Present day.

It's been another two days since my night with Merlin at Stonehenge. As much as I've been tempted to see him again, addicted to his hate and the way I can make him come apart despite it, I've resisted. I'm tired of chasing him. Other than my first couple of nights in the city where he practically came to me, it's like he's made it a point to prove me wrong. That he's not obsessed.

Unfortunately, I am.

So when he doesn't show up to our second to last gig we have in the city, I find myself pissed off all over again.

I really shouldn't be. He hasn't come to any of our shows since the one the night after the Stone Crow, but his absence this time feels different, heavier. Like what happened at Stonehenge didn't affect him as much as it did me.

And *that's* what pisses me off.

Why did it have to affect me at all? In the last thousand years, I've had at least that same amount of sexual partners. Why would Merlin be any different?

I told Merlin I'd crawl under his skin, but it turns out he's the one who crawled under mine and made a home there. How dare he make me addicted and then deny me my next fix. Is he hoping now that I helped him reclaim his magic that I'll just leave him alone? If so, he's in for a rude awakening. I'm not releasing my claws until he's gone for good back to Camelot.

Even the thought of that has a bitter taste creeping up my throat as the band and I finish up our set for the night.

At least I didn't fuck up the show. The last time I played this riled, it was a disaster.

"Your performance was a little more edgy than usual tonight," Ava says after we've loaded up the equipment in the van. "Not that I'm complaining. It was badass."

"Yeah," Anthony agrees. "Did you and Merlin not bang it out enough?"

"Apparently not." I'm still too worked up to even deny it.

"So, I guess we'll see you tomorrow then?" Will asks with a jealous edge to his voice even though he's grinning, like he knows exactly what my plans for the rest of the night are.

I shouldn't go to Merlin like some damn junkie. I should let him walk away since that's clearly what he wants to do.

But...*fuck*.

I've never done what I *should* do. Why start now?

"Yeah. Say hey to Willow for me," I say as I start walking away.

The others are going to hang out at the Crow like usual, but since Merlin wasn't there last night, I assume he won't be tonight either. As soon as I've rounded the corner where the rest of my band can't see me, I disappear and reappear right in front of Merlin's bookshop and discover my assumption was correct.

The lights downstairs in the shop are off, but the ones in the upstairs apartment are on, a shadow moving behind the curtain.

Don't go up there.
Let him go.
You're such a fucking masochist.
What the hell is wrong with—
I strangle that voice until it dies.

The next second, I'm inside Merlin's apartment, standing in the center of the small space. Merlin's back is to me as he takes clothes out of his small closet, throwing them on the couch. He must have recently showered, his hair damp, wearing nothing but a pair of sweatpants.

"Good evening, Mordred," he says without turning around.

"I see you still have all that magic I helped you find."

"I sensed you when you showed up outside."

Flopping down on the end of the couch that isn't covered in clothes, I stare at the rippling muscles in his back, a single droplet of water cascading down the curve of his spine. "Show-off."

He chuckles and turns around.

"Fuck."

My cock is instantly thickening in my jeans at the sight of my marks covering his throat. The bruises are a lighter purple now with a thin yellowish border. I knew I had latched on to every inch of his throat that I could that night, but... *damn.* His entire neck is painted with my marks. I want to cover the rest of him with them too. His bare chest would look good in the same shade of purple.

He regards me while my gaze is fixed on his throat. "I can't decide if you're angry or turned on right now."

"Both." My voice comes out somewhere between a groan and a growl. "You've been avoiding me and denying me this sight for two days."

"I'm sorry."

"You're apologizing?" I ask with mild surprise, tilting my head. "To *me*?"

Sighing, he runs a hand through his hair, hesitating before finally saying, "I've been trying to figure out how to say goodbye to you."

That mild surprise turns into pure shock.

It's all I can do to barely conceal it.

Smirking through it, I shrug and say, "I figured you'd say something similar to the last time we parted ways."

He gives me a faint grin. "I might still hate you, Mordred, but I guess I no longer wish you a slow and painful death."

"You guess?" I scoff. "Good to know."

"That's the best you're going to get."

He turns back to the closet, and I'm left staring at his back again as he digs out a few more items of clothing.

Leaning back against the cushions, I prop my right ankle up on my left knee and drum my fingers on top of my right knee anxiously. I have no idea what it is I'm feeling. Glad that Merlin was as affected as me after all? Even more possessive now that I know he was and after seeing my marks on him haven't faded? Disappointed that some of his hatred seems to have been what's faded? *Glad* that it has? Fear of saying goodbye?

Whatever it is, I'm disoriented, no idea which way is up, which way is my escape.

This is when I tend to make all my worst decisions.

"When are you leaving?" I ask, voice tight, as I watch him work.

"I'm not sure yet. I'll need to sell the place. I thought I'd get a head start on packing," he says, motioning to all the clothes thrown haphazardly on the couch beside me.

"You're taking all this with you?"

He shakes his head. "I'll give most of this stuff to charity."

I roll my eyes. "Of course you will."

Grinning, he adds, "And I'll have to find a good home for Percy."

"Maybe Willow will take him?"

"Yeah, I can ask her."

"I'd offer, but I doubt he'd do well on a tour bus. Our last show in the city is tomorrow night, then we're leaving the day after."

Merlin goes still, and the muscles in his back tense. "Right."

"You know, my offer still stands." I rise off the couch and slowly approach him. " It'd be a good way to say goodbye. If you want to beg for it…"

The moment he turns around, I'm close enough that I can press my body into his until he's backed up against the closet door. I place my hands on either side of his head, the heat between our bodies quickly rising in temperature. His bare chest immediately starts to heave as his breaths turn harsher.

"I told you." He stares into my eyes, his own giving away the lust that he's refusing to give into. "I won't beg."

"Stubborn wizard." I smirk as I lean in and brush my lips lightly against his, teasing. I skim my lips up his jaw to his ear and murmur, "If you won't beg, darling, I will."

Pulling back enough to look into his eyes that are wide, waiting for my next move, I grind my growing erection against his. I need Merlin's hate, his chaos, to fucking ground me. And *I'm* not against begging for it.

"Please, Merlin." I kiss him more forcefully this time, then whisper desperately against his lips, "Please fuck me."

17

MERLIN

"*lease fuck me.*"

I don't think three words have ever affected me the way those three do, said with so much gravity, so much urgency. It's even more potent in Mordred's deep, rough voice. It usually sounds like that after his shows, but it's even more husky right now, raw with a thirst that has nothing to do with water.

I realize I haven't said anything when Mordred grinds his hips against mine again, making me groan. He licks across my lips like he's lapping up the sound. I dart my tongue out and attempt to chase his, but he pulls back.

"Now who's needy, darling?"

"You were the one just begging." Even with that fact, the argument is still debatable.

"And I'll beg some more if that's what it takes to get your cock inside me," he says as he runs his hands down my bare chest, his palms leaving a scorching trail. "But first…"

One of his hands comes up and wraps around my throat. He ducks his head down and takes my right nipple into his mouth, sucking for one second before biting down. I hiss as I let my head fall back against the door, submitting to him and his ministrations. His other hand moves lower, sliding down my abs, then palming my dick through my sweats. I thrust against him as he soothes his assault on my nipple with his tongue before traveling to my other one and giving it the same treatment.

"Fuck, you taste amazing everywhere." He moves his tongue lazily across my chest, swirling it around one nipple, then back to the other, like he can't get enough of the flavor of my skin. When he palms my cock with harsher strokes, I moan and buck into his hand. "I fucking need you inside me, Merlin."

Trying to snap myself out of this intense lust haze Mordred always manages to put me in, I grab him by both his wrists, push him away, then turn him to shove him against the wall beside the closet. I grind against him as I pin his wrists on either side of his head.

"Beg some more."

"Please, Merlin. Show me how much you hate me. Take it all out on my ass."

I groan and seal my mouth to his, driving my tongue inside and reclaiming control. When he whimpers into my mouth, I swear I'm about to come in my sweats.

Without breaking the kiss, I haul him away from the wall and steer him backward toward the bed. My tongue continues to battle against his, our lips pressed together so tightly, moving so harshly against the other's that they're bound to bruise. It takes a burst of sheer will to pull myself away from him, and then a burst of magic to send him flying back onto the mattress so he lands exactly where I want him.

He stares up at me, eyes darkening as he pants heavily.

Glancing over at my plants that are hanging by the window, I smirk. The vines grow, crawling along the wall toward the bed as they lengthen. Striking like snakes, they wrap around Mordred's wrists, cinching tight as they hold his arms taut above him.

"Now I see why you like to restrain me," I muse as my eyes rake over him. "You look good like this. Tell me what you want."

"I want you inside me," he says breathlessly. "I want you to fuck me. As hard and rough as you can. Fill me with your cum."

"I love your dirty fucking mouth."

With a wave of my hand, Mordred's clothes vanish.

My eyes fall first to his hard, leaking cock, flushed, veins throbbing around his piercings. As my gaze drifts up, it stops at his left hip. His body is almost completely covered in tattoos, but for some reason, there are lighter and empty spaces around the scar that Arthur gave him a thousand years ago with the help of Excalibur.

Mordred squirms as he realizes what I'm looking at. In a more vulnerable voice than I've ever heard come out of his mouth, he says, "Please stop."

When I look up to peer into his face, my eyes catch on something else.

"What is that?"

He knows I'm no longer looking at his scar, and he seems to squirm even more. "You know what it is."

I do. I'm not surprised to see that his nipples are pierced too, but on his chest, covering his right pec, is a tattoo of the Pendragon crest—a red shield with a yellow dragon, all outlined in black.

Tearing my gaze away from it, I finally look up into Mordred's face. The expression in his eyes is almost...scared.

Haunted. Surely he knew I'd see all of him when he begged me to fuck him?

"Why would you get that?"

It makes no sense. He was right about how his father treated him, and in return, he treated Arthur no better. Then he killed him. Was the tattoo meant as some kind of sick mark of victory?

He quickly schools his visage and glares. "None of your fucking business."

A growl rips from my throat. "You have a bad habit of keeping secrets, Mordred. I'm getting really fucking tired of it."

"Good. Teach me a lesson then."

My pleasure.

"Bend your knees and put your feet flat on the bed."

He might have a habit of keeping things locked up tight, but he obeys my orders so beautifully when he's this desperate.

"Open your legs wider."

Again, he does exactly as I say, even lifting his hips a little, granting me a view of his hole. While he showed vulnerability when my eyes were fixed on his scar and his tattoo, he shows none of that now. He's eager, *wanting* me to see him, see exactly where he wants me to fuck him.

"Merlin, please," he begs some more when I've left him untouched for too long.

"You're not the one in control right now, Mordred." I place a knee on the foot of the bed and then crawl forward until I'm settled between his legs, staring straight into his eyes. "You want me to teach you a lesson? Haven't I told you to be careful what you wish for?" Grabbing him by the backs of his thighs, I raise his legs up and tell him, "Leave them there."

Leaning forward, I part his ass cheeks so I can swipe my tongue from his hole to his balls.

"*Fuuuck.*"

His cock jerks in front of me, but I don't touch it. I go back to his hole instead, swirling my tongue around the ring of nerves. I move back and forth between his hole and his balls, licking, sucking, nibbling until he's all slick with saliva. Taking his balls into my mouth, I suck until he's writhing and gasping and pleading. I let go of them and trail a path down his inner thigh with kisses and bites before licking my way back to his hole.

His entire body is trembling from pleasure and probably the effort of holding his legs up without having the use of his hands to help him.

When I shove my tongue inside him, his body practically spasms as he chokes on a sob. He moans my name, and it sounds like a goddamn prayer.

"Fuck, Mordred. You taste good too."

I go back to fucking him with my tongue, adding a finger alongside it. Licking at his inner walls, I drive my finger in deeper. I know I hit his prostate when he cries out my name again. I hit it again, and again. I'm rutting against the mattress, the front of my sweats becoming more and more damp with each delicious noise out of his mouth. He continues writhing, moving his hips as he meets my thrusts, demanding more.

"More, Merlin."

I don't give it to him.

I remove my finger and tongue, and he immediately starts whining. When I move my tongue upward again, skimming over his balls and straight past his cock, he starts cursing.

"Fuck you!"

Letting out a deep chuckle, I slowly lick a path up his abs, lapping up the precum gathered there. "What's the matter, little monster?"

"Fucking touch me!"

"I am touching you," I say, unable to keep the amusement out of my voice.

"I swear to god, Merlin, if you don't touch my cock—"

His words are cut off the moment my hand wraps around his throat. I hover over him, keeping distance between us as I continue denying him any friction.

"Stop trying to give orders," I growl in his face. "When I'm in control, you're going to take what I give you. Even if I decide to give you nothing, then you're going to fucking take nothing. Do you understand?"

A hint of surprise flashes in his eyes. There's a little fear there too. It's all woven together with lust and desperation.

Eventually, he nods and says a quiet, "Yes."

"Good boy."

He moans loudly, his eyes fluttering like his pulse beneath my palm. I like the way my praise affects him, and before I can stop myself, I grind my hard length against his, as though it's a reward, making him moan again. The friction feels so damn good, so I do it again.

"If I want to use you, Mordred, then I'm going to fucking use you."

"Yes," he says again as he thrusts up against me. "Use me, Merlin."

I groan and release his throat, sitting back on my heels before I rut against him until I come. I won't be coming unless it's inside him.

Holding out my hand, I conjure an item into my outstretched palm. "If you want to be used, maybe I should use this on you.

Mordred stares at the black silk blindfold in my hand, and his harsh breathing appears to cease, his eyes widening a barely perceptible degree. Slowly, he shakes his head. "You can do anything you want to me. Just…no blindfolds."

I narrow my eyes. "Why?"

He presses his lips into a thin line.

"Mordred," I snarl.

He still says nothing.

There's a part of me that knows I shouldn't push him, that I should respect there are things he doesn't want to share. But even after living for twelve hundred years, I don't take sex lightly. Even now, there's a voice screaming in my head not to cross this line with him, but even the side of my brain that hates him wants him.

If I'm going to give something up for him, he's going to give something up for me too.

"You have a choice if you want to come tonight." I toss the blindfold across the room, then bring my hand down on his right pec over his tattoo. When I dig my nails into his inked skin, he groans and his cock jerks. "The tattoo or the blindfold."

A frown creases his face, but he takes a deep breath and says, "My mother used to put me in the dark to punish me when I was a child."

Oh.

Well, that's deeper than I expected of him.

"For the record," he adds, glaring up at me to cover up whatever vulnerabilities he's feeling, "I'm not *afraid* of the dark."

I nod understandingly. "But you don't like someone else forcing you into the dark."

His expression softens, and his brow furrows with mild surprise. He looks away from me, like he doesn't like that I read him so easily, maybe afraid that I'll be able to see more of him the longer I look.

I grab him by the jaw, force his face back to mine, and kiss him softly before whispering against his lips, "Thank you for telling me."

"Like I had a choice," he mutters bitterly.

There's still a defenselessness to him, his ocean eyes open and exposed. If I wanted, I could probably jump inside and swim around, make him squirm and writhe for me in a different way. Or he could shut down completely. As much as I'd enjoy using that as an excuse to give him even more of my hate, I'm not willing to risk that.

"You did have a choice. You're just desperate for my cock in your ass." I grin, brush a strand of hair off his forehead, and kiss him again. "Do I need to be gentle with you now?"

"Fuck you. Don't you dare."

I chuckle and move lower until my face is above his dick that had only barely begun to soften. Still grinning up at him, I blow on his crown, and his cock hardens and jerks.

"Fuck. Please, Merlin. I'm fucking dying here."

"Then I've got you right where I want you."

He groans and throws his head back on the pillows. "You're so much more sadistic than I thought you'd be."

"Only when it comes to you."

Using magic again, I conjure a bottle of lube while I distract Mordred by blowing on his dick again, making him moan and whine. I pop the cap open and pour a little out onto my fingers.

"I'm seriously going to be pushing up daisies before you even get inside me if you keep going at this—*fuuuck*."

I successfully shut him up when I thrust two fingers inside him without any warning, then lick up the underside of his cock, my tongue sweeping over the piercings of his Jacob's Ladder. As he whimpers and writhes beneath me, I imagine what all that metal would feel like inside me, his apadravya hitting that spot inside me over and over and over...

"Merlin, fuck."

Mordred pulls me back from those thoughts with more of those sinful noises that slip past his parted lips. As curious as I might be, he'll never make me beg.

By the time I add a third finger, he's panting hard, tugging at the vines binding him with desperation.

"Please. Need your cock," he pleads in a choked voice, just as desperately.

"You'll get it when I give it," I growl.

He's so tight, the hot tunnel of his ass squeezing my fingers as I thrust in and out to continue stretching him. I may want to hurt him, but I don't want to *hurt* him.

Apparently, Mordred isn't as worried about that. I suddenly feel a cool rush of air beneath my waist when he magics away my sweatpants, freeing my erection that immediately leaks precum on the sheets.

"Get the fuck inside me! How much more do I have to beg?"

With my fingers still inside him, I lick my way up his body, starting at his balls, his cock, lapping up more of his precum on my way up his tattooed abs and chest. I stop to suck a pierced nipple into my mouth, tasting metal and skin as he moans, before continuing my way up until I'm once more hovering over his face.

"You're too fucking needy for your own good," I tell him as I thrust my fingers as deep as they'll go.

His eyes roll into the back of his head, and he arches his back off the bed. He's already sweating, his dark, disheveled hair damp and glistening beautifully.

"I told you you'll take what I give you. Do you want this to hurt?"

"Yes," he whimpers.

"Have it your way then." I pull my fingers out of his ass and immediately line my cock up that's already slick with lube up to his hole. When I think of something I don't normally have to consider, I ask, "Do I need to use a condom?"

As sorcerers, we're much less susceptible to illnesses and diseases that ail mortals, but we're not entirely impervious to them. I've never had anything as far as I'm aware, but I'm assuming the number of his sexual partners far exceeds my own.

He weakly shakes his head. "You're safe. I swear."

I may not trust Mordred, but for some reason, I trust him about this. Besides, he may keep secrets, but he hasn't lied to me, at least to my knowledge.

As I start to push my way inside him, I hold his gaze, keeping it hostage like I am his body. His breaths come quicker, harsher as my crown breaches the tight ring of muscle. When I thrust forward and bury myself all the way inside him to the hilt, his breaths completely cease. I think mine do too.

"Fuck," I groan as I lower my head to rest my forehead against his. "Fuck, you feel so good."

He's still staring up into my eyes, his own lost in bliss, or pain. Maybe both. And he's still not breathing.

"Breathe for me."

I bring my mouth down on his parted lips and force life back into him until he gasps. When I pull back to let him draw in air on his own, he chases after me instead, crashing his lips back to mine. I'm helpless but to stay put and let him ravage my mouth, his tongue vibrating against mine as he moans, his ass clenching gloriously around my cock.

"Fuck me hard, Merlin," he whispers raspily after he stops the kiss, his lips still brushing against mine as he brings his legs up and wraps them tight around my waist. "I want to feel you long after you're gone."

Fuck.

Just the thought of leaving, of having to withdraw from the tight, intoxicating heat of him after just one taste, has me wishing this could last forever—and wanting to give him exactly what he's asking for.

"Then hold on, little monster."

I pull almost all the way out, then drive back in with a force that has him sliding up the bed and crying out when I nail his prostate.

"Is this what you want, Mordred?" I ask as I do it again. And again. I thread my fingers through his hair and fist it harshly to keep his face toward me. "For me to fuck all my hate into you?"

"Yes," he moans. "Yes, please."

"Good. Because I have plenty of it."

As I continue to pound into him mercilessly, building a rhythm of violent, brutal thrusts, I tighten my grip in his hair and yank his head back, baring his throat. I lick up his Adam's apple and feel it move with a swallow beneath my tongue. He whimpers, a noise that still stuns me coming from him, still strikes at something in me, making me even hotter.

I lick my way to the side of his neck to a spot there's no ink and decide to take my revenge. Sinking my teeth into his flesh, I bite hard, forcing a harsh cry to rip from his throat. Latching onto him, I suck viciously as I continue to fuck him without mercy.

Past, present, and future have come together to form this bubble of hate and hunger and heat we exist in.

Even the metal in his cock feels as though it's been heated up a hundred degrees as each ball of his piercings rubs against my abs, giving him the friction I had been denying him before.

"Fuck, Merlin," he chokes out on a sob. "Gonna come."

I release my teeth from his throat and lick up his chin to find his lips again. "Come for me. I need to feel it."

Slamming my mouth down on his, I kiss him as savagely as he had done to me. It takes mere seconds of fucking him with my cock and my tongue before I feel his ass clench around me and his release pour out between our heated bodies.

The feel of him all over me has me following him quickly over the edge, and I unravel, shooting deep in his ass.

"You feel that, Mordred?" I ask as I continue to pulse inside him, the waves of my orgasm slowly ebbing. "You wanted my hate. Now you have it."

He's trembling as he stares up at me with eyes that shine with rapture and satisfaction and vulnerability.

Even though I told him before that I still hate him but don't want to kill him anymore, it truly hits me in this moment.

I adamantly, wholly no longer wish to kill Mordred le Fay.

In fact, I think I want to protect him.

18

MORDRED

I shouldn't have let Merlin fuck me. Or, rather, I shouldn't have begged him to.

I feel fucked in more ways than one.

When he pulls out of me, I feel more empty than I ever have before. And that's saying something considering I often feel like a walking void. I wince as his softening cock slips out of me. My wrists are still bound above my head, but my legs have fallen back to the mattress, my body boneless. I might as well be a puddle of imprisoned jelly on his bed.

Merlin leans back on his heels, and I can practically feel his eyes on my hole as he groans. Then his finger is there, circling my rim before he pushes past, shoving all his cum back inside me and making me moan.

Again.

I've never made this much noise before.

"I gave you all this hate, Mordred. Don't be rude and let it go."

I try to respond, but it comes out as an incoherent mumble.

Fuck, I feel drugged.

Cum drunk.

Removing his finger, he swirls it around in my own cum that's smeared all over my chest. When he brings it to his mouth and wraps his lips around it, I moan, and my spent cock twitches. Then he brings his finger to my mouth next, rubbing it over my lips before pushing past them. I suck lazily, and he groans again.

The vines around my wrists loosen and retreat, and my arms slump on the pillows like dead weight.

Merlin grabs my arms and holds them close, examining my wrists. His brow furrows, and he begins to lightly massage with slow, gentle circles of his thumbs.

"What are you doing?" I ask, my voice full of gravel.

"Your wrists are all red and raw."

Fucking hell.

"Careful, Merlin," I say, looking up at him with a languid grin. "I might start to think you hate me a little less."

"Definitely not."

Yet he doesn't stop his soothing ministrations.

And I can't take all these tender touches.

I pull my hands away from him.

He glares at me, but there's a playful undertone that makes me feel as though we've switched places. He must feel the same because he says, "So you're the one pulling away now?"

When I say nothing, he leans down, places another tender fucking touch against my lips with his, then climbs out from between my legs and off the bed. I watch his ass as he walks away toward the bathroom and find myself taking over the massaging of my wrists. Because…yeah, they're sore as fuck. But I also kind of love it.

The shower in the bathroom turns on, the sound of running water floating into the room with me. I stare at the door Merlin left open. It feels like an invitation.

Do I really want to shower with him?

Yes.

Should I?

Fuck no.

Am I?

I crawl out of the bed, and as soon as I'm on my feet, I feel Merlin's cum dripping down my thigh. Closing my eyes, I pause to enjoy the feel of it, imagining it's his claim on me.

What the fuck is wrong with me?

I got my fix—that huge dose of hate Merlin just gave me. Now I'm high off of it.

Snapping myself out of it, I cross the room to the open door and step inside. The frosted glass door of the shower is already clouded by steam, but I can make out Merlin's body as he washes himself.

As though he senses me, he pushes open the door. His bathroom is so small that I have to step to the side to avoid getting hit.

"I didn't realize your shower was this small." I was going for a more snarky tone but ended up sounding more dejected instead.

I turn away to leave the room, but Merlin darts his hand out and snatches me by the forearm before hauling me inside the shower. He closes the door, and I'm trapped beneath the spray between him and the wall.

The shower seems even smaller inside. Despite my back being pressed against one wall, there are mere inches between Merlin's body and mine.

I can't tell if the heat I feel is radiating from the water or from him.

He reaches for a washcloth off a hook and soaps it up. When he starts washing my chest and abs of cum, I stare at him as though he's grown two heads.

Looking up, he meets my gaze and grins. "What's that look for?"

"Why—" I damn near choke and have to start again. "Why are you taking care of me?"

Merlin's amusement fades, and he peers back down as he continues cleaning me. He adopts a pensive, unsettling silence while he works, a deep crease forming between his brows. Eventually, he sighs and asks, "How many sexual partners have you had?"

"In my whole life?"

"Yes."

"At least as many as the number of years I've been alive," I answer honestly. "I've kind of lost count."

He winces, and…wait.

Do I feel *bad*?

Surely not.

I've never felt ashamed for anything, let alone for acting on my carnal desires. Life gets boring. There have been times where that's all I've had going for me.

So, no. I don't feel bad. But…*maybe* I care a little at how that seems to upset Merlin.

"It's kind of turned into phases," I tell him in an attempt to dull the blow. "I've gotten bored of it plenty of times. But after the last…phase, I guess…I did get tested just as a precaution. So I was telling you the truth earlier."

He nods and gives me a faint smile. "I believed you."

Silence falls over us again as he soaps up more of my body. I give myself over to the pleasure of it, turning around when he tells me to so he can wash my back, struggling a bit in the confined space. When he moves down to my ass, dragging the cloth through my crease and over my abused and sensitive hole, I let out a moan and my head rolls back on my shoulders.

Before I can let myself fall too deep, I clear my throat. "So, what's your number then?"

A few more seconds of silence, and then, "Thirty-eight. Well, thirty-nine now."

I turn back, having to shove him a bit out of the way so I can gawk at him. "In a thousand years?!"

"Technically, over twelve hundred. That includes my life back in Camelot, and several of those are from my very young years."

"Wow…" I'm gaping at him like he's some alien creature again, but I really can't help it. "If I didn't know better, I'd take back what I said about you not being a prude."

"But you do know better," he says in a husky voice, his grin returning only briefly before he turns serious again. "The point is…sex means something to me. It's not something I take lightly or go into impulsively. *Usually*. So, yes, I fucked you hard, and now I want to take care of you. I gave you a choice, but since you followed me in here, you can deal with it."

He turns just enough to get the washcloth beneath the stream of water, washing it thoroughly, wringing it out, then soaping it back up. Facing me again, he drags the cloth up and down each of my arms, then moves to clean what he can reach of my legs considering the space is too small for him to kneel to get any lower.

"Have you ever considered you might be demisexual?" I ask him curiously.

"I had at one point, but I think that ship has sailed." He stares into my eyes as though he's blaming me for something, or maybe to make a point. "Don't demisexuals have to form an emotional bond before feeling sexual attraction?"

I shrug and attempt to suppress a smirk. "Technically, hate's an emotion."

His grin from before widens into a full-blown smile. The beautiful sight does stupid things to that useless organ in my chest whose only job has ever been to pump the black sludge moving in my veins.

"I don't think that's how it works. Although…"

Merlin's gaze falls to my throat, and I can suddenly feel that spot where he bit down and sucked on my flesh, heating and pulsing as though it's alive. His free hand comes up, and he brushes his fingertips lightly over it while he stares with a sinful gleam in his eyes.

"If we're going based on marks, it looks like you're mine now too."

As though to punctuate his point, he moves the soapy cloth to my cock, gripping it softly and giving it a stroke, being careful of my piercings. I groan at the feeling of the rough fabric and let my eyes close and my head fall back against the wall as he takes his time washing my dick and balls until I'm fucking hard again.

Fuck, I want to be his.

I guess I'm still a little high.

"Do you want me to let you come again?" Merlin whispers, his voice low and rough in my ear.

When I open my eyes, I meet his gaze as he continues rubbing the cloth along my aching length. At this rate, I'm never going to come down from this high.

Biting my bottom lip, I tug the ring there between my teeth and slowly shake my head.

He grins but doesn't stop his gentle stroking. "You like it when I edge you? You want me to deny you too?"

I nod listlessly, my eyes hooded as I stare into his, my breathing becoming shallower, harsher, more ragged. I could probably come in seconds if he stroked just a little harder, a little faster. Instead, his teasing movements bring me right to the edge but never let me take the plunge.

"Don't you dare come," Merlin growls as he keeps his same rhythm, as though all he's really doing is still washing me.

Before I can get *too* close, he pulls away, and I whine. I may have asked for it, but…damn, I really do want to come now.

After he's finished cleaning my body, Merlin somehow manages to wash my hair in the tiny space. Once he's rinsed it out, he opens the shower door, helps me out since my legs are made of jelly again, and grabs a towel to dry me off. He tosses it over my head with a chuckle before stepping back inside the shower to finish washing himself.

Wrapping the towel around my waist, I lean back against the small counter to watch him through the opaque door. Playful Merlin isn't something I'd ever thought I'd witness, and I might like it a little too much.

He finishes up, dries himself off, then takes my hand and guides me out of the bathroom while he's still completely naked. Leading me back to the bed, he replaces the sheets with a wave of his hand. With another wave, he flings my towel off and across the room before pushing me back onto the bed, practically manhandling me to the middle and then climbing in behind me.

"You want me to stay?" I ask, dazed and a little stunned as he settles in and spoons me from behind.

"Only if you want to."

The shower was already crossing a line, but staying is the absolute last thing I should do.

However, Merlin turns off the lights, throwing us into darkness except for the faint city lights filtering in through the curtains, then pulls a blanket over us. He snuggles into me with an arm slung over my waist, his nose in my hair. His warmth feels too good, and losing it right now might just make me weep.

"This doesn't feel like hate to me," I whisper into the dark.

"Consider it hate cuddles," he says, his chest rumbling against my back.

Fighting against all my instincts, I sigh and let myself relax, sinking into the pillows and into Merlin. My mind is loud, but my body is warm and comfortable. I've rarely slept with other people unless it was after passing out from drunken sex or an orgy.

This is...different.

But it's difficult to listen to the voices in my head telling me how wrong this is when it feels so right.

19

MERLIN

The bed beside me is empty and cold when I wake. Not that I was expecting anything different. Mordred made it pretty clear last night that sex doesn't mean the same to him as it does to me.

I still don't fully understand why I gave in to him. I don't...*care* about him. Sure, I may not want to kill him anymore, but I don't care about him in the same way I've cared about my previous partners.

Mordred wasn't wrong though.

Hate *is* an emotion. And as far as hate sex goes, yeah, I can see the appeal now.

I'd rather not analyze everything that happened after.

Before I head downstairs for the day, I feed Percy and finish cleaning out my closet except for a few outfits to wear until I leave. I dress in another turtleneck sweater—because the bruises on my neck still haven't faded—and head down to the shop.

I spend the morning contacting the Realtor I worked with when I bought the place. I let her know that I'm less concerned with making money off it and more so with making sure the store goes to someone who will appreciate it and make it their own. Keeping it as a bookstore would be a plus, but I'm not going to be that picky. If I do make any money off the sale, I'll just give it to charity anyway.

That afternoon, Willow comes in with our usual coffees and asks if I want to go to Dethrone the Queen's show with her tonight since it's their last one in the city.

I consider telling her no. If I don't see Mordred again, then last night could be our goodbye. That would probably be for the best...

But, of course, I tell her I'll go with her. Just to see him one last time.

I've never been addicted to anything before in my life, not until him.

Willow meets me at the shop after I close up that evening, and we take the subway to where the band's playing. As we get off and head down the street toward the bar, she links her arm with mine. I think nothing of it—my mind too full of other thoughts—until I tilt my head to see her grinning at me.

"What?"

She stares pointedly at our arms joined together.

I clear my throat and look ahead. "What about it?"

"You're not going all stiff. You weren't standing on the subway with your arms tucked into your chest. Someone bumped into you, and you didn't cringe."

"What's your point?"

She shrugs and removes her arm from mine. "I always thought you were a slight germaphobe or something. I know I shouldn't pry, but...does this change have anything to do with Mordred?"

"No."

At least, not *technically*.

It's been, well…let's just say a *long* time since I last had sex, and I think the extended period of abstinence made me somewhat averted to touch. Not drastically, but enough to where Willow noticed.

I'm realizing now that maybe my psychological well-being had been wearing thin over the last several centuries, and it simply snapped in the face of my surprising lust for Mordred. I had never been prone to panic attacks either. Maybe his intentions that night were good, maybe they weren't. But I think the truth is that he *did* help me. Not that I'd ever admit it because it was still a pretty piece-of-shit thing to do.

The poison of my hatred for him, of my own shame for failing Arthur and abandoning Camelot, has bled out of my veins just a little. I wouldn't quite call it closure, but it's something close to it.

"He and the band are leaving tomorrow," Willow says. "Are you okay?"

"Why wouldn't I be?"

"Oh, you know. Because you *hate* him so much." There's that damn sarcasm dripping off her tongue again.

"I *do*," I say with no less conviction than before.

Well, maybe a little less.

I *do* still hate him. There's no doubt in my mind about that. But I think there's something else there too, something I don't quite understand and am doing a decent job at completely ignoring and pretending doesn't exist. When I return to Camelot, I'll simply lock it up tight and forget all about it for the rest of eternity.

"Okay. Then won't you miss the hate sex?"

Yes.

"I'll live," I mutter.

That may have been the first time I admitted to having sex with Mordred out loud to her, but she doesn't make a big deal out of it. Or maybe it doesn't come as a surprise because she was already certain of it.

"What about you and Ava?" I ask as we near the bar her girlfriend is playing at tonight.

"We'll keep in touch." There's a hint of sadness in her voice. "But, actually…No. Never mind."

"What?"

She shakes her head and sighs. "It's nothing."

I'm curious, but she clearly doesn't want to say what's on her mind. So I don't push her.

When we enter the bar, Mordred's band is setting up their equipment on stage. Judging by the way Mordred's back that's facing me stiffens, he must sense me. It wasn't that long ago that *I* was the one who was constantly on edge when around *him*.

It's a puzzle to me as to why he's suddenly the one reacting that way to my presence, and if I had the time, I'd dig all the pieces out of him so I could put it together. But not only do we not have that kind of time, it's best if that puzzle remains in pieces.

Once their equipment is set up and everyone takes their places, Mordred steps up to the mic and his eyes immediately find mine.

"I'm Mordred le Fay, and we're Dethrone the Queen."

After he gives his usual quick, almost gruff introduction, the music starts. Like at the first couple of shows I went to, Mordred can't seem to take his eyes off me, but it's different this time. It's not to unsettle me or make me squirm. It feels as though he's drinking me in, taking his fill, because he knows we'll never see each other again after tonight.

Or maybe that's just why *I* can't stop staring at *him*.

Because this show is different for me too. I pay more attention to the way his body moves on stage, the way his fingers move deftly across his guitar, the deep, rich tone of his voice as he sings and occasionally screams.

He's fucking beautiful.

When they move fluidly into a song I recognize as "Sins of the Father," I listen to the lyrics again, hearing them in a different light.

"*Bow down...bow down...I was sinful at birth...this wicked legacy of mine...disease in my veins...cycle of sin and sorrow...chain that can be broken...this curse of mine...*"

I know he hated and resented his father, but since he's barged back into my life, he's shown more enmity toward his mother. His entire purpose behind helping me reclaim my magic has been to bring Arthur back and *dethrone the queen*.

What if the song isn't about Arthur at all?

There's a deep sadness in his eyes as the song finishes and he tells the crowd they have one more for them.

"I love you, Mordred!" some girl in the crowd screams during the lull.

My eyes seek her out, and I'm pretty sure it's the same girl with the black and blue hair from the band's first show at the Stone Crow.

Has she been at every single one of his shows in the city? Has she followed them their entire tour? Does she tell him she loves him at every gig? How many times has Mordred signed her tits?

When Willow elbows me in the ribs, I realize I'm scowling. I quickly clear my throat and turn back to the stage. Mordred is staring at me as Ava begins their final song with a drum solo, his lips twitching at the corner. I couldn't have possibly been any more obvious.

I'm not used to all this jealousy and possessiveness I feel toward Mordred.

Maybe he was right.

My hate did turn into obsession.

Halfway through the next song, that's only confirmed by my reaction to Will grabbing Mordred's ass as they switch places on stage. Everything around me turns a little red as the crowd goes wild. It's clearly a publicity stunt, but it has me wondering if the two of them have ever hooked up.

It wouldn't be suspicious if a bolt of lightning came down from the ceiling and struck Will clear off the stage, would it?

Fuck. As much as I claimed Mordred was mine, he can't be. Even if my demons are begging for a taste of Will's blood...

I know I can't stay until the band leaves the stage. I don't think I'd be able to say a proper goodbye to Mordred. There's a piece of me that's glad he left in the middle of the night so I wouldn't have to figure out how to tell him.

As the last song nears its end, I lean over to tell Willow I'm going to go ahead and leave, having to speak loudly over the music. She looks at me, offers a sad, understanding smile, and nods.

I turn back to the stage one last time, and my eyes lock with Mordred's. Either he heard me or he simply senses what I have to do because there are deep frown lines on his face.

I give him the best smile I can muster and mouth the words, "Goodbye, Mordred."

Even from a distance, I can see my dark purple mark on his throat as his Adam's apple bobs with a swallow.

The music fades out as I turn and head through the bar. Cool air nips at my face as I walk outside, the noise of the crowd dying as the door shuts behind me. I start heading toward the subway, though I have no plans on taking it. I'll stroll around for a bit before using magic to take myself home and finish packing up my things.

I know Mordred won't seek me out tonight.

It wasn't a proper goodbye, but it's all I have in me.

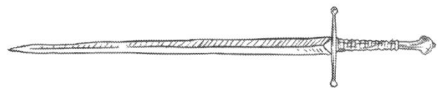

"Please, Mordred."

There's a hard surface at my back, a warm breath against my throat, a wet tongue gliding across my skin, a hard bulge grinding against mine.

The sharp sting of teeth.

The cry that rips from my throat.

Like last time, everything but Mordred is a little blurred out, though it's not as drastic this time. I can make out a little of what seems to be a hotel room.

"What do you want, darling?"

Mordred's voice holds a blend of that scratchiness after his shows and the deep huskiness of desire.

"Please fuck me."

I wake with a start, jolting up in bed.

My body is covered in a thin sheen of sweat, and my cock is rock hard, my boxers tight. I crash back down on the pillows, breathing heavily. I don't bother escaping the bed and running to the shower to wash the vision off of me like last time.

Besides, I'm certain this time it was a dream and not a premonition because there's no way *this* one is happening.

I already said goodbye.

And I *don't* beg.

20

MORDRED

It's been ten days since we left the city. Ten days since I last saw Merlin. For all I know, he's already back in Camelot.

The rest of the band and I have been making our way back home to LA, stopping along our route for the few remaining gigs of the last leg of our tour. We've had shows in Philly, Cincinnati, St. Louis, OKC, Albuquerque, and Flagstaff. Tonight, we're in Vegas for our last show before we make the final drive home tomorrow.

I'm not as eager to return home as I was a few weeks ago.

Lights from the Strip are nearly blinding as Anthony drives us in the van from our hotel to the venue, weaving his way through Friday night traffic. I sit in the back with Will, the silence in the vehicle stifling.

According to Ava, my brooding has been worse than ever since we left New York and I'm an absolute nightmare to be around.

I don't understand why she thinks that. I haven't been any different than before.

I *haven't*.

Sure, I've been spending most of our time in the tour bus not speaking to anyone, but that's only because I've been diligently working on that new song that's been plaguing me for weeks. I think it's just about finished. It turned out a bit different than I originally intended, but...it works. Really fucking well. It's *good*.

I'll share it with the others when we get back home, and maybe they'll forgive me.

Besides, Ava doesn't get it. Willow calls her every single day, *multiple* times a day. I haven't spoken to Merlin in ten days. Not that there's anything between us like what Ava and Willow seem to have...

No, fuck it.

I don't have the same denial issues as he does, so I can admit it.

I miss him.

When he showed up at our last gig in the city and said goodbye to me from the crowd, I knew that was it. He didn't want to see me again. Even if I had been tempted to see him my last night there, I don't know if my pride at always being the one to chase him down would've been enough to stop me. He did that with his silent goodbye.

Chances are he's already gone back to Camelot, and I'll never see him again.

Which is absolutely, one-hundred percent for the best.

Despite my high number of sexual partners, I've never had a legitimate relationship. Why would I want one when I'd just have to watch that person grow old and die? I've had some regular fuck buddies, but nothing more. Even when there's been the rare man or woman I started to form any kind of emotional attachment to, I always let them go because being with an immortal who never lets himself age wouldn't be fair to them.

I've lived my life avoiding the fear of losing people by never letting myself have anyone to lose.

Except, now...I feel that loss I've always evaded.

And that's exactly why it's best I never see Merlin again. He'll only ever hate me.

Anthony pulls up outside the bar we're playing at, parks the van, and we all hop out. While he goes inside to check us in, the rest of us go ahead and start unloading the equipment.

"I think I'm going to miss touring," Will says as he carefully sets his guitar case down. "But I'm excited to finally be home for a while."

"It's our last show." Ava lets out a wistful sigh, then gives me a pointed stare. "Let's make it a good one. Yeah?"

"What's that supposed to mean?" I ask. "I'm fine."

"Say it another hundred times, and I might believe it."

I can't stop my mouth from forming a grumpy pout. "I haven't said it that much."

"You're right. Probably more." Will snickers but stops abruptly when I narrow my eyes at him. "Look, man. It's perfectly okay if you're not fine. We could all tell there was something between the two of you."

There's a little less jealousy in his voice than when the topic of Merlin has come up before, which I'm grateful for.

I may have loved corrupting Merlin, but I could never do that to Will.

"Trust me, there was nothing but hate."

"Tell yourself whatever you need to, buttercup," Ava says. "Just don't let it ruin our last show."

"Have I ruined any of our last few?"

She shrugs. "Not really. Maybe it's not noticeable to the crowds watching, but the rest of us can tell you're different up there lately. Not *bad*. Nothing like that one a couple of weeks ago," she adds with a grimace. "But...I don't know. It's like you've lost a little of your spirit, that middle finger to the world you always used to throw up. If you'd ever actually open up and talk to us, maybe we could help."

"There's nothing to talk about. I swear. I'm *fine*."

Ava takes a step forward, the light from the street hitting her electric blue and neon pink striped leggings. She places a hand on my arm and gives me a sympathetic smile. "You like to pretend you feel nothing, Mordred. The truth is, I think you feel too much, and pretending you don't is just easier."

My lips part, but no noise comes out.

Here's another fucking reason I don't get close to anyone. Spend too much time with someone, and they'll start to see right through you and call you on your shit.

No.

She's wrong.

I don't care.

So much for not being in denial...

The door to the bar opens, and Anthony steps out, saving me from the pain of having to respond to that load of bullshit. He undoes the top button of his brown and teal paisley shirt, making me think it's a little warm inside. He lets us know that we can start hauling our equipment inside and put it all behind the stage while the first band plays, so that's what we do.

Ava's words keep tumbling around in my mind as we stand in the crowd to watch the first band play through their set. Those are the only words I hear, none of the lyrics coming from the singer on stage.

Of course I feel things. I'm not a damn robot.

I admitted I missed Merlin, didn't I? Just because I'd rather not say it out loud to my bandmates doesn't mean I'm pretending.

Just because I keep some secrets doesn't mean I don't live with those demons in the darkest parts of my soul.

I hate that Ava can see them at all.

The first band finishes up their set, and we wait for them to get their equipment off the stage before replacing it with our own.

Somehow, I manage not to fuck up the show even after that bit of scolding on Ava's part. In fact, as though throwing up that middle finger she accused me of having lost touch with, I make sure this is the best damned show we've played all tour.

I let myself *feel*.

Everything.

All my secrets. All my loss. All the little pieces of my soul I've sometimes struggled with blindly.

Merlin.

I find what feels like a new rhythm, a new spirit, and the crowd appears to eat it up, judging by the roaring of the noise in my ears as the last song fades out. My body is covered in sweat, my shirt sticking to me like a second skin beneath my jacket. My ears ring, and my throat feels as though I spent the entire show swallowing gravel.

But I have to admit the adrenaline still pumping through my veins is worth it.

"Now that's what I'm talking about, man!" Will exclaims as soon as we're all outside. He gives me a slap on the back before opening the cab doors.

"Good show, Mordred," Ava agrees with a knowing flash in her eyes.

I flip her the bird and mutter, "There's your fucking middle finger."

She laughs as she and Anthony start loading up her drums. "It was our last show. Should we get drunk tonight to celebrate?"

"Yes!" Will agrees enthusiastically.

"There's a bar at the hotel," Anthony says. "We could drink there so we all can."

They all look at me, probably expecting me to be a buzz-kill like usual. But they don't know just how much of my tired soul that show took from me, how hard it was to lock everything back up tight where it belongs.

I need a fucking drink. Or twelve.

I shrug. "I'm in."

After we finish loading up the van, Anthony drives us back to the hotel. We choose the Lobby Bar because we figure it'll be less crowded than the sports bar or any of the others. It's dimly lit only by the glow from television screens and the golden chandeliers from the lobby. I take a seat on a stool at the bar between Ava and Will, and we all order drinks.

A few shots in, we're all loosened up, having switched to beer, and reminiscing about the tour now that it's officially over. Ava gushes about how much she misses Willow, causing me and the other guys to groan at the sickeningly romantic hearts floating drunkenly in her eyes. But at least none of them mention Merlin again.

"I've been curious about something," Ava says, shaking the hearts away as she turns to her brother on the other side of her. "Where did you sneak off to the night of our last gig in New York? You always stay for drinks, but you left right after the show."

Anthony grimaces and stares down into his beer. "I, uh...might've hooked up."

"With who?" Ava asks incredulously.

"You know that girl who was at like every one of our shows in the city? The one with the black and blue hair?"

Ava's eyes widen comically, and I'm sure if she had any of her drink in her mouth, it would've just spewed out all over the bar. "The one who screamed how much she loves Mordred at every single show?!"

He looks up sheepishly. "That's the one."

Throwing my head back, I let out a loud boom of roaring laughter. I can't help it. I'm drunk, and that's funny as fuck.

"I can't believe you slept with a groupie," Ava says, shaking her head. "You're such a walking cliche, dude."

Will's laughing too as he throws an arm over my shoulders as we cackle drunkenly together. "Can you blame him though?" he asks between snorts. "She was kind of hot. Poor girl just wanted attention, and Mordred wasn't giving it to her."

"Because Mordred is smart enough not to sleep with groupies."

I'm really not, but I was a little too preoccupied with someone else...

"Besides," Ava continues, turning her gaze to me and Will, "how much you want to bet she's going to start stalking—" Her jaw goes slack as her eyes move past us. "Oh shit."

Will and I turn our heads at the same time to see Merlin stalking across the bar.

He's *here*, not in Camelot.

He's no longer wearing turtlenecks considering my marks all over his throat have faded, which makes me mourn. Still, he looks mouthwatering in the regular pine green sweater he's wearing that brings out his russet brown eyes.

Right now, however, those eyes are *dark*.

He marches toward us with purpose, his gaze murderous. Maybe he's finally decided to kill me because he can't bring himself to return to Camelot and leave loose ends behind.

But when Will immediately drops his arm from my shoulders, I think he's translated the truth of that look before I have.

Merlin reaches us, and he grabs onto the collar of my jacket and heaves me to my feet. The room spins as I sway on unsteady, drunken legs. That doesn't stop him as he fists both sides of my jacket, holding me up and dragging me forward before slamming our mouths together.

It's heaven.

The feel of his soft lips moving against mine, his warm tongue demanding entrance, his possessive grip, his hard body all over me. His tongue swirls around the bar in mine, making me moan into his mouth. I don't know if I'm dizzy from the alcohol or the kiss.

When he pulls us apart, I try to chase after him.

I never thought I'd see heaven, and now that I have, I don't want to leave.

"Do you have a room?" he whispers gruffly against my lips.

I realize I haven't opened my eyes, so I force them to flutter open and am greeted by the dark red-brown of his intense stare.

"Yes," I reply breathlessly.

He releases my jacket but throws an arm around my waist to hold me tight against him as he turns to my bandmates. They're all staring with either slack jaws or titillated smirks.

"Hey, Merlin." Will gives him an awkward wave, a peace offering.

Merlin grunts in brusque acknowledgment. "Goodnight, everyone."

Ava's drunken giggles follow us as Merlin hauls me away and out of the bar, giving me zero opportunity to argue or fight to stay put. Not that there's any chance in heaven or hell that would happen.

21

MERLIN

When I saw Will hanging all over Mordred, I nearly lost my shit. The thought that he had moved on so fast from...whatever the fuck it was we had...was like a shot of venom straight to my veins. I've never been a man prone to violence when it wasn't to defend my own or someone else's life, but, right then, I was tempted to send an electrifying jolt of magic through that mortal that would have him lighting up like fireworks on New Year's Eve.

Instead, I settled for staking my claim on Mordred in front of him. Fortunately, I managed to stop myself before I claimed him a little *too* thoroughly and got us both arrested.

I give him barely any slack to allow him to lead us out of the bar and across the lobby, not wanting to let him go. We get on the elevator for one of the royal towers, and he presses the button for the sixteenth floor. Unfortunately, there are other people on the lift with us, so I have to wait to ravage him.

We get a few odd stares, but I'm not surprised. We make quite the strange couple. I may only look ten years older than him instead of two hundred, but while I'm wearing a respectable pair of blue jeans and a nice sweater, Mordred's in all black—black nails, black tattoos on the backs of his hands, his black hair disheveled from his show.

The last two people with us exit the elevator on the tenth floor, and once the doors close again, I back Mordred up against the wall and seal my mouth to his again. He smells like incense and sweat and tastes like alcohol—and, yet, it's *him* that's intoxicating.

When I'm forced to come up for air, my lips travel down, feathering light kisses over his jaw to his throat. His skin rumbles beneath my mouth with each whimper and moan.

"Will is in love with you," I growl before biting into his flesh.

"He only thinks he is."

"Why do you say that?"

Mordred fists the front of my sweater in both hands and turns us until it's my back against the wall. I groan because... *fuck yes*. This is exactly how I need him.

"Because he doesn't know me," he growls back, his eyes a little glassy, but his stare no less intense. "Not really." He rolls his hips, grinding his growing erection against mine. "But I fucking love that you're jealous, darling."

"I'm not jealous."

The corners of his lips pull up in that smirk of his I love. I mean hate.

"Deny, deny, deny." He punctuates each word with a thrust.

The elevator dings, and I shove Mordred backward as soon as the doors open, causing him to stumble out into the hall.

I exit after him, and after a quick glance around to make sure we're alone, I wrap my hand around his throat. "Fine. I'm jealous. You're mine, and I'm not fucking done with you." I kiss him fast and hard. "Room. Now."

As soon as I release him, he nearly trips over his own feet as he turns and starts heading down the hallway. I walk behind him, my gaze fixed firmly on his ass, only looking up when he uses his key card to open the door to his room.

He lets me in first, and when I step inside, I'm drawn to the window on the opposite side of the room. I stroll past the king-size bed to look out at the view of the rotunda outside, the castle turrets with their red and blue and gold spires.

"Did you think you were being funny when you booked your rooms here?" I ask, peering at him over my shoulder with a grin.

He's leaning against the door, bottom lip between his teeth. "Maybe I was leaving you a clue in case you wanted to find me. Looks like it worked."

All I can do is shake my head because I'd rather not let him know that I was at his show tonight, shielding and concealing my magic so he couldn't sense me, then followed him back here to the Excalibur Hotel.

I turn back to the window, staring out at the castle lit up beneath the night sky and thinking back to his performance tonight, how it was somehow different from the others. It was like he had a fresh spark, a renewed vigor. It had me fighting against an erection from where I stood at the very back of the venue. And then when I saw him with Will at the bar, the thought that Mordred's fire had been stoked by someone else had me losing control enough to claim him in front of everyone.

"Why are you here, Merlin?"

Why am I here? Because I haven't been able to stop thinking about him, because he's like a virus in my bloodstream, a fucking parasite in my brain, the goddamn bug that crawled beneath my skin.

"I wanted to ask you something," I say, still staring out the window.

"If you shoving your tongue down my throat was the question, the answer is fuck yes."

I can't stop the twitch at the corner of my mouth, but I school my expression when I turn to face him. "Your song, 'Sins of the Father,' isn't about Arthur, is it?"

He's still leaning against the door, arms folded across his chest. He stares at me in silence for a moment before shaking his head.

"It's about Morgan."

It's not a question, so he doesn't give an answer this time.

The phrase "sins of the father" simply means generational sin, but when I first heard it, it was easy to assume he meant it literally with how much I knew he hated Arthur. Now I realize he holds even more contempt for his mother.

Moving across the room, I stop several feet in front of him. "Give me something, Mordred. Because the song, the tattoo..." I sigh and frown. "Do you regret it?"

He scoffs as he removes his jacket and tosses it over a chair. "Still looking for good where it doesn't exist, I see."

Maybe he's right. Maybe asking again, *hoping* again, was just a waste of my time. But...

"What else am I supposed to think?"

"That I hate my father and mother both. Because that's the truth. There's no deeper meaning to anything. What you see is what you get."

"What I see is a man who's still determined to rebel against his parents even after a thousand years, who's searching for a freedom he won't ever truly feel because, in truth, he's just lost."

Mordred's jaw ticks with a scowl. "Rock star was the perfect career choice then, wasn't it?"

I return his glare and take a step toward him.

He mirrors my movements as he retreats, like he's afraid of me again. "I guess I'm just a cliche after all. Except maybe for the lack of drugs besides the occasional weed," he says as he goes off on a rant to steer away from the true topic. "The hard stuff kind of loses its appeal quickly for an immortal. Not that you'd know anything about that, would you? Boring, straight-laced Merlin, always—"

I cut off his rambling with a hand around his throat as soon as his back meets the door once more. "Shut up."

Eyes still a little glassy like an iced-over sea stare back at me. His chest heaves, and I can't tell if his rapid breathing is from fear or lust.

"I can't give you what you want, Merlin. You can't save me. You can't redeem me. I killed my father, and I don't regret it. I'll *never* regret it. So if that's what this is all about—"

"I said *shut up.*"

Then I crash my lips against his. Because, at least for right now, I don't care.

Despite what he says, there *is* something deeper. He may not feel regret or guilt or shame, but he feels *something*. I may not know what it is, but I can see it, sense it. I still refuse to use dark magic to break my way into his mind to seek it out, and I can't stop him from keeping his secrets, as much as I wish he'd share them.

But, right now, it doesn't matter. Because he's still everything I loathe. I still hate him. And that's all *I* need to feel.

"I'm still a little drunk," he admits when I pull back to let him breathe, kissing up his jaw. I nip his ear, and he gasps. "Are you planning on taking advantage of me?"

"I was actually hoping you'd take advantage of *me.*"

He strikes like a snake, his hand wrapping around my wrist and yanking my hand away from his throat. Spinning me around, he twists my arm behind my back and presses my chest against the door, my other hand slapping against the surface to try to catch myself. I groan as he thrusts forward, his erection grinding against my ass through our jeans.

"Does that mean you're ready to beg, Merlin?" he growls into my ear.

I didn't want to beg. I planned on never giving into him. But that first dream I had the night I said goodbye wasn't the last, and the concerning part is I think they really were *dreams* and not premonitions.

And I haven't been able to get any of them out of my damn head.

"Please, Mordred."

"What do you want, darling?"

My front is pressed against the hard surface of the door, not my back like in that vision.

None of those visions were premonitions.

They were dreams.

This wasn't destined to happen. *I* made this happen. Because I *want* it.

"Please fuck me."

"Fuck yes."

He thrusts against my ass again. Still holding my arm behind my back, he brings his other hand up to thread into my hair. He grips it tight and yanks my head back.

"You're going to have to beg a hell of a lot more than that though for making me wait."

I didn't want to beg at all, but now that I have...

"Mordred, please," I groan as he bites the soft flesh of my ear. "I need to feel you inside me at least once. I need you to fuck me with that pierced cock of yours."

His mouth travels down the side of my neck, his warm lips and tongue feathering against my heated skin before he sinks his teeth into my throat, making me whimper.

"I need you to fill me with your cum," I continue, voice ragged and strained. "I need you to mark me. I need you to make me hate myself as much as I hate you. So that I never forget why I had to leave." A choked sob escapes me as he finds an unmarked spot on my throat to latch onto. "And why I can't keep you."

A growl rumbles from deep in his throat, and he bites down harder, sucking on my tender skin more viciously. The grips he has on my wrist and my hair both tighten, his hold and his touches all turning harsher, rougher, making me wonder just what kind of effect my words had on him.

"I don't want you to hate yourself, Merlin," he says once he's released his teeth and rests his forehead against my temple.

The clothes between us suddenly disappear. We stand there naked, skin against skin. He rolls his hips, slowly and sensually, his cock slipping against the crease of my ass until I lose the ability to breathe.

When he speaks again, it's just as husky and full of lust as before, but this time, I think there's a hint of resignation too.

"But I'll give you whatever it is you need, darling."

22

MORDRED

"I *need you to make me hate myself as much as I hate you.*"

That's his reason for finally giving in and begging me to fuck him?

Fuck, that pisses me the fuck off.

But if that's what he truly wants, then I'll make sure to do a thorough and effective job.

"Tell me what you want me to do to you." I grab his other wrist and bring it back to join his other one behind him, pressing him harder against the door. "You want me to tie you up? Hurt you?"

He moans as I thrust my cock in the crease of his ass. "Do whatever you want to me."

"Are you sure it's wise to give me free rein over your body, Merlin? You should know I have very few limits."

Tensing slightly against me, he asks in a quiet voice, "And if I ask you to stop?"

"Then I'll stop," I tell him honestly. "I'm careful with my possessions."

His taut muscles relax again, and he groans as he repeats himself. "Then do whatever you want to me."

It doesn't matter that Merlin isn't keen on the idea of no limits. As much as he wants to hate me and hate himself, I have no desire to break him, and "stop" is as good a safeword as anything else. The fact that he doesn't want to pretend not to want this, to want *me*, has me even hotter, a tendril of heat wrapping around the base of my spine.

"As you wish, darling," I growl in his ear before hauling him back by his wrists, twisting them higher up his back until he cries out.

The sound goes straight to my dick, making it jerk against his ass like it's got its sights set on the finish line and it's going for the gold.

Patience.

I've got a lot of playing to do first.

Spinning Merlin around, I push him toward the bed. I let go of his wrists and press my palm between his shoulder blades, shoving him down so he's forced to catch himself with his hands on the bed.

A moment later, the sound of hissing joins our heavy breathing.

Merlin looks up at the head of the bed. His breathing ceases, his body going rigid beneath my hand still on his back. Two black snakes weave their way over the top of the wooden headboard, their tails curled around the corners.

"Mordred…" His voice trembles with just a hint of trepidation, maybe a little anger. He struggles against my hand, but I continue to hold him down.

The twin snakes' black scales shimmer with a blue and purple iridescence—similar to the oil slick ribbon I used to follow Merlin back in New York—as they hiss and slither down the bed toward him.

"Relax, darling," I purr. "The only teeth you have to worry about are mine."

The snakes strike, wrapping around his wrists and dragging them toward the head of the bed, causing the top half of his body to crash down on the mattress, his chest flat on the sheets and his ass raised deliciously in the air. As he struggles against the slithering beasts, I drop to my knees.

"Really, Mordred? Fucking snakes of all—*oh fuuuck*."

It feels good to be the one shutting *him* up for a change as my tongue swipes a straight line up from his balls to his hole. He bucks against my face as I part his cheeks and dive in even deeper, my tongue swirling around his rim before pushing inside.

I'm feral for him, the taste of him, the feel of him.

"Fuck, Mordred," he moans, sounding damn near delirious with pleasure.

I guess he's forgotten all about the snakes...

Pulling out of him, I replace my tongue with a finger, my saliva magically turning to lube. My mouth wanders over to his left ass cheek, and I sink my teeth into the meaty flesh. Merlin lets out a choked sob before his hisses join those of the snakes.

My cock is so fucking hard and leaking, but I ignore it. If I touch it now, I'll come before I can even get inside him.

As I add a second finger, I move over to his other cheek and bite there next. I reach between his legs and grab onto his cock, his hard length pulsing in my grasp as I swipe my thumb over his slit and use his precum to slick his shaft. He moves his hips as I stroke him, grinding into my hand and fucking himself on my fingers as he lets out quiet moans and curses. I bite him harder, and the noises out of his mouth grow louder.

Releasing my teeth, I lick over the deep purple marks in his ass and shove a third finger inside him, pumping them in deep.

"Fuck, I can't wait to fill this ass."

"Then get on with it," he groans, still rolling his hips.

I growl as I squeeze the base of his dick, showing him he's not the one with the power right now. With how much he edged me last time, I should torture him more, draw this out until he's begging with tears in his eyes. But the truth is, it's *me* who enjoys that kind of torment, and I loved that more than I'll admit.

Removing my fingers and releasing his cock, I stand up and stare down at my marks on his ass as he squirms. I exhale a satisfied breath before smacking his ass hard, causing him to cry out and pitch forward.

"Get on the bed," I demand.

The snakes tug at his wrists, offering him no slack as they haul him forward until he's forced to place his knees on the mattress and crawl forward. The black serpents remain drawn tight, keeping his arms taut and the top half of his body down on the bed.

I climb up, settling between his legs behind him and taking a cheek in each of my hands, kneading them roughly. Lowering my head, I gather spit in my mouth and let it dribble down onto my dick where it once again turns to lube. I let go of one of his cheeks to slick myself with it, then line my cock up with his hole. I don't move further, remaining still, breathing heavily.

Merlin raises his head and turns to peer at me over his shoulder. "What are you doing?"

I meet his darkened gaze with my own and smirk. "I think I want you to beg some more."

With a grunt, he buries his face in the sheets. His curses are muffled, but I'm pretty sure I catch the words, "I hate you so fucking much."

He tries to push back on my cock, and I smack his ass again.

"Fuck! Please, Mordred! Fuck, I need you!"

The sincerity and desperation in his voice sends another wave of heat down my spine and has me nearly coming undone.

"You have me, Merlin."

I start to push inside him, slow and gentle at first. Our moans fill the room once my crown slips past that ring of muscle. I give him barely two seconds to adjust before I'm thrusting the rest of the way inside his tight, welcoming heat.

"Fuck," I grunt as I lean forward and rest my forehead against the back of his neck. "Fuck, Merlin. If I knew you'd feel like this, I wouldn't have made you beg."

He says nothing. His only response is to roll his hips forward and then back, trying to fuck himself on my cock. When I grip his hips tight to keep him from moving, he huffs.

"*Please* move," he pleads.

"Hmm. Unless you like to beg after all?"

He whimpers.

"Go ahead. Beg all you'd like. You want to really hate yourself? Beg me for my cock. Beg me to fuck you hard and without mercy."

"Yes. Please. Fuck me hard, Mordred. Don't hold back."

"Fuck, you're perfect like this."

I pull back, nearly all the way out, then snap my hips forward.

"Fuck!" Merlin cries out breathlessly. "More. Please."

I chuckle darkly. "Did you think that was all I was going to give you? Hold on, darling."

Tightening my grip on his hips, I pull back and slam into him harder than before, setting a brutal, relentless rhythm as I pound into him over and over.

His arms are still pulled taut above his head, the snakes slowly slithering up his forearms, his biceps, creeping their way up to his shoulders. Their mouths open wide, teeth glistening. The moment they strike, driving their teeth into the crooks of his neck and shoulders on either side, I bite down on the back of his right shoulder.

Merlin's ass clenches tight around my cock, blacking out my vision, as he releases a deep scream into the sheets.

"You...you said they wouldn't bite," he chokes out, voice pained.

I let him go and lick across my own bite mark. "They couldn't help themselves, Merlin. You're just too fucking delicious."

I didn't make him bleed, but as the snakes release their teeth, small, gleaming droplets of crimson blood drip from the puncture holes on both sides of his neck. Licking my way up, I capture them on my tongue, groaning at the metallic taste.

"Do you want to tell me to stop?"

He shakes his head weakly. "No. Please don't."

Either he really is determined to hate us both as much as possible, or he actually enjoys my ruthlessness.

I hope it's the latter.

As the snakes slink back down his arms to his wrists, I wrap my hand around his throat from behind and haul him up on his knees until his back is pressed against my front.

"Tell me how it feels, Merlin," I growl in his ear as I let my other hand roam over his chest, his abs, and back up where I pinch one of his nipples, rolling the hard bud between my fingers. "Tell me how it feels to have me fucking you."

"So good," he croaks as he leans his head back on my shoulder. "So fucking good. So full. Your piercings are—*fuck*."

"Hitting that magical little spot inside you?"

"Yes. Fucking love it."

The snakes still have his arms pulled in front of him with barely any slack, holding them stretched out so he's not able to grab his cock that bobs in front of him, red and leaking and longing to be touched.

"Do you want to come, darling?"

"Yes. Please. Fuck, please touch me. Make me come."

I don't even have to tell him to beg at this point. He does it all on his own, and he does it so beautifully.

"Wouldn't you hate yourself more if I didn't?" I taunt, never slowing my fast, rough thrusts. "If I leave you unsatisfied with the knowledge that I only fucking used you?"

"No." He sobs, shaking his head weakly where it sways on my shoulder. "Please, Mordred. Please let me come."

With my hand that's not around his throat, I give his other nipple a quick pinch before reaching around him and gripping his hard length. It throbs in my hand as I use his precum to slick his shaft. He moans as he meets me thrust for thrust, fucking into my hand.

"That's it, Merlin. Fuck, you take me so well. You were fucking made for my cock. Now come for me, darling."

As though my words trigger his orgasm, like he's just dying to obey my demands, his release shoots out of him, warm jets of silky cum making a mess of my hand and the sheets. The muscles in his ass spasm around my cock, and I growl into the crook of his neck and shoulder.

I continue to stroke him through the waves of his climax until he's hissing and whimpering. Releasing him, I bring my hand to his face, tracing his lips with my cum-coated fingers. He opens up for me, sucking them sensually into his mouth, tasting, slurping, swallowing down the evidence of his own pleasure.

The feel of his tongue swirling around my fingers and his enthusiasm at completely cleaning my fingers of his mess has me barreling over the edge into an abyss of pure ecstasy.

My hips still, and I bite down on his shoulder again as I pump deep inside of him, spurt after spurt filling him until I think it'll never stop.

When it finally does, I realize Merlin is shaking, his body trembling against me.

"Fuck," I mutter as I slowly pull out of him, immediately missing the tight heat of his ass.

The snakes recoil, slithering off his wrists and back up the bed where they disappear behind the headboard with fading hisses.

After magicking away Merlin's cum from the sheets, I lower him gently to his stomach. I mean to check on him but get distracted by the sight of my cum dripping from his ass. Groaning, I grab his cheeks, splitting him open before diving in, spearing him with my tongue and lapping up my own flavor. Merlin squirms beneath me, unintelligible noises muffled in the sheets.

I go at him for not as long as I'd like, his grumbling turning pained from overstimulation. He's had enough before I have, but I decide to show him a little mercy.

Flopping onto the bed next to him on my side, I roll him over so he's facing me. "Are you okay?"

It takes a moment for his eyes to focus, but when they do, he answers, "Better than."

The blissed-out smile on his face goes straight to something inside my chest. It can't possibly be my heart since that thing hasn't worked right in ages, but...it's *something*. A kind of fullness, almost a pleasurable ache.

"Does that mean I failed?" I asked with a smirk.

He sighs contentedly. "I don't know yet."

"I'll ask again when you're not cum drunk."

The laughter that comes bubbling out of him next has that blasted, beating organ damn near stopping to the point that if I was mortal, I wonder if I'd be flatlining right now. I can feel the rumble of the sound in my bones, sending tingles all the way down to my toes.

For several seconds, I hold my breath and stare into his eyes, his own brighter than I've ever seen them.

Before I can stop myself, I blurt out, "I want to show you something."

When I inch forward, leaning my head toward his, he pulls back, that happy, bright expression in his eyes replaced by something closer to panic.

"I'm not invading your mind again," I tell him truthfully. "I'm letting you inside mine."

His gaze softens, though there's still apprehension there.

However, this time, he lets me move in closer, resting my forehead against his to show him a piece of my soul I've kept locked up tight for a thousand years.

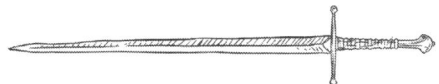

Over a thousand years ago.

I was told I've been unconscious for nearly a sennight. The excruciating pain I feel upon waking makes that difficult to believe. After seven days, should it really be hurting this badly?

Then again, I'm alive, so I guess I can't complain too much.

I wasn't afraid to die. In fact, I was prepared for it, ready to greet death with open arms after I had succeeded in stealing Arthur's life from him. But since that didn't happen, it's time to claim what my mother promised me.

The crown is mine.

As soon as the physician is confident that I'm no longer knocking on death's door, he releases me from his care with a few vials of salves and herbs and orders me to rest in my chambers.

Fuck that.

I'll rest on my throne.

I don the same chainmail I had been wearing during the battle—ruined and stained with my blood—and strap my sword around my waist, a mark of my victory, Arthur's blood still on the blade.

Every step I take to the throne room is agonizing, sharp pains and dull aches threatening to bring me to my knees. I hold onto my side as though that can staunch the unpleasant throbbing of my wound.

But the injury from Excalibur is nothing compared to the knife stabbed in my back when I enter the grand hall.

Morgan le Fay sits on the throne.

My throne.

A twisted crown of vines and thorns dipped in gold and encrusted with black and red jewels rests on top of her head over long, flowing, wavy black hair. When her gaze finds me, the sickly sweet smile she gives me is just as twisted as her crown.

"Everyone out," she says to the few knights standing in the room with us.

They move to obey. I only recognize one—Sir Gawain, my older half brother, Morgan's other son. He gives me a look of loathing and utter contempt as he brushes past me toward the double doors of the hall. He always hated me, but I thought he hated our mother more.

I guess I was wrong about a lot of things.

The moment the doors close behind me, I take a step forward, trying not to grimace from the pain, not wanting to show any sign of weakness.

"What the hell is this?" My roaring voice echoes off the stone walls.

"I'm the new queen of Camelot," my mother answers as though that should've been obvious.

It is, but that's not what I meant.

"You promised me the crown!"

"Yes, and you believed me." She tilts her head, her blood red lips pulling down into a frown of faux sympathy that mars her usually beautiful, pale face. "You played your role so perfectly. I should thank you."

I take another step. "You—"

"Careful, Mordred." She holds up a hand, her narrow fingers adorned with elegant rings, probably the previous Queen of Camelot's jewels. "You're in no state to fight me— not that you ever have been. You know what I'll do to you if you try. Do you need a reminder?"

No.

I don't get the chance to speak the word before everything goes black. I think I drop to my knees, but I can't be certain because the darkness that descends all around me presses against me on all sides like a solid wall. The weight of it is crushing, suffocating.

I can't move. I can't breathe.

Do I even exist?

Does *anything* but this darkness exist?

I'm not sure how long it lasts, but even two seconds of it is more than I can bear.

Finally, mercifully, it lifts.

I suck in a deep, ragged gasp and blink back tears. When I peer up, Morgan stands before me.

"Did you know I could keep you in the dark forever, Mordred?" Her voice is like silver and poisoned honey. She reaches out with deceptive gentleness to brush a strand of hair from my forehead that's damp with sweat—from the pain, the fear of the dark, or both. "And I will if you dare defy me."

Still panting, I choke out, "I'm your *son*."

She laughs, the sound like cursed bells sending chills down my spine.

When she whirls around, her black gown swishes behind her. She returns to the throne, reclaims her seat, and pins her piercing, cold gray eyes on me. "You were my son for one reason and one reason only. And now you've served your purpose."

I shake my head, refusing to believe what I'm hearing.

Morgan leans forward, all traces of pretense gone, any ounce of her motherly facade I once knew vanished. "The only reason you were born, the whole purpose for your existence, was to kill Arthur, to remove the obstacle in my way so I could sit on this throne."

I can't breathe again, but this time, it isn't because of the darkness.

Fuck, I think I'd rather go back to the dark.

"You're dismissed, Mordred," she snaps brusquely, leaning back once more.

Standing, my legs nearly give out from under me. When I glance down, I see a drop of blood drip from my side and splash onto the stone floor by my feet.

"You're welcome to stay and serve as one of my knights, but if you give me *any* reason, no matter how small, you will be banished from the kingdom. Is that clear?"

"Yes, *Your Grace*." I spit the words, my jaw clenched so tight I fear the bone might fracture.

Turning on my heels, I limp across the room and throw the doors open with what little strength I possess.

I shouldn't stay. I don't *want* to stay.

But I killed my father. Surely I can find a way to slaughter my mother too?

If I can't, if I'm not strong enough, I'll just run away like Merlin did.

23

MERLIN

ordred passed out right after sharing that memory with me. It could've been physical exhaustion from his vigorous fucking, mental fatigue from all the magic he used tonight, emotional drain from the memory, or a mix of all of it. It could've just as easily been an excuse to avoid the conversation we needed to have afterwards.

Either way, I let him sleep. Mainly because I need to process everything before I'd even know *what* to say to him.

For at least an hour, I lie awake on my side, facing him and feeling a bit like a creep as I watch him sleep. I can't help it. He looks so damn peaceful, despite the memory he just relived.

I could *feel* what he felt.

It wasn't just the physical pain from the wound caused by Excalibur or the suffocating dark magic that Morgan enveloped him in that I could feel. It was the betrayal and the hurt, bitterness and disappointment.

His father rejected him.

His mother manipulated and used him.

He only ever wanted at least one parent's love and approval, but they both let him down.

I could have guessed that Arthur's treatment of him contributed to his reasons for ultimately killing him, but I didn't know the whole story. I didn't know just how much it meant to him because he hid those feelings so well.

A thousand years later, he *still* hides it so well.

Watching him sleep, it's easy to believe he doesn't have a single care in the world.

I like him like this, and I could watch him sleep forever.

It's not until I turn away from him to lie on my other side that I'm finally able to fall asleep myself.

Some hours later, I'm awakened by movement, a slight rocking of the bed, rustling of sheets, and something hard rubbing against my bare ass.

My eyes blink open, and I can tell it must be early morning judging by the faint light trickling in around the edges of the blackout curtains.

Behind me, Mordred lets out quiet sighs and moans as he continues rubbing his erection against me. His arm is draped over me, his hand resting on my chest. I'm not sure if he's awake or still sleeping, so I don't stop him. I'm tempted to reach back and guide his dick to my hole because my own is starting to thicken, but before I can, he stills.

"Merlin?" His voice is deep and groggy.

The knowledge that he was definitely humping me in his sleep makes me grin. "Were you dreaming I was someone else? Because I might be just a little offended if you were."

More like fucking enraged.

I'd probably have to let my demons out to play to show him who he belongs to.

"No." He shakes his head as he buries his face in the back of my shoulder, muffling his next words. But I hear them clearly. "I don't want anyone but you."

There's a flutter in my chest, and I wonder if he can feel it beneath his hand.

Fuck. I don't want anyone but him either.

When the fuck did that happen?

I take a breath and hold it. "Come with me then."

He stops breathing too, his body freezing against my back.

"I sold the shop," I tell him. "I have to be out at the end of next week. You have time to think about it? You don't have to decide right now."

Finally, he scoffs like he thinks I'm joking. The heat of his body is taken away as he rolls onto his back, giving me the room to turn over onto my other side and see him staring up at the ceiling. The lack of a tent in the sheets must mean his erection has faded.

"Right. I'm going to leave my life here to return to a place I left eight-hundred years ago with a man who hates my very existence. Face my father, who—" He turns his head to glance briefly at me. "—I *murdered*, by the way. In case you've forgotten." Shaking his head, he blows out a breath and looks back to the ceiling. "Who will undoubtedly take his revenge by running me through with Excalibur. Again. Sounds like a great plan, Merlin."

"I wouldn't let him hurt you."

"We both know if I was there and you tried to keep him from his revenge, he wouldn't trust you."

"Morgan manipulated you, Mordred."

He bolts up into a sitting position and glares down at me, his eyes darkening with cruel fury that I've rarely seen in them. "Don't," he snarls. "I didn't show you that memory as some kind of excuse as to why I did the things I did. Did you feel any regret from me? Even after my mother stabbed me in the back, I didn't regret it. I made my own choices, and I own them. You've hoped all this time that I feel even a little guilt for what I did, haven't you? But you didn't feel any of that. Did you?"

I have to swallow an uncomfortable lump that's formed in my throat. Because he's right. He never felt shame for it, and I hoped he had.

"Why did you show it to me then?" I ask.

"To show you why Morgan needs to be stopped. Why I hate her more than I ever hated Arthur. Because you doubted my reasons for wanting you to get your magic back, and now you don't have to. And, yes, you were right. My reasons are selfish. I want that witch to fucking burn."

"Because she betrayed you? Or because she proved to be even a worse mother than Arthur was a father?"

He looks away, his shoulders slumping. "Both."

"And you killed Arthur, why? Because Morgan told you to?"

Seething, he cuts another sharp scowl my way that slices at something inside me. "I gave him a chance to save himself, and he didn't take it."

I think back to all my memories of Camelot, and one stands out. "When you asked him to crown you prince?"

"I wasn't asking him to make me prince, Merlin!" he shouts. "I was asking him to be my *fucking father*!"

Time seems to slow, the silence in the room cut only by the beating of our hearts, Mordred's a rapid, galloping pulse as his eyes widen with every ounce of vulnerability and fear he's tried with all his might to hide. The weight of his words crushes me, crumbling part of the wall I've built around myself in my own attempt to keep Mordred out.

By the time he's tossed the sheets off of him, he's covered himself in a pair of black sweatpants. He starts to scramble off the bed, but I grab firmly onto his arm to prevent him from leaving.

Maybe I shouldn't push him further than I already have, but it's time I stop letting him escape, even as he struggles against me to do exactly that.

"Let me go! I want you to leave!"

"Fuck that," I growl as I haul him back onto the bed, throwing the covers off so that I can sit up and straddle his waist, not bothering with clothes. I grab his wrists and slam them down on the pillow on either side of his head.

He bucks beneath me, still fighting. "Get off me!"

"Why? Because you're finally telling the truth? Stop fucking hiding from me!"

"No," he says as the fight bleeds out of him, at least the physical one. He still glares up at me from where I have him pinned. "Because all you'll see is what you *want* to see—a hurt little boy rejected by his father—and you'll want to try to use that to absolve me of my sins. But that's not fucking possible!"

"You're right. It's not. Because you're not a good person, Mordred. Trust me, I'm not blind to that fact. You murdered your own father. There are no excuses for that. Even though Arthur turned his back on you and Morgan manipulated you, those facts don't justify your actions. But they are your *reasons*."

"Yeah, and you didn't help."

My brows pinch. "What is that supposed to mean?"

"Nothing."

When he turns his face away, I let go of one of his wrists to grab him by the jaw, turning him back to me. The wetness gathering in his eyes, making them look even more like oceans, guts me. I lean forward and ease my grip but don't let go.

"*Stop. Hiding.*"

"Arthur trusted you," he says, voice choked with emotion. "He respected you. You could have...you could've convinced him to give me a chance."

I release him and rock back on my heels as though he struck me. The tension leaves my body, replaced by a different kind of tightness in my chest as my past words return to me.

"You have no obligation to claim him as your son considering the deceit that brought him into existence..."

While I *did* try to get Arthur to treat him better, I allowed him excuse after excuse to not see Mordred as his son. I could have tried harder. Whether or not it would have made a difference, I guess I'll never know.

"You're right."

He looks away from me again, but I let go of his other wrist to use both hands to grab each side of his face to force him to look up at me.

Leaning down close again, my words whisper against his mouth as I say, "I'm sorry."

He shakes his head, the move slight as he remains trapped between my hands. "Don't do that. This is why I didn't want to tell you any of this. You and Morgan and Arthur, you may have all played your part, but that victory was *mine*."

I wince at his choice of words. "Does that mean you want the credit or the blame?"

His jaw ticks beneath my hands. "Both."

My grip on him tightens. "So determined to cling to my hatred."

His hands move between us, his palms flat on my stomach. They move up my abs, my chest, his black nails scraping along my flesh. He digs his thumbs in where my neck meets my shoulders, the shooting pangs reminding me of where his snakes had their teeth and making me hiss just like they had.

"I've asked and wanted nothing more from you," he snarls as he presses harder against the bite marks.

I growl against the pain and release the sides of his face to hit his arms away. Both my hands return to grab him, but this time, it's around his throat. The moment I give a light squeeze, his cock twitches against mine. I realize I'm semi-hard too, probably since he reminded me of the snakes, of how he used them to restrain me last night. Truthfully, I didn't mind any of it.

"Nothing?" I ask, my voice just as harsh as his.

He stares up at me, his eyes still slightly wet. I could give him nothing if that's what he truly wanted, but with one word out of his mouth, I'd give him more. Because as much as I've been trying to fight it, there *is* more than just hate. I still don't know what to call it, but it's…*more*.

Seconds later, with his jaw set, he replies, "Nothing."

That ache in my chest returns, and I release him with a nod. "Fine."

I move to get off him, but he grabs onto my arm before I can. For a moment, I remain still and refuse to look back down at him, afraid of what he might see in my eyes. A thousand years ago, I trusted him with the king, with my best friend. I should have known better than to trust him with anything else of mine.

"Merlin."

There's a crack in his voice, a fracture that mirrors the one inside me, that has me finally peering back at him. However, I manage to disguise my true feelings with every ounce of the loathing he *wants* me to feel for him.

I don't know if it's that look in my eyes that does it or the touch of our bodies from where I'm still straddling him, but his cock fills out more. He thrusts his hips up, grinding his growing erection against mine and letting out a soft moan that I'm tempted to bottle up and wear around my neck like a keepsake.

"You said it yourself, Merlin," he whispers, voice turning breathless beneath me. "You can't keep me. But you can remind me of your hate one last time before you go."

24

MORDRED

Merlin flips me onto my stomach like I'm nothing more than a fucking rag doll, divesting me of the sweats in the blink of an eye. His weight pins against my back, pressing me into the mattress and stealing what little breath I had left.

"I shouldn't give you what you want." His warm breath ghosts across my ear, causing perspiration to bead at the back of my neck as he ruts his hard length against my ass. "But this will be my parting gift to you, Mordred. I'm going to fucking ruin you."

"Yes. Please."

I need his hate more than he knows.

"That was a clever trick last night." He brings his hand to my mouth, shoving his fingers forcefully past my lips. "Get them nice and wet because this is going to be fast and dirty."

He keeps his promise, barely letting me swirl my tongue around his fingers a couple of times before he's pulling them out of my mouth. Which is fine because I want this to hurt. I *need* this to hurt worse than the cracking of my soul.

Merlin's going to fuck me, wreck me, then vanish forever.

Two fingers push into my ass abruptly, and I cry out. They're slick with more than just spit, and I assume Merlin turned it to lube. But there wasn't much, and the sudden stretch burns.

I'm grateful that he turned me around so he can't see the way my eyes continue to leak. I wish I could say it was only from physical pain.

Even still, my balls ache, and I grind my cock against the sheets as he works me open. He pulls his fingers out all too soon, replaced by the head of his cock against my entrance. When he pushes inside me without any shred of patience or gentleness, I swear he's splitting me wide open. Ripping apart my body, tearing my soul to shreds.

Taking a fistful of my hair, he yanks my head back and licks a hot trail up my neck to my ear. "Tell me this is exactly what you wanted."

"It's exactly what I wanted," I say as though my mouth's on autopilot, my brain not yet having caught up past the pain.

As though he has no plans on letting that happen, he starts fucking me like a man possessed. Which, I suppose since I coaxed out his demons, that's exactly what he is.

"You have until I finish to come, little monster," he growls in my ear as he quite literally fucks me into the mattress. "Otherwise you don't get to."

Maybe I shouldn't.

Because now it's me who needs to hate *myself*.

Maybe I should let him use me, abuse me, hate me enough to walk away without so much as a glance back.

But he's nailing my prostate with every thrust, my cock trapped, rubbing against the sheets and smearing precum between them and my abs. My balls grow heavy as Merlin fucks me with every bit of hatred he possesses, until I feel it so deep in my bones that I know he's engraved himself within the very marrow.

Merlin. Merlin. Merlin.

I belong to Merlin.

I belong to his hate.

I think I always will.

He claims that last trace of me as he fills me, the pulsing of his cock inside of me triggering my own orgasm. The waves haven't even subsided by the time Merlin is pulling out of me, leaving me empty in more ways than one.

The sheets beneath me are wet with tears, sweat, and cum, and I'm scared to turn around, like the last memory that I deserve of Merlin is him fucking his hate into me.

But I do turn around.

Because I'm selfish.

Merlin stands at the end of the bed dressed in the same clothes he was wearing last night. His brows are pinched, a deep frown etched into his beautiful face as he stares down at me, all hints of his demons gone, locked back in their cages.

I sit up, conjuring the sweats on again. He's seen too much of me already.

It must upset him because his frown deepens as he shakes his head. "I hope you don't spend the rest of your life hiding, Mordred."

"I guess that's a step up from wishing me a slow and painful death."

He almost smiles. Almost. "It's funny how a thousand years didn't change anything, but a few weeks with you did."

I shake my head because…*fuck*. He can't say shit like that. He can't look at me with that hurt in his eyes, with regret at how I just made him treat me. He can't take care of me and give me *hate cuddles*. He can't threaten to give me more than I asked him for.

"It was just sex," I mutter pathetically.

"How many times are you going to accuse me of being in denial when you're even worse than I am?"

"Fuck you!"

Fuck him for being right.

Because it wasn't *just* sex. But denying it, letting myself be angry, is better than admitting to either of us how I truly feel and then watching him walk away.

Climbing off the bed to my feet, I keep my distance from him because if I moved any closer, I'd fall back into his orbit and be tempted to admit it all anyway.

"You've tamed your demons, Merlin!" I shout, my voice hoarse and clogged with all the emotion I wish I didn't feel. "You might let them out from time to time, but you have the control to lock them up again. All I know how to do, all I've ever done, is kill mine."

It's his turn to shake his head. "You never killed them, Mordred. You only pretended you did and allowed them to eat away at the deepest parts of you where you could ignore them."

A warm, wet drop slides down my cheek. I don't bother wiping it away because he's already seen it.

"Leave! It's what you do best."

He doesn't take the bait. He's already tamed *those* demons too.

Without a word, Merlin turns, giving me his back, and heads to the door.

No. No. No.

He was right. My own demons have spent the last thousand years gnawing on my soul, scratching and pecking, chipping away at it until it's nothing but a pale imitation of what it may have once been. Weakening it.

And now, watching him walk away, it crumbles, turning to ash.

I know I have to let him go, but I can't fucking stand it.

Rushing forward, I throw my arms around him, plastering myself to his back when he's two feet to the door.

"I'm sorry, Merlin." A sob claws its way from deep in my chest, tearing up my throat. "I'm so fucking sorry I can't come with you."

He places a hand on my arm. It's warm and gentle as it lingers there for a few seconds.

But then he grabs my wrist, pulls me off of him, and opens the door, stepping out with nothing but silence, without so much as a glance back.

Just like I knew he would.

I asked him for his hate, and that's what he leaves me with. It's what I *need*.

I've never known anything but hate. I think anything else might kill me.

25

MERLIN

Despite the demons I've lived with my entire life, I'm not a cruel man. My mother never feared my demons, didn't hate me for the nature of my conception. She taught me to be good, to be kind and loyal and wise. She loved me as any worthy mother would love their child.

I failed her when it came to Mordred.

If I had been a better man, the man my mother raised me to be, I would have carried her lesson with me and handed it down to Arthur.

It was nature versus nurture. My nature didn't make me inherently evil. Mordred's upbringing corrupted him.

And I played a part.

That last morning I saw him, five days ago, I *was* cruel.

The heartbreaking resonance of his sob, the wrenching of his body against my back with the violent sound, haunts my every waking minute.

I shouldn't have asked him to come with me. I shouldn't have put that on him, knowing how difficult it would be for him to face Arthur. It was selfish of me because…I wish I didn't have to leave. I know I can't keep him, but I would have if things were different. I still hate him for killing Arthur—I think I always will—but I can admit to myself now that I also feel…other things for him.

Possessiveness.

Protectiveness.

Passion.

The line between loathing and everything else has blurred, and sometimes it's all swirling around together that I can't locate the distinction.

Not that it matters anymore.

I'm leaving in two days.

The shop has been sold, along with everything in it. My apartment has been almost completely cleaned out except for the bed, a few clothes, and Percy and his things. Willow is supposed to be stopping by soon to take Percy. As much as I hate rehoming him, I can't exactly take him with me through the portal back to Camelot. Cats hate swimming.

There's a knock on the door, and I go over to open it. Willow flashes a smile at me before quickly moving past me to where Percy is lounging on the foot of the bed. She sits down beside him and scratches him affectionately under the chin.

"Hey, buddy," she coos. "You ready to come home with me?"

Closing the door, I turn to her with a grin. "Not even a hi? I knew you always loved the cat more than me."

She looks up and rolls her eyes. "Hi, Merlin," she says with a teasing sense of obligation.

"I have all his stuff together." I tap the bag that's on the floor with my foot. Inside is a clean litter box I bought along with bags of cat food, bowls, toys, and treats. "I really appreciate you taking him. I know you'll take care of him."

I already had the conversation with Willow about leaving, making up a story about needing to go back home to help some extended family. Which isn't exactly far from the truth. Arthur was always like a brother to me.

"Yeah, about that…" She stands, shuffling her feet. "Do you think he'll be okay making a cross-country trip?"

My brow furrows. "You're leaving too?"

She bites her lip, and that's when I notice there's something different about her. She's always been spirited and cheerful, a ray of sunshine I've welcomed in my life. But, right now, she's *glowing*.

I have my suspicions, but I still urge her on. "Willow?"

"I wanted to tell you before, but I wasn't sure if it was going to happen." She smiles brightly and practically bounces on the balls of her feet. "Ava asked me to come to LA."

"That's amazing!" I return her smile as I walk across the room to wrap my arms around her. "I'm happy for you."

Happy.

Not at all jealous.

Deny. Deny. Deny.

Fuck.

Okay, a little jealous.

Barely managing to keep my mouth from turning down, I pull back to see her eyes sparkling more than before, like she never thought she'd get a hug from me.

"Thanks, Merlin."

"Are you two moving in together? It's only been, what, a month?"

She shrugs. "One month is like six in lesbian years."

I laugh, still trying to ignore the sharp pang radiating from my chest. I *am* happy for her and Ava that they found each other, and if I could dispel this bitter resentment that's starting to fester, I would.

Moving around her, I scoop up Percy from the bed and carry him over to the cat carrier that's waiting on the kitchen counter.

"I take it things didn't end as well with you and Mordred?"

It was too much to hope that I could have hidden that from her. The last thing I want to do is bring her down when she's flying so high.

"It's okay. Really." I usher Percy into the carrier and lock the door before turning back to my friend, ignoring the cat's irate mews. "What happened between us in the past was always something neither of us would ever be able to get over. We dealt with it the best, the *only*, way we could. At least we have some closure now."

But that's not exactly true, is it?

If anything, it feels as though there's more unfinished business between us than there was before.

"That's a load of bullshit."

My eyes widen at her blunt outburst.

"I don't know what happened between you, and I won't ask again. But if you two had dealt with it the *only* way you could, you wouldn't have fallen into bed together. You did that because you *wanted* each other. It's pretty clear you still do. Sometimes you just have to learn to leave things in the past."

If she knew he murdered his own father, she might think differently.

But she is right about one thing.

I did want him anyway.

"And if he's not sorry for what happened?" I ask, well aware of how vague that is.

She shrugs. "We can forgive someone even if they're not sorry. Sometimes it's easier to just forgive and forget, or else you may never move on. Besides, actions speak louder than words. I don't know what Mordred did, but he doesn't need to say out loud how hopeless he is for you."

I let out a soft laugh.

I could feel it in the way he wrapped his arms around me that morning—something that mirrored my own feelings. Something *more*.

It's just not enough for him to face his father, or his mother, again.

I suppose I should try to understand that and accept it.

"Thanks, Willow."

She looks like she wants to say more, but she eventually nods and picks up the cat carrier in one hand and the bag of Percy's things with the other. Percy has stopped meowing bloody murder, so it gives me hope he'll be fine taking the trip with Willow.

"Take care, Merlin. Make sure you call sometime. Or write since you're old school like that."

I give her a warm smile. "I'll do my best."

If I survive, I suppose I could find a way with magic. Or even visit.

That thought has a tight knot creeping up my throat.

Probably not visit...

"Have a safe trip," I say as I open the door for her.

"You too."

Once she's gone, I turn back to my empty apartment and exhale a heavy breath.

I've never had a problem with solitude—I've often preferred it. But right now, the loneliness is a suffocating weight that's bearing down on my chest, constricting around my lungs like a couple of snakes.

When I become aware of the fact I can't breathe, it brings with it another realization that has me sliding down against the door to the floor.

I wanted so desperately to keep Mordred that I was willing to forgive him.

26

M⊛RDRED

We've been back in LA for a few days, and I've found myself often unable to breathe. Like Merlin just took all my air with him when he left.

But I got it back this morning.

I've been breathing easier since making my decision.

A stupid, reckless, foolish, insane, idiotic, suicidal—I could go on and on—decision. A decision that will undoubtedly get me killed. Be the end of me. Send me off to meet my maker.

Fuck.

Give me a break. I'm fucking terrified.

That's why I'm currently lounging on the couch in the living room of the condo I share with Ava and Anthony with my feet propped up on the coffee table and smoking the fattest joint I've ever rolled. I haven't been able to smoke in days because anytime I tried, I'd feel like my lungs would collapse. Even with knowing it wasn't real, it wasn't physical, only mental, I couldn't shake that feeling.

It took me some time to come to terms with it—what I'm truly scared of.

I don't fear much, at least I never used to. I didn't used to fear death, but now I do. I've known that for a while, though.

What I had to accept was how afraid I am of facing Arthur again, not just because I know he'll want to kill me the second he lays eyes on me.

But while both those fears are what kept me from saying yes to Merlin, from agreeing to go with him, it turns out I'm far more terrified of something else.

Losing him.

Merlin can hate me for all eternity. It doesn't matter.

He's mine, and I can't let him go.

I won't.

If I have to, I'll die to prove to him that I'm his too. Like a fucking martyr.

When I hear movement outside the door, I quickly wave my hands, one banishing the joint and the other chasing away the smoke and the stench. Ava hates when I smoke in the common areas, and I'd rather not get bitched out right before I have to deliver this news. Not that Ava's a bitch. She's actually…

Fuck, she's my…*friend.*

When she walks through the door, flanked by Anthony and Will, all of them laughing while carrying bags of Chinese food, it hits me.

When did I get attached to these people? These mere mortals?

Dammit.

I'm actually going to miss them.

I inwardly scoff at this annoying sentimentality I'm not used to feeling. I guess I have been with Ava and Anthony a bit longer than I ever was the companions I've chosen in the past. Usually, I would have run fast and far for the hills by now.

My time with them was probably coming to an end anyway…

It still sucks.

And of course Ava finds me brooding because that's almost always my default setting around them all. I'm certain she'll be glad to be rid of me.

They come over to the couch, and Ava smacks my legs. "Feet off the furniture, dog."

My lips twitch at the corners as my feet hit the floor with a thud. Has her tone always held that teasing, loving lilt even when she nags us?

My bandmates all continue chatting among themselves, dishing out take-out boxes of fried rice, noodles, chicken, pork, and spring rolls. Ava hands me a box of my own, and when I peek inside to see my favorite, steamed eggplant, I feel even more like shit because she's never gotten me my own order of it before.

I really must have been pathetic with how much she's felt the need to comfort me these last few weeks.

Opening my mouth, my words get lodged around a knot in my throat, and I have to clear it away before I can speak. "Thanks."

"Ew." Ava looks at me with wide eyes. "Did you just express *gratitude*?"

I roll my eyes and shake my head. Picking up a pair of chopsticks from the table, I dig into the eggplant and try to ignore the way she keeps glancing over at me like she's more concerned about me than before.

They continue whatever conversation they had been having before they came in, but my mind is spinning too fast to pick up what it's about. So I leave them to it while I eat my eggplant, stealing a little chicken, pork, and noodles from the other boxes. The food quickly sinks to the bottom of my gut where it churns nauseatingly, making me quit the meal before the rest of them.

I try to wait patiently while the rest of them finish, not wanting to ruin the good mood they're all in. But the second Anthony sets aside the last empty box, I blurt out, "I'm leaving."

They all turn their heads toward me with pinched brows and bemusement.

"For how long?" Anthony asks.

Sighing heavily, I stand up, turning to look out the window and giving them my back. "For good."

"You're leaving the band?"

I can hear the frown in Will's voice, and I wish it didn't affect me.

I wish I didn't *care*.

"Is this because I asked if Willow could move in?"

At Ava's question, I force myself to turn around so she can see the truth in my answer. "Absolutely not."

Will grins. "It's about Merlin."

Ever since that damn wizard showed up in Vegas, Will has been less awkward around me. No blushing, no flirtatious touches. I'm glad he's getting over his crush, and I surprisingly haven't missed the attention.

"Yes and no," I tell him with just as much honesty.

"What are we supposed to do without you?"

The wetness shining in Ava's dark brown eyes nearly kills me. I almost wish it would, that it would save me from this asinine, suicidal mission of mine.

"You're going to replace Will." At least I'm able to grin at the hurt look in *his* eyes because I know it won't last. "And Will's going to replace me."

"What?" Sure enough, his momentary distress is replaced by incredulity. "Me? A frontman?"

"You've got the skills. The voice. Why not?"

He blinks at me, struck speechless.

"I've already put some money in your account," I tell Ava as I turn back to her. "And the condo's in your name now."

That's what I spent the morning doing, as soon as I made my decision so I couldn't change my mind.

"Me?" she asks in a small voice like she can conceal the emotion in it.

"You're more responsible than these dipshits," I tease, waving my hand at the other two men.

They all stare at me with pained, confused expressions. The longer the silence goes on, the longer I take in the sight of them for possibly the last time, the *better* I feel. I should feel worse, more guilty, but the truth is they've always deserved better than me.

"Look, I've only been holding you all back." I hold up my hand when they all open their mouths to argue. I know they won't believe me because I can't tell them just how true it is, that I've been doing it on *purpose*. "But maybe this will help make up for it."

Reaching into the back pocket of my jeans, I take out a folded piece of notebook paper and hand it over to Ava. She takes it apprehensively, the crease between her brows deepening.

"What's this?" she asks as she unfolds it.

"The song I've been working on."

"You mean for the past century?" Anthony jokes with a snort.

I suppress an eye roll, but only because it feels like it's been a work in progress for more like a millennium, for my whole goddamn life.

"'When Hate's The Only Thing I've Ever Known.'" Ava looks up at me from the paper after reading the title, her mouth turned down in a frown of sympathy.

I look out the window again as though something caught my attention. The view isn't anything spectacular—mostly other condo buildings against the backdrop of a hill—but it's better than having a staring contest with my drummer while she dissects my insides. She's always had a way of seeing past my bullshit, but it's like her superpowers have increased recently.

Or maybe I've just been dropping walls.

Breaking the silence and the tension, Anthony says, "So you leaving *is* about Merlin."

"That's…" Ava's voice is still choked with emotion, preventing me from facing her still. "That's not a reflection of how you really feel, is it?"

Shit.

Taking a deep breath, I finally turn back to them. "Not when it comes to you guys."

A tear slides down Ava's cheek like she had been holding it back for as long as she could. She tosses the paper onto the coffee table, stands, and crosses the distance between us to throw her arms around me and bury her face in my shoulder.

"Do you really have to leave?"

Hugging her back, I nod. I won't change my mind. "I do."

She pulls back to meet my gaze, her eyes wet with unshed tears. "I'm going to miss you."

"We'll all miss you, man," Anthony says.

Will nods in agreement.

It's all I can do to keep my own voice steady. "I'll miss you all too."

"When do you have to leave?" Ava asks as she steps back and wipes at her cheeks with a sniffle.

Merlin said he wasn't leaving until the end of this week, so one more night won't hurt.

"Tomorrow. Promise me you'll use the song?"

Ava purses her lips in contemplation, and I imagine she's facing a dilemma, not sure if she wants to take the credit for it since I'm leaving. "Only if you teach it to us," she eventually says. "Play with us one last time before you leave?"

"Of course," I answer easily.

After we clean up the empty take-out boxes, we all head to the studio we have set up to play together as a band one last time.

27

MERLIN

Ever since saying goodbye to Willow and Percy yesterday, I haven't been able to take a single full breath of air. It's been so uncomfortable that I'd consider something medical is wrong with me if I wasn't immortal. As it is, I don't have to worry about anything like that.

It's possible that saying goodbye to my last friend and my last companion I had in this world has affected me so strongly mentally that I'm manifesting some kind of magical curse on myself.

Because I'm certain that's what it is. It's magical.

I've tried burning sage and thyme and rosemary, drinking a potion with mint and licorice and osha root, along with meditating.

None of it has helped.

It's early afternoon the day before I'm supposed to leave, and I'm lying on the bed, staring up at the ceiling because there's nothing left to do. I'm considering just leaving now. Maybe returning to Camelot will alleviate whatever the hell this is.

It's not like there's anything keeping me here anymore…

Just as that thought hits me, along with another painful attempt at breathing, there's a knock on my apartment door.

Assuming it might be the Realtor here to do a final walk-through, I climb off the bed and cross the room. If I thought I couldn't breathe before, it's nothing compared to the way all the air is sucked out of my vicinity when I open the door, leaving behind a crushing vacuum that compresses my lungs until they shrivel.

"You're still here," Mordred says on an exhale, his tone full of relief.

I don't know for how much longer if I can't fucking breathe—

He throws himself at me, wrapping his arms around my middle and crashing his mouth to mine in a desperate, hard kiss. Seconds after his lips press against mine, I'm gasping in all the air I've been deprived of for the last two days, like I've been drowning and I've finally broken the surface.

Placing my hands on Mordred's chest, I push him away to look into his eyes. The brilliant blue oceans within are so wide, so open. So oblivious to what he's done. I glare fiercely at him anyway.

I kick the door closed and then push him up against it, panting heavily with the merciful ability to finally breathe. "You little fucking shit."

He licks his lips. "What?" There's a trace of fear in his voice. "Hey, at least I used the door this time."

The uncertain grin tugging on his lips is kind of cute, as is him thinking that's the reason I'm upset.

"What were you doing yesterday morning?"

He blinks, confused. Then he bites his bottom lip and says, "Deciding to come with you."

My body relaxes, along with whatever rage is painted on my face. I brush a strand of hair off his forehead, then lean my forehead against his until we're sharing the same air, like I'm afraid he might take it all away from me again. "Were you trying to warn me not to leave without you?"

"What do you mean?"

"I haven't been able to breathe since yesterday."

His brows shoot up. "I...I felt like I couldn't either since you left that hotel in Vegas."

Wait.

Is it possible I had been doing the same thing to him?

He shakes his head, and as though reading my mind, says, "It wasn't magical. It was just..." He swallows. "I missed you."

Another sense of drowning crashes over me with a wave of emotion, but this time, I don't mind it so much. I kiss Mordred because I need to feel his lips against mine, know he's really here, that him finally not hiding from me isn't simply an illusion.

"Fuck, I missed you too," I groan before diving back in, letting him nibble at my bottom lip before licking into his mouth as he grants me entrance. I swirl my tongue around the metal ball in his a moment before pulling back for air.

When I do, he still appears bemused. "Are you saying... that..."

"You subconsciously stole your breath back because I left you without yours? Yes, that's what I'm saying." I let out a short, soft laugh and kiss him again, slower this time, taking my time before whispering against his lips, "Little monster."

Mordred leans his head back against the door, smirking. "You mean I took your breath away...literally?"

My lips twitch because, yes, he did. And I'm actually a little impressed. It's also probably why I didn't sense him when he showed up here.

I lean forward to brush my lips against his again. "In all the ways."

His smirk falls, his own breath hitching. "I should tell you, Merlin…" His voice trembles as he trips over his words. "For the record, I'm fucking terrified. Not just because I doubt your ability to stop a man hellbent on revenge, but… just of facing Arthur period. But I put this weight on your shoulders. I won't let you go it alone."

"I told you I won't let him hurt you."

"You can't risk him losing his trust in you."

"I won't," I tell him with a conviction I hope I feel when the time comes. "I'll talk to him before we let him see you."

He nods, but he doesn't appear convinced.

Not that I blame him. He's going to be facing the man he murdered a thousand years ago. Maybe I shouldn't have asked him to come with me because it'll be a miracle if I can persuade Arthur that revenge isn't necessary. But, if anything, I'll make him see that we need Mordred's magic to help us destroy Morgan.

In that moment, staring into his eyes that still show a fear he would've never shown me weeks ago, I make a decision.

If Arthur's forgiveness is something I want for Mordred, no matter how long it takes, then I have to give it to him first.

Our warm breath coalesces in the small space between us, like we've each somehow become the air the other breathes. I inhale it all, drawing it in, sucking it into my lungs greedily, needing the affirmation of *us*, of *more*, to resolve any doubt.

"I forgive you."

My words hang in the air, suspended, momentarily freezing time.

Then his eyes widen. "What?" A flash of anger. "I never asked for your forgiveness!"

"I know. I'm giving it anyway."

He starts to struggle against me, trying to get away, but I hold him against the door with my hands lowering to his arms and pinning him with my hips against his.

He gives up easily.

"Why?" he asks, voice deep and strained, as though my forgiveness causes him physical pain.

"Because I can. Because while Arthur didn't deserve to die, you deserved parents who wouldn't turn their backs on you. Because while you may not be sorry, your actions came from a place of hurt. Don't worry, I'm not giving you excuses. I know you don't want them. You may not want my forgiveness either, but I'm going to give it anyway."

His eyes turn glassy, threatening tears I can tell he's fighting against. Chest heaving, he chokes out, "You're supposed to hate me."

I grin at his addiction to my hatred, knowing by now that there's more to it. But I won't press the issue right now, not when he's already so emotionally charged. "Trust me, I can still hate you when you need it."

He bites his bottom lip and looks down.

"Just promise me one thing, Mordred." I bring a hand up to lift his chin, coaxing his gaze back to mine. "When we defeat Morgan, you won't kill Arthur again."

The little shit actually laughs, like he had never even considered it. He shakes his head. "I don't care about Arthur anymore."

It's not the complete truth, but, again, I save the prying for later.

"But I promise." He blinks back any trace of tears, eyes shining with sincerity. "I don't want to lose *you*."

I've never felt so light.

It's never been easier to breathe.

I move my hand to his throat, not squeezing, just holding. "Tell me you're mine. Tell me I can keep you."

A slow smirk creeps back onto his face as he grabs onto my sides, fingers digging into my hips. He pulls them even tighter against him, grinding against me until I can feel his growing erection. "I'd rather show you."

He shoves me backward, chasing after me as he reaches for the hem of my sweater and pulls it up and over my head, tossing it away. We've always magicked away our clothing, and something about him physically undressing me has my cock hardening, pressing painfully against my zipper.

His hands roam up my stomach to my chest. He pinches my nipples hard before shocking me even more by pushing me again. My legs hit the bed, and I go tumbling backwards onto the mattress.

"Fuck, Merlin," he groans as he shrugs out of his jacket, then his shirt. "I'm *all* yours."

My legs widen as he climbs onto the bed between them, following me again as I crawl backwards to the middle. He leans over, fingers threading in my hair as he thrusts his hips against mine. I moan, and he swallows it up with a punishing kiss. The length of his body presses me into the mattress, our bare chests brushing, sparking heat, our cocks grinding through the last layers of our clothes.

And then they're gone.

The moment his cock touches mine, both of ours already slick with copious amounts of precum, the flame of desire licking up my spine flares hotter. He sinks his teeth into my bottom lip as he continues thrusting against me.

I'm panting heavily as his mouth travels down to my throat, my jaw, kissing, biting, marking me over and over.

"Mordred," I growl as my hands find his hips, moving them more urgently as our dicks rut together. "Either get inside me or get me inside you. Right the fuck now."

He chuckles. "Relax, darling. I'm going to show you just how much I belong to you."

Sitting up on his knees, he reaches behind him, groaning a second later. When his hand comes back into view, he's holding a black anal plug.

"Fuck. How long have you had that in?"

"Just a few minutes," he says with a grin and a shrug.

"Such a fucking slut," I tease as my hands roam up his sides.

"Oh, come on, Merlin. You know I have no shame."

As though to prove it, he reaches back again. This time, the point of the toy finds my hole. It's still slick with whatever lube he conjured, and he works the widest part of it past my rim with a few gentle thrusts until it's fully seated and my eyes are rolling into the back of my head.

Mordred moves lower down the bed, sweeping up the precum that's gathered on my abs with his tongue before taking my cock into his mouth. His gaze meets mine, wide and eager, as he hollows his cheeks and sucks me down, at the same time pressing on the toy until it grazes my prostate, making me thrust up into the back of his throat. My balls ache with the need to come as he licks his way back up my shaft, eyes never wavering from mine.

"Fuck, Mordred." My hands find their way into his hair, fingers flexing with the desire I'm resisting to grip tight and fuck his face.

Then my hands are suddenly yanked back, my own vines that I hadn't been able to bring myself to get rid of appearing out of nowhere to wrap tightly around my wrists, hauling them up and over my head. I growl and struggle against the plant, even though I know magic is the only thing that would break its hold.

Truthfully, I don't want to break his hold on me.

Mordred pops off my dick with a wicked smirk, my stomach tightening at the sight. "You should've known better, darling. You're mine, too."

He crawls up my body to straddle my waist, grabbing my hard length and lining it up with his hole, his saliva already turned to lube. His gaze holds mine hostage as he slowly lowers himself, the head of my cock slipping past his rim and right into the blissful, welcoming tunnel of tight heat. I throw my head back against the bed, overcome with pleasure.

He starts to move, his hands coming down on my chest, digging his nails in as his dick leaks precum on my abs. His warm palms coast along my skin as his nails leave angry, red trails down my torso.

"Fuck," I groan as I struggle against the vines again. I want to touch him too, but I can't. "You're such a pain in my ass," I growl as I glare up at him.

He just smirks smugly down at me.

So I thrust my hips up forcefully, drawing a deep cry out of him.

He falls forward on top of me, his slick chest heaving against mine. "Yeah, well right now, you're a pain in mine."

Now it's my turn to smirk up at him. "Get up and fuck yourself on my cock, little monster."

He does just that, using his hands on my chest as leverage as he lifts himself and rocks his hips. His pace picks up, and an obscene moan escapes his parted lips as his head rolls back on his shoulders, eyes closed. More precum leaks out from him onto me, and I wish I could lap it up.

"Mordred," I breathe. When his eyes fly open to seek out mine, I look down at the pearly drops on my abs. "I want it."

"You want me to feed you, Merlin?"

"I'm fucking starving for you."

He groans and swipes up the precum on the tip of his finger before bringing it to my mouth. I suck him in, licking and lapping up the salty taste. The pleasure from that combined with the plug in my ass and my cock in *his* ass have my balls drawing up dangerously tight.

But it's him who moans, "Fuck, I'm so close."

"Don't you dare," I growl before biting down on his finger.

Crying out, he stops moving and scowls down at me. "That's going to do the opposite of what you want, Merlin."

I grin, soothing the sting of my bite with my tongue. "Such a slut for pain."

"Only a little more than you," he quips.

I can't even deny it. I love it when he bites.

"You've proven you're mine," I tell him, staring up into his eyes, completely breathless for more than one reason. "Now prove I'm yours too."

Moaning, he lifts off my cock. He moves forward until he's straddling my chest, his dick in front of my face. I open my mouth without any prompting, and he thrusts inside, the metal of his Jacob's Ladder piercings gliding across my tongue. Wrapping my lips tightly around him, I hollow my cheeks and suck as though I could siphon the very life out of his cock.

"Fucking hell, Merlin." His fingers card through my hair without grasping, letting me control the pace. "Have I told you how fucking good at that you are?"

I grin around the length of him as I coat him with as much saliva as I can.

Pulling out of my mouth with a reluctant whine, he moves back down and settles between my legs. After slowly removing the toy in my ass, he tosses it away. Grabbing the base of his cock, he lines it up with my hole, easing inside at an agonizingly slow pace. Even after his crown has pushed past my rim and our moans mingle in the thick air between our heated gazes, he makes sure I feel every inch of him, every steel ball of his piercings as they slide against my walls.

He thrusts forward the last few remaining inches, the top ball of his apadravya grazing my prostate. Precum leaks from my cock as he leans over me again, rocking his hips slowly, sensually, so I feel every stroke, every bit of him inside me.

His forehead comes down on mine, slick with sweat, his hands tangling in my hair.

"Fuck you, Merlin," he whispers in the sparse breadth between our lips. His tone isn't angry; if anything, it's tormented. "I was supposed to get under your skin, but you crawled under mine instead."

While he's distracted fucking me, eyes closed as he soaks in the pleasure, I focus on the vines around my wrists and force them to loosen and retreat back to the window.

I bring my hands up and place them on the sides of Mordred's face. He gasps, and his eyes fly open as his hips still, my touch taking him by surprise.

"You *are* beneath my skin, Mordred." Holding his gaze, I stroke my thumbs across his cheeks. "You're in my blood, my bones. You're fucking *everywhere*."

A noise between a whimper and a groan leaves his lips before they're pressing against mine, coaxing them open so he can dive his tongue into my mouth. His tongue swirls around mine as his hips move again, his thrusts turning harder and faster than before as he kisses me relentlessly.

This isn't like the other times we've fucked. There's no hate—or, at least, not like before. I'm certain this doesn't mark the end of our hate fucks, but, maybe, it marks the beginning of that word that keeps floating around in my head.

More.

"Please, Merlin," he moans above me, his grip tightening in my hair. "I'm yours. Please, tell me I can come."

"You can come. Fill me up, little monster. I'm yours too."

Another desperate noise leaves him as his mouth slams back down on mine. His tongue and his cock fuck into me in harsh, urgent thrusts and strokes, hips rocking furiously, lips massaging mine fiercely. When he comes, his dick pulsing inside of me with each spurt, he bites down on my bottom lip. The sting of his teeth, the complete fullness of him inside me, the grinding of our bodies against my cock trigger my own orgasm, one so fucking intense my vision goes black as my release fills the hair's breadth between us.

As we come down from our highs, his tongue slips inside my mouth again, this time moving languidly, tenderly.

I don't know when it happened. Or how.

But I love this softer side of Mordred as much as I do the rough one.

Wrapping my arms around him, I roll us over onto our sides as we continue kissing through our panting breaths. His spent cock slips out of me, and I swallow the whimper that spills from his mouth.

Eventually, his head falls back onto the pillow, still breathing heavily as he throws an arm over my waist. He stares at me through hooded eyes, his lips red and swollen. "Tomorrow, right?" he asks, voice raw and groggy. "We're leaving tomorrow?"

I nod because I'm not sure I can speak.

"Good." He closes his eyes. "I don't think I'll be able to walk for at least twelve hours."

I let out a breathy laugh and magic away our mess because I doubt either of us have the ability to make it to the shower right now.

With one arm still trapped beneath him, I reach up with my free hand to brush hair off his forehead. I find my voice and the strength to ask, "You'll still be here in the morning?"

His eyes slowly peel open, and they're no more guarded than they were when he arrived. He smiles. "I'm not going anywhere, darling."

I kiss him once more, a quick, light brush of my mouth on his. "Good. You're mine."

He closes his eyes again, lips still pulled up at the corners as he releases a satisfied breath. "Yours."

28

M⊗RDRED

The Lake of Avalon stretches out ahead from where I'm perched on a boulder on the far east side of the water.

It's not *actually* the Lake of Avalon, at least not in this world. Here, it's known as Llyn Ogwen. Its waters aren't quite as blue, not quite as calm, lacking that mystical serenity it holds back in the land of Camelot.

Merlin and I arrived in Wales about an hour ago. We waited until it was early afternoon in New York so the setting sun here would help disguise us from the road without the need to use magic to do it. The light cloud of fog helps too.

We stayed in bed all morning, trading messy, unhurried blowjobs. Merlin made me swallow all of his cum and mine, and it's settled in the pit of my stomach, comforting me, reminding me that no matter what happens, I'm his.

Right now, Merlin is walking along the edge of the lake, searching for where the veil between worlds is the thinnest. I would've helped, but I told him that I needed a minute with my thoughts before we left.

It was a bunch of bullshit.

Truthfully, I just wanted to watch him walk around. His brow is furrowed sexily in concentration as he waves his hands slowly over the water. His jeans hug his ass; the sight nearly makes me drool. I may not be able to make out his smooth, defined muscles beneath the sweater he wears, but he still looks good in it as always.

He's a few yards away when he calls out, "Mordred!"

I sigh now that the show is over and hop off the boulder. However, of course I can't stop myself from staring at his ass on the way over to him.

When he turns to me, I snap my gaze up to meet his. He scowls, perfectly aware of where my eyes were. I blink innocently, flashing a smile to match.

He shakes his head, not buying my act, and turns back to the lake. His hands move in slow circles above the water, the surface rippling. "I think I found it."

"I didn't doubt you for a second, darling." Standing beside him, I place my hands in the pockets of my jacket and lean my shoulder against Merlin's for a little extra heat. "Now can you hurry? It's cold as balls out here."

Turning his head toward me, he smirks. "Are your balls cold, baby?"

Baby?

Good boy.

Beautiful.

Arthur isn't going to kill me. Merlin is.

The stunning sight of his russet eyes shining with the glare of the setting sun attests to one simple truth. This man is capable of breaking my heart for the first time in a thousand years.

I clear my throat. "I hate you."

His smirk widens, and he looks back to the lake. "Hate you too."

Focusing my gaze on the water to get it off Merlin—because lord knows what I'll do if I keep staring at him—I try to think about something I actually *do* hate about him.

I come up with nothing.

I don't hate his annoyingly charitable, kind nature.

I don't hate his intimidating confidence.

I don't hate his ability to forgive and protect, even when it's not deserved.

I especially don't hate when his smiles are aimed at me.

Fuck.

I don't hate a single thing about him.

Merlin's hands on my shoulders snap me out of my dizzying revelation, and I realize he's standing behind me now. I lean back against him before I can stop myself.

The water in front of us has moved past gentle ripples. There's a wide circle of bubbling water as though it's boiling.

"Are you planning on turning me into soup, Merlin?"

He chuckles in my ear, sending tingles down my spine. "I don't need to do that to eat you up," he says before nipping at my ear.

I suck in a breath and try not to pop a damn boner.

"Are you ready, little monster?"

"As ready as I'll ever be."

And then…*Merlin fucking pushes me.*

Okay. *Now* I hate him.

The water at the edge of the lake is shallow as I splash down, but the spell that he cast over it sucks me in, pulls me under, a current forcing me deeper and deeper away from Llyn Ogwen and toward the Lake of Avalon.

At least the water isn't actually at boiling point.

The portal that Merlin created swallows me in like a vortex, and it's less like I'm swimming and more like I'm slipping through a tunnel slide. My speed increases even as the water around me appears to still. I could breathe, but I'm holding my breath with how fast my body travels.

Bubbles float around me, breaking through the walls of water to join me on the journey before gliding through the air and rejoining the magical tunnel. It's something to watch, a distraction for the way my stomach is somersaulting.

I don't remember this nausea from my last trip between the lakes, and I can't help but wonder if my surprise dive has something to do with it.

I'll have to make sure to pay Merlin back for that.

Finally, the tunnel of water curves upward, and I'm breaking through the surface of the Lake of Avalon, coughing and sputtering and gasping for air. Treading water and weighed down by my soaked clothes, I slowly make my way to the bank.

Crawling over rocks and dirt, I find a patch of dry grass and crash down onto my back, staring up at the clear, baby blue sky, chest heaving as I try to catch my breath.

A moment later, another body falls down beside me.

When I turn my head toward him with a scowl, his eyes are closed, but he's grinning like he can sense the exact expression on my face.

"I *will* be getting you back for that," I promise him.

With no warning, he leaps up and straddles my waist. Leaning over me, he shakes his head like a damn dog, pelting me with water slinging off his hair.

"Merlin!" I shout through belly-aching laughter, throwing my arms up to shield myself.

I'm still laughing when Merlin grabs my wrists and pins them to the ground on either side of my head. My eyes open, and my laughter fades as I look up at the most gorgeous smile I think I've ever seen in my life.

I *definitely* don't hate Merlin's playful side either.

When was the last time I heard such genuine laughter come from *me*?

We're both still breathing heavily, gazes locked as droplets continue to rain down on me from his hair, when reality comes swooping in like the goddamn Grim Reaper. Because my brain apparently can't fathom this happiness in my heart, it concocts this ridiculous idea that has my mood plummeting. It claws against the inside of my skull, an itch inside my head I can't scratch away.

"You didn't lure me back here on purpose, did you?" I hate how small my voice is.

Merlin's brows pinch. "What do you mean?"

The words are never going to get past the lump in my throat, so I swallow it down before answering. "You loved Arthur like a brother. I wouldn't blame you if you manipulated me to get me here so he could take his revenge." I grin, huff a laugh, and repeat what he once accused me of. "Bewitched me with dick."

His face falls further, and he releases my wrists and sits up. "Do you really think so little of me?"

I sigh and shake my head. "No, I don't. Because you're a better man than I am. It's something I would've done."

The frown on his face quickly morphs into something sinister, his voice turning deep and gravelly. "Is that what you did? Lure me here so you and Morgan can take me out? She was always afraid of me. I'm sure if you two work together, you'd stand a chance."

It's my turn to get angry.

Grabbing the front of Merlin's sweater with both hands, I pull him back down, then roll us over until I'm on top. With my hands still fisting the fabric of his top, I growl right in his face, "If *anyone* hurts you, I will slit their fucking throat before they can even blink. You're fucking mine."

His face relaxes, and a slow smile spreads across his lips. He sits us both up so that I'm situated on his lap and reaches up to sweep some of my wet hair off my forehead. My eyes flutter closed, and I lean into his touch because...fuck, I love it when he does that.

"Look at me."

I open my eyes at his command.

"I know you're not used to feeling cared about."

My jaw clenches, tightening the dam holding back the mere threat of emotion.

Why did I have to let him see me?

"Despite what you may think, you deserve to be cared about. And I *do* care about you at least enough not to want to see you dead. So get used to it, little monster."

"Is that all?" I try to keep my voice light and teasing, but fuck him for bringing out the vulnerability in me. "Just enough not to want to see me dead?"

I don't think I mean to use magic to dig deeper into his reactions, studying him from the inside out. But that must be the case because I can clearly hear his heart pounding, the rush of blood pumping through his body joining the rhythm of my own pulsing in my ears.

He lets out a breath as his hands settle on my hips, gripping them harder than necessary. "I think it might kill me."

Well, fuck.

Leaning forward, I bury my face into the crook of his neck and shoulder because I can't stand to stare into his eyes a second longer, eyes that are definitely not full of hate right now.

"Tell me you hate me," I muffle into his sweater.

"You know I don't usually have a problem with that." I can hear the grin in his voice, but it does nothing to help the way my heart is threatening to leap out of my chest. "But I won't do that right now. It's not what you need."

He's wrong, but I can't tell him that.

I can't tell him I've only ever survived off hate, that I can't survive without it.

Because...maybe I want to try.

Even if it kills me.

"Come on." He kisses my temple and smacks my thigh. "Let's get started."

I scramble off of him, clearing my throat on the way up. That was too heavy for me, and I'm ready to forget all about it.

Speaking of heavy, I don't know if the weight on my shoulders is from what just happened or from my soaked jacket. Either way, I can't stand the added load, so I peel the jacket off, struggling against the drenched material, and throw it to the ground with a wet *thwack*.

When I turn back to Merlin who's on his feet now too, I find him staring at me, his eyes taking in my dripping black jeans and black T-shirt.

"As much as I'm enjoying the sight of that shirt sticking to your sinful body..." He smirks, still not looking away. "I think we should probably change clothes."

"Right."

Despite the fact I'm shivering, I can't help but grasp the opportunity. Because teasing and taunting and seducing? Those are things I *do* know how to mentally deal with.

Gripping the bottom hem of my shirt, I slowly raise it, letting my fingertips brush over my tattooed abs. Merlin groans, encouraging me further as I lift the material up to expose my chest. His heated gaze has calmed the shivers, and because he's still staring at me, nostrils flaring with the effort of restraint, I give him a show and pinch my right nipple, rolling the steel balls of my piercing between my fingers and letting a quiet moan slip past my lips.

"Mordred," he growls with a warning.

"What?"

I pull my shirt up and over my head and drop it down on top of my jacket, flashing him that smile that's meant to be innocent but is always anything but.

Even though he's glaring at me, his eyes continue raking over my half naked body. I lower my own gaze and am greeted by a very telling bulge in his jeans. Looking back up, my smile turns into a toothy grin.

With a huff, Merlin waves his hands. His sweater and jeans are replaced with black pants, a blank tunic, and a deep, rich purple cloak hanging loosely over his shoulders.

Biting my lip, I hum, a rumble deep in my throat. "There's my wizard."

"Put some damn clothes on, Mordred," he snarls.

As much as I'd love to tease him further, see how far I can push him, that chill is starting to creep back in. Merlin's body would be an excellent source of heat, but I'm not willing to wait for however long it would take to convince him to warm me up.

Ditching the soaking jeans, I change into the last outfit I ever wore in Camelot—black pants, boots, and tunic, covered with stainless steel chainmail that falls to the middle of my thighs. A black leather belt wraps around my waist, holding a scabbard for my sword.

I wrap my hand around the hilt and draw it out, a missing piece of me finding its way back. I may be a sorcerer, but I always loved being a knight and wielding a sword.

The blade was probably dull before I conjured it, but there's no way I was going to brandish one that's rusty and blunt. Here, the sun is high in the sky, and it catches on the blade, the light glinting off the polished steel.

"It's been awhile since I handled a sword," I muse as I twirl it in the air. "But it should be like riding a bike, right?"

When I look at Merlin, he's staring at me. Still. Again? Because now, it's different. His eyes are wide, jaw slack. There's no trace of irritation left.

"What?" I ask as I lower my sword, the question and curiosity genuine this time.

He doesn't answer. Still staring. Still not blinking. Or breathing, I think.

One corner of my mouth slowly tilts up. "Merlin. Do you have a chainmail kink?"

He finally blinks. Clears his throat and shakes his head.

It's dirty thoughts he's shaking from his mind, and that knowledge has me smirking even wider.

"For the record, I never did." His eyes rove over me again. "It must be a *you in chainmail* kink."

I hum again and return my sword to its scabbard before sweeping my hand across the front of my chainmail. "Good to know."

Merlin crosses the distance between us, grabs a fistful of the links of steel, and pulls me even closer until our noses are brushing. "I'm fucking you in this later."

Then it's our lips brushing as I grin against his. "You have to keep me alive first."

He deepens the kiss, his tongue slipping into my mouth. As he pulls back, he licks over my lips. "I've got you."

Letting me go, he steps back, his radiant smile so sure and confident.

Unfortunately, I don't feel the same.

But...it turns out, I trust Merlin with my life.

29

MERLIN

I turn to the lake because if I spend one more second checking Mordred out in that chainmail, I'm going to fuck him in it *now*.

Risking getting caught by the Lady of the Lake isn't exactly on our to-do list.

Stepping up to the edge, I look out over the water. It's bluer than it was back in the world we came from. Calmer. Everything is quieter. The surface of the lake shimmers like it's coated with a fine layer of stardust.

"Nimue!"

A few seconds pass, but the water remains calm. *Too* calm.

I wait.

"Lady!"

Mordred comes to stand beside me. I see his face turn toward mine from the corner of my eye, but I can't look at him, not wanting him to see my fear.

The Lady of the Lake has always come when I've called. But it has been a thousand years…

What if we're too late?

"Nimue, *please*!"

Finally, the water ripples a few feet ahead, and I can finally breathe. The gentle waves reach the bank, and Nimue floats out of the water, breaking through the surface as delicately as a ghost. She hasn't changed a bit—white dress; long, blonde hair; glowing like an angel.

Hovering above the water, she drifts closer to us. She gives me a faint smile, a scarce nod, then turns her gaze to the man beside me.

"You sure did take your time, young sorcerer."

I look at Mordred to see him grimace. "Excuse me?"

He shuffles his feet like he wants to take a step away, but he doesn't and eventually meets my gaze. "How did you think I knew you were meant to bring Arthur back? She'd only agree to take me away from Camelot if I found you and brought you back here."

I should be upset, angry that Mordred was given a mission that he didn't complete for eight-hundred years. However, when I remember how he said he was afraid of showing himself to me the first time he saw me four-hundred years ago, I can't bring myself to be.

Turning back to look at the lake witch, he adds, "And, *technically*, she never gave me a deadline."

Nimue's lingering, blinking stare is impassive and unamused, but when she peers at me, she smiles. Her voice is light and airy with a whimsical echo when she says, "It's good to see you, Merlin."

I return her smile. "You too, Nimue."

Mordred clears his throat, and when I glance at him, I roll my eyes in response to his scowl.

"Why did you let me go?" I ask Nimue. "If I was meant to bring Arthur back?"

"Because you were hurting, and the time for that wouldn't have come soon enough. It was the only way for you to heal."

"Tell me we're not too late."

"It depends on your definition of too late."

Mordred and I share a look, and he at least has the decency to look a *little* guilty, even if he doesn't feel it.

"Obviously, many generations have suffered and passed in the time you two have been away," Nimue says. "But Morgan's reign remains long and bloody and unchallenged. Magic is outlawed, of course, save for her own. She has two bands of knights—her Dark Knights, as she calls them, and the lower knights. The Dark Knights are terribly feared. They're born of dark magic. They'll kill anyone who so much as whispers contempt for the queen, who commits any kind of crime, trials be damned. Any kind of work they're allowed must benefit the crown, and they're paid only with their lives, what's required to sustain them. Sometimes not even that. The people are prisoners in their own land. Their lives, their deaths, mean nothing."

My heart sinks into my gut, heavier than lead, and nausea threatens to bring it right back up my throat.

"She didn't have the Dark Knights when I was here," Mordred says, and he actually *does* sound remorseful. "It sounds like things have gotten worse."

"Does the kingdom remember Arthur's name?" I ask, my voice desperate and unsteady.

Arthur Pendragon was always destined to be a legend, the greatest king of Camelot, never forgotten. We may depend on the memory of him being what brings him back, returns him to the throne.

"Some do. All written records of him—ones Morgan and her Dark Knights were able to get a hold of—were destroyed long ago. But whispers of his name live on, though they are becoming fewer and further between."

"I guess it's good we weren't any later, at least," I mutter, giving Mordred another look, taking in the tension in his shoulders and the deep crease between his brow.

I shouldn't want to comfort him considering this is partly his fault, but…dammit, I do.

I've always been a protector at heart, a trait I inherited from my mother and first felt when it came to her. My magic makes me strong, stronger than most of the souls I've ever cared about—maybe for the exception of the Lady of the Lake. It was easy to fall into that role when so many needed me, needed my power and my strength.

I never expected to feel that for Mordred. But, right now, *he* needs it.

Turning back to the lake and its living spirit, I ask, "What do we need to do, Nimue? To bring Arthur back?"

"You have to get Excalibur."

"Excalibur? I threw it into this lake a thousand years ago. *You* caught it."

She nods, her hair floating around her face, like the very air around her is water. "It had to be moved. Morgan knew about the sword."

My head snaps to the side to scowl at Mordred, who's wincing again, eyes cast down. "Forget to tell me that?"

"Sorry," he mumbles to the ground.

I turn back to Nimue, jaw clenched. "Where is it now?"

"The first place it ever was."

"And how am I supposed to get it without Arthur? I can't get the sword without him, and I can't get him without the sword?"

"You know how."

Damn this lake witch and her vague ass answers.

"Bring me the sword, Merlin," she says as she begins to drift backward, voice carrying as though she's already farther away than she really is. "And I will bring you Arthur."

Nimue lowers once more into the water, leaving nothing but a calm, shimmering surface.

Taking a deep breath, I run my hand through my hair, tugging at the strands. This little shit sure did leave out some important details…

Turning to him, I grasp him by the throat and haul him toward me. "Tell me again that you didn't want me here for other reasons, Mordred. Tell me this isn't to get that sword for your mother. Or for you."

He can deny it all he wants, but there *is* guilt swimming in his eyes. But at my half accusations, anger sweeps it away.

"I didn't!" he spits back. "If you don't believe me, if you want me to leave, just say so."

When I tighten my grip just a little, fear joins the emotions on his face. I don't *want* him to fear me, but my demons sure do enjoy it.

Instead of giving into them, I lean my forehead against his, loosening my hold around his throat but keeping my hand there. "I'm choosing to trust you, Mordred. Please don't make me regret it."

"You won't." He grabs onto the edges of my cloak, holding me close. "*I swear.*"

Closing the distance between us, I press my lips to his and coax his mouth open with my tongue so I can taste him. I deepen the kiss until our teeth clash, until I can reach as far inside him as possible, like I can lick every truth he's ever hidden with the tip of my tongue, touch every secret that's never passed his lips.

He gives them up willingly. They may not form words, but they do form something that means more than words could say.

When we pull back, breathing heavily, we're no longer standing at the edge of the lake. Even though Mordred senses it, it takes him several seconds to break free from my gaze to check our new surroundings.

We're now in a dark cave, illuminated only by a small opening high up in the far wall, the glow of day barely reaching us. The spotlight shines down on a stone in the center of the cave. Sure enough, Excalibur is buried into the rock nearly to the hilt, cobwebs glistening in the stream of sunlight.

The steady drip of water reverberates off the walls, and the air is thick. We've still barely caught our breath.

"I told her about Excalibur." Mordred stares at the sword, his voice too quiet to echo. "I overheard you and Arthur talking about it one night, that the blade is capable of fighting against dark magic and that whoever wore the scabbard couldn't bleed. It's why I couldn't kill Arthur with magic and why Morgan ordered me to destroy the scabbard." He scoffs and shakes his head. "I guess I should've kept it and wore it myself."

As he speaks, I move around him, coming to stand on the other side of the stone. He doesn't look away from the sword. I watch as his Adam's apple moves with a swallow, the line between his brows so deep I fear it might crack.

"If I'm sorry for anything, it's for listening to *her*. For being her pawn. For letting her make me her fucking puppet. I should've seen right through her. Arthur was cruel, but Morgan was devious and manipulative. It should've been obvious that she never truly cared about me, that she'd never let me have the throne when she could take it for herself."

He finally looks up, our gazes meeting across the stream of light. There's a war raging within his eyes, like he doesn't know who he is on his own. Eight-hundred years hasn't been long enough for him to figure it out.

"I'm sorry, Merlin."

"I'm curious about something." I cross my arms over my chest, a sign to let him know that I'm genuinely not happy with him at the moment. "What would you have done if Morgan wasn't in the picture? If she abandoned you with Arthur and vanished forever? Would you still have killed him?"

His frown deepens, and he shrugs. "I honestly don't know. I'll never know, Merlin. The truth is I hated him too. So maybe? All I can tell you for certain is that *right now*, I want to see Arthur come back from the dead and run Morgan through with this fucking sword."

"That's good enough for me." I suppress a smile and nod at Excalibur. "Now prove it. Get the sword."

"Excuse me?" His brows shoot up. "*Me?*"

"Did you think *I* could take it out of there?"

Mordred takes a step back, looking at me as though I've lost my mind. "And you think I can? Don't you have to be worthy? Pure of heart or some shit?"

"That was only part of the myth. The only thing you have to be is the rightful king of Camelot."

He looks down at the sword and shakes his head. "But…"

"That's *you*. You might be Arthur's illegitimate son, but you are his *only* son. His only heir. Therefore, the throne does rightfully belong to you. So does Excalibur."

A dozen different emotions flit across his face, skipping around faster than I can translate them. I'd be lying if I said I wasn't tempted to dive into his mind to see for myself what he's thinking.

Fortunately, Mordred's more open to me than he's ever been before.

"I could use the sword to defeat Morgan on my own," he says, like he's thinking out loud. "I wouldn't even need to bring Arthur back. I could get rid of the witch and take her crown."

"You could," I agree, even while my heart feels as though it weighs ten times more than normal.

He peers back up at me. "I'd never see you again, would I?"

The faint smile I give him is sad. "No."

Is that true though? It *has* to be. As obsessed with Mordred as I've become, I don't think I could forgive him for killing Arthur all over again. It would hurt even worse this time.

Pain and fear mingle in his eyes as he looks at me, practically pleading. "What if the sword tempts me, Merlin? What if I'm not strong enough to resist it?"

"Remember when I said I'm choosing to trust you?"

His eyes fall back to Excalibur, and he whispers, more to himself, "I swore you wouldn't regret it."

The way he's chewing violently on his bottom lip, clearly distressed, has me concerned he's hitting some kind of existential crisis. I wish I could help him through this, but the fact is that I can't. He's the only one who can pull that sword from the stone, and whatever he chooses to do after is completely up to him.

I shouldn't be surprised that Mordred had to be here, that he *would* be here. The Lady of the Lake is a powerful seer, her premonitions far more potent than my own.

"Go ahead, Mordred." I give him another small smile when he meets my gaze. "I trust you."

A month ago, I never would've imagined speaking those words. But, now, I know they're true. He's mine, and I won't let even himself take him away from me.

Some of the tension eases from his shoulders, and he nods before stepping toward the stone between us. He stares at the sword for a long while like he's afraid to even touch it, and I swear my heart starts to match the *drip, drip, drip* of water echoing around us as I hold my breath.

Finally, he wraps one hand around the hilt and pulls.

30

MORDRED

Excalibur's blade scrapes against rock as I withdraw it from the stone, the harsh grating filling the cave and my ears and that little empty piece of my soul where any sense of worth might have once been.

I'm the rightful king of Camelot.

I hold the sword out in front of me, the bit of daylight spilling into the cave glinting off the blade. It's beautiful. As I stare at it, I don't feel its magic, its power, like I thought I might though. I don't hear it speaking to me.

What I *do* hear are those dark voices in my own head.

I could use this to defeat Morgan. I wouldn't even need to bring Arthur back.

He could stay dead.

I wouldn't have to face the father that never wanted me.

When I glance past the sword at Merlin, I see his brows drawn down as he studies me, waiting for what I'll do next.

Arthur could stay dead.

I lower the sword and hold it out. "Take it, Merlin. Please."

As he rounds the stone, his gaze never leaves mine. He takes his time, testing me, giving me the opportunity to change my mind.

"Are you sure?" he asks as he stops in front of me on the other side of the sword.

As loud as those voices in my head are, I'm not listening to them anymore. Because...

"I don't want any of it, Merlin. Not if it means I lose you."

He releases a long breath as though he had been holding it for ages. Taking the sword from me, he places it gently on top of the stone, then turns back to me. He fists the front of my chainmail and tugs me forward. I go easily, feeling weak, drained from resisting those voices in my head.

"If you need me to be the light that pulls you from the darkness, Mordred, then I will gladly be that for you." He kisses me until I'm fucking dizzy, then growls against my lips. "I'm fucking you in this chainmail now."

I grin at the drastic subject change. Some of my energy comes back to me even while my blood rushes to my cock. "Don't we need to go bring Arthur back?"

"He's waited a thousand years. He can wait one more hour."

His mouth comes back to mine, his tongue licking across my lips before I open them, inviting him in as his tongue dives inside. Moving his hands to the hem of my chainmail, he raises it up above my belt. When he grinds his hard length against mine, I never thought I'd be so happy to be back in Camelot where the clothes are made of thinner material than damn jeans.

He moans into my mouth, and I swallow it deep down into my lungs. It comes back up as a whine when he tears his mouth from mine.

"Get on your fucking knees."

I smirk, cocky, like he doesn't already have me completely breathless. "I'm the rightful king. Shouldn't you be the one kneeling?"

Merlin fucking growls again, grips my hair tight, and pushes me down until I'm where he wants me. He yanks my head back by my hair, forcing me to look up at him as he takes himself out of his pants. His cock hangs heavy in front of my face, leaking precum that makes my mouth water. When I try to lean forward to taste him, he jerks my head back.

Fuck if I don't love Merlin when he's being demanding, dominant...

My brain short circuits.

As I stare up into his darkened eyes, I know it wasn't just a fleeting, lust-drunk thought.

I don't think I've ever loved anyone before, or at least been *in* love. So my point of reference is shit. But...

Fuck. I think I'm in love with Merlin.

"Are you okay, little monster?"

I realize I'm panting heavily, as though the epiphany knocked the wind out of me, probably staring up at him with little sickening hearts in my eyes.

No. No, I'm not okay.

"Are you going to knight me with your sword, Merlin?" I ask, plastering the smirk right back on my face, trading in the pathetic mess Merlin's turned me into for my usual snarky self.

Neither one of us is ready for *that* kind of revelation.

"Sure." With one hand still keeping my head back and the other grasping the base of his dick, he brings the head of his cock to my lips, painting them with precum. "How about Sir Cockslut?"

I don't even get the chance to lick the taste of him off my lips before he's thrusting into my mouth, forcing his way in, all the way to the back of my throat. I gag from the sudden intrusion, and my eyes instantly water. He pulls back long enough to let me suck in a breath before he's ramming into my throat again.

Merlin's rough treatment has me moaning around his hard length and my own cock aching. I don't think I'll ever, ever get enough of this. Of *him*.

"Fuck, Mordred. You look so fucking beautiful on your knees with a cock in your mouth."

Merlin hates me. There's no way his compliments are lies.

I peer up at him through the blur of tears gathered in my eyes. His gaze is so intense, passionate, blazing with heat that shoots right down my spine.

I can't help it anymore. I reach down to desperately stroke my cock through my pants.

Hauling me off his dick by my hair, Merlin growls, "Don't you dare."

He heaves me to my feet, steadying me when I sway. With a bruising kiss, he licks away the saliva and precum on my lips before biting my bottom one, lip ring and all. I nip back at him until we're both groaning, then we go at each other's mouths until I'm dizzy all over again.

I don't even realize Merlin had been forcing me backward until my back hits the cave wall. His tongue remains in my mouth, battling against mine, as he lifts my chainmail again and drags my pants down around my thigh, freeing my hard, aching, dripping cock. When he takes us both into his hand, I moan loudly into his mouth.

Pulling back, he continues stroking us, slicking us with our precum and my magical spit-turned-lube. I thrust against him, making sure he feels each of my piercings along his shaft.

He groans as he looks at me through dark, hooded eyes. "I never thought I'd be so obsessed with a pierced dick."

I growl. "*My* pierced dick."

Something in him softens as he grins. "Yours."

Before I can let my possessive mouth run more, Merlin shoves three fingers inside of it. My cock jerks and leaks more precum in his hand as he thrusts his fingers over my tongue.

"I'm obsessed with this fucking pierced tongue too." He holds my gaze hostage as he continues working his fingers in my mouth, driving them in deep until I'm drooling around them, soaking them. "It feels so good on my cock."

I moan just as he withdrawals his fingers and releases us. He spins me around, presses my front against the wall, and splits me open with a rough hand on one cheek. When he pushes two fingers inside of me, I moan even louder, my back arching.

"Fuck, Merlin. Hurry up. I need you inside me. I don't care if it hurts."

"You want pain, little monster?"

"Yes—*fuuuck*."

Merlin bites down in the crook of my neck and shoulder, so hard I wouldn't be surprised if his teeth pierced skin.

It's probably payback for the snakes.

I'll gladly take it.

The pain of Merlin's bite and the pleasure of his fingers thrusting inside me send me into a desperate spiral as I start grinding against the cave wall. I don't even care that it's damp and dirty and gross. I just want fucking friction.

At the same time he adds a third finger, he bites down even harder. I cry out, drowning in all the sensations, in the heat of Merlin's body at my back, in *him*.

"Please," I beg with a whimper. "I need you, Merlin."

He finally releases his teeth, and I just know the mark he's left me with is going to be sore as fuck. That thought makes me even harder. I want to feel him all over forever.

Merlin withdrawals his fingers, and then the head of his cock is nudging against my hole. One hand comes up to grip my chin, and he forces my head to the side, his touch and mere presence demanding my eyes meet his.

He speaks in a deep, husky voice that sends another bolt of electricity down my spine as he repeats what I told him not long ago. "You have me, Mordred."

A hungry, desperate sound escapes me, and he captures it with his mouth. As his tongue dives past my lips, his cock slips past my rim. The sound still clawing its way up my throat turns more urgent and feral as he pushes inside me and swirls his tongue around mine. I try to kiss him back with as much ardent fervency as he does me, but all I can feel and focus on is his cock stretching me and filling me like he's the piece I've been missing for a thousand years.

"Fuck," he groans as he breaks the kiss and rests his forehead against my temple. "I still can't believe how fucking good you feel."

"You feel good too, Merlin." I push back against him, begging for more. "So good."

He grips my hips, driving in slowly so I feel every blessed inch of him, until he's fully sheathed inside me and we're moaning in sync.

"How do you want to be fucked, little monster?" he asks.

"Hard." Because I don't think I can handle anything else right now. "Fuck all your hate into me again."

Merlin's fingers dig hard into my hips as he pulls out and thrusts back in. *Fucking slow*. It's agonizing and blissful, devastating and fucking divine.

"I said hard," I whine as my eyes flutter closed.

"Maybe I want to fuck you slow. Maybe I don't hate you right now."

I don't hate you either.

I don't think I ever did.

I don't say it, but I think he knows. He kisses my jaw and down my neck to where he bit me, then he licks his way back up. All the while he continues fucking me slow and deep. *So* fucking deep. I don't complain again because the pleasure is all-consuming and enchanting, as if he has me under a spell.

My cock is hard and aching, and I shamelessly grind it against the wall with each of Merlin's thrusts. The rough friction every time his cock slowly strokes my prostate has the tension building, the heat in my spine burning hotter.

"Fuck, Merlin," I groan as he nips along my jaw and neck. "I'm gonna come."

He pulls me back by my hips, and I whimper as I lose the friction of the wall. Reaching around, he grasps the base of my cock and growls in my ear, "You can come when I tell you to come."

I let out a desperate, pathetic noise. "Merlin, please."

"You can beg all you want." His thrusts turn a little faster, a little harder, as he chases his release. "In fact, please do. But you'll still come when I let you. You're mine and so are your fucking orgasms."

Fuck.

I whine and try to thrust into his hand, but of course he doesn't let me. I only end up taking him deeper, each strike against my prostate both torturous and thrilling, knowing he's in control of every part of me, especially my pleasure.

"Fuck. Please." I moan as he fucks me with increased urgency. "I want to come with you inside me."

"No. I'm going to fill your ass, and then you're going to fill my stomach."

If Merlin wasn't denying me an orgasm right now, I could've come from his words alone.

He fulfills the first part of his promise, hips stuttering before going still, his cock pulsing inside me with each warm jet of cum. He grunts and growls in my ear as he releases my dick to grip my hips again, his fingers digging in so hard I know they'll leave bruises.

The second he pulls out of me, his two fingers replace his cock, never letting a drop of his release escape, fucking it all as deep into me as he can. I moan, my head rolling back on my shoulders as I rut against the wall again.

Merlin spins me around, tucks himself back into his pants, and slams his mouth to mine in a hard, filthy kiss. Before I can fall too deep into it, he's gone, and by the time I open my eyes, he's already on his knees.

He peers up at me, panting heavily. "Use me, Mordred. Come down my throat."

Fuck again.

When I grip his hair and tug his head back, he lets out the sexiest fucking moan I've ever heard, and my cock jerks in front of his face. He opens his mouth and sticks out his tongue.

I'm obsessed with the way he falls into submission so easily, even after dominating the fuck out of me. When it's exactly what he needs. Or what I need.

What we *both* need.

"You think I look beautiful with a cock in my mouth?" I bring my dick to his lips, stroking it along his warm tongue. "You're fucking hot when it's your mouth stuffed full."

Slamming my hips forward, I groan as the head of my cock hits the back of his throat. His eyes widen from the intrusion, but he doesn't even gag because he's so damn skilled, eagerly opening up for me.

I wish I could take my time with this, but I'm already so fucking close from the edging and from the sight of Merlin on his knees. Just a few thrusts have my balls drawing up, aching and pleading for release.

When Merlin moans around my cock, I'm fucking gone.

Gripping the back of his head with both hands, I hold him pressed against me with my dick so far down his throat his eyes start to water. My orgasm rips through me like a tidal wave as he swallows around my cock and my release shoots down his throat. Even after I let him go, he doesn't move, making sure he gets every last drop.

He rises to his feet, having to be the one to keep *me* steady as my body threatens to collapse.

"Are you going to let me taste myself on you this time?" I ask breathlessly.

Merlin grins, places his hands on the sides of my head, and presses his lips to mine. The kiss isn't ravenous or urgent like all our other ones have been. He kisses me slowly, softly, an unhurried sweep of lips and tongues that has me tasting every bit of myself on him. I let a quiet, satisfied noise slip into his mouth as I grip his cloak and pull him even closer to me.

He moves away sooner than I'm ready for him to, but he makes up for it by brushing hair off my forehead. I instinctively lean into his touch.

"Are you ready?"

"No," I answer honestly.

"You've come this far, Mordred. I know you can do this." He leans his forehead against mine, and I feel like I can breathe a little easier. "You've got me."

I give him a small smile. "My light."

"Whenever you need it. Always."

My heart clenches.

Always.

31

MERLIN

I stand at the edge of the Lake of Avalon again, this time with Excalibur in my hand. Mordred is hidden somewhere in the trees behind me because I need a chance to convince Arthur not to kill him. Even with having the time to persuade him before he sees Mordred, doing so will be a challenge.

I have zero misconceptions that this will be easy.

Taking a deep, steadying breath, I raise the sword and throw it through the air, releasing it out into the lake. Just like a thousand years ago, the Lady of the Lake stretches her softly glowing hand out of the water to catch the sword by the hilt before pulling it under.

This time, Excalibur resurfaces seconds later, held by a different hand. A human hand.

A head of blond hair breaks through the surface of the water next. Arthur gasps for air as though he had been held under all this time, his first living breath in a thousand years.

He slings his wet hair from his face, shimmering water droplets flying off him, returning to their magical home in the lake.

When Arthur's eyes open, they immediately find me standing at the edge of the water. He stills, staring, blinking like he can't believe what he's seeing.

"Merlin?"

"Hello, Arthur."

I hold my breath as his expression remains unchanging.

I failed him. I couldn't stop his death despite seeing it in a premonition.

Maybe he won't forgive me.

But then a wide smile breaks out on his face, and the tension in my body deflates. I watch as my resurrected friend trudges through the water toward the bank, feeling happy and maybe a little hopeful now that he's back.

However, when the water is around his knees and he places Excalibur in the scabbard at his side, I notice he's wearing the same chainmail and armor he was that day during the Battle of Camlann. It's all stained with dark blood around the broken links of chainmail.

A knot lodges in my throat. How am I supposed to convince Arthur not to kill Mordred when he wears the memories of what he did?

My uncertainty and guilt only increase when Arthur fully emerges from the lake and stands before me, his brilliant smile unwavering. His eyes shine as blue as the lake behind him.

Just like Mordred's.

If only I had seen how much of his father was in him all that time ago, maybe Arthur and I could've nurtured that side of him instead of only seeing the part that came from Morgan, instead of continuously pushing him toward his mother and her dark magic.

I can't change the past. I can only hope to do better now and in the future.

"It's good to see you, Merlin."

"It's good to see you too." My voice is choked with as much emotion as his.

We close the distance and embrace. I close my eyes and let myself bask in the joy and relief at having my friend back from the dead before all hell breaks loose.

"I missed you, Arthur," I admit.

"How long has it been?" he asks as he pulls back.

"A thousand years."

His eyes go wide. "Why am I back now?"

Here comes all hell...

Buying myself a little more time before I tell him about Mordred, I tell him about Morgan first instead. That she's taken the throne and is reigning over Camelot as a tyrannical witch. I tell him everything Nimue told us. His spirits sink lower and lower the more I speak.

"That doesn't exactly answer my question," he says once I've told him all I know, at least about Morgan. "Why am I back *now*? After a thousand years? Where have you been all this time?"

I grimace and glance away toward the glittering lake. We've made our way over to a cluster of boulders where we sit side by side facing the water. The sun is low in the sky, dipping closer to the horizon, causing the lake to glisten with a golden hue.

"I ran away," I confess with a frown as I look back at Arthur. "I failed you and couldn't face it. So I left."

"We both failed, Merlin. The blame is not solely yours."

And this is why Arthur was always destined to be the king of Camelot, why it was his fate to pull Excalibur from the stone. He's fair and honest and benevolent. He's a *good* man.

I hold that thought as close as I can.

"We failed Mordred too."

Arthur's eyes widen even more than when I told him how much time has passed. "Excuse me? You can't possibly be talking about the man who *killed me*."

I take a deep breath and let it out. "I am." When Arthur is struck by stunned silence, I continue. "A lot has changed, Arthur. I've realized that I was wrong, that I made a mistake. *We* made a mistake."

He stands as though he can't stomach the blasphemous things coming out of my mouth. "The only mistake we made was trusting him at all! Welcoming him into Camelot and making him a knight."

"No." I stand too, facing him. "Our mistake was not giving him more of a chance. You turned your back on him as his father, and I allowed you to. Hell, I justified it. Because of that, he hated you when he didn't need to."

"You're defending him?" he snarls.

"No," I say again. "I'm not giving him an excuse. I'm just saying that we gave him his reason."

"And tell me, Merlin, what's the difference?"

I sigh, considering my words carefully. "An excuse deflects the blame off of him, and that's not what I'm trying to do. Even he takes responsibility for his choices. But that's not to say we didn't play a role in them."

Arthur stares at me for a long while, his face turning redder by the second. "*Takes?* Present tense?"

Fuck.

Well, he was going to find out sooner rather than later.

I nod. "He's alive."

He fumes as his eyes dart around the area. "Is he here?"

"Arthur, listen to me." I take a step forward. "He's the one who found me and told me you were meant to come back, meant to defeat Morgan. He *wants* that. He came with me. He pulled Excalibur from the stone so we could bring you back. You're here, alive, now, *because* of him."

"Can't you see what's happening, Merlin? He's obviously tricked you. Used his dark magic to lure you here."

"That's not true."

I'm surprised by just how much conviction my words hold, how much I fully believe them. After our time in the cave, I trust Mordred even *more*. His eyes did that thing where they open up without him fully meaning them to, making him vulnerable. The truth was clear—the emotion, the feeling, the need.

He *needs* me, and I'm pretty sure I need him.

"Is a thousand years how long it takes someone to lose their mind?" Arthur snarls.

Then from the lake comes a musical voice like soft bells as Nimue calls to him. "Arthur."

His head whips to the side to peer out over the water, and something in him settles, a calm washing over his face. He stares wistfully toward the lake, as though he's remembering.

"You spent a lot of time in Avalon, Arthur," I say. "If you remember any of it, then you know just how significant you are. Very few mortals have ever visited Avalon. But you are the once and future king, and there is a reason for that. You're the best king that Camelot has ever known, *will* ever know. You are compassionate and merciful and wise. But even the wise make mistakes. Giving Mordred another chance could help right the wrong we both made."

"He *killed* me, Merlin!" Arthur shouts, whatever magic Nimue had called to him with obviously not quite hitting its mark. "Are you prepared to pronounce that my fate was deserved because I chose not to claim him as my son?"

"No, of course not. Not in the least. But as I said, a lot has changed."

Like my feelings for your son…

"I think *you've* changed." Arthur takes a step toward me, seething, and any hope I had left withers. "Maybe I shouldn't trust you any longer. If you're going to stand between me and Mordred, then maybe I should move you out of my way."

"Mordred isn't the problem right now! It's Morgan."

But Arthur's fury is unmovable. At least I know Mordred's anger doesn't come *just* from his mother.

His fists clench at his side, and I swear I hear my heart fracture. I knew this wasn't going to be easy, but I should've expected it to be impossible. I never wanted to choose between the two men I care for most, and I'm scared that's what it's going to come to.

"If you hurt Merlin, I'll kill you again."

Mordred's slow drawl attracts both our attention, our heads turning to where he leans against a tree only a few yards away, appearing bored.

Turning his scowl back to me, Arthur arches a brow. "Well, that inspires confidence."

I close my eyes and let out a heavy sigh.

Fuck.

"Mordred, you're not supposed to be here."

"It's not like you're getting anywhere with this anyway." He rolls his eyes before they find Arthur, and he gives him a smirk that I'd find sexy in literally any other situation. "Hello, Father. I see you came back from the dead in one piece. Pity."

If he was any closer, I'd wrap my hands around his throat for thinking it's a good idea to antagonize Arthur right now.

Maybe later…

If Arthur doesn't fucking kill him first.

Unsurprisingly, Arthur turns away from me and marches across the rocks and grass in Mordred's direction, withdrawing Excalibur on his way. My heart leaps into my throat, and I chase after him. Magic cracks down my arms like lightning, burning hot in my palms and tingling at the tips of my fingers.

I won't hurt Arthur, but I promised Mordred I wouldn't let him hurt him.

However, before I can catch up, Mordred holds up his hand, and my feet immediately become rooted to the ground as I hit some kind of invisible barrier.

Arthur reaches Mordred. Mordred does nothing to stop him as he brings the sharp edge of Excalibur's blade to his neck.

"Arthur!"

In a desperate attempt, magic shoots from my hands in a wisp of ashy blue smoke, but it hits the shield in front of me and disintegrates.

Arthur doesn't move. He keeps the sword against Mordred's throat, glaring down his nose at his son with red eyes, his shoulders tense with the effort it takes not to strike him down.

"What are you doing, Mordred?" I ask, voice strained as I try to fight against his magic, my heart in my fucking throat, blood rushing in my ears.

He doesn't look at me, eyes fixed on Arthur as he says, "This is between me and him."

Despite how terrified he was to come back to Camelot and face his father again, he doesn't look afraid right now.

"Arthur," I plead, panic surging through me as my body trembles with it.

Please don't take him from me.

If I let my demons out right now, I could probably draw enough power to take out this fucking wall in front of me. However, if I did that, I might end up taking Arthur out with it…

"You would keep him from saving you?" Arthur asks Mordred.

"I won't make him choose between us."

"You think he cares for you?"

Mordred's eyes flicker to mine only briefly before they're back on the man with the sword to his neck. "He cares about me more than you ever did at least."

Fuck. Don't make this more difficult, Mordred.

If I could, I'd tell them both just how much I *do* care about him, but that would surely result in more of Arthur's wrath.

Then again, I'm too fucking close to ending this problem myself.

"I'll tell you what, Mordred," Arthur snarls, pressing Excalibur a little harder against his throat. "I've always trusted Merlin with my life, but right now I'm not sure if I can do that. This sword will deflect any dark magic you attempt to use on me. I'll give you one chance and one chance only. Give me a reason not to run you through."

Mordred's Adam's apple bobs against the blade. "You need me. I can help you take down Morgan and reclaim your throne."

"Not good enough. I'd rather spill your blood."

Arthur's arm twitches, preparing to strike.

That cage door in my mind cracks open...

Before my demons can escape, the voice from the lake speaks again. "Arthur."

The King's gaze snaps back, looking past me to the water, the fury on his face faltering as the Lady of Lake tries to reach him again.

It gives Mordred a chance to move, but it's not to defend himself. He reaches up to the collar of his chainmail, pulling it and the tunic he wears beneath down as far as they'll go, revealing the right side of his chest.

When Arthur looks back, he sees the Pendragon crest inked into his skin. His anger recedes a little further, replaced by a disconcerted astonishment.

"Why do you have that?"

Mordred glances at me again where I'm still blocked by his goddamn magical barricade. There's a hint of fear in his eyes now, but I don't think it's from death. Rather, it's from the vulnerability he's always been so terrified of, what he views as a weakness, what's peeking out and about to take over.

He looks back at Arthur, swallows again, and speaks in a voice that makes it sound as though he's fighting against the words. "Because had you given me the chance, I would've rather chosen to be a Pendragon than a le Fay. It's a reminder of how much of a disappointment you were and that sometimes it's necessary to take what you want."

Arthur's jaw falls slack, a pained, stunned expression in his bright eyes.

Maybe I'm a little jealous that Mordred decided to share the secrets of the tattoo with Arthur before me, but mostly...I'm fucking proud of him.

But I don't know if it's enough.

Arthur still holds Excalibur to Mordred's throat, indecision etched all over his face. His hand tightens around the hilt of the sword, his knuckles turning white.

Nimue speaks again, her voice like an echo around us. "Remember who you are, Arthur."

The king stares at Mordred, a thousand thoughts and memories and choices no doubt racing through his mind. The quiet trickle of water against rocks, the distant call of birdsong, and the rapid beating of all our hearts are the only things that fill the otherwise tense silence.

Finally, slowly, Arthur lowers his sword and takes a step back.

As though blown down by the gust of air I exhale all at once from my lungs, the magical barrier before me falls away. The first thing I want to do is run to Mordred and hold him, kiss him. *Hard*. Punish him for that fucking stunt he pulled.

Of course, I can't do any of that. Not in front of Arthur.

Instead, I approach them both a hell of a lot more composed than I feel. I give Mordred a look, asking with my eyes if he's okay. As it usually does, his moment of vulnerability seems to have drained him some, but he nods anyway.

I turn to Arthur next. "If it means anything, he promised not to kill you again."

It was meant to lighten the mood, but it doesn't reach him past the war raging behind his eyes. I don't know what happened to his soul in Avalon or what he remembers—I may never know—but I can see the torment he's experiencing. Between being the good, gracious man he is, the part of him that the magic of Avalon would have only intensified, and facing the son who murdered him and the desire for revenge, it's difficult to know where his heart will land.

"He also promised to help us rid Camelot of Morgan," I tell him. "I know it's difficult to trust me right now, but I trust *him* to help us do that."

Arthur finally comes to his senses, sheathing Excalibur. He makes it a point to avoid looking in Mordred's direction. "And where do you propose we start?"

"If you're both interested," Mordred says, "I have an idea."

It's dark.

So fucking dark.

The darkness presses in on me, suffocating me. It's the purest form of black, a total absence of light or hope.

There's no escape.

It feels tangible, its weight like being at the deepest depths of the ocean. The pressure crushes me, burning my lungs.

Suddenly, there's light. Just enough…

"*Merlin?*"

32

M⊛RDRED

I'm awakened in the middle of the night to the disconcerting sound of Merlin gasping for air. I remain still,
lying on the hard ground a few feet away, listening and
saying nothing while pretending to still be asleep. It
sounds as though he woke from a dream, or maybe a premonition, so I wait for a clue as to which one.

Surprisingly, the guys went for my idea, even if Merlin
did have to do a little more convincing on my behalf—and
even if Arthur gave me about a hundred more death glares
throughout the day on our way to the edge of the forest just
outside the lower village of Camelot. We'll be going to the
castle before sunrise, and Arthur refused to let Merlin and
I use magic to make the journey faster. He still doesn't trust
either of us, me even less. Not that I blame him.

The stars wink down at us through the opening of the
canopy of trees surrounding the small clearing we're camped
out in. When I slowly shift my head to the side, I can see

that Merlin's eyes are open, the glow of the small fire illuminating his face. He's staring up at the sky, still breathing a
little heavily, a deep crease between his furrowed brows.

Premonition it is.

"What'd you see, Merlin?" I ask, keeping my voice quiet.

Arthur is asleep on the other side of the fire, having put
as much space between him and us as he could for the night.
Merlin and I are closer. If we both reached out, we could
touch.

Merlin turns his head to meet my gaze. The flickering
flames cast dancing shadows over his face, crackling in the
quiet night. When he smiles, the heat that licks across my skin
isn't just from the fire.

"Do you trust me?"

"Yes," I answer without hesitation.

He turns his face skyward again and says nothing else.
I frown when I realize he's not going to tell me. But I meant
what I said. I *do* trust him.

I close my eyes, expecting Merlin to go back to sleep.

"I'm surprised by how well you're behaving around
Arthur."

My eyes snap open to glare petulantly at him even
though he's still staring up at the stars.

I guess I haven't been goading or antagonizing Arthur
like I did when he first came back. I haven't been cruel or
picking fights with him like Merlin probably expected I
would—hell, like *I* would've expected myself to.

"I told you I don't care about him anymore." I wince as
soon as the words are out of my mouth. If I can hear the lie in
them, Merlin undoubtedly can too.

I think the truth is I just don't have it in me.

During my time in that other world, I witnessed a lot of
children spurned by their parents simply disown them, cut

them out of their lives, and move on. I was always jealous of how easily they seemed to get the fuck over it.

But me?

I've held a grudge against both my parents for a millennium.

Maybe there's something wrong with me.

"You were scared to come back," Merlin says, turning to look at me. "You didn't look afraid when Arthur was about to kill you."

I grin. "I almost pissed myself."

He laughs, a little louder than he intended I think. He quickly falls quiet, and we listen as Arthur shuffles around on the other side of the fire.

"I've been curious about that," he says in a lower voice as soon as Arthur falls still again. "You sure weren't afraid of death a thousand years ago. You were practically cackling in the face of it after being stabbed by Excalibur. What changed?"

It's my turn to stare up at the night sky as I shrug. "A thousand years passed. You'd think such a long existence would have me welcoming death, but…" I force myself to look back at him. "Can you honestly say that your twelve-hundred-year existence wouldn't feel completely meaningless if you were to die tomorrow?"

His brows dip, casting deeper shadows there. After a moment, an easy smile slowly stretches his lips. "I think so. My life feels pretty meaningful right now."

Well, fuck me.

I have to look away from Merlin's eyes that are burning their way right through mine, searing a path straight to my soul, the one that was all but dead not too long ago.

As I turn my face to the stars again, I try to control the rapid flutter of my heart, the rhythm rivaling one of Ava's drum solos. The stars wink down at me, letting me know I'm not hiding a damn thing. I'm sure Merlin can see the swift rise and fall of my chest, feel the pounding of my heart vibrating through the ground we lay on.

Maybe he didn't mean it like that...

Except...*my* life feels more meaningful too.

Now that Merlin's in it.

Maybe that's why I didn't show my fear in the face of Arthur's rage. Maybe I wasn't truly as afraid as I thought I'd be.

"Mordred?"

Keeping my gaze fixed skyward, I clear my throat, though my voice still comes out too thick. "Yeah?"

"Why do you go by le Fay?"

"What?"

"You told Arthur you'd rather have been a Pendragon, but you still go by le Fay."

I have to shake my head, clear it of previous thoughts to focus on his question. Forcing a grin back on my face, I peer back at him. "I don't think I agreed to twenty questions." But the genuine curiosity shining in his eyes, like he's determined to discover the very secrets of the universe, is too hard to resist. "I was in a band. Mordred le Fay sounded badass. There's nothing more to it than that. I did use Pendragon a few times, but when I did...I don't know. I felt like I was living a lie. Even more so when I wasn't going by Mordred."

"Well now I have to know some of the other names you used."

"Forget it."

But then Merlin's bottom lip pokes out in a cute-as-fuck pout that makes me want to kiss it. Maybe lick it. Bite it.

Fuck, I wish we were alone.

I give into it in another way and say, "I once went by Lancelot as a joke."

He laughs again, this time softer. "Don't tell Arthur that."

For several seconds, I simply stare at him, at the smile lingering on his face. For someone who shares his mind with demons, how the fuck does he have his shit together better than me? Sure, I rattled their cages for a while there, probably always will, but beyond that, Merlin has this carefree, easy spirit that I realize now how insanely jealous of it I am.

"You didn't have a father, right?" I ask, immediately regretting the way the eyes appear to dim a little.

"No. I had a mortal, biological mother, but I was conceived by magic, by demons."

Maybe that's why. He was never let down by shitty parents.

"You're lucky," I whisper, more to myself. But Merlin hears it.

"Because I didn't have a father?"

"Because you had a mother who loved you."

He nods. "I did. Even though I had to watch her die."

"But at least she loved you until the end."

"Mordred, the love that you deserve can never be determined by how much love was or wasn't given to you by your parents. Or anyone else for that matter."

Again, I have to look away, needing to hide the immediate burning behind my eyes. "You want to know the truth, Merlin?" I ask, trying not to choke on my words. "I meant what I told Arthur. I think if I was a son he could've loved, he would've been a good father."

"Even a good man has flaws. He *would* be a good father."

"The other truth that it's really my mother I don't care about anymore. She's the one who poisoned his mind against me when she tricked him into conceiving me. Instead of letting her poison my mind too, I should've brought him her head on a silver platter."

"You still can."

I look back at him to see him smiling at me, reaching out his hand across the stretch of ground between us.

"I'll help you."

If I tell him I'm in love with him, would he change his mind?

I don't risk it. I reach out toward him and lace my fingers with his. I don't even care if Arthur wakes and sees us. I fall asleep holding Merlin's hand.

We're all up before the sun, the clearing plunged into darkness as I kick dirt over the fire to put it out. I was tempted to kick Arthur too to wake him, but I resisted the urge.

Look at me being all mature and shit.

I don't know if it was my talk with Merlin last night or the decent rest I got once I was touching him, but I feel a renewed spark.

However, it's snuffed out just like the damn fire with the first scowl of the day from Arthur. But something about it is different today. It's less fury and more...confused? Not that I hate it any less.

Merlin must sense it because he gives my shoulder a comforting squeeze and offers a faint, reassuring smile. "You ready?"

I respond with a silent nod, then lead the way out of the clearing.

As we make our way to the edge of the forest and through the lower village of Camelot, we move quickly and quietly, though I can hear Arthur and Merlin speaking in hushed voices behind me. I don't attempt to overhear. I need to keep my head clear for what comes next.

The roads of the village are empty and dark, only a few windows lit by the glow of fires to keep their homes warm at night. Other than the wind sighing through the alleys, everything is quiet, all the villagers tucked away asleep.

When we near the castle, we spot a small patrol of knights coming our way. I've never seen Morgan's Dark Knights, but I'm fairly certain these are just the plain old regular ones.

The three of us swiftly duck behind a merchant cart, and when Arthur's foot comes down on mine, I let out an involuntary grunt. Merlin's hand slaps over my mouth, and if I wasn't too busy glaring at Arthur, my body might be reacting to him touching me right now.

Once the knights have passed, Merlin releases my mouth. The second he does, I snap at Arthur in a whisper hiss, "Fucker."

His eyes widen, then narrow as he glances between Merlin and me. "You two speak very oddly."

Am I the first person to utter the word *fuck* in Camelot? That thought makes me *oddly* satisfied.

"As I said, a lot has changed," Merlin says.

Arthur's gaze then drifts to Merlin's hand that moved from my mouth down to my shoulder, as though he was planning on holding me back lest I attack. His front is pressed against my back, and I guess our proximity is a bit suspiciously close.

"Clearly," Arthur mutters.

The temptation to turn around and plant a big, sloppy kiss on Merlin is strong.

Technically, homosexuality was never a crime in Camelot. Then again, it wasn't common either. While it would shock Arthur, I don't see him sentencing Merlin to death for being with a man. But for being with *me*?

He'd probably kill us both.

With one last scowl in Arthur's direction, I turn away and continue toward the castle. Again, they follow after me with soft murmurs reaching my ears.

I ignore them the best I can as we head around the side of the inner curtain wall where—yup—there's still a hidden entrance beneath the wall that leads underground to the southeast tower. The tunnel we enter through was carved by magic a long time ago—by *me*. It's how I escaped the castle when I needed to meet Morgan, and when I knew Merlin wasn't on a mission to follow me.

Just inside the tunnel, I grab a torch out of a bracket sticking out of the stone and light it with magic, the flames casting an orange glow off the ancient, damp walls.

When I peer back at Arthur and Merlin, they're both standing there with arms folded and one brow arched.

"What?" I snap. "Don't look so surprised. I was always the rebellious child."

When I wiggle my brows at Arthur, his jaw ticks, but, for once...he doesn't glare.

Ew, gross.

That's just great. I'm officially so fucked up that anything deviating even slightly from pure animosity from my father gives me the ick.

I roll my eyes at myself and mutter, "Come on, fuckers."

I catch one last glimpse of Arthur's dumbstruck expression before heading down the tunnel. Behind me, Merlin chuckles, and I hear him taking the second torch from the wall before the glow of his fire joins mine.

"I know you said a lot has changed, but…" Despite how softly Arthur speaks, his voice reverberates off the tunnel walls as we walk. "He's changed…*a lot*."

"He still holds onto a lot, but, I think…he's let go of a lot too."

Again, I roll my eyes. "This tunnel echoes *a lot*, assholes."

Merlin laughs again, and, goddammit, I love the sound. But I can't help but be a little jealous that he's laughed more often, been more at ease, since Arthur came back.

Maybe I should kill him again.

No. Bad Mordred.

Perhaps he's just relieved Arthur didn't kill me?

Hey, a guy can wish. Or pretend. Anything to keep the murderous urges at bay.

It's about a five minute walk to the crypts below the southeast tower, and we reach them without incident. We enter them through a small grate in the far corner, and I wave aside a large chest that was used to hide the tunnel. It's covered in cobwebs, as is everything else inside the crypt.

Merlin and I go around, lighting a few of the torches on the walls, illuminating the large space that's all arches and columns, filled with ancient and forgotten treasures of Camelot. Armor, chests, furniture, weapons, books, gold and silver knickknacks, empty coffins. The crypts to the north are where the corpses of some of the past kings reside, including Uther Pendragon, Arthur's father.

"Is that…"

Arthur's voice cracks as we step into the center of the crypt where what was once a large, round table rests in two splintered pieces, the aged oak fractured right down the middle.

"Your Round Table, Sire. Bit symbolic, isn't it?"

Arthur's frown deepens as he stares at the broken table.

"Mordred," Merlin scolds.

"Whatever. Not like I was ever welcomed to sit at it."

So much for having let go of a lot, huh, Merlin?

I'm right back there, a thousand years ago. Maybe I'm not as *angry* as I once was, but I'm still plenty fucking bitter.

I walk away, and Merlin calls after me. I ignore him because I need to put some distance between me and Arthur for at least a good sixty seconds. Besides, we're here for a reason, and it's not to rehash the past.

But then, once I've made it several arches away deeper into the shadows of the crypt, even more of the past comes crashing down on me. Literally. A body barrels into me, shoving me against a pillar, the sharp edge of a sword pressing against my throat.

Again.

This is really getting old.

Still, I can't help but grin into the face of the man before me, only one side of his scowl lit up by the glow of my torch.

"Hello, brother."

Gawain's face contorts between disgust and rage as he digs his blade into the skin of my neck. He hasn't changed a bit. His shoulder-length dirty blond hair hangs around his face as he looks down a slightly crooked nose with brown eyes.

"Mordred? You're the one who sent that message?"

"Guilty."

I sent it via crow—a very vague message to meet here without revealing my name—only hoping that Gawain was still alive.

Then again, maybe I wouldn't have minded so much if he was dead.

"If you think I'm even slightly curious to hear what you have to say, you're—"

Gawain doesn't get a chance to finish what I'm sure would've been some beautiful endearment of brotherly love before he's ripped off me and thrown against the opposite column. My heart warms a bit when I see Merlin has him pinned against the pillar.

But then recognition crosses both their faces.

"Gawain?"

"Merlin!"

With wide, bright smiles, they throw their arms around each other in an embrace, and a blood-red veil slowly descends over my vision. My jaw aches, and my fists clench as I resist the urge to yank them apart too.

"Gawain!"

Now it's Arthur looking at my half brother like he's fucking Jesus or some shit. When Gawain sees Arthur, he pales, staring with wide, unblinking eyes as though he's seen a ghost. Which…okay, yeah. I'm obviously retiring that cliche.

"Arthur." Gawain swallows, the sound audible through the crypt. He falls to his knees, the tip of his sword digging into the stone floor, and bows his head. "I…I mean…Your Grace."

"Arise, Sir Gawain."

He peers up to see Arthur extending his hand and hesitates only briefly before reaching for it, letting Arthur pull him to his feet.

"It's good to see you, old friend," Arthur says before embracing Gawain too.

When I roll my eyes, it's near painful, and I don't know if it's because I do it particularly hard this time or because I've done it so much in the past half hour. Either way, it takes a considerable amount of strength not to interrupt with a loud retching sound.

Gawain was always one of Arthur's favorite knights, one of his twelve of the Round Table. Despite the fact that *he's* Morgan's son too…

The reminder of that, the way they're laughing as they're reunited, all of it has every muscle in my body going taut. My left eye twitches. I feel as though I'm a time bomb, my heart the ticking timer counting down to the inevitable explosion.

I want to kill something.

"So it was never because I was *Morgan's* son, was it?" I blurt before I can stop myself. "It's because I was *yours*."

Arthur and Gawain break apart, both turning to look at me. My half brother glares while Arthur...looks utterly shocked. Jaw slack, eyes wide. It's the stunned expression that makes me realize something. I never spoke to him like this, never told him exactly what was on my mind or how I felt.

Would it have even changed anything?

Probably not. He would've never stopped making me feel worthless, just like he always will. Because that's another truth I failed to tell Merlin. It was less about Arthur not claiming me as his son and more about how worthless he made me feel. It's exactly what Morgan did after I did her dirty work for her. The only difference was that Morgan was more direct in her contempt.

I never should've come back to Camelot.

I'm about to give up, say fuck it, and get the fuck out of here when Merlin appears beside me, his presence immediately calming the air around me. His light touch on my arm grounds me, helping me breathe. I want to lean into him, breathe him into my lungs.

Fuck, he's my new drug.

"What are you two doing with *him*?" Gawain looks from me, to Merlin, to Arthur. "And how are you back?"

Arthur's gaze is still on me. I wish I could tell what he's thinking, but I never knew the man well enough to read him. But he still appears a bit dazed, speechless until he finally says, "Mordred helped Merlin bring me back."

Wait. What?

Is he actually giving me credit for something?

"I don't think I'd be here without him," he adds, the faintest lift at the corner of his mouth. "Then again, I wouldn't have been dead in the first place, but…" His grin widens. "We'll circle back around to that later."

He's fucking *teasing*.

What the actual hell?

Did I come back to Camelot or the fucking Twilight Zone?

"He's also going to help us take down Morgan," Arthur says. "Right?"

I have to swallow the thick knot that's lodged itself in my throat before I can reply. "Fuck yeah."

Merlin and Arthur both grin. Gawain has a similar reaction as Arthur did the first time I used the word.

I'll deal with this existential crisis later.

First, it's time to burn a witch.

33

MERLIN

On our way to the castle, Arthur told me that he dreamed of Avalon that night, that the mystical powers of that place opened his eyes to many of the truths he had been blinded to in his last life. I suspect he'll continue to have dreams and memories of Avalon return to him as time goes on.

He admitted to having misplaced trust in Lancelot, but he also said that he's forgiven him for his betrayal. Mordred's betrayal is more difficult to forgive, which I understand.

Lancelot stole his queen.

Mordred stole his life.

But then Arthur said, "I confess that I punished him for the sins of his mother. It was unfair and shortsighted of me. I just...I don't know where to go from here, Merlin."

My heart soared at that for more than one reason.

Whether it was Arthur's naturally benevolent spirit and merciful heart, the magic of Avalon, Mordred finally opening up, or some combination of it all, it doesn't matter. There's hope, and I'm going to cling to it as tightly as I can.

It also sounded as though he was once more seeking my counsel, indicating that whatever trust I may have lost is not completely irreparable. I once more confessed that we *all* made mistakes, but we'd been given another chance.

Then Arthur said, "He's quite odd, isn't he? I've never seen so many tattoos and rings on one body before."

I couldn't help but chuckle at that. "He's unique. That's for sure."

I wasn't about to tell him of all the ink and metal in places he *couldn't* see.

Tattoos and piercings weren't exactly used as art or self-expression here a thousand years ago, so I'm sure it was yet another thing that Arthur found shocking.

Of course, not as shocking as discovering that I'm in a relationship with his son would undoubtedly be...

I wasn't even ashamed of thinking of it as a relationship. In fact, the word doesn't nearly encompass it. I own him, and he owns every piece of me. One day, when this is all over, I want Arthur to know. I couldn't live in Camelot while being forced to hide my feelings, with having to pretend that Mordred isn't *mine*.

But that time is definitely not now, even if Arthur does seem to be extending a short olive branch, just out of Mordred's reach. I can practically see him fighting the urge to grasp it.

I'll make sure these two get their shit together if it's the last thing I do.

"How are you still alive?" Arthur asks Gawain, breaking through my thoughts.

"You know I refused her magic, my birthright, for a long time," he answers, pausing to cut his eyes at Mordred.

I was always friendly with Gawain, but I suddenly feel the temptation to punch him in the jaw with the way he's looking at Mordred. Instead, I give Mordred's arm a gentle squeeze to remind him I'm here.

"Morgan offered me and the other knights the chance to keep our posts, to pledge our loyalty to her in exchange for our lives and the lives of our families. There were a few, those who had no one to protect, who refused. They were all hanged a few days after the battle. The rest of us chose to accept her offer, not only to save the ones we loved, but to do what we could to protect the people of Camelot. We got many people out, helped them find their way to neighboring kingdoms. We turned our backs as often as we could when Morgan's laws were broken. It wasn't much, but we did what we could.

"One day, a sickness swept through the kingdom, taking many villagers and knights with it. We were all certain it was created by dark magic. Honestly," Gawain continues, glancing at Mordred again, "I thought it was you."

Mordred shakes his head. "It wasn't."

Gawain nods solemnly, seeming to believe him. "I was on my deathbed when Morgan came to me and made another offer. A little bit of magic, immortality, for an eternity of servitude. Truthfully, the thought of living forever was terrifying. But I accepted, only so I could continue doing what I was doing. I recruited new knights, told them of you, Arthur, and we've been trying to uphold your legacy ever since. We've saved a life here and there, kept a few souls from starving. I only wish I could have done more."

Arthur places a hand on Gawain's shoulder. "You've done more than I would have ever asked of you. I'm eternally grateful for what you've done for Camelot."

Beside me, Mordred rolls his eyes.

"Did you know?" Arthur asks, peering at his son. "What the knights were doing?"

Mordred's jaw ticks. "I knew."

"You knew?" Gawain's brow furrows in disbelief. "And you never told Morgan?"

Mordred scoffs. "I would've *helped* if I thought you'd trust me. If my leaving wasn't clear enough, I hate the witch."

"Because she claimed the throne when it was supposed to be yours after killing Arthur?" Gawain asks, the question a challenge.

Everyone looks at Mordred, me included. His jaw is still tense, a precursor to his anger.

Don't give into it, baby.

He takes a step forward, slipping out of my grasp. I follow after him, but when he peers at me over his shoulder, I see something other than rage in his eyes. It's a little sorrow and a lot of hard determination.

Turning back to Gawain, Mordred steps right up to him, ignoring the way the knight's hand goes to his sword that's been returned to the scabbard at his side.

"No, that's not why. It's because I was only bred to be her pawn. She made sure I knew that was the sole reason for my existence. Lot was a caring father to you, Gawain, so you never needed our mother's love and approval. I foolishly thought I did. She made sure I had no one so I'd always play my role as her perfect little puppet."

Gawain and Arthur both stare at Mordred, taken aback. Honestly, I am too.

I'm so fucking proud of him.

The tense, uncomfortable silence only lasts a moment before Gawain nods. "I hear you."

"We all do, Mordred," I say, stepping forward to stand beside him. I don't care what the others think as I give him a wide, heartfelt smile to let him know just how proud of him I am. "You don't have to hide anymore."

He looks at me with oceans full of emotion. The waters within are calm, like he truly understands that he's hidden so much all this time, but it's not as painful as he thought it'd be to be *seen*.

When the dam becomes a little too close to bursting, he clears his throat. "Right. So how are we doing this? Because Arthur may be a dick..." He pauses to grin, appreciating the looks of mortification on the other men's faces. "But he still deserves that throne a hell of a lot more than that fucking witch."

That look of utter torment is back in Arthur's eyes, waging a battle between everything he believed a thousand years ago, everything he learned in Avalon, and what he's coming to realize now.

"Well...."

We all turn to Gawain, who's apparently struggling to come to terms with it too.

I get it. Going from hating Mordred to...not, was one of the most difficult things I've ever done.

And, yet, it was the easiest fucking thing I've ever done.

"The problem, other than Morgan herself, is going to be getting past her Dark Knights," Gawain says. "But my knights are loyal to me, to *you*, Arthur. They'll fight with us. I have no doubts about that."

Arthur turns to me and Mordred. "Can you two fight her knights? With magic?"

I glance at Mordred, and he gives me a determined nod. "We'll do what we can. You certainly can fight them, Arthur. You have Excalibur."

"Wait," Gawain says. "Is there any way to save them?"

"Save them?"

"They were once knights of Camelot. They were human, mortal, before they were consumed by dark magic. Surely there must be a way to free them of the enchantment?"

Again, we all look at Mordred, the one of us most familiar with dark magic.

Mordred frowns and shakes his head. "I don't know. What I do know is that anyone or anything that's touched by her magic in that way, that's trapped in that darkness of hers like it sounds they are, when she dies, which she *will*..." He swallows. "They'll be imprisoned in that darkness forever."

My heart plummets, and the air around me suddenly feels too thick. The weight of the premonition I had last night suddenly feels too heavy.

"There *might* be a way to free them before she's dead," Mordred continues, this time with a slight hitch in his voice as he looks around at a few piles of dusty books. "I'd have to do some reading."

"Could you take the day?" Arthur asks.

"I don't know if that'll be enough time, but..." Mordred squares his shoulders, his sharp, sexy jaw set in resolution. "I'll do my best."

Setting my trepidation aside, I admire the way they're willingly working together, my heart swelling with joy I refuse to tamp down. Unable to help the way my mouth pulls up at the corners, I look at Mordred. "I'll help you."

Arthur nods. "It's settled then. We'll attack tomorrow. At first light."

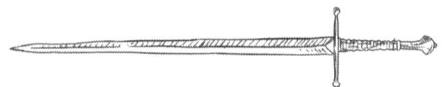

Arthur and Gawain spent the morning introducing the Knights of Camelot to their true king. I was there for the initial meeting to make sure everything went smoothly, but Gawain had been telling the truth. After all this time, he had always made sure his knights knew of King Arthur, and even in death, he had generations and generations of knights who were loyal to him. They all bowed down the moment Gawain uttered Arthur Pendragon's name.

It was truly a sight to behold, and I'd be lying if I said it didn't give me goosebumps. The way Arthur's eyes grew wet spoke volumes to his humble nature.

The rest of the day, I've been in the crypts with Mordred, both of us buried up to our necks in old, leather-bound books, their browned pages practically crumbling. Gawain has brought us several more from the royal library, but Mordred and I have begun suspecting that Morgan had most of the books concerning magic removed long ago. Our best chance is probably the books down here in the crypts.

We've also been concealing our magic the best we can since arriving at the castle, but that's even more draining. By the time the sun sets, our eyes and minds are tired.

Gawain has retired to his chambers, and Arthur is asleep in a dark corner nearby. The only sounds in the crypt are those of our breathing, the faint crackling of flames from the torches, and the rustling of pages.

Then a quiet rip breaks through the hush.

I peer up at Mordred across the table we sit at to see him folding a page from one of the books and stuffing it into a pocket in his pants. There's a deep, disconcerting crease between his brows, and a darkness to his eyes that has nothing to do with the shadows from the lit torches.

"Something you want to tell me, Mordred?" I ask, keeping my voice low.

His haunted gaze meets mine. "Do you trust me?"

Without hesitation, I answer, "I do."

It's the same question I asked him after I had that premonition last night, so I know he won't tell me whatever it is he's found.

"Good," he says, a forced smile now on his face. "I'm going to bed."

I stand when he does. "Mordred…"

He holds a hand up and glances over to where Arthur is sleeping. He's shrouded in shadow, but we can hear his steady breathing as he sleeps.

Looking back at me, he still has that damn, fake smile plastered on his face.

I hate it.

"Big day tomorrow, Merlin."

I round the table and grab him by the sides of his head. There's a brief flicker of panic in his eyes, but once my lips are on his, he melts into the kiss, into me. He fists the edges of my cloak, pulling me closer. His mouth opens when I demand entrance, my tongue swirling around the metal ball in his as he moans softly. I swallow up the sound, inhaling it deep like I can also catch all of his worries, his fears.

Breaking away, I rest my forehead against his, and whisper in the space of warm breath between us, "I promised you I wouldn't let Arthur hurt you. I won't let Morgan hurt you either."

With a quiet growl, he says, "Morgan's mine."

I grin. "Whatever you want, little monster. Come on."

We've set up a couple of cots in another corner with a non-suspicious amount of space between them. After extinguishing all of the torches but one, we lie down in the shadows. Just like the night before, we fall asleep with our hands entwined.

It feels as though no time has passed before I hear my name through the haze of sleep.

"Merlin."

A booted foot taps me on the back, rousing me. I blink my eyes open and peer up and over my shoulder to see Arthur's scowling face hovering over me.

"It's time," is all he says, voice gruff and curt as he turns away.

When I look to my other side, I see...*fuck*.

Mordred's hand is still in mine.

Gently prying myself out of his grasp so I don't wake him, I scramble off the cot. "Arthur."

I've barely caught up with him when he turns around so fast I'm forced to come to a screeching halt. The light from the torches that have been lit once more cast a haunting glow in his blue eyes. There's anger swimming somewhere in there, yes, but there's so much more.

Hurt.

Disappointment.

Betrayal.

I don't feel shame for what I have with Mordred, but I do feel guilty for causing Arthur more grief and torment. This isn't how I would've chosen him to find out.

"Don't." Arthur shakes his head, a deep frown creasing the features of his face. "I need you right now, Merlin. I need you *both*. We'll deal with the rest of it later." He pauses, the corners of his mouth pulling down further. "Big day today, Merlin."

He turns away again, and I close my eyes in defeat.

He heard us.

When we come up from the crypts, the Dark Knights are waiting for us.

While Mordred and Gawain took half our knights up through the northwest tower, Arthur and I entered the castle from the southeast crypts with the rest. Splitting up was the last thing I wanted to do, but the plan they had formed yesterday was solid.

The moment we break out onto the main floor and lay siege, it's all clashing of blades, slashing of swords and fists, the smell of sweat and blood.

The battle for King Arthur begins fast and violent and loud.

Morgan's Dark Knights are not too much unlike Camelot's own. While our men wear steel armor and only a few sport helmets, Morgan's are covered from head to toe in midnight black metal plates and gauntlets, each one with a black helmet. Even their swords are black from hilt to sharp tip.

While they appear human, the swords our knights wield are incapable of piercing their armor, a magical shield surrounding them as well, like a dark aura.

The only thing that *can* penetrate their defenses is Excalibur. Even my magic barely breaches their shields, doing little more than shoving them out of the way, hindering their advancements, and dulling their blows against our knights.

The hall fills with the clanging of metal on metal, the scent of blood spilt as one of our men goes down, and the thickening ashy blue smoke of my magic as we push the Dark

Knights back. Back in the direction of the courtyard, the center of Camelot's fortress.

About halfway there, a cry rips through the air.

My eyes immediately find Arthur as he faces off with one of the larger knights in all black. Blood drips through the chainmail on his arm beneath his pauldron.

Pushing my way through the battle, I raise my hand and hurl a burst of magic at the attacking knight. The force drives him back until he crashes into the wall behind him, the impact so strong that parts of the stone crack and crumble.

I grab Arthur by his breastplate and yell above the din of battle, "Don't hesitate, Arthur!"

"They were Knights of Camelot, Merlin!"

"They're not anymore. And I don't know if we can save them." As far as I know, our research yielded no answers. Unless that page Mordred ripped out had anything to do with it. "Do what you have to. Use the sword!"

Arthur grits his teeth but eventually concedes with a nod.

We get back to the fight, continuing our push toward the courtyard. Another of our knights joins the fallen with one quick slash of a black blade. By the time we near the outer doors, Arthur has a fresh spark of determination not to lose more.

Just as a Dark Knight brings one of our own to his knees with a hard blow, I watch as Arthur rushes to his defense, impaling the attacking knight on his sword.

Excalibur pierces through the magic barrier, the metal armor, and straight through the knight's body. A bone-chilling, inhuman shriek echoes throughout the hall a split second before the knight appears to turn to stone, cracks snaking up the armor of its arms, legs, and back. The black metal chips and breaks, and the knight crumbles in a heap of broken rock and black smoke.

Arthur is distraught. When his tortured gaze finds mine, I do my best to convey that he only did what he had to do.

When we finally enter the courtyard, I see the others are already here, pushing another legion of Dark Knights toward the center of the area as we do the same.

My eyes immediately search for Mordred through the droves of knights in combat as the harsh clanging of blades rings out into the open air under a pale blue morning sky. I find him by following the dark purple smoke of his magic. He launches brilliant violet lightning bolts toward several Dark Knights, driving them away from ours and toward the middle of the courtyard.

I take a moment to appreciate the determined set of his jaw, his black hair damp with sweat, chainmail a little splattered with blood, the fierce fire in his eyes as he fights on the right side of the battle.

I don't think he's ever been sexier.

The rest of our army begins to form a circle around the battalion of the black-clad knights, forcing them all into the center of the open space. The air around them is thick with the lingering blue and purple vapors of magic.

Mordred is on the other side of them. I can't see him, but I call out, "Mordred, now!"

As our men back away, I hold my arms out to my sides. Pale white-blue lightning shoots from my palms, the effect causing tingles up and down my arms.

The lightning ripples and cracks as it surrounds the horde of Dark Knights. They're caught off guard, following the electrical magic with eyes hidden behind visors as the lightning continues to stretch all around them. I feel it the moment my magic connects with Mordred's on both sides, blue bolts joining his purple ones with the rumble of thunder. Sparks fly and dance and arc the moment the colors link. They twist together, intertwining like a braid around the entire circle until the enchanted knights within are imprisoned by a ring of lightning.

I bring my hands together, secure the magic between them, and step back. Mordred comes jogging around the circle, a radiant smile on his face that damn near makes my heart stop. He raises both middle fingers at the trapped knights, and I can't help but grin.

"Did you see that shit?" He approaches me, practically bouncing on the balls of his feet.

"I did." I grab a fistful of his chainmail and haul him toward me until his body crashes against mine. "You did great."

His smile falters as his eyes dart to the side. "Merlin…"

"I don't care."

When his smile returns, it's even brighter than before.

I consider kissing him, right here in front of Arthur and all the Knights of Camelot. Before I can find an answer to my silent question in Mordred's eyes, Arthur interrupts.

"Merlin!"

When I turn to see Arthur starting up the steps toward the Great Hall, I expect to see more disgust and anger on his face, but there's none. Maybe he's just pumped from battle. Or I suppose he could just be more focused than I am right now…

"The throne room!"

Grabbing hold of Mordred's hand, I rush toward the stairs, dragging him with me. However, once we enter the Hall, I have to let go because we both need our hands to face the dozen or so Dark Knights guarding the throne room.

Fuck, there's so many of them.

At least we were prepared. The knights held captive in the courtyard will remain that way until we release them. Or, well…if one of us dies. But that's not an option.

Arthur and our army attack first without hesitation, rushing Morgan's knights and fighting even though they can't do much damage—or *won't* in Arthur's case.

Mordred and I join in the fray, using our magic to help push them out of the way until the doors are clear. The moment they are, we stand side by side and throw more magic at them. It combines to hit the double doors in a cloud of lightning and smoke, the colors merging into a cosmic periwinkle as the doors burst open.

While most of the knights stay behind to continue fighting, Mordred and I rush through the indigo fog, flanked by Arthur and Gawain. Breaking through the cloud, we see there are more Dark Knights lining the edges of the throne room.

On the other side of the long room sits Morgan on the throne, a twisted gold crown on her head of long, flowing black hair. She leans back with her legs crossed beneath her black dress, completely at ease.

"Hello, Mordred," she says as though she doesn't have a care in the world, like the castle she's claimed for a thousand years isn't currently under siege. "So nice of you to show up with your father and brother for a reunion."

"It won't last long, I assure you," Mordred says with just as much calm.

"You're right." Morgan stands in one fluid, graceful motion. "Because now I have to kill you all." Her eyes land on me. "Nothing personal, Merlin. You're simply on the wrong side."

"I'm right where I should be, Morgan."

But when Mordred takes several steps forward toward the center of the room, my confidence wanes, my heart stutters.

"If you hurt Merlin," he starts, his voice a darkened, threatening rumble, "I'll make sure your death lasts an entire excruciating century instead of the quick one I had planned for you."

Morgan laughs, a wicked, spine-chilling, taunting sound. "Oh, Mordred. You know it takes no effort at all for me to correct that bad attitude of yours."

Mordred screams.

"Mordred!"

He grasps his head and falls to his knees.

I start to rush forward, but Arthur grabs my arm to hold me back. I spin toward him, eyes blazing like fire just might erupt from them, tempted once again to attack him if he tries to stop me from getting to Mordred.

"I'm not letting him get trapped in that darkness, Arthur," I snarl.

He doesn't look hurt or surprised to see whatever it is he's witnessing in my eyes.

Protectiveness?

Possessiveness?

Obsessiveness?

More?

"I know, Merlin. Do what you have to. We'll give you as much time as we can."

I don't have time to be shocked or express my gratitude. Giving him a nod, I rush to where Mordred is incapacitated, still on his knees on the ground, head in his hands. I ignore the way Morgan smirks down at us in premature victory as I fall to the floor in front of him.

Our army from the hall storms inside to aid Arthur and Gawain as the Dark Knights lining the throne room attack, the battle picking right back up.

Morgan's dark magic fills the room as black lightning and smoke shoot in Arthur's direction. He easily deflects it with Excalibur.

I shouldn't be leaving, not now. I should stay and help Arthur.

But when I peer into Mordred's ashen face, all screwed up in terror and agony, I refuse to leave him alone to fight the darkness.

Leaning forward, I place my hands on the sides of his neck and rest my forehead against his.

He doesn't react. He's here, but his mind's not.

For the first time ever, I call to my demons for a little dark magic as I force my way into his mind, into the darkness.

Hold on, Mordred. I'm coming.

34

MORDRED

organ's darkness is more than just *dark*. It's hopelessness and despair, misery and agony. It's a pressing weight that crushes your lungs like they're in a vise, making it damn near impossible to breathe. It makes you question your own existence, the existence of *anything* outside of the blackness.

Fuck, I really didn't miss it here.

But I had to be here. I had to provoke Morgan so she'd send me to this darkness. It was the only way...

Of course, now that I'm here, I have no idea if I can do what I need to. I need light, and I have none. There's only darkness all around me, inside of me, embedded so deep in my soul that light could never survive there.

I've never fucking used light magic before. Why did I think I could do this?

I try and try and fucking *try*.

No matter how deeply I search for it, there's no light here.

Arthur and Merlin are going to kill Morgan, and I'm going to be trapped here forever.

A sob rips its way through my chest as the anguish and torment of the darkness weighs down on me, squeezing all the hope from my heart.

Merlin.

His face swims in front of me, and I swear I see a spark.

My light.

I think about him again, focus my thoughts solely on Merlin. There's another spark, a brief flicker of light, making my skin glow. I try to stoke it, make it catch fire.

But it's not *enough*.

The darkness is winning, wrapping me in cold chains of sorrow until I can't move. I curl in on myself and sob again.

I don't know how long I stay like that before my vision blurs with tears—

Wait.

I shouldn't be able to see anything at all.

But I can. It's like a rainy car ride at night, everything blurred through iridescent droplets on a window. There's a light, and this one isn't coming from me.

I sniff back the tears and wipe my eyes. The light is in the distance, but it's bright. I can make out a figure, a silhouette, moving in my direction.

"Merlin?" My voice chokes as more tears threaten to spill over the edge.

He shouldn't be here.

He starts rushing toward me, light pouring out of him, glowing like he's a damn human lantern. The moment he reaches me, he drops to his knees, takes my head in his hands, and kisses my damp forehead.

"Why are you here, Merlin?" I ask, my throat scratchy and dry. "*How* are you here?"

He winces. "I had to break into your mind."

My eyes widen. "You used dark magic? Why would you do that?"

I've never once known Merlin to use that kind of magic. He's too *good* for it. It'd be like him truly letting his demons out to run amok, one step toward the risk of allowing them to control him instead of the other way around.

"You shouldn't have done that, Merlin," I add, shaking my head that's still firmly grasped between his hands.

My own pain seems to be reflected in his eyes as he stares at me with a crease between his brows. But the longer I peer into those russet orbs, made brighter by the light radiating from him, I think his torment is different from mine.

"Isn't it obvious, Mordred?" He leans his forehead against mine and releases a warm breath that kisses my lips. "I'd do anything for you."

It's then I realize where his pain stems from, and I can't help but let out a soft laugh. "You hate it, don't you?"

"I do. I hate *you*."

I lower my head and wince as a stabbing pain gnaws its way straight through my chest. When the fuck did I want anything but his hate?

With one hand gripping my chin, he lifts my gaze back to his. The smile on his face is soft and effortless and achingly beautiful. I think I *feel* his words before I hear them. They come out deep and full of feeling, like he's speaking with his soul.

"I hate you for making me love you."

I can't breathe. I wait as I stare into his eyes, wait for him to take it back, say the punchline of his cruel joke, rip those words away.

But he doesn't.

When I finally suck air into my lungs, I feel as though I can breathe easier than I have in a thousand years. I thought experiencing anything but hatred would be the death of me, but...I feel more alive than I ever have.

I throw myself at him, wrapping my arms around him, holding him tight as I bring my mouth down on his. I kiss him with everything I have, everything I am. It might not be much, but everything I *feel* makes up for it.

"I love you too," I whisper against his lips. "I think I have for a while."

He kisses me again, just a gentle stroke of his lips, a tender touch. Then he rocks back on his heels, that same smile still on his face. I could admire it for the rest of eternity.

Of course, if we don't make it out of here, I might just have to.

"Now," he says as he brushes a strand of damp hair off my forehead. "Do you want to tell me why we're here?"

I shouldn't be surprised he knows I'm here on purpose.

Reaching into the pocket of my pants, I pull out the page I ripped from an ancient spellbook last night. I unfold the fragile paper carefully and hand it to Merlin.

"I thought I could do it." I frown and shake my head. "I don't have enough light magic."

Merlin looks up from the page, glowing even brighter than before. "I told you, Mordred. I'll be your light."

That damn pressure behind my eyes returns, and I smile at him even as he blurs before me. "My darling light."

The radiance emanating from him flares, shining with an intensity that's nearly blinding. Despite the battle I know must still be raging outside this darkness, Merlin's light makes me feel calm and happy. At peace.

"This spell could take a little time," I warn him. "We've already been here awhile."

He nods, his smile never faltering. "If we get trapped, at least we'll be together."

On a breath, I whisper, "Together."

Merlin takes one last look at the page before setting it aside and taking both my hands in his. I didn't think it was possible for him to glow any brighter, but he does. His light slowly swallows up the shadows around us until it's all I see, the darkness no longer caving in, trying to push its way closer.

All the while, he stares into my eyes as I stare back into his, neither of us daring to break the connection.

After a moment, Merlin's mouth lifts even higher in one corner. "I knew you had your own light in there somewhere."

I don't look away, but I don't need to to see how much brighter the glow around us is now, to feel how my skin burns, a warmth sparking in my chest.

I'm not sure if it's *my* light or rather the light that Merlin's kindled inside of me.

We stay like that for so long I'm not sure how much time has passed. Our eyes are still open, and I swear my retinas are burning with how bright it is, like we're in the center of the sun.

There's one last flare, a flash of white, a burst of a million rays.

Then the light begins to fade.

Instead of the darkness that surrounded us before, we're back in the throne room. Instead of the din of battle, everything is silent. And still.

The morning sun has risen over the horizon, and yellow light spills into the room through the windows. The knights on both sides are frozen, a moment suspended in time.

The sound of metal clanging against stone breaks through the eerie silence as the Dark Knights drop their swords. Some of them stumble back, some peer around the room as though confused.

Then they begin to remove their helmets.

Beneath are the faces of men—human, mortal men. They blink their eyes against the sunlight, as though they haven't seen it for centuries. For many of them, that may be true.

"*NO!*"

The piercing shriek echoes throughout the room, and all eyes turn to Morgan, rage twisting her face into an ugly scowl. Arthur is behind her, drenched in sweat, chest heaving from exertion. I wonder how long he's been fighting her.

Morgan whips around to glare down at me and Merlin where we're still kneeling on the floor. "How dare you! How did you—" Her eyes cut to Merlin, and I feel the urge to claw them out of her head. "Of course. *Merlin*," she spits his name. "I knew I should have gotten rid of you a long time ago, wizard."

Oh, I can't wait until this bitch is dead.

While Morgan's attention is focused on us, Arthur moves behind her, closing in as he raises his sword.

Morgan turns her back on us, and with a wave of her hand, a burst of magic hits Arthur's arm before he can deflect it with the blade. Excalibur flies out of his grasp and clatters to the floor, sliding against the stone a few feet away.

"I guess I have to do everything myself this time," Morgan says with a dramatic sigh.

"Your thousand-year reign is over, Morgan." Arthur speaks between panting breaths, his deep voice confident despite the fact he's now defenseless. "These knights never go back to serving you."

"They'll have no choice," she snarls.

"Are you certain? Because I have an heir this time."

I think my heart stops.

Dammit. That old, shriveled up organ isn't used to all these heavy emotions. I swear it's going to end up giving out on me before the end of the day, immortality be damned.

Of course, I'm sure Arthur's only purpose is to piss Morgan off and doesn't truly mean it.

Morgan scoffs. "*Him?*" She barely raises a hand in my direction, deeming me unworthy of anything more. "He'll betray you just like he did last time. I shaped him, molded him. He'll never give you his loyalty, Arthur Pendragon!"

Arthur peers down at me, his gaze lingering on where I'm still holding onto one of Merlin's hands. He grins. "I think I know exactly where his loyalties lie."

"You've made the same fatal mistake of trusting him as last time," Morgan sneers, her voice growing shrill. "He's *worthless.*"

For the first time, my mother's words don't completely ruin me. They don't make me want to rip myself open and cut out every little sliver that she could possibly deem useless and insignificant.

It might have something to do with the way Merlin grips my hand a little tighter.

If I'm worthy of Merlin's love, how could any piece of me be worthless?

My eyes snap over to where Excalibur is still lying on the floor. Arthur follows my gaze. I give him a nod.

His grin widens as he looks back at Morgan. "He's not worthless."

With a burst of light magic that won't be deflected by the sword, I aim my free hand at Excalibur, raising it off the floor. It sails through the air and lands right back in Arthur's grasp.

Letting go of Merlin's hand, I jump to my feet, at the same time withdrawing my own sword from its scabbard.

Morgan spins toward me, then back to Arthur, trying to figure out where the attack is coming from.

But she's too late.

We both drive our blades through her.

A deafening, high-pitched scream rings out. A second later, a deeper one joins it.

I think it's mine.

I don't understand the source of the stabbing pain, but I'm too busy relishing in Morgan's screams to figure it out. It's not until she's quieted, her body falling limp between me and Arthur, that I let myself look. I peer down to see that Excalibur ran right through Morgan and the tip is embedded in my left shoulder.

I grunt and pull myself off the sword, immediately falling back, my own sword withdrawing from Morgan and clattering to the ground. Merlin catches me, still on the floor, his arms wrapping around me.

"Mordred!"

"I'm fine," I groan, not feeling *fine* at all. Then again, the witch is dead, so I'm on top of the fucking world. "That sword really hates me," I mutter, ending on a choked cough.

Merlin tries to suppress a laugh, but I feel his chest rumble against my back.

A sickening sound echoes through the throne room as Arthur yanks Excalibur out of Morgan, letting her lifeless body crumple to the floor.

With my good arm, I raise a hand, sending the witch's corpse sliding across the stone, past the throne, into the corner. One last spark of magic has her body going up in flames, filling the room with the smell of burnt flesh as the blood from her wounds boils.

Burn, witch, burn.

Arthur approaches us with heavy steps, blood dripping from Excalibur's blade as he looks down at us. I think I should be afraid he's about to kill me, but...I'm not. I feel too safe in Merlin's arms to feel any fear.

"Will you live?" Arthur asks me.

I swallow as I peer up at him. "Will you let me?"

The corner of his mouth twitches. Then he lifts his sword and lays the flat of the blade on my right shoulder.

Behind me, Merlin tenses.

Fuck. He's really going to kill me while I'm in Merlin's arms? I guess if I got to choose, this is where I'd go out...

Arthur raises Excalibur, and I wince before I feel it on my other shoulder. He takes it away, sheathing it, then extends his hand out to me.

"Arise, Sir Mordred."

I stare at his hand, gawking at it.

Is this real? Did he just—

Holy fuck.

Whispered murmurs circle around the knights standing in the room. Merlin chuckles.

Well, I guess I said that out loud.

I take Arthur's hand, and he pulls me to my feet as I grunt and grimace from the pain in my shoulder. He offers Merlin his other hand and pulls him up too.

"Does this mean I get to be prince too?" I ask. Because of course I can't help but push my luck.

Arthur narrows his eyes. "We'll discuss that later."

I almost laugh. I'll take what I can get.

"I hope you'll both stay," Arthur says, looking from me to Merlin.

Merlin's mouth turns down in contemplation. He looks at me, and the corners of his lips slowly pull back up as he grabs the hand of my good arm, linking our fingers together. Turning back to Arthur, he asks, "Are you sure?"

He peers down at our hands, clearly understanding the point Merlin's making, then looks back up with a smile. "I can't do this without you, Merlin." He briefly glances at me. "I'd like to do it right this time."

I'm tempted to ask Merlin if he's sure we came back to the *right* Camelot, but the beautiful, radiant smile on his face stops me.

Letting go of my hand, Merlin reaches into some deep pocket of his cloak and pulls out a golden crown like a damn rabbit out of a hat. Each intricately carved spike of the crown is adorned with a different color jewel that catches the sunlight from the windows and reflects prismatic rays.

"I kept it safe for you, Arthur," Merlin says as he holds it out in front of him.

Arthur stares at the crown, lips parted and eyes wide.

At the sound of shuffling and shifting of armor, we all look around at the knights filling the room to see them lowering to their knees.

Arthur turns back to Merlin, his eyes wet. He bows, and Merlin places the crown on his head.

Merlin takes my hand again, guides us a step back, then says loud enough for all the knights to hear, "Long live the king!"

The knights immediately join in, chanting, "Long live the king!"

As Arthur takes his rightful seat on the throne, with the dying flames of Morgan's burning corpse behind him, Merlin turns to me. He gently tugs on my chainmail to pull me close, and I go without a shred of resistance.

"Will he, Mordred? Live long?"

I shrug, trying and failing to hold back a grin. "*I* won't be the one to take him out this time at least."

He shakes his head, his amused smile pure light. Reaching up, careful of my still-bleeding shoulder, he brushes hair from my forehead. I lean into his touch like I always do, hoping there will be many, many more touches like it for the rest of eternity.

"I love you," he says in a way I'd never be able to doubt. "And I know you hate it."

When he opens his mouth, I don't give him the chance to speak or argue or whatever it is he plans to do. I seal my mouth to his and kiss him deep. His lips move against mine as we're both completely unbothered by the chorus of "long live the king" singing out around us.

Only when I need to come up for air do I pull back and say, "I love you too, my darling light."

Then his mouth is on mine again, the chanting of the knights and the king on his throne fading into the background.

Maybe it won't be so bad in Camelot this time around.

EPILOGUE

MERLIN

A few months later.

The Round Table of King Arthur has been restored. The aged and fractured oak was no match for mine and Mordred's magic when we decided to mend it and present it to Arthur as a second coronation gift. Mordred even put his own touch on it by burning the Pendragon crest into the center. I think it served as another link in the bond that he and Arthur have slowly been building.

Slowly.

At a fucking snail's pace.

And it's a fragile bond at best.

They constantly bicker, and I often feel more like a babysitter than I do Arthur's royal advisor. But even when Mordred's antagonizing Arthur and Arthur's resisting the urge to give Excalibur a third taste of Mordred's blood, I see a growing respect between them.

Mordred may not be crown prince—*yet*, but he's earned his place at the Round Table.

However, right now, I think Arthur's reconsidering his decision.

Sir Mordred sits to Arthur's right, leaning a little sideways in his chair with his booted feet propped up on the table. He drums a beat on the oak wood with his fingers, imitating what I'm pretty sure is one of Ava's drum solos. He doesn't talk about his old bandmates much, but I can sense he misses them from time to time. I miss Willow too.

With how old we are, we're used to leaving people behind, but sometimes it still stings.

Right now, however, is not the time for Mordred to be up in his head reminiscing. Especially judging by the way Arthur's face is turning redder and redder by the second as he and the other twenty-five knights around the table stare at him with varying degrees of amusement and impatience.

From where I stand behind him, I clear my throat loudly.

Mordred stops drumming and tilts his head all the way back to peer at me upside down. He flashes me one of his smirks I used to hate, the same one I now love—though I try not to let it show.

"Hello, darling."

I clear my throat again and flick my eyes to Arthur.

"Right." Mordred rolls his eyes and drops his feet. "What did I miss?"

A few of the knights chuckle. I suppose, if anything, Mordred's antics are a source of entertainment.

"King Fergus," Arthur repeats himself from before Mordred pulled everyone's attention. "His lands were ravaged by Morgan and her Dark Knights for the last few decades. He's been recently preparing for war, but I'd like to talk peace with him instead."

"I wouldn't go without a peace offering," Mordred says. "Any ideas?"

Mordred sits up a little straighter in his chair and looks around before pointing a finger at his chest. "You're asking *me*?"

"You think you deserve to be my heir?" Arthur arches a challenging brow. "Prove it."

All traces of foolishness disappear as Mordred folds his hands together on the table. Mordred is still Mordred, but I love seeing him eager to prove himself.

"You could offer him some land," he suggests. "Food and supplies at the very least. We're still working on rebuilding Camelot, but the farms we've added are doing well and we're growing our grain stores. We could afford to spare some if it means preventing war."

The corner of Arthur's mouth twitches, but he manages to keep his face set as he nods. "I'll need someone to go to King Fergus and offer to meet with me so we can discuss a truce."

Mordred purses his lips and drops his gaze.

"Mordred?"

"Sire," Sir Gawain interrupts from where he sits on Arthur's left. "With all due respect, Your Grace, are you certain he's the best choice for this?"

Mordred scowls. "Et tu, brother? Have you already forgotten you wouldn't have your head right now if it wasn't for me?"

"No. You'll *never* let me forget it."

Apparently while they were making their way to the courtyard during the Battle for King Arthur—which is exactly what it'll go down in history known as—Mordred saved Gawain from getting his head chopped off by a Dark Knight. And he reminds him of it every chance he gets.

Arthur reaches up to rub at his temple, but I can see amusement swimming somewhere in his eyes—deep, *deep* in the waters. "Gawain," he says on a sigh. "Go with him."

Gawain grins. "Yes, Sire. We'll leave at first light."

Arthur stands, his Knights of the Round Table following suit. "Thank you, all. You're dismissed."

Mordred is the first to bolt around his chair, immediately grabbing my hand, and hauling me toward the doors out of the hall. A few snickers follow us, making my cheeks flame.

The king and all the knights are well aware that Mordred and I are together, something I thought would've been an issue among some of them but surprisingly wasn't. Just because sexuality wasn't a topic commonly discussed during my last time in Camelot doesn't mean everyone would turn their noses up at two men holding hands.

In fact, people here are more accepting than many of those I met in the last few centuries. Returning to Camelot feels like being thrown back into the past, yet it's ahead of the times compared to that other world.

Still…I'd rather be respectful and keep our relationship contained to our chambers.

Which is exactly where Mordred's dragging me.

He doesn't say anything as he pulls me through the halls of the castle, throws open the door to our room, and tugs me inside. When the door slams shut with a wave of his hand, he backs me up against it and slams his mouth to mine. I part my lips, inviting him in, because it's apparent this is one of those times where Mordred needs to be in control.

I allow him to ravage me, tongue swirling against mine as he gyrates his hips, making sure I feel every bit of his length hardening. Mine quickly thickens in response.

However, there's more to this, and he should know better than to think I'm going to let him get away with it.

Threading my fingers through his hair, I yank his head back just as his lips start moving along my jaw, meeting his gaze instead. "Mordred."

He groans. "I need you, Merlin."

"You can have me. As soon as you talk to me."

His eyes close as he whines.

"Don't hide, little monster."

When he leans forward against my hold, I release his hair, letting him bury his head in the crook of my neck and shoulder.

Sometimes he still has to hide just a little bit...

"I just...I guess I didn't think about the responsibility."

"When you decided to get on Arthur's good side?"

He nods into my shoulder.

I grin since he can't see me. "You wanted the throne once upon a time. What did you expect?"

Pulling back, he shrugs. "I imagined being fanned with palm leaves and fed grapes."

I try not to, but I can't help the laugh that slips from my lips. When a weak scowl crosses his face, I fall silent.

"Look, Mordred." I sigh and brush some hair off his forehead, a gesture I know helps calm him. Sure enough, he leans into it as his scowl falls away. "You're right. It is a lot of responsibility. But Arthur is the best influence you could ask for."

Mordred scoffs. "He was born for the crown."

"He didn't always feel that way."

His brows pinch. "Was he afraid too?" His scowl returns as he snaps, "Not that I'm afraid," like it was *me* who suggested he was.

I nod, barely concealing another grin. "He was."

"How did he get over it?"

"I helped him. I'll help you too."

He gives me a warm smile before his hands come up to fist the front of my cloak. "Are we done talking now?"

"Sure, Sir Mordred."

With a groan of appreciation, he rolls his hips, his semi-hard cock filling out once more. He hooks a thumb beneath my jaw to tilt my head back, giving him access to my throat so he can dive in with his teeth. He bites me, sucking on my skin before soothing the sting away with his tongue.

"Say it again."

Leaning my head back against the door, I let him continue his alternating rough and gentle ministrations on my throat, my breathing growing heavy. "Are you going to fuck me, Sir Mordred?"

Just saying those words has my cock leaking in my pants.

"Fuck," he grunts as he thrusts against me, still latched onto my neck. "Fuck yes."

My eyes flutter closed, then open. Then they widen when they land on something across the room, something I swear wasn't there a minute ago.

"Um, Mordred..."

"Hmm?" he asks as he viciously sucks a mark into my throat.

"What is that doing in our room?"

I can feel him smirk against my skin. "I'm going to fuck you in the stocks, darling."

My cock jerks against his. "Technically, that's a pillory."

Mordred growls. "Technically, I want you naked."

Less than a second later, my clothes are magicked right off me, leaving me with a slight chill that Mordred extinguishes with the heat of his body as he presses against me, his hot hands gripping my waist. His mouth finds mine again, his tongue licking a hot stripe across my lips.

"Tell me I can fuck you in the *pillory*, Merlin."

I meet his lustful gaze and grin. "Keep the chainmail on."

He smirks. "Kinky fucker."

Like he has room to talk.

He kisses me hard and deep as he turns us around and starts backing me up across the room. His tongue darts inside my mouth as one of his hands roams up to my chest while the other grasps my cock, giving it a long stroke as he pinches my right nipple. I moan loudly into his mouth and arch into his touch.

He suddenly releases me, and his hands come back down on my waist as he spins me around.

The top wooden slat of the pillory is open. Mordred grabs both my wrists, placing them into the slots before forcing me to bend over with a hand flat on my back until my head is resting in the middle.

Then the top shuts over my wrists and neck.

Mordred takes a step away, the heat of him disappearing from my back, and I squirm like a trapped animal.

The pillory was used as a punishment, for humiliation, and I'm understanding why.

"Mordred," I whimper.

There's a rustling of chainmail and then...

"*Fuck!*"

Teeth sink into my right ass cheek as Mordred bites into the flesh hard. I really should've seen that coming...

"Fuck, Mordred," I moan as I look down, barely able to see the tip of my flushed cock past the bottom of the pillory, a drop of precum beading at the slit.

Mordred is on his knees behind my legs, licking over the bite before moving to nip at my left ass cheek next. Then he's splitting me open with both hands a moment before his tongue swipes across my hole, making me shudder and buck against him, seeking out more of his touch. When his tongue pushes past my rim, just a little, teasing, I writhe, the wood rubbing against my wrists.

"Mordred, please."

"Tell me what you want, darling," he says before he licks up my balls back to my hole, swirling his tongue around until I swear my nerves are on fire, sending sparks all the way to my brain.

"Your cock. I want your cock."

He hums, the vibrations thrumming right through my ass. "Beg."

I groan, but I open my mouth to do exactly that— because it's much easier to give him what he wants than it used to be. However, I choke on the first word when he thrusts two fingers inside me, slick with what I know by now to be spit-turned-lube. He eases them in, stretching me open, and I moan and mumble incoherently.

"I'm so fucking obsessed with your ass, Merlin," Mordred growls as he adds a third finger. "It's fucking perfect. *Mine.* Now beg so I can fuck it."

Slowly, some of my sense returns. As I rock back on his fingers, I give him what he wants, words strained between panting breaths. "Fuck. Please. Fuck me, Mordred. Give me your fucking cock."

That's apparently enough for him because he withdrawals his fingers and stands behind me. A moment later, the slick head of his dick is pressing against my hole. Even the steel balls of his piercings feel scorching hot as his crown pushes past my rim.

He groans, the sound mingling with my moans. "Gonna fuck this ass hard, darling."

"Show me your worst, little monster."

He does.

Gripping my waist, fingers digging into the skin until I'm sure they'll leave bruises, he thrusts all the way inside, all the metal in his cock gliding against my walls as he fills me. My body rocks forward as I cry out. The pillory I'm stuck in jostles but remains stable.

"Fuck, Merlin." He pulls back, then drives forward. "You always feel so fucking good."

His chainmail brushes against the top of my ass as he pistons his hips, pounding into me in a savage, steady rhythm that has him panting and grunting behind me.

"You're going to feel me all day tomorrow while I'm gone, aren't you, Merlin?"

"Yes," I moan as I thrust my ass back as though I could really take more of him. "I'll be thinking about you all day."

"You're damn right." Then he slaps my ass, the sound ringing out along with the cry that tears past my lips. He continues fucking me right through the burning sting left behind.

It's all so much, too much.

My balls are heavy, my cock aching.

"Mordred, please touch me," I whine.

"You want to come, baby?"

I groan and nod even though he can't see me. "Yes, please."

The moment his hand wraps around my cock, I go flying toward the edge, so close to unraveling as heat rushes through my spine. His thumb swipes over my slit, collecting the precum there. He gives me a few long, tight strokes just as one of those little steel bars in his dick hits my prostate, and it's the end of me.

Ropes of cum shoot out of me, and I can see it pouring out onto the floor as shudders wrack my body and my ass clenches around his cock.

"Fuck," Mordred growls a second before his dick pulses inside me, filling me up with his release.

His hips still, and he slumps over me, his chest heaving against my back as his cock softens inside me. I give him a minute, even though I really want the fuck out of this thing. After sex, I always get the urge to touch him, hold him, and the wait is killing me.

Eventually, he stands straight, his dick slipping out of me. It's quickly replaced by two fingers as he pushes his cum back inside with a groan of, "Mine."

I can't wait for him to release me anymore, using magic to open the top of the pillory.

The moment I'm upright, Mordred grabs onto my waist to spin me around, his mouth immediately finding mine. He turns us and backs me up. My legs hit the bed, and I fall back onto the mattress.

The connection of our lips is broken for only a moment before Mordred joins me, laying the weight of his whole body across mine before his tongue is diving into my mouth. The chainmail he still wears is cool and welcome against my over-heated, bare skin.

Our breaths gradually begin to even out as we kiss slowly, softly, a languid sweep of tongues and lips.

When he pulls back, he hovers over me, staring down with his trademark smirk, damp hair hanging over his fore-head. "You look thoroughly fucked, darling."

I sigh with a smile. "I am. And you look like a wet dream."

The corners of his lips pull up even higher. "You mean a wet premonition."

Laughing, I shake my head. "Dreams too."

A low noise rumbles through his chest. "I want to hear all about them."

The rest of the evening is spent in bed with passionate kisses and gentle touches as I recount some of the dreams I've had about him—because of course he won't let that go. But I give him whatever it is he wants because, in the morning, Mordred of all people will be leaving to make peace.

EPILOGUE

MORDRED

A couple of years later.

Pleasure coils up my spine through the haze of sleep, slowly rousing me. I'm floating somewhere between sleep and awake, that place where I still remember dreaming, when I realize my hips are moving, rocking languidly as I lay on my side.

When my eyes finally flutter open, I fall still at the sight of Merlin's gaze searing straight through me. The faint glow of the morning light creeping in through the window shines around him, giving him a halo.

"Morning, little monster," he says, voice gruff and groggy like maybe I woke him.

I probably did, considering I go right back to what I was doing in my sleep—humping Merlin's thigh while we lay naked beneath the sheets. My cock is hard, and I can feel the precum I'm smearing across his skin.

This isn't the first time I've woken up like this. Okay, fine. It happens more often than I care to admit. Turns out I'm insatiable for my damn wizard.

"Don't you dare come, Mordred," Merlin's husky voice demands.

I whine but don't stop.

Merlin's lying on his back, the sheet over him tenting with a growing erection. His head is still turned toward me, his gaze still holding mine captive as I continue rutting against him, seeking the heat and contact of his body.

"Mordred," he warns, his tone turning downright scary.

But I still don't stop. I can't.

I'm so close…

"*Stop.*"

A pathetic sob claws up my throat as I finally still my hips.

"Look at that." Merlin tosses the sheets off of us and rolls over, pushing me onto my back as he throws a leg over my waist and straddles me. He grins down at me as his hands come down on my chest, thumbs brushing over my pierced nipples. "You *can* be a good boy."

I frown up at him. "I'm always good."

Except…Merlin's dick is now nestled against mine, and I swear my hips start thrusting again all on their own.

"I'm calling bullshit." Merlin leans over me and wraps a hand around my throat, his lips one warm breath from mine. "Don't do it, Mordred."

But I'm still rolling my hips, chasing the friction of his hard cock against mine, getting closer and closer. And closer…

"*Stop.*"

I do, whining, "Merlin, please."

His hand tightens around my throat as he grinds his dick against mine, torturously slow, pulling a long, low moan from me. "You know the rules. Your orgasms belong to me."

Reaching between us, I take us both in my hands and stroke us together, smirking up at him as his eyelids flutter. "I could make us both feel good, darling."

"Get on with it then." His hold on me relaxes before his hand moves up, fingertips brushing my jaw before they're in my hair. He thrusts into my hand and groans, "You're still going to come with my permission."

I open my mouth to complain, but he swallows it up, kissing me deep and hard, his morning stubble scratching at my face. He fucks me with his tongue relentlessly, lips heavy on mine, teeth clashing with wild urgency. I continue moving my hands around our cocks, our hips rocking in sync, chasing each other's touch with abandon.

Eventually, I have to yank my head back to come up for air, my panting breaths only adding to the bubble of heat surrounding us.

"Merlin," I moan breathlessly as I jerk us faster. "Merlin, please, can I come?"

"Not yet."

I whine but pick up the pace.

He's about to have to deal with it. There's no way he'd punish me. Not today...

But I don't know if I want to risk it.

Fuck, I'm so close.

"Please," I whimper as my balls draw up tight. "Merlin, please. *Please.*"

"Come for me, Mordred," he growls against my lips.

And just like that, I do. Spurt after spurt of hot cum shoots out onto my abdomen. It feels like *a lot*. Until I realize Merlin fell right over the edge into bliss with me, his release joining my own as it all coats my skin.

"Fuck." Merlin leans his forehead against mine, our chests heaving as we try to catch our breath.

Once air comes a little easier, he crawls down a little on the bed before brushing his tongue up a scorching trail over my abs, sweeping as much of our collective release into his mouth as he can. Then he's lying over me again, hands on the sides of my head as he brings his lips to mine, parting them. We kiss, sharing the taste of us.

After it's all gone, he gives me one last peck.

"Thank you," I whisper against his lips.

He hovers above, smiling down at me. "You're welcome, Prince Mordred."

I groan. "I'm not prince *yet*."

"You will be in a few hours."

Merlin rolls off me and flops down on his back beside me. We lie like that for a bit, staring up at the ceiling in silence.

Yes, it took a couple of years to get here, but that wasn't entirely because Arthur was still having a difficult time accepting me. We *both* had to trust me enough. Surprisingly, I think he trusts me more than I trust myself. However, that in itself gives me a burst of confidence.

I don't call him Father. He doesn't call me Son. But I think we've found a mutual understanding, a respect that we've worked hard for. We may never have a traditional father and son relationship, but what we have now might be even better. I've fought for him, fought by his side, fought *with* him. It's the best that things could possibly be, a healthy relationship with one of my parents that I never thought I'd have.

"You're ready," Merlin says, breaking through my thoughts. "You know that right?"

I turn my head to see him smiling at me. I smile back. "I have to believe that."

"It's *true*. You've already done so many great things, Mordred. You've proved yourself, not just to Arthur, but to Camelot. They're more than ready to accept you as their prince. As am I."

He leans over to place a soft, lingering kiss against my lips. His mouth is warm and inviting, and I could get lost in it all over again.

Instead, I pull back and say, "I want to show you something."

Sitting up, I lean my back against the pillows and wave my hand in front of me. A purplish cloud appears above the foot of the bed, vertical and swirling like a vortex that's staring straight at us. The violet hue is lighter than it once was a couple of years ago. I've been practicing light magic with Merlin's help, but I don't know if the dark will ever fully release its claws.

An image slowly appears within the vortex, growing bigger until it nears the edges of the cloud. It's a little blurry, but like adjusting the signal of an old television, it slowly comes into focus, forming a clear picture.

"Is that…" Merlin sits up straight too now, his shoulder brushing mine.

"Dethrone the Queen," I finish his thought as I watch my old band moving backstage of the venue they're in. "I check in on them every now and then. This was from last night. I had written a song before we left—well, I had been working on it for ages and finally *finished* it before we left. This was the first time they played it live since they were signed a few months ago. I haven't watched it yet. I…I was hoping you'd watch it with me."

"You know I will."

When he drapes his arm over my shoulders, I lean into him and nestle into his side.

The image coming from the magic cloud shows us Ava giving Willow a big kiss in the wings before she rushes out on stage with the rest of the band. I can practically smell the adrenaline from here. The venue they're at is larger than any of the ones I ever played in with them, but it's not difficult to imagine how that feels, just how pumped they all are.

Ava takes her place behind her drums, Will at the front of the stage. He looks good up there, oozing confidence. Merlin's hold around my shoulders tighten, and I can't help but grin.

"You're the only one I'll ever want, darling." I turn to him briefly to brush my lips against his.

He smiles and relaxes as we turn back to the cloud.

Will's finished introducing the band to the crowd, a hell of a lot more friendly and outgoing than I ever was.

Before they start their first song, Ava leans into the microphone hovering over her drums. "This one's for you, Mordred. Wherever you are. We miss you, buttercup."

I quickly clear my throat before I do something stupid like get emotional.

Will starts out the song with a slow guitar solo, fingers plucking at the strings in a kind of sad melody as the reverb fills the room with ambient sound. It lasts about twenty seconds before their new guitarist comes in, followed quickly by bass and drums as the music flows into a heavier beat.

Then Will steps back up to his mic.

"Hatred is a darkness, a shadow I've spent time in. We're intimate, all this bad blood and I. A venom in my veins, the very essence of my life."

Once more, Merlin stiffens beside me.

"I breathe it. I drink it in. It's my air, my water."

The music slows down again, drums and bass fading out as Will takes over with the same melancholy notes as before.

"I was born for this wicked hatred, closing in from all sides. You gave me life and loathed your creation. It's the

only thing I've ever known, ever known. Give me nothing else because it might just kill me now."

As the beat picks back up, spotlights of blue and purple sweep over the stage as Will, Anthony, and their new guitarist bang their heads and jump around animatedly. Merlin's hold on me is tight, comforting, as Will returns to the front of the stage, screaming the next words into the mic.

"Am I living? Or am I paralytic? Something's coming. It might just kill me now."

The song goes on, moving through the chorus again. A part of me wishes I could be there with them, but, then again, I think I'd much rather be here in Merlin's arms.

Especially as Will sings the next words.

"Hatred kept me paralyzed; love moved me. Hatred kept me in the dark; love illuminated me. Hatred kept me existing until your love brought me back to life."

When the song fades out, so does the cloud, dissolving like fog until it vanishes. Silence falls over us, but it's not awkward or tense, just heavy with the weight of that other-worldly vision. Merlin's arm is still draped over me, his thumb rubbing soft, slow circles over my shoulder.

"It's a good song," Merlin says, breaking the silence, giving my shoulder a squeeze. "It's really good. I'm glad you stopped hiding, Mordred."

"You know, being in that band wasn't the first time I played music for an audience." I continue staring out ahead, my eyes out of focus as though they're still trying to see what's no longer there. "I liked being on a stage, all eyes on me, being fawned over. It was one of the only times I didn't feel hated. I was wanted, adored."

Merlin reaches across to grab my chin, gently forcing me to face him. Both his hands move to the sides of my head. "You are wanted. And adored."

He kisses me, conveying with the lightest touch of his lips how deeply he means those words.

When he pulls back, there's a subtle glow in his eyes, the light inside him shining. "I love you."

"I love you too."

He gives me one more kiss. "Come on, my prince. It's time to go get your crown."

The butterflies he still manages to give me suddenly morph into hissing, striking snakes.

I can do this.

I can do anything as long as I have Merlin by my side.

I'll no longer live in my mother's shadow like I did for a thousand years, not when Merlin's light shines so brightly for the both of us.

We enter the throne room together. We walk through the sea of knights and neighboring royals together. We approach the king on his throne together.

When Arthur places the crown on my head, the weight of it isn't as heavy as I thought it'd be. When he introduces me as his son, the Prince of Camelot, the heir to the throne, I realize I have the life I always wanted.

But it's better than that because I have Merlin too.

It turns out there's still a lot of magic left in Camelot.

MORE BY RYLEE HALE

FAR FROM SERIES
Far From Neverland
Far From Camelot
More coming soon!

THE ECHOES DUET
Memory Lane (#1)
Echoes of the Past (#2)
Echoes: A Novella (#2.5)

ABOUT THE AUTHOR

RYLEE HALE is a pseudonym, created because her mother once told her that she'll read everything she ever writes. She's a writer with a tea addiction and a love for everything dark, twisted, haunted, and beautiful. She's written and published more appropriate books that her mother is allowed to read under her real name, but she'll always have a special place in her heart for dark romance.

Rylee's Newsletter:
https://ryleehale.com/newsletter

Join Rylee's Reader Group:
https://www.facebook.com/groups/ryleesromancereaders

instagram.com/ryleehaleauthor

tiktok.com/@ryleehaleauthor

facebook.com/ryleehaleauthor

twitter.com/ryleehaleauthor

amazon.com/Rylee-Hale/e/B0BCK7X3NL

Made in the USA
Coppell, TX
06 May 2024